No... ...ing
more than one hundred and ninety novels.
storyteller, she creates a blend of warmth, humour and
poignancy that speaks directly to her readers and has
earned her almost every award for excellence in her field.
The youngest of five children, Nora Roberts lives in western
Maryland. She has two sons.

Visit her website at www.noraroberts.com

Also available by Nora Roberts

Nora Roberts

Summer in Paradise

MILLS & BOON

This edition published in Great Britain 2018
By Mills & Boon, an imprint of HarperCollins*Publishers*
1 London Bridge Street, London, SE1 9GF

1

Risky Business © 1986 Nora Roberts
The Right Path © 1985 Nora Roberts

ISBN: 978-0-263-26719-8

09-0618

MIX
Paper from
responsible sources
FSC
www.fsc.org
FSC™ C007454

This book is produced from independently certified FSC™ paper
to ensure responsible forest management.

For more information visit: www.harpercollins.co.uk/green

Printed and bound
by CPI Group (UK) Ltd, Croydon, CR0 4YY.

Risky Business

For Michael and Darlene, good friends.

Chapter 1

"Watch your step, please. Please, watch your step. Thank you." Liz took a ticket from a sunburned man with palm trees on his shirt, then waited patiently for a woman with two bulging straw baskets to dig out another one.

"I hope you haven't lost it, Mabel. I told you to let me hold it."

"I haven't lost it," the woman said testily before she pulled out the little piece of blue cardboard.

"Thank you. Please take your seats." It was several more minutes before everyone was settled and she could take her own. "Welcome aboard the *Fantasy,* ladies and gentlemen."

With her mind on a half dozen other things, Liz began her opening monologue. She gave an absentminded nod to the man on the dock who cast off the ropes before she started the engine. Her voice was pleasant and easy as she took another look at her watch. They were already fifteen minutes behind schedule. She gave one last scan of the beach, skimming by lounge chairs, over bodies already stretched and oiled slick, like offerings to the sun. She couldn't hold the tour any longer.

The boat swayed a bit as she backed it from the dock and took an eastern course. Though her thoughts were scattered, she made the turn from the coast expertly. She could have navigated the boat with her eyes closed. The air that ruffled around her face was soft and already warming, though the hour was early. Harmless and powder-puff white, clouds dotted the horizon. The water, churned by the engine, was as blue as the guidebooks promised. Even after ten years, Liz took none of it for granted—especially her livelihood. Part of that depended on an atmosphere that made muscles relax and problems disappear.

Behind her in the long, bullet-shaped craft were eighteen people seated on padded benches. They were already murmuring about the fish and formations they saw through the glass bottom. She doubted if any of them thought of the worries they'd left behind at home.

"We'll be passing Paraiso Reef North," Liz began in a low, flowing voice. "Diving depths range from thirty to fifty feet. Visibility is excellent, so you'll be able to see star and brain corals, sea fans and sponges, as well as schools of sergeant majors, groupers and parrot fish. The grouper isn't one of your prettier fish, but it's versatile. They're all born female and produce eggs before they change sex and become functioning males."

Liz set her course and kept the speed steady. She went on to describe the elegantly colored angelfish, the shy, silvery smallmouth grunts, and the intriguing and dangerous sea urchin. Her clients would find the information useful when she stopped for two hours of snorkeling at Palancar Reef.

She'd made the run before, too many times to count. It might have become routine, but it was never monotonous. She felt now, as she always did, the freedom of open water, blue sky and the hum of engine with her at the controls. The boat was hers, as were three others, and the little concrete block dive shop close to shore. She'd worked for all of it, sweating through months when the bills were steep and the cash flow slight. She'd made it. Ten years of struggle had been a small price to pay for having something of her own. Turning her back on her country, leaving behind the familiar, had been a small price to pay for peace of mind.

The tiny, rustic island of Cozumel in the Mexican Caribbean promoted peace of mind. It was her home now, the only one that mattered. She was accepted there, respected. No one on the island knew of the humiliation and pain she'd gone through before she'd fled to Mexico. Liz rarely thought of it, though she had a vivid reminder.

Faith. Just the thought of her daughter made her smile. Faith was small and bright and precious, and so far away. Just six weeks, Liz thought, and she'd be home from school for the summer.

Sending her to Houston to her grandparents had been for the best, Liz reminded herself whenever the ache of loneliness became acute. Faith's education was more important than a mother's needs. Liz had worked, gambled, struggled so that Faith could have everything she was entitled to, everything she would have had if her father...

Determined, Liz set her mind on other things. She'd

promised herself a decade before that she would cut Faith's father from her mind, just as he had cut her from his life. It had been a mistake, one made in naïveté and passion, one that had changed the course of her life forever. But she'd won something precious from it: Faith.

"Below, you see the wreck of a forty-passenger Convair airliner lying upside down." She slowed the boat so that her passengers could examine the wreck and the divers out for early explorations. Bubbles rose from air tanks like small silver disks. "The wreck's no tragedy," she continued. "It was sunk for a scene in a movie and provides divers with easy entertainment."

Her job was to do the same for her passengers, she reminded herself. It was simple enough when she had a mate on board. Alone, she had to captain the boat, keep up the light, informative banter, deal with snorkel equipment, serve lunch and count heads. It just hadn't been possible to wait any longer for Jerry.

She muttered to herself a bit as she increased speed. It wasn't so much that she minded the extra work, but she felt her paying customers were entitled to the best she could offer. She should have known better than to depend on him. She could have easily arranged for someone else to come along. As it was, she had two men on the dive boat and two more in the shop. Because her second dive boat was due to launch at noon, no one could be spared to mate the glass bottom on a day trip. And Jerry had come through before, she reminded herself. With him on board, the women passengers were so charmed that Liz didn't think they even noticed the watery world the boat passed over.

Who could blame them? she thought with a half smile. If she hadn't been immune to men in general, Jerry might have had her falling over her own feet. Most women had a difficult time resisting dark, cocky looks, a cleft chin and smoky gray eyes. Add to that a lean, muscular build and a glib tongue, and no female was safe.

But that hadn't been why Liz had agreed to rent him a room, or give him a part-time job. She'd needed the extra income, as well as the extra help, and she was shrewd enough to recognize an operator when she saw one. Previous experience had taught her that it made good business sense to have an operator on your side. She told herself he'd better have a good excuse for leaving her without a crew, then forgot him.

The ride, the sun, the breeze relaxed her. Liz continued to speak of the sea life below, twining facts she'd learned while studying marine biology in college with facts she'd learned firsthand in the waters of the Mexican Caribbean. Occasionally one of her passengers would ask a question or call out in excitement over something that skimmed beneath them. She answered, commented and instructed while keeping the flow light. Because three of her passengers were Mexican, she repeated all her information in Spanish. Because there were several children on board, she made certain the facts were fun.

If things had been different, she would have been a teacher. Liz had long since pushed that early dream from her mind, telling herself she was more suited to the business world. Her business world. She glanced over where the clouds floated lazily over the horizon. The sun danced white and sharp on the surface of blue water. Below, coral rose like castles or waved like fans. Yes, she'd chosen her world and had no regrets.

When a woman screamed behind her, Liz let off the throttle. Before she could turn, the scream was joined by another. Her first thought was that perhaps they'd seen one of the sharks that occasionally visited the reefs. Set to calm and soothe, Liz let the boat drift in the current. A woman was weeping in her husband's arms, another held her child's face protectively against her shoulder. The rest were staring down through the clear glass. Liz took off her sunglasses as she walked down the two steps into the cabin.

"Please try to stay calm. I promise you, there's nothing down there that can hurt you in here."

A man with a Nikon around his neck and an orange sun visor over a balding dome gave her a steady look.

"Miss, you'd better radio the police."

Liz looked down through the clear glass, through the crystal blue water. Her heart rose to her throat. She saw now why Jerry had stood her up. He was lying on the white sandy bottom with an anchor chain wrapped around his chest.

The moment the plane finished its taxi, Jonas gathered his garment bag and waited impatiently for the door to be opened. When it did, there was a whoosh of hot air and the drone of engines. With a quick nod to the flight attendant he strode down the steep metal stairs. He didn't have the time or the inclination to appreciate the palm trees, the bursts of flowers or the dreamy blue sky. He walked purposefully, eyes straight ahead and narrowed against the sun. In his dark suit and trim tie he could have been a businessman, one who'd come to Cozumel to work, not to play. Whatever grief, whatever anger he felt were carefully masked by a calm, unapproachable expression.

The terminal was small and noisy. Americans on vacation stood in groups laughing or wandered in confusion. Though he knew no Spanish, Jonas passed quickly through customs then into a small, hot alcove where men waited at podiums to rent cars and Jeeps. Fifteen minutes after landing, Jonas was backing a compact out of a parking space and heading toward town with a map stuck in the sun visor. The heat baked right through the windshield.

Twenty-four hours before, Jonas had been sitting in his large, elegantly furnished, air-conditioned office. He'd just won a long, tough case that had taken all his skill and mountains of research. His client was a free man, acquitted of a felony charge that carried a minimum sentence of ten years. He'd accepted his fee, accepted the gratitude and avoided as much publicity as possible.

Jonas had been preparing to take his first vacation in eighteen months. He'd felt satisfied, vaguely tired and optimistic. Two weeks in Paris seemed like the perfect reward for so many months of ten-hour days. Paris, with its ageless sophistication and cool parks, its stunning museums and incomparable food was precisely what suited Jonas Sharpe.

When the call had come through from Mexico, it had taken him several moments to understand. When he'd answered that he did indeed have a brother Jeremiah, Jonas's predominant thought had been that Jerry had gotten himself into trouble again, and he was going to have to bail him out.

By the time he'd hung up the phone, Jonas couldn't think at all. Numb, he'd given his secretary instructions to cancel his Paris arrangements and to make new ones for a flight to Cozumel the next day. Then Jonas had picked up the phone to call his parents and tell them their son was dead.

He'd come to Mexico to identify the body and take his brother home to bury. With a fresh wave of grief, Jonas experienced a sense of inevitability. Jerry had always lived on the edge of disaster. This time he'd stepped over. Since childhood Jerry had courted trouble—charmingly. He'd once joked that Jonas had taken to law so he could find the most efficient way to get his brother out of jams. Perhaps in a sense it had been true.

Jerry had been a dreamer. Jonas was a realist. Jerry had been unapologetically lazy, Jonas a workaholic. They were—had been—two sides of a coin. As Jonas drew up to the police station in San Miguel it was with the knowledge that part of himself had been erased.

The scene at port should have been painted. There were small fishing boats pulled up on the grass. Huge gray ships sat complacently at dock while tourists in flowered shirts or skimpy shorts strolled along the sea wall. Water lapped and scented the air.

Jonas got out of the car and walked to the police station to begin to wade through the morass of paperwork that accompanied a violent death.

Captain Moralas was a brisk, no-nonsense man who had been born on the island and was passionately dedicated to protecting it. He was approaching forty and awaiting the birth of his fifth child. He was proud of his position, his education and his family, though the order often varied. Basically, he was a quiet man who enjoyed classical music and a movie on Saturday nights.

Because San Miguel was a port, and ships brought sailors on leave, tourists on holiday, Moralas was no stranger to trouble or the darker side of human nature. He did, however, pride himself on the low percentage of violent crime on his island. The murder of the American bothered him in the way a pesky fly bothered a man sitting contentedly on his porch swing. A cop didn't have to work in a big city to recognize a professional hit. There was no room for organized crime on Cozumel.

But he was also a family man. He understood love, and he understood grief, just as he understood certain men were compelled to conceal both. In the cool, flat air of the morgue, he waited beside Jonas. The American stood a head taller, rigid and pale.

"This is your brother, Mr. Sharpe?" Though he didn't have to ask.

Jonas looked down at the other side of the coin. "Yes."

In silence, he backed away to give Jonas the time he needed.

It didn't seem possible. Jonas knew he could have stood for hours staring down at his brother's face and it would never seem possible. Jerry had always looked for the easy way, the biggest deal, and he hadn't always been an admirable man. But he'd always been so full of life. Slowly, Jonas laid his hand on his brother's. There was no life there now, and nothing he could do; no amount of maneuvering or pulling of strings would bring it back. Just as slowly he removed his hand. It didn't seem possible, but it was.

Moralas nodded to the attendant. "I'm sorry."

Jonas shook his head. Pain was like a dull-edged knife through the base of his skull. He coated it with ice. "Who killed my brother, Captain?"

"I don't know. We're investigating."

"You have leads?"

Moralas gestured and started down the corridor. "Your brother had been in Cozumel only three weeks, Mr. Sharpe. At the moment, we are interviewing everyone who had contact with him during that time." He opened a door and stepped out into the air, breathing deeply of the fresh air and the flowers. The man beside him didn't seem to notice the change. "I promise you, we will do everything possible to find your brother's killer."

The rage Jonas had controlled for so many hours bubbled toward the surface. "I don't know you." With a steady hand he drew out a cigarette, watching the captain with narrowed eyes as he lit it. "You didn't know Jerry."

"This is my island." Moralas's gaze remained locked with Jonas's. "If there's a murderer on it, I'll find him."

"A professional." Jonas blew out smoke that hung in the air with no breeze to brush it away. "We both know that, don't we?"

Moralas said nothing for a moment. He was still waiting to receive information on Jeremiah Sharpe. "Your brother was shot, Mr. Sharpe, so we're investigating to find out why, how and who. You could help me by giving me some information."

Jonas stared at the door a moment—the door that led down the stairs, down the corridor and to his brother's body. "I've got to walk," he murmured.

Moralas waited until they'd crossed the grass, then the road. For a moment, they walked near the sea wall in silence. "Why did your brother come to Cozumel?"

"I don't know." Jonas drew deeply on the cigarette until it burned into the filter. "Jerry liked palm trees."

"His business? His work?"

With a half laugh Jonas ground the smoldering filter underfoot. Sunlight danced in diamonds on the water. "Jerry liked to call himself a free-lancer. He was a drifter." And he'd brought complications to Jonas's life as often as he'd brought pleasure. Jonas stared hard at the water, remembering shared lives, diverse opinions. "For Jerry, it was always the next town and the next deal. The last I heard—two weeks ago—he was giving diving lessons to tourists."

"The Black Coral Dive Shop," Moralas confirmed. "Elizabeth Palmer hired him on a part-time basis."

"Palmer." Jonas's attention shifted away from the water. "That's the woman he was living with."

"Miss Palmer rented your brother a room," Moralas corrected, abruptly proper. "She was also among the group to discover your brother's body. She's given my department her complete cooperation."

Jonas's mouth thinned. How had Jerry described this Liz Palmer in their brief phone conversation weeks before? A sexy little number who made great tortillas. She sounded like another one of Jerry's tough ladies on the lookout for a good time and the main chance. "I'll need her address." At the captain's quiet look he only raised a brow. "I assume my brother's things are still there."

"They are. I have some of your brother's personal effects, those that he had on him, in my office. You're welcome to collect them and what remains at Miss Palmer's. We've already been through them."

Jonas felt the rage build again and smothered it. "When can I take my brother home?"

"I'll do my best to complete the paperwork today. I'll need you to make a statement. Of course, there are forms." He looked at Jonas's set profile and felt a new tug of pity. "Again, I'm sorry."

He only nodded. "Let's get it done."

Liz let herself into the house. While the door slammed behind her, she flicked switches, sending two ceiling fans whirling. The sound, for the moment, was company enough. The headache she'd lived with for over twenty-four hours was a dull, nagging thud just under her right temple. Going into the bathroom, she washed down two aspirin before turning on the shower.

She'd taken the glass bottom out again. Though it was off season, she'd had to turn a dozen people away. It wasn't every day a body was found off the coast, and the curious had come in force. Morbid, she thought, then stripped and stepped under the cold spray of the shower. How long would it take, she wondered, before she stopped seeing Jerry on the sand beneath the water?

True, she'd barely known him, but he'd been fun and interesting and good company. He'd slept in her daughter's bed and eaten in her kitchen. Closing her eyes, she let the water sluice over her, willing the headache away. She'd be better, she thought, when the police finished the investigation. It had been hard, very hard, when they'd come to her house and searched through Jerry's things. And the questions.

How much had she known about Jerry Sharpe? He'd been American, an operator, a womanizer. She'd been able to use all three to her benefit when he'd given diving lessons or acted as mate on one of her boats. She'd thought him harmless—sexy, attractive and basically lazy. He'd boasted of making it big, of wheeling a deal that would set him up in style. Liz had considered it so much hot air. As far as she was concerned, nothing set you up in style but years of hard work—or inherited wealth.

But Jerry's eyes had lit up when he'd talked of it, and his grin had been appealing. If she'd been a woman who allowed herself dreams, she would have believed him. But dreams were for the young and foolish. With a little tug of regret, she realized Jerry Sharpe had been both.

Now he was gone, and what he had left was still scattered in her daughter's room. She'd have to box it up, Liz decided as she turned off the taps. It was something, at least. She'd box up Jerry's things and ask that Captain Moralas what to do about them. Certainly his family would want whatever he'd left behind. Jerry had spoken of a brother, whom he'd affectionately referred to as "the stuffed shirt." Jerry Sharpe had been anything but stuffy.

As she walked to the bedroom, Liz wrapped her hair in the towel. She remembered the way Jerry had tried to talk his way between her sheets a few days after he'd moved in. Smooth talk, smooth hands. Though he'd had her backed into the doorway, kissing her before she'd evaded it, Liz had easily brushed him off. He'd taken her refusal good-naturedly, she recalled, and they'd remained on comfortable terms. Liz pulled on an oversized shirt that skimmed her thighs.

The truth was, Jerry Sharpe had been a good-natured, comfortable man with big dreams. She wondered, not for the first time, if his dreams had had something to do with his death.

She couldn't go on thinking about it. The best thing to do was to pack what had belonged to Jerry back into his suitcase and take it to the police.

It made her feel gruesome. She discovered that after only five minutes. Privacy, for a time, had been all but her only possession. To invade someone else's made her uneasy. Liz folded a faded brown T-shirt that boasted the wearer had hiked the Grand Canyon and tried not to think at all. But she kept seeing him there, joking about sleeping with one of Faith's collection of dolls. He'd fixed the window that had stuck and had cooked paella to celebrate his first paycheck.

Without warning, Liz felt the first tears flow. He'd been so alive, so young, so full of that cocky sense of confidence. She'd hardly had time to consider him a friend, but he'd slept in her daughter's bed and left clothes in her closet.

She wished now she'd listened to him more, been friendlier, more approachable. He'd asked her to have drinks with him and she'd brushed him off because she'd had paperwork to do. It seemed petty now, cold. If she'd given him an hour of her life, she might have learned who he was, where he'd come from, why he'd died.

When the knock at the door sounded, she pressed her hands against her cheeks. Silly to cry, she told herself, when tears never solved anything. Jerry Sharpe was gone, and it had nothing to do with her.

She brushed away the tears as she walked to the door. The headache was easing. Liz decided it would be best if she called Moralas right away and arranged to have the clothes picked up. She was telling herself she really wasn't involved at all when she opened the door.

For a moment she could only stare. The T-shirt she hadn't been aware of still holding slipped from her fingers. She took one stumbling step back as she felt a rushing sound fill her head. Because her vision dimmed, she blinked to clear it. The man in the doorway stared back at her accusingly.

"Jer-Jerry," she managed and nearly screamed when he took a step forward.

"Elizabeth Palmer?"

She shook her head, numb and terrified. She had no superstitions. She believed in action and reaction on a purely practical level. When someone died, they couldn't come back. And yet she stood in her living room with the fans whirling and watched Jerry Sharpe step over her threshold. She heard him speak to her again.

"Are you Liz Palmer?"

"I saw you." She heard her own voice rise with nerves but couldn't take her eyes from his face. The cocky good looks, the cleft chin, the smoky eyes under thick dark brows. It was a face that appealed to a woman's need to risk, or to her dreams of risking. "Who are you?"

"Jonas Sharpe. Jerry was my brother. My twin brother."

When she discovered her knees were shaking, she sat down quickly. No, not Jerry, she told herself as her heartbeat leveled. The hair was just as dark, just as full, but it lacked Jerry's unkempt shagginess. The face was just as attractive, just as ruggedly hewn, but she'd never seen Jerry's eyes so hard, so cold. And this man wore a suit as though he'd been born in one. His stance was one of restrained passion and impatience. It took her a moment, only a moment, before anger struck.

"You did that on purpose." Because her palms were damp she rubbed them against her knees. "It was a hideous thing to do. You knew what I'd think when I opened the door."

"I needed a reaction."

She sat back and took a deep, steadying breath. "You're a bastard, Mr. Sharpe."

For the first time in hours, his mouth curved...only slightly. "May I sit down?"

She gestured to a chair. "What do you want?"

"I came to get Jerry's things. And to talk to you."

As he sat, Jonas took a long look around. His was not the polite, casual glance a stranger indulges himself in when he walks into someone else's home, but a sharp-eyed, intense study of what belonged to Liz Palmer. It was a small living area, hardly bigger than his office. While he preferred muted colors and clean lines, Liz chose bright, contrasting shades and odd knickknacks. Several Mayan masks hung on the walls, and rugs of different sizes and hues were scattered over the floor. The sunlight, fading now, came in slats through red window blinds. There was a big blue pottery vase on a woven mat on the table, but the butter-yellow flowers in it were losing their petals. The table itself didn't gleam with polish, but was covered with a thin layer of dust.

The shock that had had her stomach muscles jumping had eased. She said nothing as he looked around the room because she was looking at him. A mirror image of Jerry, she thought. And weren't mirror images something like negatives? She didn't think he'd be fun to have around. She had a frantic need to order him out, to pitch him out quickly and finally. Ridiculous, she told herself. He was just a man, and nothing to her. And he had lost his brother.

"I'm sorry, Mr. Sharpe. This is a very difficult time for you."

His gaze locked on hers so quickly that she tensed again. She'd barely been aware of his inch-by-inch study of her room, but she couldn't remain unmoved by his study of her.

She wasn't what he'd expected. Her face was all angles—wide cheekbones, a long narrow nose and a chin that came to a suggestion of a point. She wasn't beautiful, but stunning in an almost uncomfortable way. It might have been the eyes, a deep haunted brown, that rose a bit exotically at the outer edge. It might have been the mouth, full and vulnerable. The shirt overwhelmed her body with its yards of material, leaving only long, tanned legs bare. Her hands, resting on the arms of her chair, were small, narrow and ringless. Jonas had thought he knew his brother's taste as well as his own. Liz Palmer didn't suit Jerry's penchant for the loud and flamboyant, or his own for the discreet sophisticate.

Still, Jerry had lived with her. Jonas thought grimly that she was taking the murder of her lover very well. "And a difficult time for you."

His long study had left her shaken. It had gone beyond natural curiosity and made her feel like a specimen, filed and labeled for further research. She tried to remember that grief took different forms in different people. "Jerry was a nice man. It isn't easy to—"

"How did you meet him?"

Words of sympathy cut off, Liz straightened in her chair. She never extended friendliness where it wasn't likely to be accepted. If he wanted facts only, she'd give him facts. "He came by my shop a few weeks ago. He was interested in diving."

Jonas's brow lifted as in polite interest but his eyes remained cold. "In diving."

"I own a dive shop on the beach—rent equipment, boat rides, lessons, day trips. Jerry was looking for work. Since he knew what he was doing, I gave it to him. He crewed on the dive boat, gave some of the tourists lessons, that sort of thing."

Showing tourists how to use a regulator didn't fit with Jonas's last conversation with his brother. Jerry had talked about cooking up a big deal. Big money, big time. "He didn't buy in as your partner?"

Something came into her face—pride, disdain, amusement. Jonas couldn't be sure. "I don't take partners, Mr. Sharpe. Jerry worked for me, that's all."

"All?" The brow came up again. "He was living here."

She caught the meaning, had dealt with it from the police. Liz decided she'd answered all the questions she cared to and that she'd given Jonas Sharpe more than enough of her time. "Jerry's things are in here." Rising, she walked out of the room. Liz waited at the doorway to her daughter's room until Jonas joined her. "I was just beginning to pack his clothes. You'd probably prefer to do that yourself. Take as much time as you need."

When she started to turn away, Jonas took her arm. He wasn't looking at her, but into the room with the shelves of dolls, the pink walls and lacy curtains. And at his brother's clothes tossed negligently over the back of a painted white chair and onto a flowered spread. It hurt, Jonas discovered, all over again.

"Is this all?" It seemed so little.

"I haven't been through the drawers or the closet yet. The police have." Suddenly weary, she pulled the towel from her head. Dark blond hair, still damp, tumbled around her face and shoulders. Somehow her face seemed even more vulnerable. "I don't know anything about Jerry's personal life, his personal belongings. This is my daughter's room." She turned her head until their eyes met. "She's away at school. This is where Jerry slept." She left him alone.

Twenty minutes was all he needed. His brother had traveled light. Leaving the suitcase in the living room, Jonas walked through the house. It wasn't large. The next bedroom was dim in the early evening light, but he could see a splash of orange over a rattan bed and a desk cluttered with files and papers. It smelled lightly of spice and

talcum powder. Turning away, he walked toward the back
and found the kitchen. And Liz.

It was when he smelled the coffee that Jonas remembered he hadn't eaten since morning. Without turning
around, Liz poured a second cup. She didn't need him to
speak to know he was there. She doubted he was a man
who ever had to announce his presence. "Cream?"

Jonas ran a hand through his hair. He felt as though he
were walking through someone else's dream. "No, black."

When Liz turned to offer the cup, he saw the quick
jolt. "I'm sorry," she murmured, taking up her own cup.
"You look so much like him."

"Does that bother you?"

"It unnerves me."

He sipped the coffee, finding it cleared some of the
mists of unreality. "You weren't in love with Jerry."

Liz sent him a look of mild surprise. She realized he'd
thought she'd been his brother's lover, but she hadn't
thought he'd have taken the next step. "I only knew him
a few weeks." Then she laughed, remembering another
time, another life. "No, I wasn't in love with him. We had
a business relationship, but I liked him. He was cocky
and well aware of his own charms. I had a lot of repeat
female customers over the past couple of weeks. Jerry
was quite an operator," she murmured, then looked up,
horrified. "I'm sorry."

"No." Interested, Jonas stepped closer. She was a tall
woman, so their eyes stayed level easily. She smelled of
the talcum powder and wore no cosmetics. Not Jerry's
type, he thought again. But there was something about

the eyes. "That's what he was, only most people never caught on."

"I've known others." And her voice was flat. "Not so harmless, not so kind. Your brother was a nice man, Mr. Sharpe. And I hope whoever... I hope they're found."

She watched the gray eyes ice over. The little tremor in her stomach reminded her that cold was often more dangerous than heat. "They will be. I may need to talk with you again."

It seemed a simple enough request, but she backed away from it. She didn't want to talk to him again, she didn't want to be involved in any way. "There's nothing else I can tell you."

"Jerry was living in your house, working for you."

"I don't know anything." Her voice rose as she spun away to stare out the window. She was tired of the questions, tired of people pointing her out on the beach as the woman who'd found the body. She was tired of having her life turned upside down by the death of a man she had hardly known. And she was nervous, she admitted, because Jonas Sharpe struck her as a man who could keep her life turned upside down as long as it suited him. "I've talked to the police again and again. He worked for me. I saw him a few hours out of the day. I don't know where he went at night, who he saw, what he did. It wasn't my business as long as he paid for the room and showed up to work." When she looked back, her face was set. "I'm sorry for your brother, I'm sorry for you. But it's not my business."

He saw the nerves as her hands unclenched but interpreted them in his own way. "We disagree, Mrs. Palmer."

"Miss Palmer," she said deliberately, and watched his slow, acknowledging nod. "I can't help you."

"You don't know that until we talk."

"All right. I won't help you."

He inclined his head and reached for his wallet. "Did Jerry owe you anything on the room?"

She felt the insult like a slap. Her eyes, usually soft, usually sad, blazed. "He owed me nothing, and neither do you. If you've finished your coffee…"

Jonas set the cup on the table. "I've finished. For now." He gave her a final study. Not Jerry's type, he thought again, or his. But she had to know something. If he had to use her to find out, he would. "Good night."

Liz stayed where she was until the sound of the front door closing echoed back at her. Then she shut her eyes. None of her business, she reminded herself. But she could still see Jerry under her boat. And now, she could see Jonas Sharpe with grief hard in his eyes.

Chapter 2

Liz considered working in the dive shop the next thing to taking a day off. Taking a day off, actually staying away from the shop and the boats, was a luxury she allowed herself rarely, and only when Faith was home on holiday. Today, she'd indulged herself by sending the boats out without her so that she could manage the shop alone. Be alone. By noon, all the serious divers had already rented their tanks so that business at the shop would be sporadic. It gave Liz a chance to spend a few hours checking equipment and listing inventory.

The shop was a basic cinder-block unit. Now and again, she toyed with the idea of having the outside painted, but could never justify the extra expense. There was a cubbyhole she wryly referred to as an office where she'd crammed an old gray steel desk and one swivel chair. The rest of the room was crowded with equipment that lined the floor, was stacked on shelves or hung from hooks.

Her desk had a dent in it the size of a man's foot, but her equipment was top grade and flawless.

Masks, flippers, tanks, snorkels could be rented individually or in any number of combinations. Liz had learned that the wider the choice, the easier it was to move items out and draw the customer back. The equipment was the backbone of her business. Prominent next to the wide square opening that was only closed at night with a heavy wooden shutter was a list, in English and Spanish, of her equipment, her services and the price.

When she'd started eight years before, Liz had stocked enough tanks and gear to outfit twelve divers. It had taken every penny she'd saved—every penny Marcus had given a young, dewy-eyed girl pregnant with his child. The girl had become a woman quickly, and that woman now had a business that could accommodate fifty divers from the skin out, dozens of snorkelers, underwater photographers, tourists who wanted an easy day on the water or gung-ho deep-sea fishermen.

The first boat she'd gambled on, a dive boat, had been christened *Faith,* for her daughter. She'd made a vow when she'd been eighteen, alone and frightened, that the child she carried would have the best. Ten years later, Liz could look around her shop and know she'd kept her promise.

More, the island she'd fled to for escape had become home. She was settled there, respected, depended on. She no longer looked over the expanses of white sand, blue water, longing for Houston or a pretty house with a flowing green lawn. She no longer looked back at the education she'd barely begun, or what she might have been.

She'd stopped pining for a man who didn't want her or the child they'd made. She'd never go back. But Faith could. Faith could learn how to speak French, wear silk dresses and discuss wine and music. One day Faith would go back and mingle unknowingly with her cousins on their own level.

That was her dream, Liz thought as she carefully filled tanks. To see her daughter accepted as easily as she herself had been rejected. Not for revenge, Liz mused, but for justice.

"Howdy there, missy."

Crouched near the back wall, Liz turned and squinted against the sun. She saw a portly figure stuffed into a black-and-red wet suit, topped by a chubby face with a fat cigar stuck in the mouth.

"Mr. Ambuckle. I didn't know you were still on the island."

"Scooted over to Cancun for a few days. Diving's better here."

With a smile, she rose to go to her side of the opening. Ambuckle was a steady client who came to Cozumel two or three times a year and always rented plenty of tanks. "I could've told you that. See any of the ruins?"

"Wife dragged me to Tulum." He shrugged and grinned at her with popping blue eyes. "Rather be thirty feet down than climbing over rocks all day. Did get some snorkeling in. But a man doesn't fly all the way from Dallas just to paddle around. Thought I'd do some night diving."

Her smile came easily, adding something soft and approachable to eyes that were usually wary. "Fix you right up. How much longer are you staying?" she asked as she checked an underwater flash.

"Two more weeks. Man's got to get away from his desk."

"Absolutely." Liz had often been grateful so many people from Texas, Louisiana and Florida felt the need to get away.

"Heard you had some excitement while we were on the other side."

Liz supposed she should be used to the comment by now, but a shiver ran up her spine. The smile faded, leaving her face remote. "You mean the American who was murdered?"

"Put the wife in a spin. Almost couldn't talk her into coming back over. Did you know him?"

No, she thought, not as well as she should have. To keep her hands busy, she reached for a rental form and began to fill it out. "As a matter of fact, he worked here a little while."

"You don't say?" Ambuckle's small blue eyes sparkled a bit. But Liz supposed she should be used to that, as well.

"You might remember him. He crewed the dive boat the last time you and your wife went out."

"No kidding?" Ambuckle's brow creased as he chewed on the cigar. "Not that good-looking young man—Johnny, Jerry," he remembered. "Had the wife in stitches."

"Yes, that was him."

"Shame," Ambuckle murmured, but looked rather pleased to have known the victim. "Had a lot of zip."

"Yes, I thought so, too." Liz lugged the tanks through

the door and set them on the stoop. "That should take care of it, Mr. Ambuckle."

"Add a camera on, missy. Want to get me a picture of one of those squids. Ugly things."

Amazed, Liz plucked one from the shelf and added it to the list on a printed form. She checked her watch, noted down the time and turned the form for Ambuckle's signature. After signing, he handed her bills for the deposit. She appreciated the fact that Ambuckle always paid in cash, American. "Thanks. Glad to see you back, Mr. Ambuckle."

"Can't keep me away, missy." With a whoosh and a grunt, he hefted the tanks on his shoulders. Liz watched him cross to the walkway before she filed the receipt. Unlocking her cash box, she stored the money.

"Business is good."

She jolted at the voice and looking up again stared at Jonas Sharpe.

She'd never again mistake him for Jerry, though his eyes were almost hidden this time with tinted glasses, and he wore shorts and an open shirt in lieu of a suit. There was a long gold chain around his neck with a small coin dangling. She recalled Jerry had worn one. But something in the way Jonas stood, something in the set of his mouth made him look taller and tougher than the man she'd known.

Because she didn't believe in polite fencing, Liz finished relocking the cash box and began to check the straps and fasteners on a shelf of masks. No faulty equipment went out of her shop. "I didn't expect to see you again."

"You should have." Jonas watched her move down the

shelf. She seemed stronger, less vulnerable than she had when he'd seen her a week ago. Her eyes were cool, her voice remote. It made it easier to do what he'd come for. "You have quite a reputation on the island."

She paused long enough to look over her shoulder. "Really?"

"I checked," he said easily. "You've lived here for ten years. Built this place from the first brick and have one of the most successful businesses on the island."

She examined the mask in her hand meticulously. "Are you interested in renting some equipment, Mr. Sharpe? I can recommend the snorkeling right off this reef."

"Maybe. But I think I'd prefer to scuba."

"Fine. I can give you whatever you need." She set the mask down and chose another. "It isn't necessary to be certified to dive in Mexico; however, I'd recommend a few basic lessons before you go down. We offer two different courses—individual or group."

He smiled at her for the first time, a slow, appealing curving of lips that softened the toughness around his mouth. "I might take you up on that. Meantime, when do you close?"

"When I'm ready to." The smile made a difference, she realized, and she couldn't let it. In defense, she shifted her weight on one hip and sent him a look of mild insolence. "This is Cozumel, Mr. Sharpe. We don't run nine to five here. Unless you want to rent some equipment or sign up for a tour, you'll have to excuse me."

He reached in to close his hand over hers. "I didn't come back to tour. Have dinner with me tonight. We can talk."

She didn't attempt to free her hand but stared at him. Running a business had taught her to be scrupulously polite in any circumstances. "No, thank you."

"Drinks, then."

"No."

"Miss Palmer..." Normally, Jonas was known for his deadly, interminable patience. It was a weapon, he'd learned, in the courtroom and out of it. With Liz, he found it difficult to wield it. "I don't have a great deal to go on at this point, and the police haven't made any progress at all. I need your help."

This time Liz did pull away. She wouldn't be sucked in, that she promised herself, not by quiet words or intense eyes. She had her life to lead, a business to run, and most important, a daughter coming home in a matter of weeks. "I won't get involved. I'm sorry, even if I wanted to, there'd be nothing I could do to help."

"Then it won't hurt to talk to me."

"Mr. Sharpe." Liz wasn't known for her patience. "I have very little free time. Running this business isn't a whim or a lark, but a great deal of work. If I have a couple of hours to myself in the evening, I'm not going to spend them being grilled by you. Now—"

She started to brush him off again when a young boy came running up to the window. He was dressed in a bathing suit and slick with suntan lotion. With a twenty-dollar bill crumpled in his hand, he babbled a request for snorkeling equipment for himself and his brother. He spoke in quick, excited Spanish as Liz checked out the equipment, asking if she thought they'd see a shark.

She answered him in all seriousness as she exchanged

money for equipment. "Sharks don't live in the reef, but they do visit now and again." She saw the light of adventure in his eyes. "You'll see parrot fish." She held her hands apart to show him how big. "And if you take some bread crumbs or crackers, the sergeant majors will follow you, lots of them, close enough to touch."

"Will they bite?"

She grinned. "Only the bread crumbs. Adios."

He dashed away, kicking up sand.

"You speak Spanish like a native," Jonas observed, and thought it might come in handy. He'd also noticed the pleasure that had come into her eyes when she'd talked with the boy. There'd been nothing remote then, nothing sad or haunted. Strange, he mused, he'd never noticed just how much a barometer of feeling the eyes could be.

"I live here," she said simply. "Now, Mr. Sharpe—"

"How many boats?"

"What?"

"How many do you have?"

She sucked in a deep breath and decided she could humor him for another five minutes. "I have four. The glass bottom, two dive boats and one for deep-sea fishing."

"Deep-sea fishing." That was the one, Jonas decided. A fishing boat would be private and isolated. "I haven't done any in five or six years. Tomorrow." He reached in his wallet. "How much?"

"It's fifty dollars a person a day, but I don't take the boat out for one man, Mr. Sharpe." She gave him an easy smile. "It doesn't make good business sense."

"What's your minimum?"

"Three. And I'm afraid I don't have anyone else lined up. So—"

He set four fifty-dollar bills on the counter. "The extra fifty's to make sure you're driving the boat." Liz looked down at the money. An extra two hundred would help buy the aqua bikes she'd been thinking about. Several of the other dive shops already had them and she kept a constant eye on competition. Aqua biking and wind surfing were becoming increasingly popular, and if she wanted to keep up... She looked back at Jonas Sharpe's dark, determined eyes and decided it wasn't worth it.

"My schedule for tomorrow's already set. I'm afraid I—"

"It doesn't make good business sense to turn down a profit, Miss Palmer." When she only moved her shoulders, he smiled again, but this time it wasn't so pleasant. "I'd hate to mention at the hotel that I couldn't get satisfaction at The Black Coral. It's funny how word of mouth can help or damage a small business."

Liz picked up the money, one bill at a time. "What business are you in, Mr. Sharpe?"

"Law."

She made a sound that might have been a laugh as she pulled out a form. "I should've guessed. I knew someone studying law once." She thought of Marcus with his glib, calculating tongue. "He always got what he wanted, too. Sign here. We leave at eight," she said briskly. "The price includes a lunch on board. If you want beer or liquor, you bring your own. The sun's pretty intense on the water, so you'd better buy some sunscreen." She glanced beyond him. "One of my dive boats is coming back. You'll have to excuse me."

"Miss Palmer..." He wasn't sure what he wanted to say to her, or why he was uncomfortable having completed a successful maneuver. In the end, he pocketed his receipt. "If you change your mind about dinner—"

"I won't."

"I'm at the El Presidente."

"An excellent choice." She walked through the doorway and onto the dock to wait for her crew and clients.

By seven-fifteen, the sun was up and already burning off a low ground mist. What clouds there were, were thin and shaggy and good-natured.

"Damn!" Liz kicked the starter on her motorbike and turned in a little U toward the street. She'd been hoping for rain.

He was going to try to get her involved. Even now, Liz could imagine those dark, patient gray eyes staring into hers, hear the quietly insistent voice. Jonas Sharpe was the kind of man who took no for an answer but was dogged enough to wait however long it took for the yes. Under other circumstances, she'd have admired that. Being stubborn had helped her start and succeed in a business when so many people had shaken their heads and warned her against it. But she couldn't afford to admire Jonas Sharpe. Budgeting her feelings was every bit as important as budgeting her accounts.

She couldn't help him, Liz thought again, as the soft air began to play around her face. Everything she'd known about Jerry had been said at least twice. Of course she was sorry, and had grieved a bit herself for a man she'd hardly known, but murder was a police matter. Jonas Sharpe was out of his element.

She was in hers, Liz thought as her muscles began to relax with the ride. The street was bumpy, patched in a good many places. She knew when to weave and sway. There were houses along the street with deep green grass and trailing vines. Already clothes were waving out on lines. She could hear an early newscast buzzing through someone's open window and the sound of children finishing chores or breakfast before school. She turned a corner and kept her speed steady.

There were a few shops here, closed up tight. At the door of a market, Señor Pessado fumbled with his keys. Liz tooted her horn and exchanged waves. A cab passed her, speeding down the road to the airport to wait for the early arrivals. In a matter of moments, Liz caught the first scent of the sea. It was always fresh. As she took the last turn, she glanced idly in her rearview mirror. Odd, she thought—hadn't she seen that little blue car yesterday? But when she swung into the hotel's parking lot, it chugged past.

Liz's arrangement with the hotel had been of mutual benefit. Her shop bordered the hotel's beach and encouraged business on both sides. Still, whenever she went inside, as she did today to collect the lunch for the fishing trip, she always remembered the two years she'd spent scrubbing floors and making beds.

"*Buenos días,* Margarita."

The young woman with a bucket and mop started to smile. "*Buenos días,* Liz. *¿Cómo està?*"

"*Bien*. How's Ricardo?"

"Growing out of his pants." Margarita pushed the button of the service elevator as they spoke of her son. "Faith comes home soon. He'll be glad."

"So will I." They parted, but Liz remembered the months they'd worked together, changing linen, hauling towels, washing floors. Margarita had been a friend, like so many others she'd met on the island who'd shown kindness to a young woman who'd carried a child but had no wedding ring.

She could have lied. Even at eighteen Liz had been aware she could have bought a ten-dollar gold band and had an easy story of divorce or widowhood. She'd been too stubborn. The baby that had been growing inside her belonged to her. Only to her. She'd feel no shame and tell no lies.

By seven forty-five, she was crossing the beach to her shop, lugging a large cooler packed with two lunches and a smaller one filled with bait. She could already see a few tubes bobbing on the water's surface. The water would be warm and clear and uncrowded. She'd like to have had an hour for snorkeling herself.

"Liz!" The trim, small-statured man who walked toward her was shaking his head. There was a faint, pencil-thin mustache above his lip and a smile in his dark eyes. "You're too skinny to carry that thing."

She caught her breath and studied him up and down. He wore nothing but a skimpy pair of snug trunks. She knew he enjoyed the frank or surreptitious stares of women on the beach. "So're you, Luis. But don't let me stop you."

"So you take the fishing boat today?" He hefted the

larger cooler and walked with her toward the shop. "I changed the schedule for you. Thirteen signed up for the glass bottom for the morning. We got both dive boats going out, so I told my cousin Miguel to help fill in today. Okay?"

"Terrific." Luis was young, fickle with women and fond of his tequila, but he could be counted on in a pinch. "I guess I'm going to have to hire someone on, at least part-time."

Luis looked at her, then at the ground. He'd worked closest with Jerry. "Miguel, he's not dependable. Here one day, gone the next. I got a nephew, a good boy. But he can't work until he's out of school."

"I'll keep that in mind," Liz said absently. "Let's just put this right on the boat. I want to check the gear."

On board, Liz went through a routine check on the tackle and line. As she looked over the big reels and massive rods, she wondered, with a little smirk, if the lawyer had ever done any big-game fishing. Probably wouldn't know a tuna if it jumped up and bit his toe, she decided.

The decks were clean, the equipment organized, as she insisted. Luis had been with her the longest, but anyone who worked for Liz understood the hard and fast rule about giving the clients the efficiency they paid for.

The boat was small by serious sport fishing standards, but her clients rarely went away dissatisfied. She knew the waters all along the Yucatan Peninsula and the habits of the game that teemed below the surface. Her boat might not have sonar and fish finders and complicated equipment, but she determined to give Jonas Sharpe the ride of his life. She'd keep him so busy, strapped in a fighting chair, that he wouldn't have time to bother her. By the time they docked again, his arms would ache, his back would hurt and the only thing he'd be interested in would be a hot bath and bed. And if he wasn't a complete fool, she'd see to it that he had a trophy to take back to wherever he'd come from.

Just where was that? she wondered as she checked the gauges on the bridge. She'd never thought to ask Jerry. It hadn't seemed important. Yet now she found herself wondering where Jonas came from, what kind of life he led there. Was he the type who frequented elegant restaurants with an equally elegant woman on his arm? Did he watch foreign films and play bridge? Or did he prefer noisy clubs and hot jazz? She hadn't been able to find his slot as easily as she did with most people she met, so she wondered, perhaps too much. Not my business, she reminded herself and turned to call to Luis.

"I'll take care of everything here. Go ahead and open the shop. The glass bottom should be ready to leave in half an hour."

But he wasn't listening. Standing on the deck, he stared back at the narrow dock. She saw him raise a shaky hand to cross himself. *"Madre de Dios."*

"Luis?" She came down the short flight of stairs to join him. "What—"

Then she saw Jonas, a straw hat covering his head, sunglasses shading his eyes. He hadn't bothered to shave, so that the light growth of beard gave him a lazy, vagrant look accented by a faded T-shirt and brief black trunks. He didn't, she realized, look like a man who'd play bridge.

Knowing what was going through Luis's mind, Liz shook his arm and spoke quickly.

"It's his brother, Luis. I told you they were twins."

"Back from the dead," Luis whispered.

"Don't be ridiculous." She shook off the shudder his words brought her. "His name is Jonas and he's nothing like Jerry at all, really. You'll see when you talk to him. You're prompt, Mr. Sharpe," she called out, hoping to jolt Luis out of his shock. "Need help coming aboard?"

"I can manage." Hefting a small cooler, Jonas stepped lightly on deck. "The *Expatriate*." He referred to the careful lettering on the side of the boat. "Is that what you are?"

"Apparently." It was something she was neither proud nor ashamed of. "This is Luis—he works for me. You gave him a jolt just now."

"Sorry." Jonas glanced at the slim man hovering by Liz's side. There was sweat beading on his lip. "You knew my brother?"

"We worked together," Luis answered in his slow, precise English. "With the divers. Jerry, he liked best to take out the dive boat. I'll cast off." Giving Jonas a wide berth, Luis jumped onto the dock.

"I seem to affect everyone the same way," Jonas observed. "How about you?" He turned dark, direct eyes to her. Though he no longer made her think of Jerry, he unnerved her just the same. "Still want to keep me at arm's length?"

"We pride ourselves in being friendly to all our clients. You've hired the *Expatriate* for the day, Mr. Sharpe. Make yourself comfortable." She gestured toward a deck chair before climbing the steps to the bridge and calling out to

Luis. "Tell Miguel he gets paid only if he finishes out the day." With a final wave to Luis, she started the engine, then cruised sedately toward the open sea.

The wind was calm, barely stirring the water. Liz could see the dark patches that meant reefs and kept the speed easy. Once they were in deeper water, she'd open it up a bit. By midday the sun would be stunningly hot. She wanted Jonas strapped in his chair and fighting two hundred pounds of fish by then.

"You handle a wheel as smoothly as you do a customer."

A shadow of annoyance moved in her eyes, but she kept them straight ahead. "It's my business. You'd be more comfortable on the deck in a chair, Mr. Sharpe."

"Jonas. And I'm perfectly comfortable here." He gave her a casual study as he stood beside her. She wore a fielder's cap over her hair with white lettering promoting her shop. On her T-shirt, the same lettering was faded from the sun and frequent washings. He wondered, idly, what she wore under it. "How long have you had this boat?"

"Almost eight years. She's sound." Liz pushed the throttle forward. "The waters are warm, so you'll find tuna, marlin, swordfish. Once we're out you can start chumming."

"Chumming?"

She sent him a quick look. So she'd been right—he didn't know a line from a pole. "Bait the water," she began. "I'll keep the speed slow and you bait the water, attract the fish."

"Seems like taking unfair advantage. Isn't fishing supposed to be luck and skill?"

"For some people it's a matter of whether they'll eat or not." She turned the wheel a fraction, scanning the water for unwary snorkelers. "For others, it's a matter of another trophy for the wall."

"I'm not interested in trophies."

She shifted to face him. No, he wouldn't be, she decided, not in trophies or in anything else without a purpose. "What are you interested in?"

"At the moment, you." He put his hand over hers and let off the throttle. "I'm in no hurry."

"You paid to fish." She flexed her hand under his.

"I paid for your time," he corrected.

He was close enough that she could see his eyes beyond the tinted lenses. They were steady, always steady, as if he knew he could afford to wait. The hand still over hers wasn't smooth as she'd expected, but hard and worked. No, he wouldn't play bridge, she thought again. Tennis, perhaps, or hand ball, or something else that took sweat and effort. For the first time in years she felt a quick thrill race through her—a thrill she'd been certain she was immune to. The wind tossed the hair back from her face as she studied him.

"Then you wasted your money."

Her hand moved under his again. Strong, he thought, though her looks were fragile. Stubborn. He could judge that by the way the slightly pointed chin stayed up. But there was a look in her eyes that said I've been hurt, I won't be hurt again. That alone was intriguing, but added to it was a quietly simmering sexuality that left him wondering how it was his brother hadn't been her lover. Not, Jonas was sure, for lack of trying.

"If I've wasted my money, it won't be the first time. But somehow I don't think I have."

"There's nothing I can tell you." Her hand jerked and pushed the throttle up again.

"Maybe not. Or maybe there's something you know without realizing it. I've dealt in criminal law for over ten years. You'd be surprised how important small bits of information can be. Talk to me." His hand tightened briefly on hers. "Please."

She thought she'd hardened her heart, but she could feel herself weakening. Why was it she could haggle for hours over the price of scuba gear and could never refuse a softly spoken request? He was going to cause her nothing but trouble. Because she already knew it, she sighed.

"We'll talk." She cut the throttle so the boat would drift. "While you fish." She managed to smile a bit as she stepped away. "No chum."

With easy efficiency, Liz secured the butt of a rod into the socket attached to a chair. "For now, you sit and relax," she told him. "Sometimes a fish is hot enough to take the hook without bait. If you get one, you strap yourself in and work."

Jonas settled himself in the chair and tipped back his hat. "And you?"

"I go back to the wheel and keep the speed steady so we tire him out without losing him." She gathered her hair in one hand and tossed it back. "There're better spots than this, but I'm not wasting my gas when you don't care whether you catch a fish or not."

His lips twitched as he leaned back in the chair. "Sensible. I thought you would be."

"Have to be."

"Why did you come to Cozumel?" Jonas ignored the rod in front of him and took out a cigarette.

"You've been here for a few days," she countered. "You shouldn't have to ask."

"Parts of your own country are beautiful. If you've been here ten years, you'd have been a child when you left the States."

"No, I wasn't a child." Something in the way she said it had him watching her again, looking for the secret she held just beyond her eyes. "I came because it seemed like the right thing to do. It was the right thing. When I was a girl, my parents would come here almost every year. They love to dive."

"You moved here with your parents?"

"No, I came alone." This time her voice was flat. "You didn't pay two hundred dollars to talk about me, Mr. Sharpe."

"It helps to have some background. You said you had a daughter. Where is she?"

"She goes to school in Houston—that's where my parents live."

Toss a child, and the responsibility, onto grandparents and live on a tropical island. It might leave a bad taste in his mouth, but it wasn't something that would surprise him. Jonas took a deep drag as he studied Liz's profile. It just didn't fit. "You miss her."

"Horribly," Liz murmured. "She'll be home in a few weeks, and we'll spend the summer together. September always comes too soon." Her gaze drifted off as she spoke, almost to herself. "It's for the best. My parents take wonderful care of her and she's getting an excellent education—taking piano lessons and ballet. They sent me pictures from a recital, and..." Her eyes filled with tears so quickly that she hadn't any warning. She shifted into the wind and fought them back, but he'd seen them. He sat smoking silently to give her time to recover.

"Ever get back to the States?"

"No." Liz swallowed and called herself a fool. It had been the pictures, she told herself, the pictures that had come in yesterday's mail of her little girl wearing a pink dress.

"Hiding from something?"

She whirled back, tears replaced with fury. Her body was arched like a bow ready to launch. Jonas held up a hand.

"Sorry. I have a habit of poking into secrets."

She forced herself to relax, to strap back passion as she'd taught herself so long ago. "It's a good way to lose your fingers, Mr. Sharpe."

He chuckled. "That's a possibility. I've always considered it worth the risk. They call you Liz, don't they?"

Her brow lifted under the fringe that blew around her brow. "My friends do."

"It suits you, except when you try to be aloof. Then it should be Elizabeth."

She sent him a smoldering look, certain he was trying to annoy her. "No one calls me Elizabeth."

He merely grinned at her. "Why weren't you sleeping with Jerry?"

"I beg your pardon?"

"Yes, definitely Elizabeth. You're a beautiful woman

in an odd sort of way." He tossed out the compliment as casually as he tossed the cigarette into the water. "Jerry had a…fondness for beautiful women. I can't figure out why you weren't lovers."

For a moment, only a moment, it occurred to her that no one had called her beautiful in a very long time. She'd needed words like that once. Then she leaned back on the rail, planted her hands and aimed a killing look. She didn't need them now.

"I didn't choose to sleep with him. It might be difficult for you to accept, as you share the same face, but I didn't find Jerry irresistible."

"No?" As relaxed as she was tensed, Jonas reached into the cooler, offering her a beer. When she shook her head, he popped the top on one for himself. "What did you find him?"

"He was a drifter, and he happened to drift into my life. I gave him a job because he had a quick mind and a strong back. The truth was, I never expected him to last over a month. Men like him don't."

Though he hadn't moved a muscle, Jonas had come to attention. "Men like him?"

"Men who look for the quickest way to easy street. He worked because he liked to eat, but he was always looking for the big strike—one he wouldn't have to sweat for."

"So you did know him," Jonas murmured. "What was he looking for here?"

"I tell you I don't know! For all I know he was looking for a good time and a little sun." Frustration poured out of her as she tossed a hand in the air. "I let him have a room because he seemed harmless and I could use the money. I wasn't intimate with him on any level. The closest he came to talking about what he was up to was bragging about diving for big bucks."

"Diving? Where?"

Fighting for control, she dragged a hand through her hair. "I wish you'd leave me alone."

"You're a realistic woman, aren't you, Elizabeth?"

Her chin was set when she looked back at him. "Yes."

"Then you know I won't. Where was he going to dive?"

"I don't know. I barely listened to him when he got started on how rich he was going to be."

"What did he say?" This time Jonas's voice was quiet, persuading. "Just try to think back and remember what he told you."

"He said something about making a fortune diving, and I joked about sunken treasure. And he said…" She strained to remember the conversation. It had been late in the evening, and she'd been busy, preoccupied. "I was working at home," Liz remembered. "I always seem to handle the books better at night. He'd been out, partying I thought, because he was a little unsteady when he came in. He pulled me out of the chair. I remember I started to swear at him but he looked so damn happy, I let it go. Really, I hardly listened because I was picking up all the papers he'd scattered, but he was saying something about the big time and buying champagne to celebrate. I told him he'd better stick to beer on his salary. That's when he talked about deals coming through and diving for big bucks. Then I made some comment about sunken treasure…."

"And what did he say?"

"Sometimes you make more putting stuff in than taking it out." With a line between her brows, she remembered how he'd laughed when she'd told him to go sleep it off. "He made a pass neither one of us took seriously, and then… I think he made a phone call. I went back to work."

"When was this?"

"A week, maybe one week after I took him on."

"That must have been when he called me." Jonas looked out to sea. And he hadn't paid much attention, either, he reminded himself. Jerry had talked about coming home in style. But then he had always been talking about coming home in style. And the call, as usual, had been collect.

"Did you ever see him with anyone? Talking, arguing?"

"I never saw him argue with anyone. He flirted with the women on the beach, made small talk with the clients and got along just fine with everyone he worked with. I assumed he spent most of his free time in San Miguel. I think he cruised a few bars with Luis and some of the others."

"What bars?"

"You'll have to ask them, though I'm sure the police already have." She took a deep breath. It was bringing it all back again, too close. "Mr. Sharpe, why don't you let the police handle this? You're running after shadows."

"He was my brother." And more, what he couldn't explain, his twin. Part of himself had been murdered. If he were ever to feel whole again, he had to know why. "Haven't you wondered why Jerry was murdered?"

"Of course." She looked down at her hands. They were empty and she felt helpless. "I thought he must've gotten into a fight, or maybe he bragged to the wrong person. He had a bad habit of tossing what money he had around."

"It wasn't robbery or a mugging, Elizabeth. It was professional. It was business."

Her heart began a slow, painful thud. "I don't understand."

"Jerry was murdered by a pro, and I'm going to find out why."

Because her throat was suddenly dry, she swallowed. "If you're right, then that's all the more reason to leave it to the police."

He drew out his cigarettes again, but stared ahead to where the sky met the water. "Police don't want revenge. I do." In his voice, she heard the calm patience and felt a shiver.

Staring, she shook her head. "Even if you found the person who did it, what could you do?"

He took a long pull from his beer. "As a lawyer, I suppose I'd be obliged to see they had their day in court. As a brother..." He trailed off and drank again. "We'll have to see."

"I don't think you're a very nice man, Mr. Sharpe."

"I'm not." He turned his head until his eyes locked on hers. "And I'm not harmless. Remember, if I make a pass, we'll both take it seriously."

She started to speak, then saw his line go taut. "You've got a fish, Mr. Sharpe," she said dryly. "You'd better strap in or he'll pull you overboard."

Turning on her heel, she went back to the bridge, leaving Jonas to fend for himself.

Chapter 3

It was sundown when Liz parked her bike under the lean-to beside her house. She was still laughing. However much trouble Jonas had caused her, however much he had annoyed her in three brief meetings, she had his two hundred dollars. And he had a thirty-pound marlin—whether he wanted it or not. We deliver, she thought as she jingled her keys.

Oh, it had been worth it, just to see his face when he'd found himself on the other end of the wire from a big, bad-tempered fish. Liz believed he'd have let it go if she hadn't taken the time for one last smirk. Stubborn, she thought again. Yes, any other time she'd have admired it, and him.

Though she'd been wrong about his not being able to handle a rod, he'd looked so utterly perplexed with the fish lying at his feet on the deck that she'd nearly felt sorry for him. But his luck, or the lack of it, had helped her make an easy exit once they'd docked. With all the people crowding around to get a look at his catch and congratulate him, Jonas hadn't been able to detain her.

Now she was ready for an early evening, she thought. And a rainy one if the clouds moving in from the east delivered. Liz let herself into the house, propping the door open to bring in the breeze that already tasted of rain. After the fans were whirling, she turned on the radio automatically. Hurricane season might be a few months off, but the quick tropical storms were unpredictable. She'd been through enough of them not to take them lightly.

In the bedroom she prepared to strip for the shower that would wash the day's sweat and salt from her skin. Because it was twilight, she was already reaching for the light switch when a stray thought stopped her. Hadn't she left the blinds up that morning? Liz stared at them, tugged snugly over the windowsill. Odd, she was sure she'd left them up, and why wasn't the cord wrapped around its little hook? She was fanatical about that kind of detail, she supposed because ropes on a boat were always secured.

She hesitated, even after light spilled into the room. Then she shrugged. She must have been more distracted that morning than she'd realized. Jonas Sharpe, she decided, was taking up too much of her time, and too many of her thoughts. A man like him was bound to do so, even under different circumstances. But she'd long since passed the point in her life where a man could dominate it. He only worried her because he was interfering in her time, and her time was a precious commodity. Now that he'd had his way, and his talk, there should be no more visits. She remembered, uncomfortably, the way he'd smiled at her. It would be best, she decided, if he went back to where he'd come from and she got on with her own routine.

To satisfy herself, Liz walked over to the first shade and secured the cord. From the other room, the radio announced an evening shower before music kicked in. Humming along with it, she decided to toss together a chicken salad before she logged the day's accounts.

As she straightened, the breath was knocked out of her by an arm closing tightly around her neck. The dying sun caught a flash of silver. Before she could react, she felt the quick prick of a knife blade at her throat.

"Where is it?"

The voice that hissed in her ear was Spanish. In reflex, she brought her hands to the arm around her neck. As her nails dug in, she felt hard flesh and a thin metal band. She gasped for air, but stopped struggling when the knife poked threateningly at her throat.

"What do you want?" In terror her mind skimmed forward. She had less than fifty dollars cash and no jewelry of value except a single strand of pearls left by her grandmother. "My purse is in on the table. You can take it."

The vicious yank on her hair had her gasping in pain. "Where did he put it?"

"Who? I don't know what you want."

"Sharpe. Deal's off, lady. If you want to live, you tell me where he put the money."

"I don't know." The knife point pricked the vulnerable skin at her throat. She felt something warm trickle down her skin. Hysteria bubbled up behind it. "I never saw any money. You can look—there's nothing here."

"I've already looked." He tightened his hold until her

vision grayed from lack of air. "Sharpe died fast. You won't be so lucky. Tell me where it is and nothing happens."

He was going to kill her. The thought ran in her head. She was going to die for something she knew nothing about. Money…he wanted money and she only had fifty dollars. Faith. As she felt herself on the verge of unconsciousness, she thought of her daughter. Who would take care of her? Liz bit down on her lip until the pain cleared her mind. She couldn't die.

"Please…" She let herself go limp in his arms. "I can't tell you anything. I can't breathe."

His hold loosened just slightly. Liz slumped against him and when he shifted, she brought her elbow back with all her strength. She didn't bother to turn around but ran blindly. A rug slid under her feet, but she stumbled ahead, too terrified to look back. She was already calling for help when she hit the front door.

Her closest neighbor was a hundred yards away. She vaulted the little fence that separated the yards and sprinted toward the house. She stumbled up the steps, sobbing. Even as the door opened, she heard the sound of a car squealing tires on the rough gravel road behind her.

"He tried to kill me," she managed, then fainted.

"There is no further information I can give you, Mr. Sharpe." Moralas sat in his neat office facing the waterfront. The file on his desk wasn't as thick as he would have liked. Nothing in his investigation had turned up a reason for Jerry Sharpe's murder. The man who sat across from him stared straight ahead. Moralas had a photo of the victim in the file, and a mirror image a few feet away. "I wonder, Mr. Sharpe, if your brother's death was a result of something that happened before his coming to Cozumel."

"Jerry wasn't running when he came here."

Moralas tidied his papers. "Still, we have asked for the cooperation of the New Orleans authorities. That was your brother's last known address."

"He never had an address," Jonas murmured. Or a conventional job, a steady woman. Jerry had been a comet, always refusing to burn itself out. "I've told you what Miss Palmer said. Jerry was cooking up a deal, and he was cooking it up in Cozumel."

"Yes, having to do with diving." Always patient, Moralas drew out a thin cigar. "Though we've already spoken with Miss Palmer, I appreciate your bringing me the information."

"But you don't know what the hell to do with it."

Moralas flicked on his lighter, smiling at Jonas over the flame. "You're blunt. I'll be blunt as well. If there was a trail to follow to your brother's murder, it's cold. Every day it grows colder. There were no fingerprints, no murder weapon, no witnesses." He picked up the file, gesturing with it. "That doesn't mean I intend to toss this in a drawer and forget about it. If there is a murderer on my island, I intend to find him. At the moment, I believe the murderer is miles away, perhaps in your own country. Procedure now is to backtrack on your brother's activities until we find something. To be frank, Mr. Sharpe, you're not doing yourself or me any good by being here."

"I'm not leaving."

"That is, of course, your privilege—unless you interfere with police procedure." At the sound of the buzzer on his desk, Moralas tipped his ash and picked up the phone.

"Moralas." There was a pause. Jonas saw the captain's thick, dark brows draw together. "Yes, put her on. Miss Palmer, this is Captain Moralas."

Jonas stopped in the act of lighting a cigarette and waited. Liz Palmer was the key, he thought again. He had only to find what lock she fit.

"When? Are you injured? No, please stay where you are, I'll come to you." Moralas was rising as he hung up the phone. "Miss Palmer has been attacked."

Jonas was at the door first. "I'm coming with you."

His muscles ached with tension as the police car raced out of town toward the shore. He asked no questions. In his mind, Jonas could see Liz as she'd been on the bridge hours before—tanned, slim, a bit defiant. He remembered the self-satisfied smirk she'd given him when he'd found himself in a tug-of-war with a thirty-pound fish. And how neatly she'd skipped out on him the moment they'd docked.

She'd been attacked. Why? Was it because she knew more than she'd been willing to tell him? He wondered if she were a liar, an opportunist or a coward. Then he wondered how badly she'd been hurt.

As they pulled down the narrow drive, Jonas glanced toward Liz's house. The door was open, the shades drawn. She lived there alone, he thought, vulnerable and unprotected. Then he turned his attention to the little stucco building next door. A woman in a cotton dress and apron came onto the porch. She carried a baseball bat.

"You are the police." She nodded, satisfied, when Moralas showed his identification. "I am Señora Alderez. She's inside. I thank the Virgin we were home when she came to us."

"Thank you."

Jonas stepped inside with Moralas and saw her. She was sitting on a patched sofa, huddled forward with a glass of wine in both hands. Jonas saw the liquid shiver back and forth as her hands trembled. She looked up slowly when they came in, her gaze passing over Moralas to lock on Jonas. She stared, with no expression in those deep, dark eyes. Just as slowly, she looked back at her glass.

"Miss Palmer." With his voice very gentle, Moralas sat down beside her. "Can you tell me what happened?"

She took the smallest of drinks, pressed her lips together briefly, then began as though she were reciting. "I came home at sunset. I didn't close the front door or lock it. I went straight into the bedroom. The shades were down, and I thought I'd left them up that morning. The cord wasn't secured, so I went over and fixed it. That's when he grabbed me—from behind. He had his arm around my neck and a knife. He cut me a little." In reflex, she reached up to touch the inch-long scratch her neighbor had already cleaned and fussed over. "I didn't fight because he had the knife at my throat and I thought he would kill me. He was going to kill me." She brought her head up to look directly into Moralas's eyes. "I could hear it in his voice."

"What did he say to you, Miss Palmer?"

"He said, 'Where is it?' I didn't know what he wanted.

I told him he could take my purse. He was choking me and he said, 'Where did he put it?' He said Sharpe." This time she looked at Jonas. When she lifted her head, he saw that bruises were already forming on her throat. "He said the deal was off and he wanted the money. If I didn't tell him where it was he'd kill me, and I wouldn't die quickly, the way Jerry had. He didn't believe me when I said I didn't know anything." She spoke directly to Jonas. As she stared at him he felt the guilt rise.

Patient, Moralas touched her arm to bring her attention back to him. "He let you go?"

"No, he was going to kill me." She said it dully, without fear, without passion. "I knew he would whether I told him anything or not, and my daughter—she needs me. I slumped as if I'd fainted, then I hit him. I think I hit him in the throat with my elbow. And I ran."

"Can you identify the man?"

"I never saw him. I never looked."

"His voice."

"He spoke Spanish. I think he was short because his voice was right in my ear. I don't know anything else. I don't know anything about money or Jerry or anything else." She looked back into her glass, abruptly terrified she would cry. "I want to go home."

"As soon as my men make certain it's safe. You'll have police protection, Miss Palmer. Rest here. I'll come back for you and take you home."

She didn't know if it had been minutes or hours since she'd fled through the front door. When Moralas took her back, it was dark with the moon just rising. An officer would remain outside in her driveway and all her doors and windows had been checked. Without a word, she went through the house into the kitchen.

"She was lucky." Moralas gave the living room another quick check. "Whoever attacked her was careless enough to be caught off guard."

"Did the neighbors see anything?" Jonas righted a table that had been overturned in flight. There was a conch shell on the floor that had cracked.

"A few people noticed a blue compact outside the house late this afternoon. Señora Alderez saw it drive off when she opened the door to Miss Palmer, but she couldn't identify the make or the plates. We will, of course, keep Miss Palmer under surveillance while we try to track it down."

"It doesn't appear my brother's killer's left the island."

Moralas met Jonas's gaze blandly. "Apparently whatever deal your brother was working on cost him his life. I don't intend for it to cost Miss Palmer hers. I'll drive you back to town."

"No. I'm staying." Jonas examined the pale pink shell with the crack spreading down its length. He thought of the mark on Liz's throat. "My brother involved her." Carefully, he set the damaged shell down. "I can't leave her alone."

"As you wish." Moralas turned to go when Jonas stopped him.

"Captain, you don't still think the murderer's hundreds of miles away."

Moralas touched the gun that hung at his side. "No, Mr. Sharpe, I don't. *Buenas noches.*"

Jonas locked her door himself, then rechecked the windows before he went back to the kitchen. Liz was pouring her second cup of coffee. "That'll keep you up."

Liz drank half a cup, staring at him. She felt nothing at the moment, no anger, no fear. "I thought you'd gone."

"No." Without invitation, he found a mug and poured coffee for himself.

"Why are you here?"

He took a step closer, to run a fingertip gently down the mark on her throat. "Stupid question," he murmured.

She backed up, fighting to maintain the calm she'd clung to. If she lost control, it wouldn't be in front of him, in front of anyone. "I want to be alone."

He saw her hands tremble before she locked them tighter on the cup. "You can't always have what you want. I'll bunk in your daughter's room."

"No!" After slamming the cup down, she folded her arms across her chest. "I don't want you here."

With studied calm, he set his mug next to hers. When he took her shoulders, his hands were firm, not gentle. When he spoke, his voice was brisk, not soothing. "I'm not leaving you alone. Not now, not until they find Jerry's killer. You're involved whether you like it or not. And so, damn it, am I."

Her breath came quickly, too quickly, though she fought to steady it. "I wasn't involved until you came back and started hounding me."

He'd already wrestled with his conscience over that. Neither one of them could know if it were true. At the moment, he told himself it didn't matter. "However you're involved, you are. Whoever killed Jerry thinks you know something. You'll have an easier time convincing me you don't than you will them. It's time you started thinking about cooperating with me."

"How do I know you didn't send him here to frighten me?"

His eyes stayed on hers, cool and unwavering. "You don't. I could tell you that I don't hire men to kill women, but you wouldn't have to believe it. I could tell you I'm sorry." For the first time, his tone gentled. He lifted a hand to brush the hair back from her face and his thumb slid lightly over her cheekbone. Like the conch shell, she seemed delicate, lovely and damaged. "And that I wish I could walk away, leave you alone, let both of us go back to the way things were a few weeks ago. But I can't. We can't. So we might as well help each other."

"I don't want your help."

"I know. Sit down. I'll fix you something to eat."

She tried to back away. "You can't stay here."

"I am staying here. Tomorrow, I'm moving my things from the hotel."

"I said—"

"I'll rent the room," he interrupted, turning away to rummage through the cupboards. "Your throat's probably raw. This chicken soup should be the best thing."

She snatched the can from his hand. "I can fix my own dinner, and you're not renting a room."

"I appreciate your generosity." He took the can back from her. "But I'd rather keep it on a business level. Twenty dollars a week seems fair. You'd better take it, Liz," he added before she could speak. "Because I'm staying, one way or the other. Sit down," he said again and looked for a pot.

She wanted to be angry. It would help keep everything else bottled up. She wanted to shout at him, to throw him bodily out of her house. Instead she sat because her knees were too weak to hold her any longer.

What had happened to her control? For ten years she'd been running her own life, making every decision by herself, for herself. For ten years, she hadn't asked advice, she hadn't asked for help. Now something had taken control and decisions out of her hands, something she knew nothing about. Her life was part of a game, and she didn't know any of the rules.

She looked down and saw the tear drop on the back of her hand. Quickly, she reached up and brushed others from her cheeks. But she couldn't stop them. One more decision had been taken from her.

"Can you eat some toast?" Jonas asked her as he dumped the contents of the soup in a pan. When she didn't answer, he turned to see her sitting stiff and pale at the table, tears running unheeded down her face. He swore and turned away again. There was nothing he could do for her, he told himself. Nothing he could offer. Then, saying nothing, he came to the table, pulled a chair up beside her and waited.

"I thought he'd kill me." Her voice broke as she pressed a hand to her face. "I felt the knife against my throat and thought I was going to die. I'm so scared. Oh God, I'm so scared."

He drew her against him and let her sob out the fear. He wasn't used to comforting women. Those he knew well were too chic to shed more than a delicate drop or two. But he held her close during a storm of weeping that shook her body and left her gasping.

Her skin was icy, as if to prove the fact that fear made the blood run cold. She couldn't summon the pride to draw herself away, to seek a private spot as she'd always done in a crisis. He didn't speak to tell her everything would be fine; he didn't murmur quiet words of comfort. He was simply there. When she was drained, he still held her. The rain began slowly, patting the glass of the windows and pinging on the roof. He still held her.

When she shifted away, he rose and went back to the stove. Without a word, he turned on the burner. Minutes later he set a bowl in front of her then went back to ladle some for himself. Too tired to be ashamed, Liz began to eat. There was no sound in the kitchen but the slow monotonous plop of rain on wood, tin and glass.

She hadn't realized she could be hungry, but the bowl was empty almost before she realized it. With a little sigh, she pushed it away. He was tipped back in his chair, smoking in silence.

"Thank you."

"Okay." Her eyes were swollen, accentuating the vulnerability that always haunted them. It tugged at him, making him uneasy. Her skin, with its ripe, warm honey glow was pale, making her seem delicate and defenseless. She was a woman, he realized, that a man had to keep an emotional distance from. Get too close and you'd be sucked right in. It wouldn't do to care about her too much when he needed to use her to help both of them. From this point on, he'd have to hold the controls.

"I suppose I was more upset than I realized."

"You're entitled."

She nodded, grateful he was making it easy for her to skim over what she considered an embarrassing display of weakness. "There's no reason for you to stay here."

"I'll stay anyway."

She curled her hand into a fist, then uncurled it slowly. It wasn't possible for her to admit she wanted him to, or that for the first time in years she was frightened of being alone. Since she had to cave in, it was better to think of the arrangement on a practical level.

"All right, the room's twenty a week, first week in advance."

He grinned as he reached for his wallet. "All business?"

"I can't afford anything else." After putting the twenty on the counter, she stacked the bowls. "You'll have to see to your own food. The twenty doesn't include meals."

He watched her take the bowls to the sink and wash them. "I'll manage."

"I'll give you a key in the morning." She took a towel and meticulously dried the bowls. "Do you think he'll be back?" She tried to make her voice casual, and failed.

"I don't know." He crossed to her to lay a hand on her shoulder. "You won't be alone if he does."

When she looked at him, her eyes were steady again. Something inside him unknotted. "Are you protecting me, Jonas, or just looking for your revenge?"

"I do one, maybe I'll get the other." He twined the ends of her hair around his finger, watching the dark gold spread over his skin. "You said yourself I'm not a nice man."

"What are you?" she whispered.

"Just a man." When his gaze lifted to hers, she didn't believe him. He wasn't just a man, but a man with patience, with power and with violence. "I've wondered the same about you. You've got secrets, Elizabeth."

She was breathless. In defense, she lifted her hand to his. "They've got nothing to do with you."

"Maybe they don't. Maybe you do."

It happened very slowly, so slowly she could have stopped it. Yet she seemed unable to move. His arms slipped around her, drawing her close with an arrogant sort of laziness that should have been his undoing. Instead, Liz watched, fascinated, as his mouth lowered to hers.

She'd just thought of him as a violent man, but his lips were soft, easy, persuading. It had been so long since she'd allowed herself to be persuaded. With barely any pressure, with only the slightest hint of power, he sapped the will she'd always relied on. Her mind raced with questions, then clouded over to a fine, smoky mist. She wasn't aware of how sweetly, how hesitantly her mouth answered his.

Whatever impulse had driven him to kiss her was lost in the reality of mouth against mouth. He'd expected her to resist, or to answer with fire and passion. To find her so soft, yielding, unsteady, had his own desire building in a way he'd never experienced. It was as though she'd never been kissed before, never been held close to explore what man and woman have for each other. Yet she had a daughter, he reminded himself. She'd had a child, she was young, beautiful. Other men had held her like this. Yet he felt like the first and had no choice but to treat her with care.

The more she gave, the more he wanted. He'd known needs before. The longer he held her, the longer he wanted to. He understood passions. But a part of himself he couldn't understand held back, demanded restraint. She wanted him—he could feel it. But even as his blood began to swim, his hands, as if under their own power, eased her away.

Needs, so long unstirred, churned in her. As she stared back at him, Liz felt them spring to life, with all their demands and risks. It wouldn't happen to her again. But even as she renewed the vow she felt the soft, fluttering longings waltz through her. It couldn't happen again. But the eyes that were wide and on his reflected confusion and hurt and hope. It was a combination that left Jonas shaken.

"You should get some sleep," he told her, and took care not to touch her again.

So that was all, Liz thought as the flicker of hope died. It was foolish to believe, even for a moment, anything could change. She brought her chin up and straightened her shoulders. Perhaps she'd lost control of many things, but she could still control her heart. "I'll give you a receipt for the rent and the key in the morning. I get up at six." She took the twenty-dollar bill she'd left on the counter and walked out.

Chapter 4

The jury was staring at him. Twelve still faces with blank eyes were lined behind the rail. Jonas stood before them in a small, harshly lit courtroom that echoed with his own voice. He carried stacks of law books, thick, dusty and heavy enough to make his arms ache. But he knew he couldn't put them down. Sweat rolled down his temples, down his back as he gave an impassioned closing plea for his client's acquittal. It was life and death, and his voice vibrated with both. The jury remained unmoved, disinterested. Though he struggled to hold them, the books began to slip from his grasp. He heard the verdict rebound, bouncing off the courtroom walls.

Guilty. Guilty. Guilty.

Defeated, empty-handed, he turned to the defendant. The man stood, lifting his head so that they stared, eye to eye, twin images. Himself? Jerry. Desperate, Jonas walked to the bench. In black robes, Liz sat above him, aloof with distance. But her eyes were sad as she slowly shook her head. "I can't help you."

Slowly, she began to fade. He reached up to grab her hand, but his fingers passed through hers. All he could see were her dark, sad eyes. Then she was gone, his brother was gone, and he was left facing a jury—twelve cold faces who smiled smugly back at him.

Jonas lay still, breathing quickly. He found himself staring back at the cluster of gaily dressed dolls on the shelf beside the bed. A flamenco dancer raised her castanets. A princess held a glass slipper. A spiffily dressed Barbie relaxed in a pink convertible, one hand raised in a wave.

Letting out a long breath, Jonas ran a hand over his face and sat up. It was like trying to sleep in the middle of a party, he decided. No wonder he'd had odd dreams. On the opposing wall was a collection of stuffed animals ranging from the dependable bear to something that looked like a blue dust rag with eyes.

Coffee, Jonas thought, closing his own. He needed coffee. Trying to ignore the dozens of smiling faces surrounding him, he dressed. He wasn't sure how or where to begin. The coin on his chain dangled before he pulled a shirt over his chest. Outside, birds were sending up a clatter. At home there would have been the sound of traffic as Philadelphia awoke for the day. He could see a bush close to the window where purple flowers seemed to crowd each other for room. There were no sturdy elms, no tidy evergreen hedges or chain-link fences. No law books would help him with what he had to do. There was nothing familiar, no precedents to follow. Each step he took would be taken blindly, but he had to take them. He smelled the coffee the moment he left the room.

Liz was in the kitchen dressed in a T-shirt and what appeared to be the bottoms of a skimpy bikini. Jonas wasn't a man who normally awoke with all batteries charged, but he didn't miss a pair of long, honey-toned legs. Liz finished buttering a piece of toast.

"Coffee's on the stove," she said without turning around. "There're some eggs in the refrigerator. I don't stock cereal when Faith's away."

"Eggs are fine," he mumbled, but headed for the coffee.

"Use what you want, as long as you replace it." She turned up the radio to listen to the weather forecast. "I leave in a half hour, so if you want a ride to your hotel, you'll have to be ready."

Jonas let the first hot taste of coffee seep into his system. "My car's in San Miguel."

Liz sat down at the table to go over that day's schedule. "I can drop you by the El Presidente or one of the other hotels on the beach. You'll have to take a cab from there."

Jonas took another sip of coffee and focused on her fully. She was still pale, he realized, so that the marks on her neck stood out in dark relief. The smudges under her eyes made him decide she'd slept no better than he had. He tossed off his first cup of coffee and poured another.

"Ever consider taking a day off?"

She looked at him for the first time. "No," she said simply and lowered her gaze to her list again.

So they were back to business, all business, and don't cross the line. "Don't you believe in giving yourself a break, Liz?"

"I've got work to do. You'd better fix those eggs if you want to have time to eat them. The frying pan's in the cupboard next to the stove."

He studied her for another minute, then with a restless movement of his shoulders prepared to cook his breakfast. Liz waited until she was sure his back was to her before she looked up again.

She'd made a fool of herself the night before. She could almost accept the fact that she'd broken down in front of him because he'd taken it so matter-of-factly. But when she added the moments she'd stood in his arms, submissive, willing, hoping, she couldn't forgive herself. Or him.

He'd made her feel something she hadn't felt in a decade. Arousal. He'd made her want what she'd been convinced she didn't want from a man. Affection. She hadn't backed away or brushed him aside as she'd done with any other man who'd approached her. She hadn't even tried. He'd made her feel soft again, then he'd shrugged her away.

So it would be business, she told herself. Straight, impersonal business as long as he determined to stay. She'd put the rent money aside until she could manage the down payment on the aqua bikes. Jonas sat at the table with a plate of eggs that sent steam rising toward the ceiling.

"Your key." Liz slid it over to him. "And your receipt for the first week's rent."

Without looking at it, Jonas tucked the paper in his pocket. "Do you usually take in boarders?"

"No, but I need some new equipment." She rose to pour another cup of coffee and wash her plate. The radio announced the time before she switched it off. She was ten minutes ahead of schedule, but as long as she continued to get up early enough, they wouldn't have to eat together. "Do you usually rent a room in a stranger's house rather than a hotel suite?"

He tasted the eggs and found himself vaguely dissatisfied with his own cooking. "No, but we're not strangers anymore."

Liz watched him over the rim of her cup. He looked a little rough around the edges this morning, she decided. It added a bit too much sexuality to smooth good looks. She debated offering him a razor, then rejected the notion. Too personal. "Yes, we are."

He continued to eat his eggs so that she thought he'd taken her at her word. "I studied law at Notre Dame, apprenticed with Neiram and Barker in Boston, then opened my own practice five years ago in Philadelphia." He added some salt, hoping it would jazz up his cooking. "I specialize in criminal law. I'm not married, and live alone. In an apartment," he added. "On weekends I'm remodeling an old Victorian house I bought in Chadd's Ford."

She wanted to ask him about the house—was it big, did it have those wonderful high ceilings and rich wooden floors? Were the windows tall and mullioned? Was there a garden where roses climbed on trellises? Instead she turned to rinse out her cup. "That doesn't change the fact that we're strangers."

"Whether we know each other or not, we have the same problem."

The cup rattled in the sink as it slipped from her hand. Silently, Liz picked it up again, rinsed it off and set it in the drainer. She'd chipped it, but that was a small matter at the moment. "You've got ten minutes," she said, but he took her arm before she could skirt around him.

"We do have the same problem, Elizabeth." His voice was quiet, steady. She could have hated him for that alone.

"No, we don't. You're trying to avenge your brother's death. I'm just trying to make a living."

"Do you think everything would settle down quietly if I were back in Philadelphia?"

She tugged her arm uselessly. "Yes!" Because she knew she lied, her eyes heated.

"One of the first impressions I had of you was your intelligence. I don't know why you're hiding on your pretty little island, Liz, but you've got a brain, a good one. We both know that what happened to you last night would have happened with or without me."

"All right." She relaxed her arm. "What happened wasn't because of you, but because of Jerry. That hardly makes any difference to my position, does it?"

He stood up slowly, but didn't release her arm. "As long as someone thinks you knew what Jerry was into, you're the focus. As long as you're the focus, I'm standing right beside you, because directly or indirectly, you're going to lead me to Jerry's killer."

Liz waited a moment until she was sure she could speak calmly. "Is that all people are to you, Jonas? Tools? Means to an end?" She searched his face and found it set and remote. "Men like you never look beyond their own interests."

Angry without knowing why, he cupped her face in his hand. "You've never known a man like me."

"I think I have," she said softly. "You're not unique,

Jonas. You were raised with money and expectations, you went to the best schools and associated with the best people. You had your goal set and if you had to step on or over a few people on the way to it, it wasn't personal. That's the worst of it," she said on a long breath. "It's never personal." Lifting her chin, she pushed his hand from her face. "What do you want me to do?"

Never in his life had anyone made him feel so vile. With a few words she'd tried and condemned him. He remembered the dream, and the blank, staring eyes of the jury. He swore at her and turned to pace to the window. He couldn't back away now, no matter how she made him feel because he was right—whether he was here or in Philadelphia, she was still the key.

There was a hammock outside, bright blue and yellow strings stretched between two palms. He wondered if she ever gave herself enough time to use it. He found himself wishing he could take her hand, walk across the yard and lie with her on the hammock with nothing more important to worry about than swatting at flies.

"I need to talk to Luis," he began. "I want to know the places he went with Jerry, the people he may have seen Jerry talk to."

"I'll talk to Luis." When Jonas started to object, Liz shook her head. "You saw his reaction yesterday. He wouldn't be able to talk to you because you make him too nervous. I'll get you a list."

"All right." Jonas fished for his cigarettes and found with some annoyance that he'd left them in the bedroom. "I'll need you to go with me, starting tonight, to the places Luis gives you."

A feeling of stepping into quicksand came strongly. "Why?"

He wasn't sure of the answer. "Because I have to start somewhere."

"Why do you need me?"

And even less sure of this one. "I don't know how long it'll take, and I'm not leaving you alone."

She lifted a brow. "I have police protection."

"Not good enough. In any case, you know the language, the customs. I don't. I need you." He tucked his thumbs in his pockets. "It's as simple as that."

Liz walked over to turn off the coffee and move the pot to a back burner. "Nothing's simple," she corrected. "But I'll get your list, and I'll go along with you under one condition."

"Which is?"

She folded her hands. Jonas was already certain by her stance alone that she wasn't set to bargain but to lay down the rules. "That no matter what happens, what you find out or don't find out, you're out of this house and out of my life when my daughter comes home. I'll give you four weeks, Jonas—that's all."

"It'll have to be enough."

She nodded and started out of the room. "Wash your dishes. I'll meet you out front."

The police car still sat in the driveway when Jonas walked out the front door. A group of children stood on the verge of the road and discussed it in undertones. He heard Liz call one of them by name before she took out a handful of coins. Jonas didn't have to speak Spanish to recognize a business transaction. Moments later, coins in hand, the boy raced back to his friends.

"What was that about?"

Liz smiled after them. Faith would play with those same children throughout the summer. "I told them they were detectives. If they see anyone but you or the police around the house, they're to run right home and call Captain Moralas. It's the best way to keep them out of trouble."

Jonas watched the boy in charge pass out the coins. "How much did you give them?"

"Twenty pesos apiece."

He thought of the current rate of exchange and shook his head. "No kid in Philadelphia would give you the time of day for that."

"This is Cozumel," she said simply and wheeled out her bike.

Jonas looked at it, then at her. The bike would have sent a young teenager into ecstasies. "You drive this thing?"

Something in his tone made her want to smile. Instead, she kept her voice cool. "This thing is an excellent mode of transportation."

"A BMW's an excellent mode of transportation."

She laughed. He hadn't heard her laugh so easily since he'd met her. When she looked back at him, her eyes were warm and friendly. Jonas felt the ground shift dangerously under his feet. "Try to take your BMW on some of the back roads to the coast or into the interior." She swung a leg over the seat. "Hop on, Jonas, unless you want to hike back to the hotel."

Though he had his doubts, Jonas sat behind her. "Where do I put my feet?"

She glanced down and didn't bother to hide the grin. "Well, if I were you, I'd keep them off the ground." With this she started the engine then swung the bike around in the driveway. After adjusting for the added weight, Liz kept the speed steady. Jonas kept his hands lightly at her hips as the bike swayed around ruts and potholes.

"Are there roads worse than this?"

Liz sped over a bump. "What's wrong with this?"

"Just asking."

"If you want sophistication, try Cancun. It's only a few minutes by air."

"Ever get there?"

"Now and again. Last year Faith and I took the *Expatriate* over and spent a couple of days seeing the ruins. We have some shrines here. They're not well restored, but you shouldn't miss them. Still, I wanted her to see the pyramids and walled cities around Cancun."

"I don't know much about archaeology."

"You don't have to. All you need's an imagination."

She tooted the horn. Jonas saw an old, bent man straighten from the door of a shop and wave. "Señor Pessado," she said. "He gives Faith candy they both think I don't know about."

Jonas started to ask her about her daughter, then decided to wait for a better time. As long as she was being expansive, it was best to keep things less personal. "Do you know a lot of people on the island?"

"It's like a small town, I suppose. You don't necessarily have to know someone to recognize their face. I don't know a lot of people in San Miguel or on the east coast. I know a few people from the interior because we worked at the hotel."

"I didn't realize your shop was affiliated with the hotel."

"It's not." She paused at a stop sign. "I used to work in the hotel. As a maid." Liz gunned the engine and zipped across the intersection.

He looked at her hands, lean and delicate on the handlebars. He studied her slender shoulders, thought of the slight hips he was even now holding. It was difficult to imagine her lugging buckets and pails. "I'd have thought you more suited to the front desk or the concierge."

"I was lucky to find work at all, especially during the off season." She slowed the bike a bit as she started down the long drive to El Presidente. She'd indulge herself for a moment by enjoying the tall elegant palms that lined the road and the smell of blooming flowers. She was taking one of the dive boats out today, with five beginners who'd need instruction and constant supervision, but she wondered about the people inside the hotel who came to such a place to relax and to play.

"Is it still gorgeous inside?" she asked before she could stop herself.

Jonas glanced ahead to the large stately building. "Lots of glass," he told her. "Marble. The balcony of my room looks out over the water." She steered the bike to the curb. "Why don't you come in? See for yourself."

She was tempted. Liz had an affection for pretty things, elegant things. It was a weakness she couldn't allow herself. "I have to get to work."

Jonas stepped onto the curb, but put his hand over hers before she could drive away. "I'll meet you at the house. We'll go into town together."

She only nodded before turning the bike back toward the road. Jonas watched her until the sound of the motor died away. Just who was Elizabeth Palmer? he wondered. And why was it becoming more and more important that he find out?

By evening she was tired. Liz was used to working long hours, lugging equipment, diving, surfacing. But after a fairly easy day, she was tired. It should have made her feel secure to have had the young policeman identify himself to her and join her customers on the dive boat. It should have eased her mind that Captain Moralas was keeping his word about protection. It made her feel caged.

All during the drive home, she'd been aware of the police cruiser keeping a discreet distance. She'd wanted to run into her house, lock the door and fall into a dreamless, private sleep. But Jonas was waiting. She found him on the phone in her living room, a legal pad on his lap and a scowl on his face. Obviously a complication at his office had put him in a nasty mood. Ignoring him, Liz went to shower and change.

Because her wardrobe ran for the most part to beachwear, she didn't waste time studying her closet. Without enthusiasm, she pulled out a full cotton skirt in peacock blue and matched it with an oversized red shirt. More to prolong her time alone than for any other reason, she fiddled with her little cache of makeup. She was stalling, brushing out her braided hair, when Jonas knocked on her door. He didn't give her time to answer before he pushed it open.

"Did you get the list?"

Liz picked up a piece of notepaper. She could, of course, snap at him for coming in, but the end result wouldn't change. "I told you I would."

He took the paper from her to study it. He'd shaved, she noticed, and wore a casually chic jacket over bone-colored slacks. But the smoothness and gloss didn't mesh with the toughness around his mouth and in his eyes. "Do you know these places?"

"I've been to a couple of them. I don't really have a lot of time for bar-or club-hopping."

He glanced up and his curt answer slipped away. The shades behind her were up as she preferred them, but the light coming through the windows was pink with early evening. Though she'd buttoned the shirt high over her throat, her hair was brushed back, away from her face. She'd dawdled over the makeup, but her hand was always conservative. Her lashes were darkened, the lids lightly touched with shadow. She'd brushed some color over her cheeks but not her lips.

"You should be careful what you do to your eyes," Jonas murmured, absently running his thumb along the top curve of her cheek. "They're a problem."

She felt the quick, involuntary tug but stood still. "A problem?"

"My problem." Uneasy, he tucked the paper in his pocket and glanced around the room. "Are you ready?"

"I need my shoes."

He didn't leave her as she'd expected, instead wandering around her room. It was, as was the rest of the house, furnished simply but with jarring color. The spicy scent he'd noticed before came from a wide green bowl filled with potpourri. On the wall were two colored sketches, one of a sunset very much like the quietly brilliant one outside the window, and another of a storm-tossed beach. One was all serenity, the other all violence. He wondered how much of each were inside Elizabeth Palmer. Prominent next to the bed was a framed photograph of a young girl.

She was all smiles in a flowered blouse tucked at the shoulders. Her hair came to a curve at her jawline, black and shiny. A tooth was missing, adding charm to an oval, tanned face. If it hadn't been for the eyes, Jonas would never have connected the child with Liz. They were richly, deeply brown, slightly tilted. Still, they laughed out of the photo, open and trusting, holding none of the secrets of her mother's.

"This is your daughter."

"Yes." Liz slipped on the second shoe before taking the photo out of Jonas's hand and setting it down again.

"How old is she?"

"Ten. Can we get started? I don't want to be out late."

"Ten?" A bit stunned, Jonas stopped her with a look. He'd assumed Faith was half that age, a product of a relationship Liz had fallen into while on the island. "You can't have a ten-year-old child."

Liz glanced down at the picture of her daughter. "I do have a ten-year-old child."

"You'd have been a child yourself."

"No. No, I wasn't." She started to leave again, and again he stopped her.

"Was she born before you came here?"

Liz gave him a long, neutral look. "She was born six months after I moved to Cozumel. If you want my help, Jonas, we go now. Answering questions about Faith isn't part of our arrangement."

But he didn't let go of her hand. As it could become so unexpectedly, his voice was gentle. "He was a bastard, wasn't he?"

She met his eyes without wavering. Her lips curved, but not with humor. "Yes. Oh yes, he was."

Without knowing why he was compelled to, Jonas bent and just brushed her lips with his. "Your daughter's lovely, Elizabeth. She has your eyes."

She felt herself softening again, too much, too quickly. There was understanding in his voice without pity. Nothing could weaken her more. In defense she took a step back. "Thank you. Now we have to go. I have to be up early tomorrow."

The first club they hit was noisy and crowded with a high percentage of American clientele. In a corner booth, a man in a tight white T-shirt spun records on a turntable and announced each selection with a display of colored lights. They ordered a quick meal in addition to drinks while Jonas hoped someone would have a reaction to his face.

"Luis said they came in here a lot because Jerry liked hearing American music." Liz nibbled on hot nachos as she looked around. It wasn't the sort of place she normally chose to spend an evening. Tables were elbow to elbow, and the music was pitched to a scream. Still, the crowd seemed good-natured enough, shouting along with the music or just shouting to each other. At the table beside them a group of people experimented with a bottle of tequila and a bowl of lemon wedges. Since they were a group of young gringos, she assumed they'd be very sick in the morning.

It was definitely Jerry's milieu, Jonas decided. Loud, just this side of wild and crammed to the breaking point. "Did Luis say if he spoke with anyone in particular?"

"Women." Liz smiled a bit as she sampled a tortilla. "Luis was very impressed with Jerry's ability to…interest the ladies."

"Any particular lady?"

"Luis said there was one, but Jerry just called her baby."

"An old trick," Jonas said absently.

"Trick?"

"If you call them all baby, you don't mix up names and complicate the situation."

"I see." She sipped her wine and found it had a delicate taste.

"Could Luis describe her?"

"Only that she was a knockout—a Mexican knockout, if that helps. She had lots of hair and lots of hip. Luis's words," Liz added when Jonas gave her a mild look. "He also said there were a couple of men Jerry talked to a few times, but he always went over to them, so Luis didn't know what they spoke about. One was American, one was Mexican. Since Luis was more interested in the ladies, he didn't pay any attention. But he did say Jerry would cruise the bars until he met up with them, then he'd usually call it a night."

"Did he meet them here?"

"Luis said it never seemed to be in the same place twice."

"Okay, finish up. We'll cruise around ourselves."

By the fourth stop, Liz was fed up. She noticed that Jonas no more than toyed with a drink at each bar, but she was tired of the smell of liquor. Some places were quiet, and on the edge of seamy. Others were raucous and lit with flashing lights. Faces began to blur together. There were young people, not so young people. There were Americans out for exotic nightlife, natives celebrating a night on the town. Some courted on dance floors or over tabletops. She saw those who seemed to have nothing but time and money, and others who sat alone nursing a bottle and a black mood.

"This is the last one," Liz told him as Jonas found a table at a club with a crowded dance floor and recorded music.

Jonas glanced at his watch. It was barely eleven. Action rarely heated up before midnight. "All right," he said easily, and decided to distract her. "Let's dance."

Before she could refuse, he was pulling her into the crowd. "There's no room," she began, but his arms came around her.

"We'll make some." He had her close, his hand trailing up her back. "See?"

"I haven't danced in years," she muttered, and he laughed.

"There's no room anyway." Locked together, jostled by the crowd, they did no more than sway.

"What's the purpose in all this?" she demanded.

"I don't know until I find it. Meantime, don't you ever relax?" He rubbed his palm up her back again, finding the muscles taut.

"No."

"Let's try it this way." His gaze skimmed the crowd as he spoke. "What do you do when you're not working?"

"I think about working."

"Liz."

"All right, I read—books on marine life mostly."

"Busman's holiday?"

"It's what interests me."

Her body shifted intimately against his. Jonas forgot to keep his attention on the crowd and looked down at her. "*All* that interests you?"

He was too close. Liz tried to ease away and found his arms very solid. In spite of her determination to remain unmoved, her heart began to thud lightly in her head. "I don't have time for anything else."

She wore no perfume, he noted, but carried the scent of powder and spice. He wondered if her body would look as delicate as it felt against his. "It sounds as though you limit yourself."

"I have a business to run," she murmured. Would it be the same if he kissed her again? Sweet, overpowering. His lips were so close to hers, closer still when he ran his hand through her hair and drew her head back. She could almost taste him.

"Is making money so important?"

"It has to be," she managed, but could barely remember why. "I need to buy some aqua bikes."

Her eyes were soft, drowsy. They made him feel invulnerable. "Aqua bikes?"

"If I don't keep up with the competition…" He pressed a kiss to the corner of her mouth.

"The competition?" he prompted.

"I…the customers will go someplace else. So I…" The kiss teased the other corner.

"So?"

"I have to buy the bikes before the summer season."

"Of course. But that's weeks away. I could make love with you dozens of times before then. Dozens," he repeated as she stared at him. Then he closed his mouth over hers.

He felt her jolt—surprise, resistance, passion—he couldn't be sure. He only knew that holding her had led to wanting her and wanting to needing. By nature, he was a man who preferred his passion in private, quiet spots of his own choosing. Now he forgot the crowded club, loud music and flashing lights. They no longer swayed, but were hemmed into a corner of the dance floor, surrounded, pressed close. Oblivious.

She felt her head go light, heard the music fade. The heat from his body seeped into hers and flavored the kiss. Hot, molten, searing. Though they stood perfectly still, Liz had visions of racing. The breath backed up in her lungs until she released it with a shuddering sigh. Her body, coiled like a spring, went lax on a wave of confused pleasure. She strained closer, reaching up to touch his face. Abruptly the music changed from moody to rowdy. Jonas shifted her away from flailing arms.

"Poor timing," he murmured.

She needed a minute. "Yes." But she meant it in a more general way. It wasn't a matter of time and place, but a matter of impossibility. She started to move away when Jonas's grip tightened on her. "What is it?" she began, but only had to look at his face.

Cautiously, she turned to see what he stared at. A woman in a skimpy red dress stared back at him. Liz recognized the shock in her eyes before the woman turned and fled, leaving her dance partner gaping.

"Come on." Without waiting for her, Jonas sprinted through the crowd. Dodging, weaving and shoving when she had to, Liz dashed after him.

The woman had barely gotten out to the street when Jonas caught up to her. "What are you running away from?" he demanded. His fingers dug into her arms as he held her back against a wall.

"Por favor, no comprendo," she murmured and shook like a leaf.

"Oh yes, I think you do." With his fingers bruising her arms, Jonas towered over her until she nearly squeaked in fear. "What do you know about my brother?"

"Jonas." Appalled, Liz stepped between them. "If this is the way you intend to behave, you'll do without my help." She turned away from him and touched the woman's shoulder. *"Lo siento mucho,"* she began, apologizing for Jonas. "He's lost his brother. His brother, Jerry Sharpe. Did you know him?"

She looked at Liz and whispered. "He has Jerry's face. But he's dead—I saw in the papers."

"This is Jerry's brother, Jonas. We'd like to talk to you."

As Liz had, the woman had already sensed the difference between Jonas and the man she'd known. She'd never have cowered away from Jerry for the simple reason that she'd known herself to be stronger and more clever. The man looming over her now was a different matter.

"I don't know anything."

"*Por favor.* Just a few minutes."

"Tell her I'll make it worth her while," Jonas added before she could refuse again. Without waiting for Liz to translate, he reached for his wallet and took out a bill. He saw fear change to speculation.

"A few minutes," she agreed, but pointed to an outdoor café. "There."

Jonas ordered two coffees and a glass of wine. "Ask her her name," he told Liz.

"I speak English." The woman took out a long, slim cigarette and tapped it on the tabletop. "I'm Erika. Jerry and I were friends." More relaxed, she smiled at Jonas. "You know, good friends."

"Yes, I know."

"He was very good-looking," she added, then caught her bottom lip between her teeth. "Lots of fun."

"How long did you know him?"

"A couple of weeks. I was sorry when I heard he was dead."

"Murdered," Jonas stated.

Erika took a deep drink of wine. "Do you think it was because of the money?"

Every muscle in his body tensed. Quickly, he shot Liz a warning look before she could speak. "I don't know—it looks that way. How much did he tell you about it?"

"Oh, just enough to intrigue me. You know." She smiled again and held out her cigarette for a light. "Jerry was very charming. And generous." She remembered the little gold bracelet he'd bought for her and the earrings with the pretty blue stones. "I thought he was very rich, but he said he would soon be much richer. I like charming men, but I especially like rich men. Jerry said when he had the money, we could take a trip." She blew out smoke again before giving a philosophical little shrug. "Then he was dead."

Jonas studied her as he drank coffee. She was, as Luis had said, a knockout. And she wasn't stupid. He was also certain her mind was focusing on one point, and one point alone. "Do you know when he was supposed to have the money?"

"Sure, I had to take off work if we were going away. He called me—it was Sunday. He was so excited. 'Erika,' he said, 'I hit the jackpot.' I was a little mad because he hadn't shown up Saturday night. He told me he'd done some quick business in Acapulco and how would I like to spend a few weeks in Monte Carlo?" She gave Jonas a lash-fluttering smile. "I decided to forgive him. I was packed," she added, blowing smoke past Jonas's shoulder. "We were supposed to leave Tuesday afternoon. I saw in the papers Monday night that he was dead. The papers said nothing about the money."

"Do you know who he had business with?"

"No. Sometimes he would talk to another American,

a skinny man with pale hair. Other times he would see a Mexican. I didn't like him—he had *mal ojo*."

"Evil eye," Liz interpreted. "Can you describe him?"

"Not pretty," she said offhandedly. "His face was pitted. His hair was long in the back, over his collar and he was very thin and short." She glanced at Jonas again with a sultry smile that heated the air. "I like tall men."

"Do you know his name?"

"No. But he dressed very nicely. Nice suits, good shoes. And he wore a silver band on his wrist, a thin one that crossed at the ends. It was very pretty. Do you think he knows about the money? Jerry said it was lots of money."

Jonas merely reached for his wallet. "I'd like to find out his name," he told her and set a fifty on the table. His hand closed over hers as she reached for it. "His name, and the name of the American. Don't hold out on me, Erika."

With a toss of her head, she palmed the fifty. "I'll find out the names. When I tell you, it's another fifty."

"When you tell me." He scrawled Liz's number on the back of a business card. "Call this number when you have something."

"Okay." She slipped the fifty into her purse as she stood up. "You know, you don't look as much like Jerry as I thought." With the click of high heels, she crossed the pavement and went back into the club.

"It's a beginning," Jonas murmured as he pushed his coffee aside. When he looked over, he saw Liz studying him. "Problem?"

"I don't like the way you work."

He dropped another bill on the table before he rose. "I don't have time to waste on amenities."

"What would you have done if I hadn't calmed her down? Dragged her off to the nearest alley and beaten it out of her?"

He drew out a cigarette, struggling with temper. "Let's go home, Liz."

"I wonder if you're any different from the men you're looking for." She pushed back from the table. "Just as a matter of interest, the man who broke into my house and attacked me wore a thin band at his wrist. I felt it when he held the knife to my throat."

She watched as his gaze lifted from the flame at the end of the cigarette and came to hers. "I think you two might recognize each other when the time comes."

Chapter 5

"Always check your gauges," Liz instructed, carefully indicating each one on her own equipment as she spoke. "Each one of these gauges is vital to your safety when you dive. That's true if it's your first dive or your fiftieth. It's very easy to become so fascinated not only by the fish and coral, but the sensation of diving itself, that you can forget you're dependent on your air tank. Always be certain you start your ascent while you have five or ten minutes of air left."

She'd covered everything, she decided, in the hour lesson. If she lectured any more, her students would be too impatient to listen. It was time to give them a taste of what they were paying for.

"We'll dive as a group. Some of you may want to explore on your own, but remember, always swim in pairs. As a final precaution, check the gear of the diver next to you."

Liz strapped on her own weight belt as her group of

novices followed instructions. So many of them, she knew, looked on scuba diving as an adventure. That was fine, as long as they remembered safety. Whenever she instructed, she stressed the what ifs just as thoroughly as the how tos. Anyone who went down under her supervision would know what steps to take under any circumstances. Diving accidents were most often the result of carelessness. Liz was never careless with herself or with her students. Most of them were talking excitedly as they strapped on tanks.

"This group." Luis hefted his tank. "Very green."

"Yeah." Liz helped him with the straps. As she did with all her employees, Liz supplied Luis's gear. It was checked just as thoroughly as any paying customer's. "Keep an eye on the honeymoon couple, Luis. They're more interested in each other than their regulators."

"No problem." He assisted Liz with her tank, then stepped back while she cinched the straps. "You look tired, kid."

"No, I'm fine."

When she turned, he glanced at the marks on her neck. The story had already made the rounds. "You sure? You don't look so fine."

She lifted a brow as she hooked on her diving knife. "Sweet of you."

"Well, I mean it. You got me worried about you."

"No need to worry." As Liz pulled on her mask, she glanced over at the roly-poly fatherly type who was struggling with his flippers. He was her bodyguard for the day. "The police have everything under control," she said, and hoped it was true. She wasn't nearly as sure about Jonas.

He hadn't shocked her the night before. She'd sensed that dangerously waiting violence in him from the first. But seeing his face as he'd grabbed Erika, hearing his voice, had left her with a cold, flat feeling in her stomach. She didn't know him well enough to be certain if he would choose to control the violence or let it free. More, how could she know he was capable of leashing it? Revenge, she thought, was never pretty. And that's what he wanted. Remembering the look in his eyes, Liz was very much afraid he'd get it.

The boat listed, bringing her back to the moment. She couldn't think about Jonas now, she told herself. She had a business to run and customers to satisfy.

"Miss Palmer." A young American with a thin chest and a winning smile maneuvered over to her. "Would you mind giving me a check?"

"Sure." In her brisk, efficient way, Liz began to check gauges and hoses.

"I'm a little nervous," he confessed. "I've never done this sort of thing before."

"It doesn't hurt to be a little nervous. You'll be more careful. Here, pull your mask down. Make sure it's comfortable but snug."

He obeyed, and his eyes looked wide and pale through the glass. "If you don't mind, I think I'll stick close to you down there."

She smiled at him. "That's what I'm here for. The depth here is thirty feet," she told the group in general. "Remember to make your adjustments for pressure and gravity as you descend. Please keep the group in sight at all times." With innate fluidity, she sat on the deck and rolled into the water. With Luis on deck, and Liz treading a few feet away, they waited until each student made his dive. With a final adjustment to her mask, Liz went under.

She'd always loved it. The sensation of weightlessness, the fantasy of being unimpeded, invulnerable. From near the surface, the sea floor was a spread of white. She loitered there a moment, enjoying the cathedral like view. Then, with an easy kick, she moved down with her students.

The newlyweds were holding hands and having the time of their lives. Liz reminded herself to keep them in sight. The policeman assigned to her was plodding along like a sleepy sea turtle. He'd keep her in sight. Most of the others remained in a tight group, fascinated but cautious. The thin American gave her a wide-eyed look that was a combination of pleasure and nerves and stuck close by her side. To help him relax, Liz touched his shoulder and pointed up. In an easy motion, she turned on her back so that she faced the surface. Sunlight streaked thinly through the water. The hull of the dive boat was plainly visible. He nodded and followed her down.

Fish streamed by, some in waves, some on their own. Though the sand was white, the water clear, there was a montage of color. Brain coral rose up in sturdy mounds, the color of saffron. Sea fans, as delicate as lace, waved pink and purple in the current. She signaled to her companion and watched a school of coral sweepers, shivering with metallic tints, turn as a unit and skim through staghorn coral.

It was a world she understood as well as, perhaps better, than the one on the surface. Here, in the silence, Liz often found the peace of mind that eluded her from day to day. The scientific names of the fish and formations they passed were no strangers to her. Once she'd studied them diligently, with dreams of solving mysteries and bringing the beauty of the world of the sea to others. That had been another life. Now she coached tourists and gave them, for hourly rates, something memorable to take home after a vacation. It was enough.

Amused, she watched an angelfish busy itself by swallowing the bubbles rising toward the surface. To entertain her students, she poked at a small damselfish. The pugnacious male clung to his territory and nipped at her. To the right, she saw sand kick up and cloud the water. Signaling for caution, Liz pointed out the platelike ray that skimmed away, annoyed by the intrusion.

The new husband showed off a bit, turning slow somersaults for his wife. As divers gained confidence, they spread out a little farther. Only her bodyguard and the nervous American stayed within an arm span at all times. Throughout the thirty-minute dive, Liz circled the group, watching individual divers. By the time the lesson was over, she was satisfied that her customers had gotten their money's worth. This was verified when they surfaced.

"Great!" A British businessman on his first trip to Mexico clambered back onto the deck. His face was reddened by the sun but he didn't seem to mind. "When can we go down again?"

With a laugh, Liz helped other passengers on board. "You have to balance your down time with your surface time. But we'll go down again."

"What was that feathery-looking stuff?" someone else asked. "It grows like a bush."

"It's a gorgonian, from the Gorgons of mythology." She slipped off her tanks and flexed her muscles. "If you remember, the Gorgons had snakes for hair. The whip gorgonian has a resilient skeletal structure and undulates like a snake with the current."

More questions were tossed out, more answers supplied. Liz noticed the American who'd stayed with her, sitting by himself, smiling a little. Liz moved around gear then dropped down beside him.

"You did very well."

"Yeah?" He looked a little dazed as he shrugged his shoulders. "I liked it, but I gotta admit, I felt better knowing you were right there. You sure know what you're doing."

"I've been at it a long time."

He sat back, unzipping his wet suit to his waist. "I don't mean to be nosy, but I wondered about you. You're American, aren't you?"

It had been asked before. Liz combed her fingers through her wet hair. "That's right."

"From?"

"Houston."

"No kidding." His eyes lit up. "Hell, I went to school in Texas. Texas A and M."

"Really?" The little tug she felt rarely came and went. "So did I, briefly."

"Small world," he said, pleased with himself. "I like Texas. Got a few friends in Houston. I don't suppose you know the Dresscots?"

"No."

"Well, Houston isn't exactly small-town U.S.A." He stretched out long, skinny legs that were shades paler than his arms but starting to tan. "So you went to Texas A and M."

"That's right."

"What'd you study?"

She smiled and looked out to sea. "Marine biology."

"Guess that fits."

"And you?"

"Accounting." He flashed his grin again. "Pretty dry stuff. That's why I always take a long breather after tax time."

"Well, you chose a great place to take it. Ready to go down again?"

He took a long breath as if to steady himself. "Yeah. Hey, listen, how about a drink after we get back in?"

He was attractive in a mild sort of way, pleasant enough. She gave him an apologetic smile as she rose. "It sounds nice, but I'm tied up."

"I'll be around for a couple of weeks. Some other time?"

"Maybe. Let's check your gear."

By the time the dive boat chugged into shore, the afternoon was waning. Her customers, most of them pleased with themselves, wandered off to change for dinner or spread out on the beach. Only a few loitered near the boat, including her bodyguard and the accountant from America. It occurred to Liz that she might have been a bit brisk with him.

"I hope you enjoyed yourself, Mr...."

"Trydent. But it's Scott, and I did. I might just try it again."

Liz smiled at him as she helped Luis and another of her employees unload the boat. "That's what we're here for."

"You, ah, ever give private lessons?"

Liz caught the look. Perhaps she hadn't been brisk enough. "On occasion."

"Then maybe we could—"

"Hey, there, missy."

Liz shaded her eyes. "Mr. Ambuckle."

He stood on the little walkway, his legs bulging out of the short wet suit. What hair he had was sleeked wetly back. Beside him, his wife stood wearily in a bathing suit designed to slim down wide hips. "Just got back in!" he shouted. "Had a full day of it."

He seemed enormously pleased with himself. His wife looked at Liz and rolled her eyes. "Maybe I should take you out as crew, Mr. Ambuckle."

He laughed, slapping his side. "Guess I'd rather dive than anything." He glanced at his wife and patted her shoulder. "Almost anything. Gotta trade in these tanks, honey, and get me some fresh ones."

"Going out again?"

"Tonight. Can't talk the missus into it."

"I'm crawling into bed with a good book," she told Liz. "The only water I want to see is in the tub."

With a laugh, Liz jumped down to the walkway. "At the moment, I feel the same way. Oh, Mr. and Mrs. Ambuckle, this is Scott Trydent. He just took his first dive."

"Well now." Expansive, Ambuckle slapped him on the back. "How'd you like it?"

"Well, I—"

"Nothing like it, is there? You want try it at night, boy. Whole different ball game at night."

"I'm sure, but—"

"Gotta trade in these tanks." After slapping Scott's back again, Ambuckle hefted his tanks and waddled off toward the shop.

"Obsessed," Mrs. Ambuckle said, casting her eyes to the sky. "Don't let him get started on you, Mr. Trydent. You'll never get any peace."

"No, I won't. Nice meeting you, Mrs. Ambuckle." Obviously bemused, Scott watched her wander back toward the hotel. "Quite a pair."

"That they are." Liz lifted her own tanks. She stored them separately from her rental equipment. "Goodbye, Mr. Trydent."

"Scott," he said again. "About that drink—"

"Thanks anyway," Liz said pleasantly and left him standing on the walkway. "Everything in?" she asked Luis as she stepped into the shop.

"Checking it off now. One of the regulators is acting up."

"Set it aside for Jose to look at." As a matter of habit, she moved into the back to fill her tanks before storage. "All the boats are in, Luis. We shouldn't have too much more business now. You and the rest can go on as soon as everything's checked in. I'll close up."

"I don't mind staying."

"You closed up last night," she reminded him. "What do you want?" She tossed a grin over her shoulder. "Overtime? Go on home, Luis. You can't tell me you don't have a date."

He ran a fingertip over his mustache. "As a matter of fact…"

"A hot date?" Liz lifted a brow as air hissed into her tank.

"Is there any other kind?"

Chuckling, Liz straightened. She noticed Ambuckle trudging across the sand with his fresh tanks. Her other employees talked among themselves as the last of the gear was stored. "Well, go make yourself beautiful then. The only thing I have a date with is the account books."

"You work too much," Luis mumbled.

Surprised, Liz turned back to him. "Since when?"

"Since always. It gets worse every time you send Faith back to school. Better off if she was here."

That her voice cooled only slightly was a mark of her affection for Luis. "No, she's happy in Houston with my parents. If I thought she wasn't, she wouldn't be there."

"She's happy, sure. What about you?"

Her brows drew together as she picked her keys from a drawer. "Do I look unhappy?"

"No." Tentatively, he touched her shoulder. He'd known Liz for years, and understood there were boundaries she wouldn't let anyone cross. "But you don't look happy either. How come you don't give one of these rich American tourists a spin? That one on the boat—his eyes popped out every time he looked at you."

The exaggeration made her laugh, so she patted his cheek. "So you think a rich American tourist is the road to happiness?"

"Maybe a handsome Mexican."

"I'll think about it—after the summer season. Go home," she ordered.

"I'm going." Luis pulled a T-shirt over his chest. "You look out for that Jonas Sharpe," he added. "He's got a different kind of look in his eyes."

Liz waved him off. *"Hasta luego."*

When the shop was empty, Liz stood, jingling her keys and looking out onto the beach. People traveled in couples, she noted, from the comfortably married duo stretched out on lounge chairs, to the young man and woman curled together on a beach towel. Was it an easy feeling, she wondered, to be half of a set? Or did you automatically lose part of yourself when you joined with another?

She'd always thought of her parents as separate people, yet when she thought of one, the other came quickly to mind. Would it be a comfort to know you could reach out your hand and someone else's would curl around it?

She held out her own and remembered how hard, how strong, Jonas's had been. No, he wouldn't make a relationship a comfortable affair. Being joined with him would be demanding, even frightening. A woman would have to be strong enough to keep herself intact, and soft enough to allow herself to merge. A relationship with a man like Jonas would be a risk that would never ease.

For a moment, she found herself dreaming of it, dreaming of what it had been like to be held close and kissed as though nothing and no one else existed. To be kissed like that always, to be held like that whenever the need moved you—it might be worth taking chances for.

Stupid, she thought quickly, shaking herself out of it. Jonas wasn't looking for a partner, and she wasn't looking for a dream. Circumstances had tossed them together temporarily. Both of them had to deal with their own realities. But she felt a sense of regret and a stirring of wishes.

Because the feeling remained, just beyond her grasp, Liz concentrated hard on the little details that needed attending to before she could close up. The paperwork and the contents of the cash box were transferred to a canvas portfolio. She'd have to swing out of her way to make a night deposit, but she no longer felt safe taking the cash or the checks home. She spent an extra few minutes meticulously filling out a deposit slip.

It wasn't until she'd picked up her keys again that she remembered her tanks. Tucking the portfolio under the counter, she turned to deal with her own gear.

It was perhaps her only luxury. She'd spent more on her personal equipment than she had on all the contents of her closet and dresser. To Liz, the wet suit was more exciting than any French silks. All her gear was kept separate from the shop's inventory. Unlocking the door to the closet, Liz hung up her wet suit, stored her mask, weight belt, regulator. Her knife was sheathed and set on a shelf. After setting her tanks side by side, she shut the door and prepared to lock it again. After she'd taken two steps away she looked down at the keys again. Without knowing precisely why, she moved each one over the ring and identified it.

The shop door, the shop window, her bike, the lock for the chain, the cash box, the front and back doors of her house, her storage room. Eight keys for eight locks. But there was one more on her ring, a small silver key that meant nothing to her at all.

Puzzled, she counted off the keys again, and again found one extra. Why should there be a key on her ring that didn't belong to her? Closing her fingers over it, she tried to think if anyone had given her the key to hold. No, it didn't make sense. Brows drawn together, she studied the key again. Too small for a car or door key, she decided. It looked like the key to a locker, or a box or... Ridiculous, she decided on a long breath. It wasn't her key but it was on her ring. Why?

Because someone put it there, she realized, and opened her hand again. Her keys were often tossed in the drawer at the shop for easy access for Luis or one of the other men. They needed to open the cash box. And Jerry had often worked in the shop alone.

With a feeling of dread, Liz slipped the keys into her pocket. Jonas's words echoed in her head. *"You're involved, whether you want to be or not."*

Liz closed the shop early.

Jonas stepped into the dim bar to the scent of garlic and the wail of a squeaky jukebox. In Spanish, someone sang of endless love. He stood for a moment, letting his eyes adjust, then skimmed his gaze over the narrow booths. As agreed, Erika sat all the way in the back, in the corner.

"You're late." She waved an unlit cigarette idly as he joined her.

"I passed it the first time. This place isn't exactly on the tourist route."

She closed her lips over the filter as Jonas lit her cigarette. "I wanted privacy."

Jonas glanced around. There were two men at the bar, each deep in separate bottles. Another couple squeezed themselves together on one side of a booth. The rest of the bar was deserted. "You've got it."

"But I don't have a drink."

Jonas slid out from the booth and bought two drinks at the bar. He set tequila and lime in front of Erika and settled for club soda. "You said you had something for me."

Erica twined a string of colored beads around her finger. "You said you would pay fifty for a name."

In silence, Jonas took out his wallet. He set fifty on the table, but laid his hand over it. "You have the name."

Erika smiled and sipped at her drink. "Maybe. Maybe you want it bad enough to pay another fifty."

Jonas studied her coolly. This was the type his brother had always been attracted to. The kind of woman whose hard edge was just a bit obvious. He could give her another fifty, Jonas mused, but he didn't care to be taken for a sucker. Without a word, he picked up the bill and tucked it into his pocket. He was halfway out of the booth when Erika grabbed his arm.

"Okay, don't get mad. Fifty." She sent him an easy smile as he settled back again. Erika had been around too long to let an opportunity slip away. "A girl has to make a living, *sí?* The name is Pablo Manchez—he's the one with the face."

"Where can I find him?"

"I don't know. You got the name."

With a nod, Jonas took the bill out and passed it to her.

Erika folded it neatly into her purse. "I'll tell you something else, because Jerry was a sweet guy." Her gaze skimmed the bar again as she leaned closer to Jonas. "This Manchez, he's bad. People got nervous when I asked about him. I heard he was mixed up in a couple of murders in Acapulco last year. He's paid, you know, to…" She made a gun out of her hand and pushed down her thumb. "When I hear that, I stop asking questions."

"What about the other one, the American?"

"Nothing. Nobody knows him. But if he hangs out with Manchez, he's not a Boy Scout." Erika tipped back her drink. "Jerry got himself in some bad business."

"Yeah."

"I'm sorry." She touched the bracelet on her wrist. "He gave me this. We had some good times."

The air in the bar was stifling him. Jonas rose and hesitated only a moment before he took out another bill and set it next to her drink. "Thanks."

Erika folded the bill as carefully as the first. *"De nada."*

She'd wanted him to be home. When Liz found the house empty, she made a fist over the keys in her hand and swore in frustration. She couldn't sit still; her nerves had been building all during the drive home. Outside, Moralas's evening shift was taking over.

For how long? she wondered. How long would the police sit patiently outside her house and follow her through her daily routine? In her bedroom, Liz closed the canvas bag of papers and cash in her desk. She regretted not having a lock for it, as well. Sooner or later, she thought, Moralas would back off on the protection. Then where would she be? Liz looked down at the key again. She'd be alone, she told herself bluntly. She had to do something.

On impulse, she started into her daughter's room. Perhaps Jerry had left a case, a box of some kind that the police had overlooked. Systematically she searched Faith's closet. When she found the little teddy bear with the worn ear, she brought it down from the shelf. She'd bought it for Faith before she'd been born. It was a vivid shade of purple, or had been so many years before. Now it was faded a bit, a little loose at the seams. The ear had been worn down to a nub because Faith had always carried him by it. They'd never named it, Liz recalled. Faith had merely called it *mine* and been satisfied.

On a wave of loneliness that rocked her, Liz buried her face against the faded purple pile. "Oh, I miss you, baby," she murmured. "I don't know if I can stand it."

"Liz?"

On a gasp of surprise, Liz stumbled back against the closet door. When she saw Jonas, she put the bear behind her back. "I didn't hear you come in," she said, feeling foolish.

"You were busy." He came toward her to gently pry the bear from her fingers. "He looks well loved."

"He's old." She cleared her throat and took the toy back again. But she found it impossible to stick it back on the top shelf. "I keep meaning to sew up the seams before the stuffing falls out." She set the bear down on Faith's dresser. "You've been out."

"Yes." He'd debated telling her of his meeting with Erika, and had decided to keep what he'd learned to himself, at least for now. "You're home early."

"I found something." Liz reached in her pocket and drew out her keys. "This isn't mine."

Jonas frowned at the key she indicated. "I don't know what you mean."

"I mean this isn't my key, and I don't know how it got on my ring."

"You just found it today?"

"I found it today, but it could have been put on any-time. I don't think I would've noticed." With the vain hope of distancing herself, Liz unhooked it from the others and handed it to Jonas. "I keep these in a drawer at the shop when I'm there. At home, I usually toss them on the kitchen counter. I can't think of any reason for someone to put it with mine unless they wanted to hide it."

Jonas examined the key. "'The Purloined Letter,'" he murmured.

"What?"

"It was one of Jerry's favorite stories when we were kids. I remember when he tested out the theory by put-ting a book he'd bought for my father for Christmas on the shelf in the library."

"So do you think it was his?"

"I think it would be just his style."

Liz picked up the bear again, finding it comforted her. "It doesn't do much good to have a key when you don't have the lock."

"It shouldn't be hard to find it." He held the key up by the stem. "Do you know what it is?"

"A key." Liz sat on Faith's bed. No, she hadn't distanced herself. The quicksand was bubbling again.

"To a safe-deposit box." Jonas turned it over to read the numbers etched into the metal.

"Do you think Captain Moralas can trace it?"

"Eventually," Jonas murmured. The key was warm in his hand. It was the next step, he thought. It had to be. "But I'm not telling him about it."

"Why?"

"Because he'd want it, and I don't intend to give it to him until I open the lock myself."

She recognized the look easily enough now. It was still revenge. Leaving the bear on her daughter's bed, Liz rose. "What are you going to do, go from bank to bank and ask if you can try the key out? You won't have to call the police, they will."

"I've got some connections—and I've got the serial number." Jonas pocketed the key. "With luck, I'll have the name of the bank by tomorrow afternoon. You may have to take a couple of days off."

"I can't take a couple of days off, and if I could, why should I need to?"

"We're going to Acapulco."

She started to make some caustic comment, then stopped. "Because Jerry told Erika he'd had business there?"

"If Jerry was mixed up in something, and he had something important or valuable, he'd tuck it away. A safe-deposit box in Acapulco makes sense."

"Fine. If that's what you believe, have a nice trip." She started to brush past him. Jonas only had to shift his body to bar the door.

"We go together."

The word "together" brought back her thoughts on couples and comfort. And it made her remember her conclusion about Jonas. "Look, Jonas, I can't drop everything and follow you on some wild-goose chase. Acapulco is very cosmopolitan. You won't need an interpreter."

"The key was on your ring. The knife was at your throat. I want you where I can see you."

"Concerned?" Her face hardened, muscle by muscle. "You're not concerned with me, Jonas. And you're certainly not concerned *about* me. The only thing you care about is your revenge. I don't want any part of it, or you."

He took her by the shoulders until she was backed against the door. "We both know that's not true. We've started something." His gaze skimmed down, lingered on her lips. "And it's not going to stop until we're both finished with it."

"I don't know what you're talking about."

"Yes, you do." He pressed closer so that their bodies met and strained, one against the other. He pressed closer to prove something, perhaps only to himself. "Yes, you do," he repeated. "I came here to do something, and I intend to do it. I don't give a damn if you call it revenge."

Her heart was beating lightly at her throat. She wouldn't call it fear. But his eyes were cold and close. "What else?"

"Justice."

She felt an uncomfortable twinge, remembering her own feelings on justice. "You're not using your law books, Jonas."

"Law doesn't always equal justice. I'm going to find out what happened to my brother and why." He skimmed his hand over her face and tangled his fingers in her hair.

He didn't find silk and satin, but a woman of strength. "But there's more now. I look at you and I want you." He reached out, taking her face in his hand so that she had no choice but to look directly at him. "I hold you and I forget what I have to do. Damn it, you're in my way."

At the end of the words, his mouth was crushed hard on hers. He hadn't meant to. He hadn't had a choice. Before he'd been gentle with her because the look in her eyes requested it. Now he was rough, desperate, because the power of his own needs demanded it.

He frightened her. She'd never known fear could be a source of exhilaration. As her heart pounded in her throat, she let him pull her closer, still closer to the edge. He dared her to jump off, to let herself tumble down into the unknown. To risk.

His mouth drew desperately from hers, seeking passion, seeking submission, seeking strength. He wanted it all. He wanted it mindlessly from her. His hands were reaching for her as if they'd always done so. When he found her, she stiffened, resisted, then melted so quickly that it was nearly impossible to tell one mood from the next. She smelled of the sea and tasted of innocence, a combination of mystery and sweetness that drove him mad.

Forgetting everything but her, he drew her toward the bed and fulfillment.

"No." Liz pushed against him, fighting to bring herself back. They were in her daughter's room. "Jonas, this is wrong."

He took her by the shoulders. "Damn it, it may be the only thing that's right."

She shook her head, and though unsteady, backed away.

His eyes weren't cold now. A woman might dream of having a man look at her with such fire and need. A woman might toss all caution aside if only to have a man want her with such turbulent desire. She couldn't.

"Not for me. I don't want this, Jonas." She reached up to push back her hair. "I don't want to feel like this."

He took her hand before she could back away. His head was swimming. There had been no other time, no other place, no other woman that had come together to make him ache. "Why?"

"I don't make the same mistake twice."

"This is now, Liz."

"And it's my life." She took a long, cleansing breath and found she could face him squarely. "I'll go with you to Acapulco because the sooner you have what you want, the sooner you'll go." She gripped her hands together tightly, the only outward sign that she was fighting herself. "You know Moralas will have us followed."

He had his own battles to fight. "I'll deal with that."

Liz nodded because she was sure he would. "Do what you have to do. I'll make arrangements for Luis to take over the shop for a day or two."

When she left him alone, Jonas closed his hands over the key again. It would open a lock, he thought. But there was another lock that mystified and frustrated him. Idly, he picked up the bear Liz had left on the bed. He looked from it to the key in his hand. Somehow he'd have to find a way to bring them together.

Chapter 6

Acapulco wasn't the Mexico Liz understood and loved. It wasn't the Mexico she'd fled to a decade before, nor where she'd made her home. It was sophisticated and ultra modern with spiraling high-rise hotels crowded together and gleaming in tropical sunlight. It was swimming pools and trendy shops. Perhaps it was the oldest resort in Mexico, and boasted countless restaurants and nightclubs, but Liz preferred the quietly rural atmosphere of her own island.

Still she had to admit there was something awesome about the city, cupped in the mountains and kissed by a magnificent bay. She'd lived all her life in flat land, from Houston to Cozumel. The mountains made everything else seem smaller, and somehow protected. Over the water, colorful parachutes floated, allowing the adventurous a bird's-eye view and a stunning ride. She wondered fleetingly if skimming through the sky would be as liberating as skimming through the water.

The streets were crowded and noisy, exciting in their own way. It occurred to her that she'd seen more people in the hour since they'd landed at the airport than she might in a week on Cozumel. Liz stepped out of the cab and wondered if she'd have time to check out any of the dive shops.

Jonas had chosen the hotel methodically. It was luxuriously expensive—just Jerry's style. The villas overlooked the Pacific and were built directly into the mountainside. Jonas took a suite, pocketed the key and left the luggage to the bellman.

"We'll go to the bank now." It had taken him two days to match the key with a name. He wasn't going to waste any more time.

Liz followed him out onto the street. True, she hadn't come to enjoy herself, but a look at their rooms and a bite of lunch didn't seem so much to ask. Jonas was already climbing into a cab. "I don't suppose you'd considered making that a request."

He gave her a brief look as she slammed the cab door. "No." After giving the driver their direction, Jonas settled back. He could understand Jerry drifting to Acapulco, with its jet-set flavor, frantic nightlife and touches of luxury. When Jerry landed in a place for more than a day, it was a city that had the atmosphere of New York, London, Chicago. Jerry had never been interested in the rustic, serene atmosphere of a spot like Cozumel. So since he'd gone there, stayed there, he'd had a purpose. In Acapulco, Jonas would find out what it was.

As to the woman beside him, he didn't have a clue. Was she caught up in the circumstances formed before they'd ever met, or was he dragging her in deeper than he had a right to? She sat beside him, silent and a little sulky. Probably thinking about her shop, Jonas decided, and wished he could send her safely back to it. He wished he could turn around, go back to the villa and make love with her until they were both sated.

She shouldn't have appealed to him at all. She wasn't witty, flawlessly polished or classically beautiful. But she did appeal to him, so much so that he was spending his nights awake and restless, and his days on the edge of frustration. He wanted her, wanted to fully explore the tastes of passion she'd given him. He wanted to arouse her until she couldn't think of accounts or customers or schedules. Perhaps it was a matter of wielding power—he could no longer be sure. But mostly, inexplicably, he wanted to erase the memory of how she'd looked when he'd walked into her daughter's room and found her clutching a stuffed bear.

When the cab rolled up in front of the bank, Liz stepped out on the curb without a word. There were shops across the streets, boutiques where she could see bright, wonderful dresses on cleverly posed mannequins. Even with the distance, she caught the gleam and glimmer of jewelry. A limousine rolled by, with smoked glass windows and quiet engine. Liz looked beyond the tall, glossy buildings to the mountains, and space.

"I suppose this is the sort of place that appeals to you."

He'd watched her survey. She didn't have to speak for him to understand that she'd compared Acapulco with her corner of Mexico and found Acapulco lacking. "Under certain circumstances." Taking her arm, Jonas led her inside.

The bank was, as banks should be, quiet and sedate. Clerks wore neat suits and polite smiles. What conversation there was, was carried on in murmurs. Jerry, he thought, had always preferred the ultraconservative in storing his money, just as he'd preferred the wild in spending it. Without hesitation, Jonas strolled over to the most attractive teller. "Good afternoon."

She glanced up. It only took a second for her polite smile to brighten. "Mr. Sharpe, *Buenos días.* It's nice to see you again."

Beside him, Liz stiffened. He's been here before, she thought. Why hadn't he told her? She sent a long, probing look his way. Just what game was he playing?

"It's nice to see you." He leaned against the counter, urbane and, she noted, flirtatious. The little tug of jealousy was as unexpected as it was unwanted. "I wondered if you'd remember me."

The teller blushed before she glanced cautiously toward her supervisor. "Of course. How can I help you today?"

Jonas took the key out of his pocket. "I'd like to get into my box." He simply turned and stopped Liz with a look when she started to speak.

"I'll arrange that for you right away." The teller took a form, dated it and passed it to Jonas. "If you'll just sign here."

Jonas took her pen and casually dashed off a signature. Liz read: *Jeremiah C. Sharpe.* Though she looked up quickly, Jonas was smiling at the teller. Because her supervisor was hovering nearby, the teller stuck to procedure and checked the signature against the card in the files. They matched perfectly.

"This way, Mr. Sharpe."

"Isn't that illegal?" Liz murmured as the teller led them from the main lobby.

"Yes." Jonas gestured for her to precede him through the doorway.

"And does it make me an accessory?"

He smiled at her, waiting while the teller drew the long metal box from its slot. "Yes. If there's any trouble, I'll recommend a good lawyer."

"Great. All I need's another lawyer."

"You can use this booth, Mr. Sharpe. Just ring when you're finished."

"Thanks." Jonas nudged Liz inside, shut, then locked, the door.

"How did you know?"

"Know what?" Jonas set the box on a table.

"To go to that clerk? When she first spoke to you, I thought you'd been here before."

"There were three men and two women. The other woman was into her fifties. As far as Jerry would've been concerned, there would have been only one clerk there."

That line of thinking was clear enough, but his actions weren't. "You signed his name perfectly."

Key in hand, Jonas looked at her. "He was part of me. If we were in the same room, I could have told you what he was thinking. Writing his name is as easy as writing my own."

"And was it the same for him?"

It could still hurt, quickly and unexpectedly. "Yes, it was the same for him."

But Liz remembered Jerry's good-natured description of his brother as a stuffed shirt. The man Liz was beginning to know didn't fit. "I wonder if you understood each other as well as both of you thought." She looked down at the box again. None of her business, she thought, and wished it were as true as she'd once believed. "I guess you'd better open it."

He slipped the key into the lock, then turned it soundlessly. When he drew back the lid, Liz could only stare. She'd never seen so much money in her life. It sat in neat stacks, tidily banded, crisply American. Unable to resist, Liz reached out to touch.

"God, it looks like thousands." She swallowed. "Hundreds of thousands."

His face expressionless, Jonas flipped through the stacks. The booth became as quiet as a tomb. "Roughly three hundred thousand, in twenties and fifties."

"Do you think he stole it?" she murmured, too overwhelmed to notice Jonas's hands tighten on the money. "This must be the money the man who broke into my house wanted."

"I'm sure it is." Jonas set down a stack of bills and picked up a small bag. "But he didn't steal it." He forced his emotions to freeze. "I'm afraid he earned it."

"How?" she demanded. "No one earns this kind of money in a matter of days, and I'd swear Jerry was nearly broke when I hired him. I know Luis lent him ten thousand pesos before his first paycheck."

"I'm sure he was." He didn't bother to add that he'd

wired his brother two hundred before Jerry had left New Orleans. Carefully, Jonas reached under the stack of money and pulled out a small plastic bag, dipped in a finger and tasted. But he'd already known.

"What is that?"

His face expressionless, Jonas sealed the bag. He couldn't allow himself any more grief. "Cocaine."

Horrified, Liz stared at the bag. "I don't understand. He lived in my house. I'd have known if he were using drugs."

Jonas wondered if she realized just how innocent she was of the darker side of humanity. Until that moment, he hadn't fully realized just how intimate he was with it. "Maybe, maybe not. In any case, Jerry wasn't into this sort of thing. At least not for himself."

Liz sat down slowly. "You mean he sold it?"

"Dealt drugs?" Jonas nearly smiled. "No, that wouldn't have been exciting enough." In the corner of the box was a small black address book. Jonas took it out to leaf through it. "But smuggling," he murmured. "Jerry could have justified smuggling. Action, intrigue and fast money."

Her mind was whirling as she tried to focus back on the man she'd known so briefly. Liz had thought she'd understood him, categorized him, but he was more of a stranger now than when he'd been alive. It didn't seem to matter anymore who or what Jerry Sharpe had been. But the man in front of her mattered. "And you?" she asked. "Can you justify it?"

He glanced down at her, over the book in his hands. His eyes were cold, so cold that she could read nothing in them at all. Without answering, Jonas went back to the book.

"He'd listed initials, dates, times and some numbers. It looks as though he made five thousand a drop. Ten drops."

Liz glanced over at the money again. It no longer seemed crisp and neat but ugly and ill used. "That only makes fifty thousand. You said there was three hundred."

"That's right." Plus a bag of uncut cocaine with a hefty street value. Jonas took out his own book and copied down the pages from his brother's.

"What are we going to do with this?"

"Nothing."

"Nothing?" Liz rose again, certain she'd stepped into a dream. "Do you mean just leave it here? Just leave it here in this box and walk away?"

With the last of the numbers copied, Jonas replaced his brother's book. "Exactly."

"Why did we come if we're not going to do anything with it?"

He slipped his own book into his jacket. "To find it."

"Jonas." Before he could close the lid she had her hand on his wrist. "You have to take it to the police. To Captain Moralas."

In a deliberate gesture, he removed her hand, then picked up the bag of coke. She understood rejection and braced herself against it. But it wasn't rejection she saw in his face; it was fury. "You want to take this on the plane, Liz? Any idea on what the penalty is in Mexico for carrying controlled substances?"

"No."

"And you don't want to." He closed the lid, locked it. "For now, just forget you saw anything. I'll handle this in my own way."

"No."

His emotions were raw and tangled, his patience thin. "Don't push me, Liz."

"Push you?" Infuriated, she grabbed his shirtfront and planted her feet. "You've pushed me for days. Pushed me right into the middle of something that's so opposed to the way I've lived I can't even take it all in. Now that I'm over my head in drug smuggling and something like a quarter of a million dollars, you tell me to forget it. What do you expect me to do, go quietly back and rent tanks? Maybe you've finished using me now, Jonas, but I'm not ready to be brushed aside. There's a murderer out there who thinks I know where the money is." She stopped as her skin iced over. "And now I do."

"That's just it," Jonas said quietly. For the second time, he removed her hands, but this time he held on to her wrists. Frightened, he thought. He was sure her pulse beat with fear as well as anger. "Now you do. The best thing for you to do now is stay out of it, let them focus on me."

"Just how am I supposed to do that?"

The anger was bubbling closer, the anger he'd wanted to lock in the box with what had caused it. "Go to Houston, visit your daughter."

"How can I?" she demanded in a whisper that vibrated in the little room. "They might follow me." She looked down at the long, shiny box. "They would follow me. I won't risk my daughter's safety."

She was right, and because he knew it, Jonas wanted to rage. He was boxed in, trapped between love and loyalty and right and wrong. Justice and the law. "We'll talk to

Moralas when we get back." He picked up the box again, hating it.

"Where are we going now?"

Jonas unlocked the door. "To get a drink."

Rather than going with Jonas to the lounge, Liz took some time for herself. Because she felt he owed her, she went into the hotel's boutique, found a simple one-piece bathing suit and charged it to the room. She hadn't packed anything but a change of clothes and toiletries. If she was stuck in Acapulco for the rest of the evening, she was going to enjoy the private pool each villa boasted.

The first time she walked into the suite, she was dumbfounded. Her parents had been reasonably successful, and she'd been raised in a quietly middle-class atmosphere. Nothing had prepared her for the sumptuousness of the two-bedroom suite overlooking the Pacific. Her feet sank cozily into the carpet. Softly colored paintings were spaced along ivory-papered walls. The sofa, done in grays and greens and blues, was big enough for two to sprawl on for a lazy afternoon nap.

She found a phone in the bathroom next to a tub so wide and deep that she was almost tempted to take her dip there. The sink was a seashell done in the palest of pinks.

So this is how the rich play, she mused as she wandered to the bedroom where her overnight bag was set at the end of a bed big enough for three. The drapes of her balcony were open so that she could see the tempestuous surf of the Pacific hurl up and spray. She pulled the glass doors open, wanting the noise.

This was the sort of world Marcus had told her of so

many years before. He'd made it seem like a fairy tale with gossamer edges. Liz had never seen his home, had never been permitted to, but he'd described it to her. The white pillars, the white balconies, the staircase that curved up and up. There were servants to bring you tea in the afternoons, a stable where grooms waited to saddle glossy horses. Champagne was drunk from French crystal. It had been a fairy tale, and she hadn't wanted it for herself. She had only wanted him.

A young girl's foolishness, Liz thought now. In her naive way, she'd made a prince out of a man who was weak and selfish and spoiled. But over the years she had thought of the house he'd talked of and pictured her daughter on those wide, curving stairs. That had been her sense of justice.

The image wasn't as clear now, not now that she'd seen wealth in a long metal box and understood where it had come from. Not when she'd seen Jonas's eyes when he'd spoken of his kind of justice. That hadn't been a fairy tale with gossamer edges, but grimly real. She had some thinking to do. But before she could plan for the rest of her life, and for her daughter's, she had to get through the moment.

Jonas. She was bound to him through no choice of her own. And perhaps he was bound to her in the same way. Was that the reason she was drawn to him? Because they were trapped in the same puzzle? If she could only explain it away, maybe she could stop the needs that kept swimming through her. If she could only explain it away, maybe she would be in control again.

But how could she explain the feelings she'd experienced on the silent cab ride back to the hotel? She had had to fight the desire to put her arms around him, to offer comfort when nothing in his manner had indicated he needed or wanted it. There were no easy answers—no answers at all to the fact that she was slowly, inevitably falling in love with him.

It was time to admit that, she decided, because you could never face anything until it was admitted. You could never solve anything until it was faced. She'd lived by that rule years before during the biggest crisis of her life. It still held true.

So she loved him, or very nearly loved him. She was no longer naive enough to believe that love was the beginning of any answer. He would hurt her. There were no ifs about that. He'd steal from her the one thing she'd managed to hold fast to for ten years. And once he'd taken her heart, what would it mean to him? She shook her head. No more than such things ever mean to those who take them.

Jonas Sharpe was a man on a mission, and she was no more to him than a map. He was ruthless in his own patient way. When he had finished what he'd come to do, he would turn away from her, go back to his life in Philadelphia and never think of her again.

Some women, Liz thought, were doomed to pick the men who could hurt them the most. Making her mind a blank, Liz stripped and changed to her bathing suit. But Jonas, thoughts of Jonas, kept slipping through the barriers.

Maybe if she talked to Faith—if she could touch her greatest link with normality, things would snap back into focus. On impulse, Liz picked up the phone beside her bed and began the process of placing the call. Faith would just be home from school, Liz calculated, growing more excited as she heard the clinks and buzzes on the receiver. When the phone began to ring, she sat on the bed. She was already smiling.

"Hello?"

"Mom?" Liz felt the twin surges of pleasure and guilt as she heard her mother's voice. "It's Liz."

"Liz!" Rose Palmer felt identical surges. "We didn't expect to hear from you. Your last letter just came this morning. Nothing's wrong, is it?"

"No, no, nothing's wrong." Everything's wrong. "I just wanted to talk to Faith."

"Oh, Liz, I'm so sorry. Faith's not here. She has her piano lesson today."

The letdown came, but she braced herself against it. "I forgot." Tears threatened, but she forced them back. "She likes the lessons, doesn't she?"

"She loves them. You should hear her play. Remember when you were taking them?"

"I had ten thumbs." She managed to smile. "I wanted to thank you for sending the pictures. She looks so grown up. Momma, is she…looking forward to coming back?"

Rose heard the need, felt the ache. She wished, not for the first time, that her daughter was close enough to hold. "She's marking off the days on her calendar. She bought you a present."

Liz had to swallow. "She did?"

"It's supposed to be a surprise, so don't tell her I told you."

"I won't." She dashed tears away, grateful she could

keep her voice even. It hurt, but was also a comfort to be able to speak to someone who knew and understood Faith as she did. "I miss her. The last few weeks always seem the hardest."

Her voice wasn't as steady as she thought—and a mother hears what others don't. "Liz, why don't you come home? Spend the rest of the month here while she's in school?"

"No, I can't. How's Dad?"

Rose fretted impatiently at the change of subject, then subsided. She'd never known anyone as thoroughly stubborn as her daughter. Unless it was her granddaughter. "He's fine. Looking forward to coming down and doing some diving."

"We'll take one of the boats out—just the four of us. Tell Faith I...tell her I called," she finished lamely.

"Of course I will. Why don't I have her call you back when she gets home? The car pool drops her off at five."

"No. No, I'm not home. I'm in Acapulco—on business." Liz let out a long breath to steady herself. "Just tell her I miss her and I'll be waiting at the airport. You know I appreciate everything you're doing. I just—"

"Liz." Rose interrupted gently. "We love Faith. And we love you."

"I know." Liz pressed her fingers to her eyes. She did know, but was never quite sure what to do about it. "I love you, too. It's just that sometimes things get so mixed up."

"Are you all right?"

She dropped her hand again, and her eyes were dry. "I will be when you get there. Tell Faith I'm marking off the days too."

"I will."

"Bye, Momma."

She hung up and sat until the churning emptiness had run its course. If she'd had more confidence in her parents' support, more trust in their love, would she have fled the States and started a new life on her own? Liz dragged a hand through her hair. She'd never be sure of that, nor could she dwell on it. She'd burned her own bridges. The only thing that was important was Faith, and her happiness.

An hour later, Jonas found her at the pool. She swam laps in long, smooth strokes, her body limber. She seemed tireless, and oddly suited to the private luxury. Her suit was a flashy red, but the cut so simple that it relied strictly on the form it covered for style.

He counted twenty laps before she stopped, and wondered how many she'd completed before he'd come down. It seemed to him as if she swam to drain herself of some tension or sorrow, and that with each lap she'd come closer to succeeding. Waiting, he watched her tip her head back in the water so that her hair slicked back. The marks on her neck had faded. As she stood, water skimmed her thigh.

"I've never seen you relaxed," Jonas commented. But even as he said the words, he could see her muscles tense again. She turned away from her contemplation of the mountains and looked at him.

He was tired, she realized, and wondered if she should have seen it before. There was a weariness around his eyes that hadn't been there that morning. He hadn't changed his clothes, and had his hands tucked into the pockets of bone-colored slacks. She wondered if he'd been up to the suite at all.

"I didn't bring a suit with me." Liz pushed against the side of the pool and hitched herself out. Water rained from her. "I charged this one to the room."

The thighs were cut nearly to the waist. Jonas caught himself wondering just how the skin would feel there. "It's nice."

Liz picked up her towel. "It was expensive."

He only lifted a brow. "I could deduct it from the rent."

Her lips curved a little as she rubbed her hair dry. "No, you can't. But since you're a lawyer, I imagine you can find a way to deduct it from something else. I saved the receipt."

He hadn't thought he could laugh. "I appreciate it. You know, I get the impression you don't think much of lawyers."

Something came and went in her eyes. "I try not to think of them at all."

Taking the towel from her, he gently dried her face. "Faith's father's a lawyer?"

Without moving, she seemed to shift away from him. "Leave it alone, Jonas."

"You don't."

"Actually I do, most of the time. Maybe it's been on my mind the past few weeks, but that's my concern."

He draped the towel around her shoulders and, holding the ends, drew her closer. "I'd like you to tell me about it."

It was his voice, she thought, so calm, so persuasive, that nearly had her opening both mind and heart. She could almost believe as she looked at him that he really wanted to know, to understand. The part of her that was already in love with him needed to believe he might care. "Why?"

"I don't know. Maybe it's that look that comes into your eyes. It makes a man want to stroke it away."

Her chin came up a fraction. "There's no need to feel sorry for me."

"I don't think sympathy's the right word." Abruptly weary, he dropped his forehead to hers. He was tired of fighting demons, of trying to find answers. "Damn."

Uncertain, she stood very still. "Are you all right?"

"No. No, I'm not." He moved away from her to walk to the end of the path where a plot of tiny orange flowers poked up through white gravel. "A lot of things you said today were true. A lot of things you've said all along are true. I can't do anything about them."

"I don't know what you want me to say now."

"Nothing." Hideously tired, he ran both hands over his face. "I'm trying to live with the fact that my brother's dead, and that he was murdered because he decided to make some easy money drug-trafficking. He had a good brain, but he always chose to use it in the wrong way. Every time I look in the mirror, I wonder why."

Liz was beside him before she could cut off her feelings. He hurt. It was the first time she'd seen below the surface to the pain. She knew what it was like to live with pain. "He was different, Jonas. I don't think he was bad, just weak. Mourning him is one thing—blaming yourself for what he did, or for what happened to him, is another."

He hadn't known he needed comfort, but her hand resting on him had something inside him slowly uncurling. "I was the only one who could reach him, keep him on some kind of level. There came a point where I just got tired of running both our lives."

"Do you really believe you could have prevented him from doing what he did?"

"Maybe. That's something else I have to live with."

"Just a minute." She took his shirtfront in much the same way she had that afternoon. There was no sympathy now, but annoyance on her face. He hadn't known he needed that, as well. "You were brothers, twins, but you were separate people. Jerry wasn't a child to be guided and supervised. He was a grown man who made his decisions."

"That's the trouble. Jerry never grew up."

"And you did," she tossed back. "Are you going to punish yourself for it?"

He'd been doing just that, Jonas realized. He'd gone home, buried his brother, comforted his parents and blamed himself for not preventing something he knew in his heart had been inevitable. "I have to find out who killed him, Liz. I can't set the rest aside until I do."

"We'll find them." On impulse, she pressed her cheek to his. Sometimes the slightest human contact could wash away acres of pain. "Then it'll be over."

He wasn't sure he wanted it to be, not all of it. He ran a hand down her arm, needing the touch of her skin. He found it chilled. "The sun's gone down." He wrapped the towel around her in a gesture that would have been mere politeness with another woman. With Liz, it was for protection. "You'd better get out of that wet suit. We'll have dinner."

"Here?"

"Sure. The restaurant's supposed to be one of the best."

Liz thought of the elegance of their suite and the contents of her overnight bag. "I didn't bring anything to wear."

He laughed and swung an arm around her. It was the first purely frivolous thing he'd heard her say. "Charge something else."

"But—"

"Don't worry, I've got the best crooked accountant in Philadelphia."

Chapter 7

Because she'd been certain she would never sleep away from home, in a hotel bed, Liz was surprised to wake to full sunlight. Not only had she slept, she realized, she'd slept like a rock for eight hours and was rested and ready to go. True, it was just a little past six, and she had no business to run, but her body was tuned to wake at that hour. A trip to Acapulco didn't change that.

It had changed other things, she reminded herself as she stretched out in the too-big bed. Because of it, she'd become inescapably tangled in murder and smuggling. Putting the words together made her shake her head. In a movie, she might have enjoyed watching the melodrama. In a book, she'd have turned the page to read more. But in her own life, she preferred the more mundane. Liz was too practical to delude herself into believing she could distance herself from any part of the puzzle any longer. For better or worse, she was personally involved in this melodrama. That included Jonas Sharpe. The only question now was which course of action to take.

She couldn't run. That had never been a choice. Liz had already concluded she couldn't hide behind Moralas and his men forever. Sooner or later the man with the knife would come back, or another man more determined or more desperate. She wouldn't escape a second time. The moment she'd looked into the safe-deposit box, she'd become a full-fledged player in the game. Which brought her back full circle to Jonas. She had no choice but to put her trust in him now. If he were to give up on his brother's murder and return to Philadelphia she would be that much more alone. However much she might wish it otherwise, Liz needed him just as much as he needed her.

Other things had changed, she thought. Her feelings for him were even more undefined and confusing than they had started out to be. Seeing him as she had the evening before, hurt and vulnerable, had touched off more than impersonal sympathy or physical attraction. It had made her feel a kinship, and the kinship urged her to help him, not only for her own welfare, but for his. He suffered, for his brother's loss, but also for what his brother had done. She'd loved once, and had suffered, not only because of loss but because of disillusionment.

A lifetime ago? Liz wondered. Did we ever really escape from one lifetime to another? It seemed years could pass, circumstances could change, but we carried our baggage with us through each phase. If anything, with each phase we had to carry a bit more. There was little use in thinking, she told herself as she climbed from the bed. From this point on, she had little choice but to act.

Jonas heard her the moment she got up. He'd been awake since five, restless and prowling. For over an hour he'd been racking his brain and searching his conscience for a way to ease Liz out of a situation his brother, and he himself had locked her into. He'd already thought of several ways to draw attention away from her to himself, but that wouldn't guarantee Liz's safety. She wouldn't go to Houston, and he understood her feelings about endangering her daughter in any way.

As the days passed, he felt he was coming to understand her better and better. She was a loner, but only because she saw it as the safest route. She was a businesswoman, but only because she looked to her daughter's welfare first. Inside, he thought, she was a woman with dreams on hold and love held in bondage. She had steered both toward her child and denied herself. And, Jonas added, she'd convinced herself she was content.

That was something else he understood, because until a few weeks before he had also convinced himself he was content. It was only now, after he'd had the opportunity to look at his life from a distance that he realized he had merely been drifting. Perhaps, when the outward trimmings were stripped away, he hadn't been so different from his brother. For both of them, success had been the main target, they had simply aimed for it differently. Though Jonas had a steady job, a home of his own, there had never been an important woman. He'd put his career first. Jonas wasn't certain he'd be able to do so again. It had taken the loss of his brother to make him realize he needed something more, something solid. Exploring the law was only a job. Winning cases was only a transitory satisfaction. Perhaps he'd known it for some time. After all, he'd bought the old house in Chadd's Ford to give himself something permanent. When had he started thinking about sharing it?

Still, thinking about his own life didn't solve the problem of Liz Palmer and what he was going to do with her. She couldn't go to Houston, he thought again, but there were other places she could go until he could assure her that her life could settle back the way she wanted it. His parents were his first thought, and the quiet country home they'd retired to in Lancaster. If he could find a way to slip her out of Mexico, she would be safe there. It would even be possible to have her daughter join her. Then his conscience would ease. Jonas had no doubt that his parents would accept them both, then dote on them.

Once he'd done what he'd come to do, he could go to Lancaster himself. He'd like to see Liz there, in surroundings he was used to. He wanted time to talk with her about simple things. He wanted to hear her laugh again, as she had only once in all the days he'd known her. Once they were there, away from the ugliness, he might understand his feelings better. Perhaps by then he'd be able to analyze what had happened inside him when she'd pressed her cheek against his and had offered unconditional support.

He'd wanted to hold on to her, to just hold on and the hell with the world. There was something about her that made him think of lazy evenings on cool porches and long Sunday afternoon walks. He couldn't say why. In Philadelphia he rarely took time for such things. Even socializing had become business. And he'd seen for himself that she never gave herself an idle hour. Why should he, a man dedicated to his work, think of lazing days away with a woman obsessed by hers?

She remained a mystery to him, and perhaps that was an answer in itself. If he thought of her too often, too deeply, it was only because while his understanding was growing, he still knew so little. If it sometimes seemed that discovering Liz Palmer was just as important as discovering his brother's killer, it was only because they were tied together. How could he take his mind off one without taking his mind off the other? Yet when he thought of her now, he thought of her stretched out on his mother's porch swing, safe, content and waiting for him.

Annoyed with himself, Jonas checked his watch. It was after nine on the East Coast. He'd call his office, he thought. A few legal problems might clear his mind. He'd no more than picked up the receiver when Liz came out from her bedroom.

"I didn't know you were up," she said, and fiddled nervously with her belt. Odd, she felt entirely different about sharing the plush little villa with him than she did her home. After all, she reasoned, at home he was paying rent.

"I thought you'd sleep longer." He replaced the receiver again. The office could wait.

"I never sleep much past six." Feeling awkward, she wandered to the wide picture window. "Terrific view."

"Yes, it is."

"I haven't stayed in a hotel in…in years," she finished. "When I came to Cozumel, I worked in the same hotel where I'd stayed with my parents. It was an odd feeling. So's this."

"No urge to change the linen or stack the towels?"

When she chuckled, some of the awkwardness slipped away. "No, not even a twinge."

"Liz, when we're finished with all this, when it's behind us, will you talk to me about that part of your life?"

She turned to him, away from the window, but they both felt the distance. "When we're finished with this, there won't be any reason to."

He rose and came to her. In a gesture that took her completely by surprise, he took both of her hands. He lifted one, then the other, to his lips and watched her eyes cloud. "I can't be sure of that," he murmured. "Can you?"

She couldn't be sure of anything when his voice was quiet, his hands gentle. For a moment, she simply absorbed the feeling of being a woman cared for by a man. Then she stepped back, as she knew she had to. "Jonas, you told me once we had the same problem. I didn't want to believe it then, but it was true. It is true. Once that problem is solved, there really isn't anything else between us. Your life and mine are separated by a lot more than miles."

He thought of his house and his sudden need to share it. "They don't have to be."

"There was a time I might have believed that."

"You're living in the past." He took her shoulders, but this time his hands weren't as gentle. "You're fighting ghosts."

"I may have my ghosts, but I don't live in the past. I can't afford to." She put her hands to his wrists, but let them lie there only a moment before she let go. "I can't afford to pretend to myself about you."

He wanted to demand, he wanted to pull her with him

to the sofa and prove to her that she was wrong. He resisted. It wasn't the first time he'd used courtroom skill, courtroom tactics, to win on a personal level. "We'll leave it your way for now," he said easily. "But the case isn't closed. Are you hungry?"

Unsure whether she should be uneasy or relieved, Liz nodded. "A little."

"Let's have breakfast. We've got plenty of time before the plane leaves."

She didn't trust him. Though Jonas kept the conversation light and passionless throughout breakfast, Liz kept herself braced for a countermove. He was a clever man, she knew. He was a man, she was certain, who made sure he got his own way no matter how long it took. Liz considered herself a woman strong enough to keep promises made, even when they were to herself. No man, not even Jonas, was going to make her change the course she'd set ten years before. There was only room enough for two loves in her life. Faith and her work.

"I can't get used to eating something at this hour of the morning that's going to singe my stomach lining."

Liz swallowed the mixture of peppers, onions and eggs. "Mine's flame resistant. You should try my chili."

"Does that mean you're offering to cook for me?"

When Liz glanced up she wished he hadn't been smiling at her in just that way. "I suppose I could make enough for two as easily as enough for one. But you don't seem to have any trouble in the kitchen."

"Oh, I can cook. It's just that once I've finished, it never seems worth the bother." He leaned forward to run a finger down her hand from wrist to knuckle. "Tell you what—I'll buy the supplies and even clean up the mess if you handle the chili."

Though she smiled, Liz drew her hand away. "The question is, can you handle the chili? It might burn right through a soft lawyer's stomach."

Appreciating the challenge, he took her hand again. "Why don't we find out? Tonight."

"All right." She flexed her fingers, but he merely linked his with them. "I can't eat if you have my hand."

He glanced down. "You have another one."

He made her laugh when she'd been set to insist. "I'm entitled to two."

"I'll give it back. Later."

"Hey, Jerry!"

The easy smile on Jonas's face froze. Only his eyes changed, locking on to Liz's, warning and demanding. His hand remained on hers, but the grip tightened. The message was very clear—she was to do nothing, say nothing until he'd tallied the odds. He turned, flashing a new smile. Liz's stomach trembled. It was Jerry's smile, she realized. Not Jonas's.

"Why didn't you tell me you were back in town?" A tall, tanned man with sandy blond hair and a trim beard dropped a hand on Jonas's shoulder. Liz caught the glint of a diamond on his finger. He was young, she thought, determined to store everything she could, barely into his thirties, and dressed with slick, trendy casualness.

"Quick trip," Jonas said as, like Liz, he took in every detail. "Little business…" He cast a meaningful glance toward Liz. "Little pleasure."

The man turned and stared appreciatively at Liz. "Is there any other way?"

Thinking fast, Liz offered her hand. "Hello. Since Jerry's too rude to introduce us, we'll have to do it ourselves. I'm Liz Palmer."

"David Merriworth." He took her hand between both of his. They were smooth and uncallused. "Jerry might have trouble with manners, but he's got great taste."

She smiled, hoping she did it properly. "Thank you."

"Pull up a chair, Merriworth." Jonas took out a cigarette. "As long as you keep your hands off my lady." He said it in the good-natured, only-kidding tone Jerry had inevitably used, but his eyes were Jonas's, warning her to tread carefully.

"Wouldn't mind a quick cup of coffee." David pulled over a chair after he checked his watch. "Got a breakfast meeting in a few minutes. So how are things on Cozumel?" He inclined his head ever so slightly. "Getting in plenty of diving?"

Jonas allowed his lips to curve and kept his eyes steady. "Enough."

"Glad to hear it. I was going to check in with you myself, but I've been in the States for a couple weeks. Just got back in last night." He used two sugars after the waiter set a fresh cup of coffee beside him. "Business is good, buddy. Real good."

"What business are you in, Mr. Merriworth?"

He gave Liz a big grin before he winked at Jonas. "Sales, sweetheart. Imports, you might say."

"Really." Because her throat was dry she drank more coffee. "It must be fascinating."

"It has its moments." He turned in his chair so that he could study her face. "So where did Jerry find you?"

"On Cozumel." She sent Jonas a steady look. "We're partners."

David lowered his cup. "That so?"

They were in too deep, Jonas thought, for him to contradict her. "That's so," he agreed.

David picked up his cup again with a shrug. "If it's okay with the boss, it doesn't bother me."

"I do things my way," Jonas drawled. "Or I don't do them."

Amused, and perhaps admiring, David broke into a smile. "That never changes. Look, I've been out of touch for a few weeks. The drops still going smooth?"

With those words, Jonas's last hopes died. What he'd found in the safe-deposit box had been real, and it had been Jerry's. He buttered a roll as though he had all the time in the world. Beneath the table, Liz touched his leg once, hoping he'd take it as comfort. He never looked at her. "Why shouldn't they?"

"It's the classiest operation I've ever come across," David commented, taking a cautious glance around to other tables. "Wouldn't like to see anything screw it up."

"You worry too much."

"You're the one who should worry," David pointed out. "I don't have to deal with Manchez. You weren't around last year when he took care of those two Colombians. I was. You deal with supplies, I stick with sales. I sleep better."

"I just dive," Jonas said, and tapped out his cigarette. "And I sleep fine."

"He's something, isn't he?" David sent Liz another grin.

"I knew Jerry here was just the man the boss was looking for. You keep diving, kid." He tipped his cup at Jonas. "It makes me look good."

"Sounds like you two have known each other for a while," Liz said with a smile. Under the table, she twisted the napkin in her lap.

"Go way back, don't we, Jer?"

"Yeah. We go back."

"First time we hooked up was six, no, seven years ago. We were working a pigeon drop in L.A. We'd have had that twenty thousand out of that old lady if her daughter hadn't caught on." He took out a slim cigarette case. "Your brother got you out of that one, didn't he? The East Coast lawyer."

"Yeah." Jonas remembered posting the bond and pulling the strings.

"Now I've been working out of here for almost five. A real businessman." He slapped Jonas's arm. "Hell of a lot better than the pigeon drop, huh, Jerry?"

"Pays better."

David let out a roar of laughter. "Why don't I show you two around Acapulco tonight?"

"Gotta get back." Jonas signaled for the check. "Business."

"Yeah, I know what you mean." He nodded toward the restaurant's entrance. "Here's my customer now. Next time you drop down, give a call."

"Sure."

"And give my best to old Clancy." With another laugh, David gave them each a quick salute. They watched him stride across the room and shake hands with a dark-suited man.

"Don't say anything here," Jonas murmured as he signed the breakfast check. "Let's go."

Liz's crumpled napkin slid to the floor as she rose to walk out with him. He didn't speak again until they had the door of the villa closed behind them.

"You had no business telling him we were partners."

Because she'd been ready for the attack, she shrugged it off. "He said more once I did."

"He'd have said just as much if you'd made an excuse and left the table."

She folded her arms. "We have the same problem, remember?"

He didn't care to have his own words tossed back at him. "The least you could have done was to give him another name."

"Why? They know who I am. Sooner or later he's going to talk to whoever's in charge and get the whole story."

She was right. He didn't care for that either. "Are you packed?"

"Yes."

"Then let's check out. We'll go to the airport."

"And then?"

"And then we go straight to Moralas."

"You've been very busy." Moralas held on to his temper as he rocked back in his chair. "Two of my men wasted their valuable time looking for you in Acapulco. You might have told me, Mr. Sharpe, that you planned to take Miss Palmer on a trip."

"I thought a police tail in Acapulco might be inconvenient."

"And now that you have finished your own investigation, you bring me this." He held up the key and examined it. "This which Miss Palmer discovered several days ago. As a lawyer, you must understand the phrase 'withholding evidence.'"

"Of course." Jonas nodded coolly. "But neither Miss Palmer nor myself could know the key was evidence. We speculated, naturally, that it might have belonged to my brother. Withholding a speculation is hardly a crime."

"Perhaps not, but it is poor judgment. Poor judgment often translates into an offense."

Jonas leaned back in his chair. If Moralas wanted to argue law, they'd argue law. "If the key belonged to my brother, as executor of his estate, it became mine. In any case, once it was proved to me that the key did indeed belong to Jerry, and that the contents of the safe-deposit box were evidence, I brought both the key and a description of the contents to you."

"Indeed. And do you also speculate as to how your brother came to possess those particular items?"

"Yes."

Moralas waited a beat, then turned to Liz. "And you, Miss Palmer—you also have your speculations?"

She had her hands gripped tightly in her lap, but her voice was matter-of-fact and reasonable. "I know that whoever attacked me wanted money, obviously a great deal of money. We found a great deal."

"And a bag of what Mr. Sharpe…speculates is cocaine." Moralas folded his hands on the desk with the key under them. "Miss Palmer, did you at any time see Mr. Jeremiah Sharpe in possession of cocaine?"

"No."

"Did he at any time speak to you of cocaine or drug-trafficking?"

"No, of course not. I would have told you."

"As you told me about the key?" When Jonas started to protest, Moralas waved him off. "I will need a list of your customers for the past six weeks, Miss Palmer. Names and, wherever possible, addresses."

"My customers? Why?"

"It's more than possible that Mr. Sharpe used your shop for his contacts."

"My shop." Outraged, she stood up. "My boats? Do you think he could have passed drugs under my nose without me being aware?"

Moralas took out a cigar and studied it. "I very much hope you were unaware, Miss Palmer. You will bring me the list of clients by the end of the week." He glanced at Jonas. "Of course, you are within your rights to demand a warrant. It will simply slow down the process. And I, of course, am within my rights to hold Miss Palmer as a material witness."

Jonas watched the pale blue smoke circle toward the ceiling. It was tempting to call Moralas's bluff simply as an exercise in testing two ends of the law. And in doing so, he and the captain could play tug-of-war with Liz for hours. "There are times, Captain, when it's wiser not to employ certain rights. I think I'm safe in saying that the three of us in this room want basically the same thing." He rose and flicked his lighter at the end of Moralas's cigar. "You'll have your list, Captain. And more."

Moralas lifted his gaze and waited.

"Pablo Manchez," Jonas said, and was gratified to see Moralas's eyes narrow.

"What of Manchez?"

"He's on Cozumel. Or was," Jonas stated. "My brother met with him several times in local bars and clubs. You may also be interested in David Merriworth, an American working out of Acapulco. Apparently he's the one who put my brother onto his contacts in Cozumel. If you contact the authorities in the States, you'll find that Merriworth has an impressive rap sheet."

In his precise handwriting, Moralas noted down the names, though he wasn't likely to forget them. "I appreciate the information. However, in the future, Mr. Sharpe, I would appreciate it more if you stayed out of my way. *Buenas tardes,* Miss Palmer."

Moments later, Liz strode out to the street. "I don't like being threatened. That's what he was doing, wasn't it?" she demanded. "He was threatening to put me in jail."

Very calm, even a bit amused, Jonas lit a cigarette. "He was pointing out his options, and ours."

"He didn't threaten to put you in jail," Liz muttered.

"He doesn't worry as much about me as he does about you."

"Worry?" She stopped with her hand gripping the handle of Jonas's rented car.

"He's a good cop. You're one of his people."

She looked back toward the police station with a scowl. "He has a funny way of showing it." A scruffy little boy scooted up to the car and gallantly opened the door for her. Even as he prepared to hold out a hand, Liz was digging for a coin.

"Gracias."

He checked the coin, grinned at the amount and nodded approval. *"Buenas tardes, señorita."* Just as gallantly he closed the door for her while the coin disappeared into a pocket.

"It's a good thing you don't come into town often," Jonas commented.

"Why?"

"You'd be broke in a week."

Liz found a clip in her purse and pulled back her hair. "Because I gave a little boy twenty-five pesos?"

"How much did you give the other kid before we went in to Moralas?"

"I bought something from him."

"Yeah." Jonas swung away from the curb. "You look like a woman who can't go a day without a box of Chiclets."

"You're changing the subject."

"That's right. Now tell me where I can find the best place for buying ingredients for chili."

"You want me to cook for you tonight?"

"It'll keep your mind off the rest. We've done everything we can do for the moment," he added. "Tonight we're going to relax."

She would have liked to believe he was right. Between nerves and anger, she was wound tight. "Cooking's supposed to relax me?"

"Eating is going to relax you. It's just an unavoidable circumstance that you have to cook it first."

It sounded so absurd that she subsided. "Turn left at the next corner. I tell you what to buy, you buy it, then you stay out of my way."

"Agreed."

"And you clean up."

"Absolutely."

"Pull over here," she directed. "And remember, you asked for it."

Liz never skimped when she cooked, even taking into account that authentic Mexican spices had more zing than the sort sold in the average American supermarket. She'd developed a taste for Mexican food and Yucatán specialties when she'd been a child, exploring the peninsula with her parents. She wasn't an elaborate cook, and when alone would often make do with a sandwich, but when her heart was in it, she could make a meal that would more than satisfy.

Perhaps, in a way, she wanted to impress him. Liz found she was able to admit it while she prepared a Mayan salad for chilling. It was probably very natural and harmless to want to impress someone with your cooking. After peeling and slicing an avocado, she found, oddly enough, she was relaxing.

So much of what she'd done in the past few days had been difficult or strange. It was a relief to make a decision no more vital than the proper way to slice her fruits and vegetables. In the end, she fussed with the arrangement a bit more, pleased with the contrasting colors of greens and oranges and cherry tomatoes. It was, she recalled, the only salad she could get Faith to eat because it was the only one Faith considered pretty enough. Liz didn't realize she was smiling as she began to sauté onions and peppers. She added a healthy dose of garlic and let it all simmer.

"It already smells good," Jonas commented as he strode through the doorway.

She only glanced over her shoulder. "You're supposed to stay out of my way."

"You cook, I take care of the table."

Liz only shrugged and turned back to the stove. She measured, stirred and spiced until the kitchen was filled with a riot of scent. The sauce, chunky with meat and vegetables, simmered and thickened on low heat. Pleased with herself, she wiped her hands on a cloth and turned around. Jonas was sitting comfortably at the table watching her.

"You look good," he told her. "Very good."

It seemed so natural, their being together in the kitchen with a pot simmering and a breeze easing its way through the screen. It made her remember how hard it was not to want such simple things in your life. Liz set the cloth down and found she didn't know what to do with her hands. "Some men think a woman looks best in front of a stove."

"I don't know. It's a toss-up with the way you looked at the wheel of a boat. How long does that have to cook?"

"About a half hour."

"Good." He rose and went to the counter where he'd left two bottles. "We have time for some wine."

A little warning signal jangled in her brain. Liz decided she needed a lid for the chili. "I don't have the right glasses."

"I already thought of that." From a bag beside the bottle, he pulled out two thin-stemmed wineglasses.

"You've been busy," she murmured.

"You didn't like me hovering over you in the market. I had to do something." He drew out the cork, then let the wine breathe.

"These candles aren't mine."

He turned to see Liz fiddling with the fringe of one of the woven mats he'd set on the table. In the center were two deep blue tapers that picked up the color in the border of her dishes.

"They're ours," Jonas told her.

She twisted the fringe around one finger, let it go, then twisted it again. The last time she'd burned candles had been during a power failure. These didn't look sturdy, but slender and frivolous. "There wasn't any need to go to all this trouble. I don't—"

"Do candles and wine make you uneasy?"

Dropping the fringe, she let her hands fall to her sides. "No, of course not."

"Good." He poured rich red wine into both glasses. Walking to her, he offered one. "Because I find them relaxing. We did agree to relax."

She sipped, and though she wanted to back away, held her ground. "I'm afraid you may be looking for more than I can give."

"No." He touched his glass to hers. "I'm looking for exactly what you can give."

Recognizing when she was out of her depth, Liz turned toward the refrigerator. "We can start on the salad."

He lit the candles and dimmed the lights. She told herself it didn't matter. Atmosphere was nothing more than a pleasant addition to a meal.

"Very pretty," Jonas told her when she'd mixed the dressing and arranged avocado slices. "What's it called?"

"It's a Mayan salad." Liz took the first nibble and was satisfied. "I learned the recipe when I worked at the hotel. Actually, that's where most of my cooking comes from."

"Wonderful," Jonas decided after the first bite. "It makes me wish I'd talked you into cooking before."

"A one time only." She relaxed enough to smile. "Meals aren't—"

"Included in the rent," Jonas finished. "We might negotiate."

This time she laughed at him and chose a section of grapefruit. "I don't think so. How do you manage in Philadelphia?"

"I have a housekeeper who'll toss together a casserole on Wednesdays." He took another bite, enjoying the contrast of crisp greens and spicy dressing. "And I eat out a lot."

"And parties? I suppose you go to a lot of parties."

"Some business, some pleasure." He'd almost forgotten what it was like to sit in a kitchen and enjoy a simple meal. "To be honest, it wears a bit. The cruising."

"Cruising?"

"When Jerry and I were teenagers, we might hop in the car on a Friday night and cruise. The idea was to see what teenage girls had hopped in their cars to cruise. The party circuit's just adult cruising."

She frowned a bit because it didn't seem as glamorous as she'd imagined. "It seems rather aimless."

"Doesn't seem. Is."

"You don't appear to be a man who does anything without a purpose."

"I've had my share of aimless nights," he murmured. "You come to a point where you realize you don't want too many more." That was just it, he realized. It wasn't the work, the hours spent closeted with law books or in a courtroom. It was the nights without meaning that left him wanting more. He lifted the wine to top off her glass, but his eyes stayed on hers. "I came to that realization very recently."

Her blood began to stir. Deliberately, Liz pushed her wine aside and rose to go to the stove. "We all make decisions at certain points in our lives, realign our priorities."

"I have the feeling you did that a long time ago."

"I did. I've never regretted it."

That much was true, he thought. She wasn't a woman for regrets. "You wouldn't change it, would you?"

Liz continued to spoon chili into bowls. "Change what?"

"If you could go back eleven years and take a different path, you wouldn't do it."

She stopped. From across the room he could see the flicker of candlelight in her eyes as she turned to him. More, he could see the strength that softness and shadows couldn't disguise. "That would mean I'd have to give up Faith. No, I wouldn't do it."

When she set the bowls on the table, Jonas took her hand. "I admire you."

Flustered, she stared down at him. "What for?"

"For being exactly what you are."

Chapter 8

No smooth phrases, no romantic words could have affected her more deeply. She wasn't used to flattery, but flattery, Liz was sure, could be brushed easily aside by a woman who understood herself. Sincere and simple approval was a different matter. Perhaps it was the candlelight, the wine, the intimacy of the small kitchen in the empty house, but she felt close to him, comfortable with him. Without being aware of it happening, Liz dropped her guard.

"I couldn't be anything else."

"Yes, you could. I'm glad you're not."

"What are you?" she wondered as she sat beside him.

"A thirty-five-year-old lawyer who's just realizing he's wasted some time." He lifted his glass and touched it to hers. "To making the best of whatever there is."

Though she wasn't certain she understood him, Liz drank, then waited for him to eat.

"You could fuel an engine with this stuff." Jonas dipped

his spoon into the chili again and tasted. Hot spice danced on his tongue. "It's great."

"Not too hot for your Yankee stomach?"

"My Yankee stomach can handle it. You know, I'm surprised you haven't opened a restaurant, since you can cook like this."

She wouldn't have been human if the compliment hadn't pleased her. "I like the water more than I like the kitchen."

"I can't argue with that. So you picked this up in the kitchen when you worked at the hotel?"

"That's right. We'd take a meal there. The cook would show me how much of this and how much of that. He was very kind," Liz remembered. "A lot of people were kind."

He wanted to know everything—the small details, the feelings, the memories. Because he did, he knew he had to probe with care. "How long did you work there?"

"Two years. I lost count of how many beds I made."

"Then you started your own business?"

"Then I started the dive shop." She took a thin cracker and broke it in two. "It was a gamble, but it was the right one."

"How did you handle it?" He waited until she looked over at him. "With your daughter?"

She withdrew. He could hear it in her voice. "I don't know what you mean."

"I wonder about you." He kept the tone light, knowing she'd never respond to pressure. "Not many women could have managed all you've managed. You were alone, pregnant, making a living."

"Does that seem so unusual?" It made her smile to think of it. "There are only so many choices, aren't there?"

"A great many people would have made a different one."

With a nod, she accepted. "A different one wouldn't have been right for me." She sipped her wine as she let her mind drift back. "I was frightened. Quite a bit at first, but less and less as time when on. People were very good to me. It might have been different if I hadn't been lucky. I went into labor when I was cleaning room 328." Her eyes warmed as if she'd just seen something lovely. "I remember holding this stack of towels in my hand and thinking, 'Oh God, this is it, and I've only done half my rooms.'" She laughed and went back to her meal. Jonas's bowl sat cooling.

"You worked the day your baby was born?"

"Of course. I was healthy."

"I know men who take the day off if they need a tooth filled."

She laughed again and passed him the crackers. "Maybe women take things more in stride."

Only some women, he thought. Only a few exceptional women. "And afterward?"

"Afterward I was lucky again. A woman I worked with knew Señora Alderez. When Faith was born, her youngest had just turned five. She took care of Faith during the day, so I was able to go right back to work."

The cracker crumbled in his hand. "It must have been difficult for you."

"The only hard part was leaving my baby every morning, but the señora was wonderful to Faith and to me. That's how I found this house. Anyway, one thing led to another. I started the dive shop."

He wondered if she realized that the more simply she described it, the more poignant it sounded. "You said the dive shop was a gamble."

"Everything's a gamble. If I'd stayed at the hotel, I never would have been able to give Faith what I wanted to give her. And I suppose I'd have felt cheated myself. Would you like some more?"

"No." He rose to take the bowls himself while he thought out how to approach her. If he said the wrong thing, she'd pull away again. The more she told him, the more he found he needed to know. "Where did you learn to dive?"

"Right here in Cozumel, when I was just a little older than Faith." As a matter of habit she began to store the leftovers while Jonas ran water in the sink. "My parents brought me. I took to it right away. It was like, I don't know, learning to fly I suppose."

"Is that why you came back?"

"I came back because I'd always felt peaceful here. I needed to feel peaceful."

"But you must have still been in school in the States."

"I was in college." Crouching, Liz shifted things in the refrigerator to make room. "My first year. I was going to be a marine biologist, a teacher who'd enlighten class after class on the mysteries of the sea. A scientist who'd find all the answers. It was such a big dream. It overwhelmed everything else to the point where I studied constantly and rarely went out. Then I—" She caught herself. Straightening slowly, she closed the refrigerator. "You'll want the lights on to do those dishes."

"Then what?" Jonas demanded, taking her shoulder as she hit the switch.

She stared at him. Light poured over them without the shifting shadows of candles. "Then I met Faith's father, and that was the end of dreams."

The need to know eclipsed judgment. He forgot to be careful. "Did you love him?"

"Yes. If I hadn't, there'd have been no Faith."

It wasn't the answer he'd wanted. "Then why are you raising her alone?"

"That's obvious, isn't it?" Anger surged as she shoved his hand aside. "He didn't want me."

"Whether he did or didn't, he was responsible to you and the child."

"Don't talk to me about responsibility. Faith's my responsibility."

"The law sees things otherwise."

"Keep your law," she snapped. "He could quote it chapter and verse, and it didn't mean a thing. We weren't wanted."

"So you let pride cut you off from your rights?" Impatient with her, he stuck his hands in his pockets and strode back to the sink. "Why didn't you fight for what you were entitled to?"

"You want the details, Jonas?" Memory brought its own particular pain, its own particular shame. Liz concentrated on the anger. Going back to the table, she picked up her glass of wine and drank deeply.

"I wasn't quite eighteen. I was going to college to study exactly what I wanted to study so I could do exactly what I wanted to do. I considered myself a great deal more

mature than some of my classmates who flitted around
from class to class more concerned about where the action would be that night. I spent most of my evenings in
the library. That's where I met him. He was in his last
year and knew if he didn't pass the bar there'd be hell to
pay at home. His family had been in law or politics since
the Revolution. You'd understand about family honor,
wouldn't you?"

The arrow hit the mark, but he only nodded.

"Then you should understand the rest. We saw each
other every night in the library, so it was natural that we
began to talk, then have a cup of coffee. He was smart,
attractive, wonderfully mannered and funny." Almost violently, she blew out the candles. The scent carried over
and hung in the room. "I fell hard. He brought me flowers and took me for long quiet drives on Saturday nights.
When he told me he loved me, I believed him. I thought
I had the world in the palm of my hand."

She set the wine down again, impatient to be finished.
Jonas said nothing. "He told me we'd be married as soon
as he established himself. We'd sit in his car and look at
the stars and he'd tell me about his home in Dallas and
the wonderful rooms. The parties and the servants and
the chandeliers. It was like a story, a lovely happily-ever-
after story. Then one day his mother came." Liz laughed,
but gripped the back of her chair until her knuckles were
white. She could still feel the humiliation.

"Actually, she sent her driver up to the dorm to fetch
me. Marcus hadn't said a thing about her visiting, but I
was thrilled that I was going to meet her. At the curb was
this fabulous white Rolls, the kind you only see in mov-

ies. When the driver opened the door for me, I was floating. Then I got in and she gave me the facts of life. Her son had a certain position to maintain, a certain image to project. She was sure I was a very nice girl, but hardly suitable for a Jensann of Dallas."

Jonas's eyes narrowed at the name, but he said nothing. Restless, Liz went to the stove and began to scrub the surface. "She told me she'd already spoken with her son and he understood the relationship had to end. Then she offered me a check as compensation. I was humiliated, and worse, I was pregnant. I hadn't told anyone yet, because I'd just found out that morning. I didn't take her money. I got out of the Rolls and went straight to Marcus. I was sure he loved me enough to toss it all aside for me, and for our baby. I was wrong."

Her eyes were so dry that they hurt. Liz pressed her fingers to them a moment. "When I went to see him, he was very logical. It had been nice; now it was over. His parents held the purse strings and it was important to keep them happy. But he wanted me to know we could still see each other now and again, as long as it was on the side. When I told him about the baby, he was furious. How could I have done such a thing? *I*."

Liz tossed the dishrag into the sink so that hot, soapy water heaved up. "It was as though I'd conceived the baby completely on my own. He wouldn't have it, he wouldn't have some silly girl who'd gotten herself pregnant messing up his life. He told me I had to get rid of it. It—as though Faith were a thing to be erased and forgotten. I was hysterical. He lost his temper. There were threats. He said he'd spread word that I was sleeping around and his friends would back him up. I'd never be able to prove the baby was his. He said my parents would be embarrassed, perhaps sued if I tried to press it. He tossed around a lot of legal phrases that I couldn't understand, but I understood he was finished with me. His family had a lot of pull at the college, and he said he'd see that I was dismissed. Because I was foolish enough to believe everything he said, I was terrified. He gave me a check and told me to go out of state—better, out of the country—to take care of things. That way no one would have to know.

"For a week I did nothing. I went through my classes in a daze, thinking I'd wake up and find out it had all been a bad dream. Then I faced it. I wrote my parents, telling them what I could. I sold the car they'd given me when I graduated from high school, took the check from Marcus and came to Cozumel to have my baby."

He'd wanted to know, even demanded, but now his insides were raw. "You could have gone to your parents."

"Yes, but at the time Marcus had convinced me they'd be ashamed. He told me they'd hate me and consider the baby a burden."

"Why didn't you go to his family? You were entitled to be taken care of."

"Go to them?" He'd never heard venom in her voice before. "Be taken care of by them? I'd have gone to hell first."

He waited a moment, until he was sure he could speak calmly. "They don't even know, do they?"

"No. And they never will. Faith is mine."

"And what does Faith know?"

"Only what she has to know. I'd never lie to her."

"And do you know that Marcus Jensann has his sights set on the senate, and maybe higher?"

Her color drained quickly and completely. "You know him?"

"By reputation."

Panic came and went, then returned in double force. "He doesn't know Faith exists. None of them do. They can't."

Watching her steadily, he took a step closer. "What are you afraid of?"

"Power. Faith is mine, she's going to stay mine. None of them will ever touch her."

"Is that why you stay here? Are you hiding from them?"

"I'll do whatever's necessary to protect my child."

"He's still got you running scared." Furious for her, Jonas took her arms. "He's got a frightened teenager strapped inside of you who's never had the chance to stretch and feel alive. Don't you know a man like that wouldn't even remember who you are? You're still running away from a man who wouldn't recognize you on the street."

She slapped him hard enough to make his head snap back. Breathing fast, she backed away from him, appalled by a show of violence she hadn't been aware of possessing. "Don't tell me what I'm running from," she whispered. "Don't tell me what I feel." She turned and fled. Before she'd reached the front door he had her again, whirling her around, gripping her hard. He no longer knew why his anger was so fierce, only that he was past the point of controlling it.

"How much have you given up because of him?" Jonas demanded. "How much have you cut out of your life?"

"It's my life!" she shouted at him.

"And you won't share it with anyone but your daughter. What the hell are you going to do when she's grown? What the hell are you going to do in twenty years when you have nothing but your memories?"

"Don't." Tears filled her eyes too quickly to be blinked away.

He grabbed her close again, twisting until she had to look at him. "We all need someone. Even you. It's about time someone proved it to you."

"No."

She tried to turn her head but he was quick. With his mouth crushed on hers she struggled, but her arms were trapped between their bodies and his were ironlike around her. Emotions already mixed with fear and anger became more confused with passion. Liz fought not to give in to any of them as his mouth demanded both submission and response.

"You're not fighting me," he told her. His eyes were close, searing into hers. "You're fighting yourself. You've been fighting yourself since the first time we met."

"I want you to let me go." She wanted her voice to be strong, but it trembled.

"Yes. You want me to let you go just as much as you want me not to. You've been making your own decisions for a long time, Liz. This time I'm making one for you."

Her furious protest was lost against his mouth as he pressed her down to the sofa. Trapped under him, her body began to heat, her blood began to stir. Yes, she was fighting herself. She had to fight herself before she could fight him. But she was losing.

She heard her own moan as his lips trailed down her throat, and it was a moan of pleasure. She felt the hard line of his body against hers as she arched under him, but it wasn't a movement of protest. Want me, she seemed to say. Want me for what I am.

Her pulse began to thud in parts of her body that had been quiet for so many years. Life burst through her like a torrid wind through thin glass until every line of defense was shattered. With a desperate groan, she took his face in her hands and dragged his mouth back to hers.

She could taste the passion, the life, the promises. She wanted them all. Recklessness, so long chained within, tore free and ruled. A sound bubbled in her throat she wasn't even aware was a laugh as she wrapped herself around him. She wanted. He wanted. The hell with the rest.

He wasn't sure what had driven him—anger, need, pain. All he knew now was that he had to have her, body, soul and mind. She was wild beneath him, but no longer in resistance. Every movement was a demand that he take more, give more, and nothing seemed fast enough. She was a storm set to rage, a fire desperate to consume. Whatever he'd released inside of her had whipped out and taken him prisoner.

He pulled the shirt over her head and tossed it aside. His heartbeat thundered. She was so small, so delicate. But he had a beast inside him that had been caged too long. He took her breast in his mouth and sent them both spinning. She tasted so fresh: a cool, clear glass of water.

She smelled of woman at her most unpampered and most seductive. He felt her body arch against his, taut as a bowstring, hot as a comet. The innocence that remained so integral a part of her trembled just beneath wanton passion. No man alive could have resisted it; any man alive might have wished for it. His mouth was buried at her throat when he felt the shirt rip away from his back.

She hardly knew what she was doing. Touching him sent demands to her brain that she couldn't deny. She wanted to feel him against her, flesh to flesh, to experience an intimacy she'd so long refused to allow herself. There'd been no one else. As Liz felt her skin fused to his she understood why. There was only one Jonas. She pulled his mouth back to hers to taste him again.

He drew off her slacks so that she was naked, but she didn't feel vulnerable. She felt invulnerable. Hardly able to breathe, she struggled with his. Then she gave him no choice. Desperate for that final release, she wrapped her legs around him and drew him into her until she was filled. At the shock of that first ragged peak, her eyes flew open. Inches away, he watched her face. Her mouth trembled open, but before she could catch her breath, he was driving her higher, faster. She couldn't tell how long they balanced on the edge, trapped between pleasure and fulfillment. Then his arms came around her, hers around his. Together, they broke free.

She didn't speak. Her system leveled slowly, and she was helpless to hurry it. He didn't move. He'd shifted his weight, but his arms had come around her and stayed there. She needed him to speak, to say something that would put what had happened in perspective. She'd only had one other lover and had learned not to expect.

Jonas rested his forehead against her shoulder a moment. He was wrestling with his own demons. "I'm sorry, Liz."

He could have said nothing worse. She closed her eyes and forced her emotions to drain. She nearly succeeded. Steadier, she reached for the tangle of clothes on the floor. "I don't need an apology." With her clothes in a ball in her arm, she walked quickly to the bedroom.

On a long breath, Jonas sat up. He couldn't seem to find the right buttons on Liz Palmer. Every move he made seemed to be a move in reverse. It still stunned him that he'd been so rough with her, left her so little choice in the final outcome. He'd be better off hiring her a private bodyguard and moving himself back to the hotel. It was true he didn't want to see her hurt and felt a certain responsibility for her welfare, but he didn't seem to be able to act on it properly. When she'd stood in the kitchen telling him what she'd been through, something had begun to boil in him. That it had taken the form of passion in the end wasn't something easily explained or justified. His apology had been inadequate, but he had little else.

Drawing on his pants, Jonas started for his room. It snouldn't have surprised him to find himself veering toward Liz's. She was just pulling on a robe. "It's late, Jonas."

"Did I hurt you?"

She sent him a look that made guilt turn over in his stomach. "Yes. Now I want to take a shower before I go to bed."

"Liz, there's no excuse for being so rough, and there's no making it up to you, but—"

"Your apology hurt me," she interrupted. "Now if you've said all you have to say, I'd like to be alone."

He stared at her a moment, then dragged a hand through his hair. How could he have convinced himself he understood her when she was now and always had been an enigma? "Damn it, Liz, I wasn't apologizing for making love to you, but for the lack of finesse. I practically tossed you on the ground and ripped your clothes off."

She folded her hands and tried to keep calm. "I ripped yours."

His lips twitched, then curved. "Yeah, you did."

Humor didn't come into her eyes. "And do you want an apology?"

He came to her then and rested his hands on her shoulders. Her robe was cotton and thin and whirling with bright color. "No. I guess what I'd like is for you to say you wanted me as much as I wanted you."

Her courage weakened, so she looked beyond him. "I'd have thought that was obvious."

"Liz." His hand was gentle as he turned her face back to his.

"All right. I wanted you. Now—"

"Now," he interrupted. "Will you listen?"

"There's no need to say anything."

"Yes, there is." He walked with her to the bed and drew her down to sit. Moonlight played over their hands as he took hers. "I came to Cozumel for one reason. My feelings on that haven't changed but other things have. When I first met you I thought you knew something, were hiding something. I linked everything about you to Jerry. It didn't take long for me to see there was something else. I wanted to know about you, for myself."

"Why?"

"I don't know. It's impossible not to care about you." At her look of surprise, he smiled. "You project this image of pure self-sufficiency and still manage to look like a waif. Tonight, I purposely maneuvered you into talking about Faith and what had brought you here. When you told me I couldn't handle it."

She drew her hand from his. "That's understandable. Most people have trouble handling unwed mothers."

Anger bubbled as he grabbed her hand again. "Stop putting words in my mouth. You stood in the kitchen talking and I could see you, young, eager and trusting, being betrayed and hurt. I could see what it had done to you, how it had closed you off from things you wanted to do."

"I told you I don't have any regrets."

"I know." He lifted her hand and kissed it. "I guess for a moment I needed to have them for you."

"Jonas, do you think anyone's life turns out the way they plan it as children?"

He laughed a little as he slipped an arm around her and drew her against him. Liz sat still a moment, unsure how to react to the casual show of affection. Then she leaned her head against his shoulder and closed her eyes. "Jerry and I were going to be partners."

"In what?"

"In anything."

She touched the coin on the end of his chain. "He had one of these."

"Our grandparents gave them to us when we were kids. They're identical five-dollar gold pieces. Funny, I always wore mine heads up. Jerry wore his heads down." He closed his fingers over the coin. "He stole his first car when we were sixteen."

Her fingers crept up to his. "I'm sorry."

"The thing was he didn't need to—we had access to any car in the garage. He told me he just wanted to see if he could get away with it."

"He didn't make life easy for you."

"No, he didn't make life easy. Especially for himself. But he never did anything out of meanness. There were times I hated him, but I never stopped loving him."

Liz drew closer. "Love hurts more than hate."

He kissed the top of her head. "Liz, I don't suppose you've ever talked to a lawyer about Faith."

"Why should I?"

"Marcus has a responsibility, a financial responsibility at the least, to you and Faith."

"I took money from Marcus once. Not again."

"Child support payments could be set up very quietly. You could stop working seven days a week."

Liz took a deep breath and pulled away until she could see his face. "Faith is my child, has been my child only since the moment Marcus handed me a check. I could have had the abortion and gone back to my life as I'd planned it. I chose not to. I chose to have the baby, to raise the baby, to support the baby. She's never given me anything but pleasure from the moment she was born, and I have no intention of sharing her."

"One day she's going to ask you for his name."

Liz moistened her lips, but nodded. "Then one day I'll tell her. She'll have her own choice to make."

He wouldn't press her now, but there was no reason he couldn't have his law clerk begin to investigate child support laws and paternity cases. "Are you going to let me meet her? I know the deal is for me to be out of the house and out of your life when she gets back. I will, but I'd like the chance to meet her."

"If you're still in Mexico."

"One more question."

The smile came more easily. "One more."

"There haven't been any other men, have there?"

The smile faded. "No."

He felt twin surges of gratitude and guilt. "Then let me show you how it should be."

"There's no need—"

Gently, he brushed the hair back from her face. "Yes, there is. For both of us." He kissed her eyes closed. "I've wanted you from the first." His mouth on hers was as sweet as spring rain and just as gentle. Slowly, he slipped the robe from her shoulders, following the trail with warm lips. "Your skin's like gold," he murmured, then traced a finger over her breasts where the tone changed. "And so pale. I want to see all of you."

"Jonas—"

"All of you," he repeated, looking into her eyes until the heat kindled again. "I want to make love with all of you."

She didn't resist. Never in her life had anyone ever touched her with such reverence, looked at her with such need. When he urged her back, Liz lay on the bed, naked and waiting.

"Lovely," Jonas murmured. Her body was milk and honey in the moonlight. And her eyes were dark—dark and open and uncertain. "I want you to trust me." He began a slow journey of exploration at her ankles. "I want to know when I look at you that you're not afraid of me."

"I'm not afraid of you."

"You have been. Maybe I've even wanted you to be. No more."

His tongue slid over her skin and teased the back of her knees. The jolt of power had her rising up and gasping. "Jonas."

"Relax." He ran a hand lightly up her hip. "I want to feel your bones melt. Lie back, Liz. Let me show you how much you can have."

She obeyed, only because she hadn't the strength to resist. He murmured to her, stroking, nibbling, until she was too steeped in what he gave to give in return. But he wanted her that way, wanted to take her as though she hadn't been touched before. Not by him, not by anyone. Slowly, thoroughly and with great, great patience he seduced and pleasured. He thought as his mouth skimmed up her thigh that he could hear her skin hum.

She'd never known anything could be like this—so deep, so dark. There was a freedom here, she discovered, that she'd once only associated with diving down through silent fathoms. Her body could float, her limbs could be weightless, but she could feel every touch, every movement. Dreamlike, sensations drifted over her, so soft, so misty, each blended into the next. How long could it go on? Perhaps, after all, there were forevers.

She was lean, with muscles firm in her legs. Like a

dancer's he thought, disciplined and trained. The scent from the bowl on her dresser spiced the air, but it was her fragrance, cool as a waterfall, that swam in his head. His mind emptied of everything but the need to delight her. Love, when unselfish, has incredible power.

His tongue plunged into the heat and his hands gripped hers as she arched, stunned at being flung from a floating world to a churning one. He drew from her, both patient and relentless, until she shuddered to climax and over. When her hands went limp in his, he brought them back to his body and pleasured himself.

She hadn't known passion could stretch so far or a body endure such a barrage of sensations. His hands, rough at the palm, showed her secrets she'd never had the chance to imagine. His lips, warmed from her own skin, opened mysteries and whispered the answers. He gentled her, he enticed her, he stroked with tenderness and he devoured. Gasping for air, she had no choice but to allow him whatever he wanted, and to strain for him to show her more.

When he was inside of her she thought it was all, and more, than she could ever want. If this was love, she'd never tasted it. If this was passion, she'd only skimmed its surface. Now it was time to risk the depths. Willing, eager, she held on to him.

It was trust he felt from her, and trust that moved him unbearably. He thought he'd needed before, desired before, but never so completely. Though he knew what it was to be part of another person, he'd never expected to feel the merger again. Strong, complex, unavoidable, the emotion swamped him. He belonged to her as fully as he'd wanted her to belong to him.

He took her slowly, so that the thrill that coursed through her seemed endless. His skin was moist when she pressed her lips to his throat. The pulse there was as quick as her own. A giddy sense of triumph moved through her, only to be whipped away with passion before it could spread.

Then he drew her up to him, and her body, liquid and limber with emotion, rose like a wave to press against his. Wrapped close, mouths fused, they moved together. Her hair fell like rain down her back. She could feel his heartbeat fast against her breast.

Still joined, they lowered again. The rhythm quickened. Desperation rose. She heard him breathe her name before the gates burst open and she was lost in the flood.

Chapter 9

She woke slowly, with a long, lazy stretch. Keeping her eyes closed, Liz waited for the alarm to ring. It wasn't often she felt so relaxed, even when waking, so she pampered herself and absorbed the luxury of doing nothing. In an hour, she mused, she'd be at the dive shop shifting through the day's schedule. The glass bottom, she thought, frowning a little. Was she supposed to take it out? Odd that she couldn't remember. Then with a start, it occurred to her that she didn't remember because she didn't know. She hadn't handled the schedule in two days. And last night...

She opened her eyes and looked into Jonas's.

"I could watch your mind wake up." He bent over and kissed her. "Fascinating."

Liz closed her fingers over the sheet and tugged it a little higher. What was she supposed to say? She'd never spent the night with a man, never awoken with one. She cleared her throat and wondered if every man awoke as sexily disheveled as Jonas Sharpe. "How did you sleep?" she managed, and felt ridiculous.

"Fine." He smiled as he brushed her hair from her cheek with a fingertip. "And you?"

"Fine." Her fingers moved restlessly on the sheet until he closed his hands over them. His eyes were warm and heavy and made her heart pound.

"It's a little late to be nervous around me, Elizabeth."

"I'm not nervous." But color rose to her cheeks when he pressed his lips to her naked shoulder.

"Still, it's rather flattering. If you're nervous…" He turned his head so the tip of his tongue could toy with her ear. "Then you're not unmoved. I wouldn't like to think you felt casually about being with me—yet."

Was it possible to want so much this morning what she'd sated herself with the night before? She didn't think it should be, and yet her body told her differently. She would, as she always did, listen to her intellect first. "It must be almost time to get up." One hand firmly on the sheets, she rose on her elbows to look at the clock. "That's not right." She blinked and focused again. "It can't be eight-fifteen."

"Why not?" He slipped a hand beneath the sheet and stroked her thigh.

"Because." His touch had her pulses speeding. "I always set it for six-fifteen."

Finding her a challenge, Jonas brushed light kisses over her shoulder, down her arm. "You didn't set it last night."

"I always—" She cut herself off. It was hard enough to try to think when he was touching her, but when she remembered the night before, it was nearly impossible to understand why she had to think. Her mind hadn't been on alarms and schedules and customers when her body had curled into Jonas's to sleep. Her mind, as it was now, had been filled with him.

"Always what?"

She wished he wouldn't distract her with fingertips sliding gently over her skin. She wished he could touch her everywhere at once. "I always wake up at six, whether I set it or not."

"You didn't this time." He laughed as he eased her back down. "I suppose I should be flattered again."

"Maybe I flatter you too much," she murmured and started to shift away. He simply rolled her back to him. "I have to get up."

"No, you don't."

"Jonas, I'm already late. I have to get to work."

Sunlight dappled over her face. He wanted to see it over the rest of her. "The only thing you have to do is make love with me." He kissed her fingers, then slowly drew them from the sheet. "I'll never get through the day without you."

"The boats—"

"Are already out, I'm sure." He cupped her breast, rubbing his thumb back and forth over the nipple. "Luis seems competent."

"He is. I haven't been in for two days."

"One more won't hurt."

Her body vibrated with need that slowly wound itself into her mind. Her arms came up to him, around him. "No, I guess it won't."

She hadn't stayed in bed until ten o'clock since she'd been a child. Liz felt as irresponsible as one as she started the coffee. True, Luis could handle the shop and the boats as well as she, but it wasn't his job. It was hers. Here she was, brewing coffee at ten o'clock, with her body still warm from loving. Nothing had been the same since Jonas Sharpe had arrived on her doorstep.

"It's useless to give yourself a hard time for taking a morning off," Jonas said from behind her.

Liz popped bread into the toaster. "I suppose not, since I don't even know today's schedule."

"Liz." Jonas took her by the arms and firmly turned her around. He studied her, gauging her mood before he spoke. "You know, back in Philadelphia I'm considered a workaholic. I've had friends express concern over the workload I take on and the hours I put in. Compared to you, I'm retired."

Her brows drew together as they did when she was concentrating. Or annoyed. "We each do what we have to do."

"True enough. It appears what I have to do is harass you until you relax."

She had to smile. He said it so reasonably and his eyes were laughing. "I'm sure you have a reputation for being an expert on harassment."

"I majored in it at college."

"Good for you. But I'm an expert at budgeting my own time. And there's my toast." He let her pluck it out, waited until she'd buttered it, then took a piece for himself.

"You mentioned diving lessons."

She was still frowning at him when she heard the coffee begin to simmer. She reached for one cup, then relented and took two. "What about them?"

"I'll take one. Today."

"Today?" She handed him his coffee, drinking her own standing by the stove. "I'll have to see what's scheduled. The way things have been going, both dive boats should already be out."

"Not a group lesson, a private one. You can take me out on the *Expatriate*."

"Luis usually takes care of the private lessons."

He smiled at her. "I prefer dealing with the management."

Liz dusted crumbs from her fingers. "All right then. It'll cost you."

He lifted his cup in salute. "I never doubted it."

Liz was laughing when Jonas pulled into a narrow parking space at the hotel. "If he'd picked your pocket, why did you defend him?"

"Everyone's entitled to representation," Jonas reminded her. "Besides, I figured if I took him on as a client, he'd leave my wallet alone."

"And did he?"

"Yeah." Jonas took her hand as they crossed the sidewalk to the sand. "He stole my watch instead."

She giggled, a foolish, girlish sound he'd never heard from her. "And did you get him off?"

"Two years probation. There, it looks like business is good."

Liz shielded her eyes from the sun and looked toward the shop. Luis was busily fitting two couples with snorkel gear. A glance to the left showed her only the *Expatriate* remained in dock. "Cozumel's becoming very popular," she murmured.

"Isn't that the idea?"

"For business?" She moved her shoulders. "I'd be a fool to complain."

"But?"

"But sometimes I think it would be nice if I could block out the changes. I don't want to see the water choked with suntan oil. *Hola,* Luis."

"Liz!" His gaze passed over Jonas briefly before he grinned at her. "We thought maybe you deserted us. How did you like Acapulco?"

"It was…different," she decided, and was already scooting behind the counter to find the daily schedule. "Any problems?"

"Jose took care of a couple repairs. I brought Miguel back to fill in, but I keep an eye on him. Got this—what do you call it—brochure on the aqua bikes." He pulled out a colorful pamphlet, but Liz only nodded.

"The Brinkman party's out diving. Did we take them to Palancar?"

"Two days in a row. Miguel likes them. They tip good."

"Hmm. You're handling the shop alone."

"No problem. Hey, there was a guy." He screwed up his face as he tried to remember the name. "Skinny guy, American. You know the one you took out on the beginners' trip?"

She flipped through the receipts and was satisfied. "Trydent?"

"*Sí,* that was it. He came by a coupla times."

"Rent anything?"

"No." Luis wiggled his eyebrows at her. "He was looking for you."

Liz shrugged it off. If he hadn't rented anything, he

didn't interest her. "If everything's under control here, I'm going to take Mr. Sharpe out for a diving lesson."

Luis looked quickly at Jonas, then away. The man made him uneasy, but Liz looked happier than she had in weeks. "Want me to get the gear?"

"No, I'll take care of it." She looked up and smiled at Jonas. "Write Mr. Sharpe up a rental form and give him a receipt for the gear, the lesson and the boat trip. Since it's…" She trailed off as she checked her watch. "Nearly eleven, give him the half-day rate."

"You're all heart," Jonas murmured as she went to the shelves to choose his equipment.

"You got the best teacher," Luis told him, but couldn't manage more than another quick look at Jonas.

"I'm sure you're right." Idly, Jonas swiveled the newspaper Luis had tossed on the counter around to face him. He missed being able to sit down with the morning paper over coffee. The Spanish headlines told him nothing. "Anything going on I should know about?" Jonas asked, indicating the paper.

Luis relaxed a bit as he wrote. Jonas's voice wasn't so much like Jerry's when you weren't looking at him. "Haven't had a chance to look at it yet. Busy morning."

Going with habit, Jonas turned the paper over. There, in a faded black-and-white picture, was Erika. Jonas's fingers tightened. He glanced back and saw that Liz was busy, her back to him. Without a word, he slid the paper over the receipt Luis was writing.

"Hey, that's the—"

"I know," Jonas said in an undertone. "What does it say?"

Luis bent over the paper to read. He straightened again

very slowly, and his face was ashen. "Dead," he whispered. "She's dead."

"How?"

Luis's fingers opened and closed on the pen he held. "Stabbed."

Jonas thought of the knife held at Liz's throat. "When?"

"Last night." Luis had to swallow twice. "They found her last night."

"Jonas," Liz called from the back, "how much do you weigh?"

Keeping his eyes on Luis, Jonas turned the paper over again. "One seventy. She doesn't need to hear this now," he added under his breath. He pulled bills from his wallet and laid them on the counter. "Finish writing the receipt."

After a struggle, Luis mastered his own fear and straightened. "I don't want anything to happen to Liz."

Jonas met the look with a challenge that held for several humming seconds before he relaxed. The smaller man was terrified, but he was thinking of Liz. "Neither do I. I'm going to see nothing does."

"You brought trouble."

"I know." His gaze shifted beyond Luis to Liz. "But if I leave, the trouble doesn't."

For the first time, Luis forced himself to study Jonas's face. After a moment, he blew out a long breath. "I liked your brother, but I think it was him who brought trouble."

"It doesn't matter anymore who brought it. I'm going to look out for her."

"Then you look good," Luis warned softly. "You look real good."

"First lesson," Liz said as she unlocked her storage

closet. "Each diver carries and is responsible for his own gear." She jerked her head back to where Jonas's was stacked. With a last look at Luis, he walked through the doorway to gather it up.

"Preparing for a dive is twice as much work as diving itself," she began as she hefted her tanks. "It's a good thing it's worth it. We'll be back before sundown, Luis. *Hasta luego.*"

"Liz." She stopped, turning back to where Luis hovered in the doorway. His gaze passed over Jonas, then returned to her. *"Hasta luego,"* he managed, and closed his fingers over the medal he wore around his neck.

The moment she was on board, Liz restacked her gear. As a matter of routine, she checked all the *Expatriate*'s gauges. "Can you cast off?" she asked Jonas.

He ran a hand down her hair, surprising her. She looked so competent, so in charge. He wondered if by staying close he was protecting or endangering. It was becoming vital to believe the first. "I can handle it."

She felt her stomach flutter as he continued to stare at her. "Then you'd better stop looking at me and do it."

"I like looking at you." He drew her close, just to hold her. "I could spend years looking at you."

Her arms came up, hesitated, then dropped back to her sides. It would be so easy to believe. To trust again, give again, be hurt again. She wanted to tell him of the love growing inside her, spreading and strengthening with each moment. But if she told him she'd no longer have even the illusion of control. Without control, she was defenseless.

"I clocked you on at eleven," she said, but couldn't resist breathing deeply of his scent and committing it to memory.

Because she made him smile again, he drew her back. "I'm paying the bill, I'll worry about the time."

"Diving lesson," she reminded him. "And you can't dive until you cast off."

"Aye, aye, sir." But he gave her a hard, breath-stealing kiss before he jumped back on the dock.

Liz drew air into her lungs and let it out slowly before she turned on the engines. All she could hope was that she looked more in control than she felt. He was winning a battle, she mused, that he didn't even know he was fighting. She waited for Jonas to join her again before she eased the throttle forward.

"There are plenty of places to dive where we don't need the boat, but I thought you'd enjoy something away from the beaches. Palancar is one of the most stunning reefs in the Caribbean. It's probably the best place to start because the north end is shallow and the wall slopes rather than having a sheer vertical drop-off. There are a lot of caves and passageways, so it makes for an interesting dive."

"I'm sure, but I had something else in mind."

"Something else?"

Jonas took a small book out of his pocket and flipped through it. "What do these numbers look like to you?"

Liz recognized the book. It was the same one he'd used in Acapulco to copy down the numbers from his brother's book in the safe-deposit box. He still had his priorities, she reminded herself, then drew back on the throttle to let the boat idle.

The numbers were in precise, neat lines. Any child

who'd paid attention in geography class would recognize them. "Longitude and latitude."

He nodded. "Do you have a chart?"

He'd planned this since he'd first seen the numbers, she realized. Their being lovers changed nothing else. "Of course, but I don't need it for this. I know these waters. That's just off the coast of Isla Mujeres." Liz adjusted her course and picked up speed. Perhaps, she thought, the course had already been set for both of them long before this. They had no choice but to see it through. "It's a long trip. You might as well relax."

He put his hands on her shoulders to knead. "We won't find anything, but I have to go."

"I understand."

"Would you rather I go alone?"

She shook her head violently, but said nothing.

"Liz, this had to be his drop point. By tomorrow, Moralas will have the numbers and send his own divers down. I have to see for myself."

"You're chasing shadows, Jonas. Jerry's gone. Nothing you can do is going to change that."

"I'll find out why. I'll find out who. That'll be enough."

"Will it?" With her hand gripping the wheel hard, she looked over her shoulder. His eyes were close, but they held that cool, set look again. "I don't think so—not for you." Liz turned her face back to the sea. She would take him where he wanted to go.

Isla Mujeres, Island of Women, was a small gem in the water. Surrounded by reefs and studded with untouched lagoons, it was one of the perfect retreats of the Caribbean. Party boats from the continental coast or one of the other islands cruised there daily to offer their customers snorkeling or diving at its best. It had once been known by pirates and blessed by a goddess. Liz anchored the boat off the southwest coast. Once again, she became the teacher.

"It's important to know and understand both the name and the use of every piece of equipment. It's not just a matter of stuffing in a mouthpiece and strapping on a tank. No smoking," she added as Jonas took out a cigarette. "It's ridiculous to clog up your lungs in the first place, and absurd to do it before a dive."

Jonas set the pack on the bench beside him. "How long are we going down?"

"We'll keep it under an hour. The depth here ranges to eighty feet. That means the nitrogen in your air supply will be over three times denser than what your system's accustomed to. In some people at some depths, this can cause temporary imbalances. If you begin to feel lightheaded, signal to me right away. We'll descend in stages to give your body time to get used to the changes in pressure. We ascend the same way in order to give the nitrogen time to expel. If you come up too quickly, you risk decompression sickness. It can be fatal." As she spoke, she spread out the gear with the intention of explaining each piece. "Nothing is to be taken for granted in the water. It is not your milieu. You're dependent on your equipment and your own good sense. It's beautiful and it's exciting, but it's not an amusement park."

"Is this the same lecture you give on the dive boat?"

"Basically."

"You're very good."

"Thank you." She picked up a gauge. "Now—"

"Can we get started?" he asked and reached for his wet suit.

"We are getting started. You can't dive without a working knowledge of your equipment."

"That's a depth gauge." He nodded toward her hand as he stripped down to black briefs. "A very sophisticated one. I wouldn't think most dive shops would find it necessary to stock that quality."

"This is mine," she murmured. "But I keep a handful for rentals."

"I don't think I mentioned that you have the best-tended equipment I've ever seen. It isn't in the same league with your personal gear, but it's quality. Give me a hand, will you?"

Liz rose to help him into the tough, stretchy suit. "You've gone down before."

"I've been diving since I was fifteen." Jonas pulled up the zipper before bending over to check the tanks himself.

"Since you were fifteen." Liz yanked off her shirt and tossed it aside. Fuming, she pulled off her shorts until she wore nothing but a string bikini and a scowl. "Then why did you let me go on that way?"

"I liked hearing you." Jonas glanced up and felt his blood surge. "Almost as much as I like looking at you."

She wasn't in the mood to be flattered, less in the mood to be charmed. Without asking for assistance, she tugged herself into her wet suit. "You're still paying for the lesson."

Jonas grinned as he examined his flippers. "I never doubted it."

She strapped on the rest of her gear in silence. It was difficult even for her to say if she were really angry. All she knew was the day, and dive, weren't as simple as they had started out to be. Lifting the top of a bench, she reached into a compartment and took out two short metal sticks shaped like bats.

"What's this for?" Jonas asked as she handed him one.

"Insurance." She adjusted her mask. "We're going down to the caves where the sharks sleep."

"Sharks don't sleep."

"The oxygen content in the water in the cave keeps them quiescent. But don't think you can trust them."

Without another word, she swung over the side and down the ladder.

The water was as clear as glass, so she could see for more than a hundred feet. As she heard Jonas plunge in beside her, Liz turned to assure herself he did indeed know what he was doing. Catching her skeptical look, Jonas merely circled his thumb and forefinger, then pointed down.

He was tense. Liz could feel it from him, though she understood it had nothing to do with his skill underwater. His brother had dived here once—she was as certain of it as Jonas. And the reason for his dives had been the reason for his death. She no longer had to think whether she was angry. In a gesture as personal as a kiss, she reached out a hand and took his.

Grateful, Jonas curled his fingers around hers. He didn't know what he was looking for, or even why he continued to look when already he'd found more than he'd wanted to. His brother had played games with the rules and had lost. Some would say there was justice in that. But they'd shared birth. He had to go on looking, and go on hoping.

Liz saw the first of the devilfish and tugged on Jonas's hand. Such things never failed to touch her spirit. The giant manta rays cruised together, feeding on plankton and unconcerned with the human intruders. Liz kicked forward, delighted to swim among them. Their huge mouths could crush and devour crustaceans. Their wingspan of twenty feet and more was awesome. Without fear, Liz reached out to touch. Pleasure came easily, as it always did to her in the sea. Her eyes were laughing as she reached out again for Jonas.

They descended farther, and some of his tension began to dissolve. There was something different about her here, a lightness, an ease that dissolved the sadness that always seemed to linger in her eyes. She looked free, and more, as happy as he'd ever seen her. If it were possible to fall in love in a matter of moments, Jonas fell in love in those, forty feet below the surface with a mermaid who'd forgotten how to dream.

Everything she saw, everything she could touch fascinated her. He could see it in the way she moved, the way she looked at everything as though it were her first dive. If he could have found a way, he would have stayed with her there, surrounded by love and protected by fathoms.

They swam deeper, but leisurely. If something evil had been begun, or been ended there, it had left no trace. The sea was calm and silent and full of life too lovely to exist in the air.

When the shadow passed over, Liz looked up. In all her dives, she'd never seen anything so spectacular. Thousands upon thousands of silvery grunts moved together in a wave so dense that they might have been one creature. Eyes wide with the wonder of it, Liz lifted her arms and took her body up. The wave swayed as a unit, avoiding intrusion. Delighted, she signaled for Jonas to join her. The need to share the magic was natural. This was the pull of the sea that had driven her to study, urged to explore and invited her once to dream. With her fingers linked with Jonas's, she propelled them closer. The school of fish split in half so that it became two unified forms swirling on either side of them. The sea teemed with them, thick clouds of silver so tightly grouped that they seemed fused together.

For a moment she was as close to her own fantasies as she had ever been, floating free, surrounded by magic, with her lover's hand in hers. Impulsively, she wrapped her arms around Jonas and held on. The clouds of fish swarmed around them, linked into one, then swirled away.

He could feel her pulse thud when he reached for her wrist. He could see the fascinated delight in her eyes. Hampered by his human frailty in the water, he could only touch his hand to her cheek. When she lifted her own to press it closer, it was enough. Side by side they swam toward the seafloor.

The limestone caves were eerie and compelling. Once Jonas saw the head of a moray eel slide out and curve, either in curiosity or warning. An old turtle with barnacles crusting his back rose from his resting place beneath a rock and swam between them. Then at the entrance to a cave, Liz pointed and shared another mystery.

The shark moved across the sand, as a dog might on a hearth rug. His small, black eyes stared back at them as his gills slowly drew in water. While they huddled just inside the entrance, their bubbles rising up through the porous limestone and toward the surface, the shark shifted restlessly. Jonas reached for Liz's hand to draw her back, but she moved a bit closer, anxious to see.

In a quick move, the shark shot toward the entrance. Jonas was grabbing for Liz and his knife, when she merely poked at the head with her wooden bat. Without pausing, the shark swam toward the open sea and vanished.

He wanted to strangle her. He wanted to tell her how fascinating she was to watch. Since he could do neither, Jonas merely closed a hand over her throat and gave her a mock shake. Her laughter had bubbles dancing.

They swam on together, parting from time to time to explore separate interests. He decided she'd forgotten his purpose in coming, but thought it was just as well. If she could take this hour for personal freedom, he was glad of it. For him, there were demands.

The water and the life in it were undeniably beautiful, but Jonas noticed other things. They hadn't seen another diver and their down time was nearly up. The caves where the sharks slept were also a perfect place to conceal a cache of drugs. Only the very brave or the very foolish would swim in their territory at night. He thought of his brother and knew Jerry would have considered it the best kind of adventure. A man with a reason could swim into one of the caves while the sharks were out feeding, and leave or take whatever he liked.

Liz hadn't forgotten why Jonas had come. Because she thought she could understand a part of what he was feeling, she gave him room. Here, eighty feet below the surface, he was searching for something, anything, to help him accept his brother's death. And his brother's life.

It would come to an end soon, Liz reflected. The police had the name of the go-between in Acapulco. And the other name that Jonas had given them, she remembered suddenly. Where had he gotten that one? She looked toward him and realized there were things he wasn't telling her. That, too, would end soon, she promised herself. Then she found herself abruptly out of air.

She didn't panic. Liz was too well trained to panic. Immediately, she checked her gauge and saw that she had ten full minutes left. Reaching back, she ran a hand down her hose and found it unencumbered. But she couldn't draw air.

Whatever the gauge said, her life was on the line. If she swam toward the surface, her lungs would be crushed by the pressure. Forcing herself to stay calm, she swam in a diagonal toward Jonas. When she caught his ankle, she tugged sharply. The smile he turned with faded the moment he saw her eyes. Recognizing her signal, he immediately removed his regulator and passed it to her. Liz drew in air. Nodding, she handed it back to him. Their bodies brushing, her hand firm on his shoulder, they began their slow ascent.

Buddy-breathing, they rose closer to the surface, restraining themselves from rushing. What took only a matter of minutes seemed to drag on endlessly. The moment Liz's head broke water, she pushed back her mask and gulped in fresh air.

"What happened?" Jonas demanded, but when he felt her begin to shake, he only swore and pulled her with him to the ladder. "Take it easy." His hand was firm at her back as she climbed up.

"I'm all right." But she collapsed on a bench, without the energy to draw off her tanks. Her body shuddered once with relief as Jonas took the weight from her. With her head between her knees, she waited for the mists to clear. "I've never had anything like that happen," she managed. "Not at eighty feet."

He was rubbing her hands to warm them. "What did happen?"

"I ran out of air."

Enraged, he took her by the shoulders and dragged her back to a sitting position. "Ran out of air? That's unforgivably careless. How can you give lessons when you haven't the sense to watch your own gauges?"

"I watched my gauge." She drew air in and let it out slowly. "I should have had another ten minutes."

"You rent diving equipment, for God's sake! How can you be negligent with your own? You might've died."

The insult to her competence went a long way toward smothering the fear. "I'm never careless," she snapped at him. "Not with rental equipment or my own." She dragged the mask from her head and tossed it on the bench. "Look at my gauge. I should have had ten minutes left."

He looked, but it didn't relieve his anger. "Your equipment should be checked. If you go down with a faulty gauge you're inviting an accident."

"My equipment has been checked. I check it myself after every dive, and it was fine before I stored it. I filled those tanks myself." The alternative came to her even as she finished speaking. Her face, already pale, went white.

"God, Jonas, I filled them myself. I checked every piece of equipment the last time I went down."

He closed a hand over hers hard enough to make her wince. "You keep it in the shop, in that closet."

"I lock it up."

"How many keys?"

"Mine—and an extra set in the drawer. They're rarely used because I always leave mine there when I go out on the boats."

"But the extra set would have been used when we were away?"

The shaking was starting again. This time it wasn't as simple to control it. "Yes."

"And someone used the key to the closet to get in and tamper with your equipment."

She moistened her lips. "Yes."

The rage ripped inside him until he was nearly blind with it. Hadn't he just promised to watch out for her, to keep her safe? With intensely controlled movements, he pulled off his flippers and discarded his mask. "You're going back. You're going to pack, then I'm putting you on a plane. You can stay with my family until this is over."

"No."

"You're going to do exactly what I say."

"No," she said again and managed to draw the strength to stand. "I'm not going anywhere. This is the second time someone's threatened my life."

"And they're not going to have a chance to do it again."

"I'm not leaving my home."

"Don't be a fool." He rose. Knowing he couldn't touch her, he unzipped his wet suit and began to strip it off.

"Your business isn't going to fall apart. You can come back when it's safe."

"I'm not leaving." She took a step toward him. "You came here looking for revenge. When you have it, you can leave and be satisfied. Now I'm looking for answers. I can't leave because they're here."

Struggling to keep his hands gentle, he took her face between them. "I'll find them for you."

"You know better than that, don't you, Jonas? Answers don't mean anything unless you find them yourself. I want my daughter to be able to come home. Until I find those answers, until it's safe, she can't." She lifted her hands to his face so that they stood as a unit. "We both have reasons to look now."

He sat, took his pack of cigarettes and spoke flatly. "Erika's dead."

The anger that had given her the strength to stand wavered. "What?"

"Murdered." His voice was cold again, hard again. "A few days ago I met her, paid her for a name."

Liz braced herself against the rail. "The name you gave to the captain."

Jonas lit his cigarette, telling himself he was justified to put fear back into her eyes. "That's right. She asked some questions, got some answers. She told me this Pablo Manchez was bad, a professional killer. Jerry was killed by a pro. So, it appears, was Erika."

"She was shot?"

"Stabbed," Jonas corrected and watched Liz's hand reach involuntarily for her own neck. "That's right." He drew violently on the cigarette then hurled it overboard before he rose. "You're going back to the States until this is all over."

She turned her back on him a moment, needing to be certain she could be strong. "I'm not leaving, Jonas. We have the same problem."

"Liz—"

"No." When she turned back her chin was up and her eyes were clear. "You see, I've run from problems before, and it doesn't work."

"This isn't a matter of running, it's a matter of being sensible."

"You're staying."

"I don't have a choice."

"Then neither do I."

"Liz, I don't want you hurt."

She tilted her head as she studied him. She could believe that, she realized, and take comfort in it. "Will you go?"

"I can't. You know I can't."

"Neither can I." She wrapped her arms around him, pressed her cheek to his shoulder in a first spontaneous show of need or affection. "Let's go home," she murmured. "Let's just go home."

Chapter 10

Every morning when Liz awoke she was certain Captain Moralas would call to tell her it was all over. Every night when she closed her eyes, she was certain it was only a matter of one more day. Time went on.

Every morning when Liz awoke she was certain Jonas would tell her he had to leave. Every night when she slept in his arms, she was certain it was the last time. He stayed.

For over ten years her life had had a certain purpose. Success. She'd started the struggle toward it in order to survive and to provide for her child. Somewhere along the way she'd learned the satisfaction of being on her own and making it work. In over ten years, Liz had gone steadily forward without detours. A detour could mean failure and the loss of independence. It had been barely a month since Jonas had walked into her house and her life. Since that time the straight road she had followed had forked. Ignoring the changes hadn't helped, fighting them hadn't worked. Now it no longer seemed she had the choice of which path to follow.

Because she had to hold on to something, she worked every day, keeping stubbornly to her old routine. It was the only aspect of her life that she could be certain she could control. Though it brought some semblance of order to her life, it didn't keep Liz's mind at rest. She found herself studying her customers with suspicion. Business thrived as the summer season drew closer. It didn't seem as important as it had even weeks before, but she kept the shop open seven days a week.

Jonas had taken the fabric of her life, plucked at a few threads and changed everything. Liz had come to the point that she could admit nothing would ever be quite the same again, but she had yet to come to the point that she knew what to do about it. When he left, as she knew he would, she would have to learn all over again how to suppress longings and black out dreams.

They would find Jerry Sharpe's killer. They would find the man with the knife. If she hadn't believed that, Liz would never have gone on day after day. But after the danger was over, after all questions were answered, her life would never be as it had been. Jonas had woven himself into it. When he went away, he'd leave a hole behind that would take all her will to mend.

Her life had been torn before. Liz could comfort herself that she had put it together again. The shape had been different, the texture had changed, but she had put it together. She could do so again. She would have to.

There were times when she lay in bed in the dark, in

the early hours of the morning, restless, afraid she would have to begin those repairs before she was strong enough.

Jonas could feel her shift beside him. He'd come to understand she rarely slept peacefully. Or she no longer slept peacefully. He wished she would lean on him, but knew she never would. Her independence was too vital, and opposingly, her insecurity was too deep to allow her to admit a need for another. Even the sharing of a burden was difficult for her. He wanted to soothe. Through his adult life, Jonas had carefully chosen companions who had no problems, required no advice, no comfort, no support. A woman who required such things required an emotional attachment he had never been willing to make. He wasn't a selfish man, simply a cautious one. Throughout his youth, and through most of his adult life, he'd picked up the pieces his brother had scattered. Consciously or unconsciously, Jonas had promised himself he'd never be put in the position of having to do so for anyone else.

Now he was drawing closer and closer to a woman who elicited pure emotion, then tried to deflect it. He was falling in love with a woman who needed him but refused to admit it. She was strong and had both the intelligence and the will to take care of herself. And she had eyes so soft, so haunted, that a man would risk anything to protect her from any more pain.

She had completely changed his life. She had altered the simple, tidy pattern he'd been weaving for himself. He *needed* to soothe, to protect, to share. There was nothing he could do to change that. Whenever he touched her, he came closer to admitting there was nothing he would do.

The bed was warm and the room smelled of the flowers that grew wild outside the open window. Their scent mixed with the bowl of potpourri on Liz's dresser. Now and then the breeze ruffled through palm fronds so that the sound whispered but didn't disturb. Beside him was a woman whose body was slim and restless. Her hair spread over her pillow and onto his, carrying no more fragrance than wind over water. The moonlight trickled in, dipping into corners, filtering over the bed so he could trace her silhouette. As she tossed in sleep, he drew her closer. Her muscles were tense, as though she were prepared to reject the gift of comfort even before it was offered. Slowly, as her breath whispered at his throat, he began to massage her shoulders. Strong shoulders, soft skin. He found the combination irresistible. She murmured, shifting toward him, but he didn't know if it was acceptance or request. It didn't matter.

She felt so good there; she felt right there. All questions, all doubts could wait for the sunrise. Before dawn they would share the need that was in both of them. In the moonlight, in the quiet hours, each would have what the other could offer. He touched his mouth lightly, ever so lightly, to hers.

She sighed, but it was only a whisper of a sound— a sigh in sleep as her body relaxed against his. If she dreamed now, she dreamed of easy things, calm water, soft grass. He trailed a hand down her back, exploring the shape of her. Long, lean, slender and strong. He felt his own body warm and pulse. Passion, still sleepy, began to stir.

She seemed to wake in stages. First her skin, then her

blood, then muscle by muscle. Her body was alert and throbbing before her mind raced to join it. She found herself wrapped around Jonas, already aroused, already hungry. When his mouth came to hers again, she answered him.

There was no hesitation in her this time, no moment of doubt before desire overwhelmed reason. She wanted to give herself to him as fully as it was possible to give. It wouldn't be wise to speak her feelings out loud. It couldn't be safe to tell him with words that her heart was stripped of defenses and open for him. But she could show him, and by doing so give them both the pleasure of love without restrictions.

Her arms tightened around him as her mouth roamed madly over his. She drew his bottom lip inside the heat, inside the moistness of her mouth and nibbled, sucked until his breath came fast and erratic. She felt the abrupt tension as his body pressed against hers and realized he, too, could be seduced. He, too, could be aroused beyond reason. And she realized with a heady sort of wonder that she could be the seducer, she could arouse.

She shifted her body under his, tentatively, but with a slow rhythm that had him murmuring her name and grasping for control. Instinctively she sought out vulnerabilities, finding them one by one, learning from them, taking from them. Her tongue flicked over his throat, seeking then enjoying the subtle, distinct taste of man. His pulse was wild there, as wild as hers. She shifted again until she lay across him and his body was hers for the taking.

Her hands were inexperienced so that her stroking was soft and hesitant. It drove him mad. No one had ever been so sweetly determined to bring him pleasure. She pressed kisses over his chest, slowly, experimentally, then rubbed her cheek over his skin so that the touch both soothed and excited.

His body was on fire, yet it seemed to float free so that he could feel the passage of air breathe cool over his flesh. She touched, and the heat spread like brushfire. She tasted and the moistness from her lips was like the whisper of a night breeze, cooling, calming.

"Tell me what you want." She looked up and her eyes were luminous in the moonlight, dark and beautiful. "Tell me what to do."

It was almost more than he could bear, the purity of the request, the willingness to give. He reached up so that his hands were lost in her hair. He could have kept her there forever, arched above him with her skin glowing gold in the thin light, her hair falling pale over her shoulders, her eyes shimmering with need. He drew her down until their lips met again. Hunger exploded between them. She didn't need to be told, she didn't need to be taught. Her body took over so that her own desire drove them both.

Jonas let reason go, let control be damned. Gripping her hips, he drew her up, then brought her to him, brought himself into her with a force that had her gasping in astonished pleasure. As she shuddered again, then again, he reached for her hands. Their fingers linked as she arched back and let her need set the pace. Frantic. Desperate. Uncontrollable. Pleasure, pain, delight, terror all whipped through her, driving her on, thrusting her higher.

He couldn't think, but he could feel. Until that moment, he wouldn't have believed it possible to feel so much so intensely. Sensations racked him, building and building and threatening to explode until the only sound he could hear was the roar of his own heart inside his head. With his eyes half open he could see her above him, naked and glorious in the moonlight. And when she plunged him beyond sensation, beyond sight and reason, he could still see her. He always would.

It didn't seem possible. It didn't, Liz thought, seem reasonable that she could be managing the shop, dealing with customers, stacking equipment when her system was still soaking up every delicious sensation she'd experienced just before dawn. Yet she was there, filling out forms, giving advice, quoting prices and making change. Still it was all mechanical. She'd been wise to delegate the diving tours and remain on shore.

She greeted her customers, some old and some new, and tried not to think too deeply about the list she'd been forced to give Moralas. How many of them would come to the Black Coral for equipment or lessons if they knew that by doing only that they were under police investigation? Jerry Sharpe's murder, and her involvement in it, could endanger her business far more than a slow season or a rogue hurricane.

Over and above her compassion, her sympathy and her hopes that Jonas could put his mind and heart at rest was a desperate need to protect her own, to guard what she'd built from nothing for her daughter. No matter how she tried to bury it, she couldn't completely block out the resentment she felt for being pulled into a situation that had been none of her making.

Yet there was a tug-of-war waging inside of her. Resentment for the disruption of her life battled against the longing to have Jonas remain in it. Without the disruption, he never would have come to her. No matter how much she tried, she could never regret the weeks they'd had together. She promised herself that she never would. It was time to admit that she had a great scope of love that had been trapped inside her. Rejected once, it had refused to risk again. But Jonas had released it, or perhaps she'd released it herself. Whatever happened, however it ended, she'd been able to love again.

"You're a hard lady to pin down."

Startled out of her own thoughts, Liz looked up. It took her a moment to remember the face, and a moment still to link a name with it. "Mr. Trydent." She rose from her desk to go to the counter. "I didn't realize you were still on the island."

"I only take one vacation a year, so I like to make the most of it." He set a tall paper cup that bounced with ice on the counter. "I figured this was the only way to get you to have a drink with me."

Liz glanced at the cup and wondered if she'd been businesslike or rude. At the moment she would have liked nothing better than to be alone with her own thoughts, but a customer was a customer. "That's nice of you. I've been pretty tied up."

"No kidding." He gave her a quick smile that showed straight teeth and easy charm. "You're either out of town or out on a boat. So I thought about the mountain and Mohammed." He glanced around. "Things are pretty quiet now."

"Lunchtime," Liz told him. "Everyone who's going out

is already out. Everyone else is grabbing some food or a siesta before they decide how to spend the afternoon."

"Island living."

She smiled back. "Exactly. Tried any more diving?"

He made a face. "I let myself get talked into a night dive with Mr. Ambuckle before he headed back to Texas. I'm planning on sticking to the pool for the rest of my vacation."

"Diving's not for everyone."

"You can say that again." He drank from the second cup he'd brought, then leaned on the counter. "How about dinner? Dinner's for everyone."

She lifted a brow, a little surprised, a little flattered that he seemed bent on a pursuit. "I rarely eat out."

"I like home cooking."

"Mr. Trydent—"

"Scott," he corrected.

"Scott, I appreciate the offer, but I'm…" How did she put it? Liz wondered. "I'm seeing someone."

He laid a hand on hers. "Serious?"

Not sure whether she was embarrassed or amused, Liz drew her hand away. "I'm a serious sort of person."

"Well." Scott lifted his cup, watching her over the rim as he drank. "I guess we'd better stick to business then. How about explaining the snorkeling equipment to me?"

With a shrug, Liz glanced over her shoulder. "If you can swim, you can snorkel."

"Let's just say I'm cautious. Mind if I come in and take a look?"

She'd been ungracious enough for one day, Liz decided. She sent him a smile. "Sure, look all you want." When he'd skirted around the counter and through the door, she walked with him to the back shelves. "The snorkel's just a hollow tube with a mouthpiece," she began as she took one down to offer it. "You put this lip between your teeth and breathe normally through your mouth. With the tube attached to a face mask, you can paddle around on the surface indefinitely."

"Okay. How about all the times I see these little tubes disappear under the water?"

"When you want to go down, you hold your breath and let out a bit of air to help you descend. The trick is to blow out and clear the tube of water when you surface. Once you get the knack, you can go down and up dozens of times without ever taking your face out of the water."

Scott turned the snorkel over in his hand. "There's a lot to see down there."

"A whole world."

He was no longer looking at the snorkel, but at her. "I guess you know a lot about the water and the reefs in this area. Know much about Isla Mujeres?"

"Excellent snorkeling and diving." Absently, Liz took down a mask to show him how to attach the snorkel. "We offer full-and half-day trips. If you're adventurous enough, there are caves to explore."

"And some are fairly remote," he said idly.

"For snorkeling you'd want to stay closer to the reefs, but an experienced diver could spend days around the caves."

"And nights." Scott passed the snorkel through his fingers as he watched her. "I imagine a diver could go down there at night and be completely undisturbed."

She wasn't certain why she felt a trickle of alarm. Automatically, she glanced over his shoulder to where her police guard half dozed in the sun. Silly, she told herself with a little shrug. She'd never been one to jump at shadows. "It's a dangerous area for night diving."

"Some people prefer danger, especially when it's profitable."

Her mouth was dry, so she swallowed as she replaced the mask on the shelf. "Perhaps. I don't."

This time his smile wasn't so charming or his eyes so friendly. "Don't you?"

"I don't know what you mean."

"I think you do." His hand closed over her arm. "I think you know exactly what I mean. What Jerry Sharpe skimmed off the top and dumped in that safe-deposit box in Acapulco was petty cash, Liz." He leaned closer as his voice lowered. "There's a lot more to be made. Didn't he tell you?"

She had a sudden, fierce memory of a knife probing against her throat. "He didn't tell me anything. I don't know anything." Before she could evade, he had her backed into a corner. "If I scream," she managed in a steady voice, "there'll be a crowd of people here before you can take a breath."

"No need to scream." He held up both hands as if to show her he meant no harm. "This is a business discussion. All I want to know is how much Jerry told you before he made the mistake of offending the wrong people."

When she discovered she was trembling, Liz forced herself to stop. He wouldn't intimidate her. What weapon could he hide in a pair of bathing trunks and an open shirt? She straightened her shoulders and looked him directly in the eye. "Jerry didn't tell me anything. I said the same thing to your friend when he had the knife at my throat. It didn't satisfy him, so he put a damaged gauge on my tanks."

"My partner doesn't understand much about finesse," Scott said easily. "I don't carry knives, and I don't know enough about your diving equipment to mess with the gauges. What I know about is you, and I know plenty. You work too hard, Liz, getting up at dawn and hustling until sundown. I'm just trying to give you some options. Business, Liz. We're just going to talk business."

It was his calm, reasonable attitude that had her temper whipping out. He could be calm, he could be reasonable, and people were dead. "I'm not Jerry and I'm not Erika, so keep that in mind. I don't know anything about the filthy business you're into, but the police do, and they'll know more. If you think you can frighten me by threatening me with a knife or damaging my equipment, you're right. But that doesn't stop me from wishing every one of you to hell. Now get out of my shop and leave me alone."

He studied her face for a long ten seconds, then backed an inch or two away. "You've got me wrong, Liz. I said this was a business discussion. With Jerry gone, an experienced diver would come in handy, especially one who knows the waters around here. I'm authorized to offer you five thousand dollars. Five thousand American dollars for doing what you do best. Diving. You go down, drop off one package and pick up another. No names, no faces. Bring the package back to me unopened and I hand you five thousand in cash. Once or twice a week, and you can build up a nice little nest egg. I'd say a woman raising a kid alone could use some extra money."

Fear had passed into fury; she clenched her hands together. "I told you to get out," she repeated. "I don't want your money."

He smiled and touched a finger to her cheek. "Give it some thought. I'll be around if you change your mind."

Liz waited for her breathing to level as she watched him walk away. With deliberate movements, she locked the shop, then walked directly to her police guard. "I'm going home," she told him as he sprang to attention. "Tell Captain Moralas to meet me there in half an hour." Without waiting for a reply, she strode across the sand.

Fifteen minutes later, Liz slammed into her house. The ride home hadn't calmed her. At every turn she'd been violated. At every turn, her privacy and peace had been disrupted. This last incident was the last she'd accept. She might have been able to handle another threat, another demand. But he'd offered her a job. Offered to pay her to smuggle cocaine, to take over the position of a man who'd been murdered. Jonas's brother.

A nightmare, Liz thought as she paced from window to window. She wished she could believe it was a nightmare. The cycle was drawing to a close, and she felt herself being trapped in the center. What Jerry Sharpe had started, she and Jonas would be forced to finish, no matter how painful. No matter how deadly. Finish it she would, Liz promised herself. The cycle would be broken, no matter what she had to do. She would be finished with it so her daughter could come home safely. Whatever she had to do, she would see to that.

At the sound of a car approaching, Liz went to the front window. Jonas, she thought, and felt her heart sink. Did she tell him now that she'd met face-to-face with the man who might have killed his brother? If he had the name, if he knew the man, would he race off in a rage for the revenge he'd come so far to find? And if he found his revenge, could the cycle ever be broken? Instead, she was afraid it would revolve and revolve around them, smothering everything else. She saw Jonas, a man of the law, a man of patience and compassion, shackled forever within the results of his own violence. How could she save him from that and still save herself?

Her hand was cold as she reached for the door and opened it to meet him. He knew there was something wrong before he touched her. "What are you doing home? I went by the shop and it was closed."

"Jonas." She did the only thing she knew how. She drew him against her and held on. "Moralas is on his way here."

"What happened?" A little skip of panic ran through him before he could stop it. He held her away, searching her face. "Did something happen to you? Were you hurt?"

"No, I'm not hurt. Come in and sit down."

"Liz, I want to know what happened."

She heard the sound of a second engine and looked down the street to see the unmarked car. "Moralas is here," she murmured. "Come inside, Jonas. I'd rather go through this only once."

There was really no decision to be made, Liz told herself as she moved away from the door to wait. She would give Moralas and Jonas the name of the man who had approached her. She would tell them exactly what he'd said. By doing so she would take herself one step further away from the investigation. They would have a name, a face, a location. They would have motive. It was what the police wanted, it was what she wanted. She glanced at Jonas as Moralas came up the front walk. It was what Jonas wanted. What he needed. And by giving it to him, she would take herself one step further way from him.

"Miss Palmer." Moralas took off his hat as he entered, glanced briefly at Jonas and waited.

"Captain." She stood by a chair but didn't sit. "I have some information for you. There's an American, a man named Scott Trydent. Less than an hour ago he offered me five thousand dollars to smuggle cocaine off the reef of Isla Mujeres."

Moralas's expression remained impassive. He tucked his hat under his arm. "And have you had previous dealings with this man?"

"He joined one of my diving classes. He was friendly. Today he came by the shop to talk to me. Apparently he believed that I..." She trailed off to look at Jonas. He stood very still and very quiet just inside the door. "He thought that Jerry had told me about the operation. He'd found out about the safe-deposit box. I don't know how. It was as though he knew every move I've made for weeks." As her nerves began to fray, she dragged a hand through her hair. "He told me that I could take over Jerry's position, make the exchange in the caves near Isla Mujeres and be rich. He knows..." She had to swallow to keep her voice from trembling. "He knows about my daughter."

"You would identify him?"

"Yes. I don't know if he killed Jerry Sharpe." Her gaze shifted to Jonas again and pleaded. "I don't know, but I could identify him."

Moralas watched the exchange before crossing the room. "Please sit down, Miss Palmer."

"You'll arrest him?" She wanted Jonas to say something, anything, but he continued to stand in silence. "He's part of the cocaine ring. He knows about Jerry's Sharpe's murder. You have to arrest him."

"Miss Palmer." Moralas urged her down on the sofa, then sat beside her. "We have names. We have faces. The smuggling ring currently operating in the Yucatan Peninsula is under investigation by both the Mexican and the American governments. The names you and Mr. Sharpe have given me are not unfamiliar. But there is one we don't have. The person who organizes, the person who undoubtedly ordered the murder of Jerry Sharpe. This is the name we need. Without it, the arrest of couriers, of salesmen, is nothing. We need this name, Miss Palmer. And we need proof."

"I don't understand. You mean you're just going to let Trydent go? He'll just find someone else to make the drops."

"It won't be necessary for him to look elsewhere if you agree."

"No." Before Liz could take in Moralas's words, Jonas was breaking in. He said it quietly, so quietly that chills began to race up and down her spine. He took out a cigarette. His hands were rock steady. Taking his time, he flicked his lighter and drew until the tip glowed red. He blew out a stream of smoke and locked his gaze on Moralas. "You can go to hell."

"Miss Palmer has the privilege to tell me so herself."

"You're not using her. If you want someone on the inside, someone closer to the names and proof, I'll make the drop."

Moralas studied him, saw the steady nerves and untiring patience along with simmering temper. If he'd had a choice, he'd have preferred it. "It isn't you who has been asked."

"Liz isn't going down."

"Just a minute." Liz pressed both hands to her temples. "Are you saying you want me to see Trydent again, to tell him I'll take the job? That's crazy. What purpose could there be?"

"You would be a decoy." Moralas glanced down at her hands. Delicate, yes, but strong. There was nothing about Elizabeth Palmer he didn't know. "The investigation is closing in. We don't want the ring to change locations at this point. If the operation appears to go smoothly, there should be no move at this time. You've been the stumbling block, Miss Palmer, for the ring, and the investigation."

"How?" Furious, she started to stand. Moralas merely put a hand on her arm.

"Jerry Sharpe lived with you, worked for you. He had a weakness for women. Neither the police nor the smugglers have been sure exactly what part you played. Jerry Sharpe's brother is now living in your home. The key to the safe-deposit box was found by you."

"Guilty by association, Captain?" Her voice took on that ice-sharp edge Jonas had heard only once or twice before. "Have I had police protection, or have I been under surveillance?"

Moralas's tone never altered. "One serves the same purpose as the other."

"If I'm under suspicion, haven't you considered that I might simply take the money and run?"

"That's precisely what we want you to do."

"Very clever." Jonas wasn't certain how much longer he could hold on to his temper. It would have given him great satisfaction to have picked Moralas up bodily and thrown him out of the house. Out of Liz's life. "Liz double-crosses them, annoying the head of the operation. It's then necessary to eliminate her the way my brother was eliminated."

"Except that Miss Palmer will be under police protection at all times. If this one drop goes as we plan, the investigation will end, and the smugglers, along with your brother's killer, will be caught and punished. This is what you want?"

"Not if it means risking Liz. Plant your own pigeon, Moralas."

"There isn't time. With your cooperation, Miss Palmer, we can end this. Without it, it could take months."

Months? she thought. Another day would be a lifetime. "I'll do it."

Jonas was beside her in a heartbeat, pulling her off the couch. "Liz—"

"My daughter comes home in two weeks." She put her hands on his arms. "She won't come back to anything like this."

"Take her someplace else." Jonas gripped her shoulders until his fingers dug into flesh. "We'll go someplace else."

"Where?" she demanded. "Every day I tell myself I'm pulling away from this thing and every day it's a lie. I've been in it since Jerry walked in the door. We can't change that. Until it's over, really over, nothing's going to be right."

He knew she was right, had known it from the first moment. But too much had changed. There was a desperation in him now that he'd never expected to feel. It was all for her. "Come back to the States with me. It will be over."

"Will it? Will you forget your brother was murdered? Will you forget the man who killed him?" His fingers tightened, his eyes darkened, but he said nothing. Her breath came out in a sigh of acceptance. "No, it won't be over until we finish it. I've run before, Jonas. I promised myself I'd never run again."

"You could be killed."

"I've done nothing and they've nearly killed me twice." She dropped her head on his chest. "Please help me."

He couldn't force her to bend his way. Two of the things he most admired in her were her capacity to give and her will to stand firm. He could plead with her, he could argue, but he could never lie. If she ran, if they ran, they'd never be free of it. His arm came around her. Her hair smelled of summer and sea air. And before the summer ended, he promised himself, she'd be free. They'd both be free.

"I go with her." He met Moralas's eyes over her head.

"That may not be possible."

"I'll make it possible."

Chapter 11

She'd never been more frightened in her life. Every day she worked in the shop, waiting for Scott Trydent to approach. Every evening she locked up, went home and waited for the phone to ring. Jonas said little. She no longer knew what he did with the hours they were apart, but she was aware that he was planning his own move, in his own time. It only frightened her more.

Two days passed until her nerves were stretched thinner and tighter than she would have believed possible. On the beach, people slept or read novels, lovers walked by arm in arm. Children chattered and ran. Snorkelers splashed around the reef. She wondered why nothing seemed normal, or if it ever would again. At sundown she emptied her cash box, stacked gear and began to lock up.

"How about that drink?"

Though she'd thought she'd braced herself for the moment when it would begin, Liz jolted. Her head began to throb in a slow, steady rhythm she knew would last for hours. In the pit of her stomach she felt the twist come and go from panicked excitement. From this point on, she reminded herself, she had no room to panic. She turned and looked at Scott. "I was wondering if you'd come back."

"Told you I'd be around. I always figure people need a couple of days to mull things over."

She had a part to play, Liz reminded herself. She had to do it well. Carefully, she finished locking up, then turned back to him. She didn't smile. It was to be a business discussion, cut-and-dried. "We can get a drink over there." She pointed to the open-air thatched-roof restaurant overhanging the reef. "It's public."

"Suits me." Though he offered his hand, she ignored it and began to walk.

"You used to be friendlier."

"You used to be a customer." She sent him a sideways look. "Not a business partner."

"So…" She saw him glance right, then left. "You've mulled."

"You need a diver, I need money." Liz walked up the two wooden stairs and chose a chair that had her back to the water. Seconds after she sat, a man settled himself into a corner table. One of Moralas's, she thought, and ordered herself to be calm. She'd been briefed and rebriefed. She knew what to say, how to say it, and that the waiter who would serve them carried a badge and a gun. "Jerry didn't tell me a great deal," she began, and ordered an American soft drink. "Just that he made the drop and collected the money."

"He was a good diver."

Liz swallowed the little bubble of fear. "I'm better."

Scott grinned at her. "So I'm told."

A movement beside her had her glancing over, then freezing. A dark man with a pitted face took the chair beside her. Liz knew he wore a thin silver band on his wrist before she looked for it.

"Pablo Manchez, Liz Palmer. Though I think you two have met."

"Señorita." Manchez's thin mouth curved as he took her hand.

"Tell your friend to keep his hands to himself." Calmly, Jonas pulled a chair up to the table. "Why don't you introduce me, Liz?" When she could do no more than stare at him, he settled back. "I'm Jonas Sharpe. Liz and I are partners." He leveled his gaze to Manchez. This was the man, he thought, whom he'd come thousands of miles to see. This was the man he'd kill. Jonas felt the hatred and the fury rise. But he knew how to strap the emotions and wait. "I believe you knew my brother."

Manchez's hand dropped from Liz's and went to his side. "Your brother was greedy and stupid."

Liz held her breath as Jonas reached in his pocket. Slowly, he pulled out his cigarettes. "I'm greedy," he said easily as he lit one. "But I'm not stupid. I've been looking for you." He leaned across the table. With a slow smile, he offered Manchez the cigarettes.

Manchez took one and broke off the filter. His hands were beautiful, with long spidery fingers and narrow palms. Liz fought back a shudder as she looked at them. "So you found me."

Jonas was still smiling as he ordered a beer. "You need a diver."

Scott sent Manchez a warning look. "We have a diver."

"What you have is a team. Liz and I work together." Jonas blew out a stream of smoke. "Isn't that right, Liz?"

He wanted them. He wasn't going to back off until he had them. And she had no choice. "That's right."

"We don't need no team." Manchez started to rise.

"You need us." Jonas took his beer as it was served. "We already know a good bit about your operation. Jerry wasn't good at keeping secrets." Jonas took a swig from the bottle. "Liz and I are more discreet. Five thousand a drop?"

Scott waited a beat, then held a hand up, signaling Manchez. "Five. If you want to work as a team, it's your business how you split it."

"Fifty-fifty." Liz spread her fingers around Jonas's beer. "One of us goes down, one stays in the dive boat."

"Tomorrow night. Eleven o'clock. You come to the shop. Go inside. You'll find a waterproof case. It'll be locked."

"So will the shop," Liz put in. "How does the case get inside?"

Manchez blew smoke between his teeth. "I got no problem getting in."

"Just take the case," Scott interrupted. "The coordinates will be attached to the handle. Take the boat out, take the case down, leave it. Then come back up and wait exactly an hour. That's when you dive again. All you have to do is take the case that's waiting for you back to the shop and leave it."

"Sounds smooth," Jonas decided. "When do we get paid?"

"After you do the job."

"Half up front." Liz took a long swallow of beer and hoped her heart would settle. "Leave twenty-five hundred with the case or I don't dive."

Scott smiled. "Not as trusting as Jerry."

She gave him a cold, bitter look. "And I intend to stay alive."

"Just follow the rules."

"Who makes them?" Jonas took the beer back from Liz. Her hand slipped down to his leg and stayed steady.

"You don't want to worry about that," Manchez advised. The cigarette was clamped between his teeth as he smiled. "He knows who you are."

"Just follow the coordinates and keep an eye on your watch." Scott dropped bills on the table as he rose. "The rest is gravy."

"Stay smart, Jerry's brother." Manchez gave them both a slow smile. *"Adios, señorita."*

Jonas calmly finished his beer as the two men walked away.

"You weren't supposed to interfere during the meeting," Liz began in a furious undertone. "Moralas said—"

"The hell with Moralas." He crushed out his cigarette, watching as the smoke plumed up. "Is that the man who put the bruises on your neck?"

Her hand moved up before she could stop it. Halfway to her throat, Liz curled her fingers into a ball and set her hand on the table. "I told you I didn't see him."

Jonas turned his head. His eyes, as they had before, reminded her of frozen smoke. "Was it the man?"

He didn't need to be told. Liz leaned closer and spoke softly. "I want it over, Jonas. And I don't need revenge. You were supposed to let me meet with Scott and set things up by myself."

In an idle move, he tilted the candle on the table toward him and lit it. "I changed my mind."

"Damn you, you could've messed everything up. I don't want to be involved but I am. The only way to get uninvolved is to finish it. How do we know they won't just back off now that you've come into it?"

"Because you're right in the middle, and you always have been." Before she could speak, he took her arm. His face was close, his voice cool and steady. "I was going to use you. From the minute I walked into your house, I was going to use you to get to Jerry's killer. If I had to walk all over you, if I had to knock you out of the way or drag you along with me, I was going to use you. Just the way Moralas is going to use you. Just the way the others are going to use you." The heat of the candle flickered between them as he drew her closer. "The way Jerry used you."

She swallowed the tremor and fought against the pain. "And now?"

He didn't speak. They were so close that he could see himself reflected in her eyes. In them, surrounding his own reflection, he saw the doubts and the defiance. His hand came to the back of her neck, held there until he could feel the rhythm of her pulse. With a simmering violence, he pulled her against him and covered her mouth with his. A flare that was passion, a glimmer that was hope—he didn't know which to reach for. So he let her go.

"No one's going to hurt you again," he murmured. "Especially not me."

It was the longest day of her life. Liz worked and waited as the hours crawled by. Moralas's men mixed with the vacationers on the beach. So obviously, it seemed to Liz, that she wondered everyone else didn't notice them as though they wore badges around their necks. Her boats went out, returned and went out again. Tanks and equipment were checked and rented. She filled out invoices and accepted credit cards as if there were some importance to daily routine. She wished for the day to end. She hoped the night would never come.

A thousand times she thought of telling Moralas she couldn't go through with it. A thousand times she called herself a coward. But as the sun went down and the beach began to clear, she realized courage wasn't something that could be willed into place. She would run, if she had the choice. But as long as she was in danger, Faith was in danger. When the sun went down, she locked the shop as if it were the end of any ordinary day. Before she'd pocketed her keys, Jonas was beside her.

"There's still time to change your mind."

"And do what? Hide?" She looked out at the beach, at the sea, at the island that was her home. And her prison. Why had she never seen it as a prison until Jonas had come to it? "You've already told me how good I am at hiding."

"Liz—"

She shook her head to stop him. "I can't talk about it. I just have to do it."

They drove home in silence. In her mind, Liz went over her instructions, every point, every word Moralas had pushed at her. She was to follow the routine, make the exchange, then turn the case with the money over to the police who'd be waiting near the dock. She'd wait for the next move. And while she waited, she'd never be more than ten feet away from a cop. It sounded foolproof. It made her stomach churn.

There was a man walking a dog along the street in front of her house. One of Moralas's men. The man whittling on her neighbor's porch had a gun under his denim vest. Liz tried to look at neither of them.

"You're going to have a drink, some food and a nap," Jonas ordered as he steered her inside.

"Just the nap."

"The nap first then." After securing the lock, Jonas followed her into the bedroom. He lowered the shades. "Do you want anything?"

It was still so hard to ask. "Would you lie down with me?"

He came to her. She was already curled on her side, so he drew her back against him and wrapped her close. "Will you sleep?"

"I think so." In sleep she could find escape, if only temporarily. But she didn't close her eyes. "Jonas?"

"Hmm?"

"After tonight—after we've finished, will you hold me like this again?"

He pressed his lips to her hair. He didn't think he could love her any more. He was nearly certain if he told her she'd pull away. "As long as you want. Just sleep."

Liz let her eyes close and her mind empty.

The case was small, the size of an executive briefcase. It seemed too inconspicuous to be the catalyst for so much danger. Beside it, on the counter of Liz's shop, was an envelope. Inside was a slip of paper with longitude and latitude printed. With the slip of paper were twenty-five one-hundred-dollar bills.

"They kept their part of the bargain," Jonas commented.

Liz merely shoved the envelope into a drawer. "I'll get my equipment."

Jonas watched her. She'd rather do this on her own, he reflected. She'd rather not think she had someone to lean on, to turn to. He took her tanks before she could heft them. She was going to learn, he reminded himself, that she had a great deal more than that. "The coordinates?"

"The same that were in Jerry's book." She found herself amazingly calm as she waited to lock the door behind him. They were being watched. She was aware that Moralas had staked men in the hotel. She was just as certain Manchez was somewhere close. She and Jonas didn't speak again until they were on the dive boat and had cast off. "This could end it." She glanced at him as she set her course.

"This could end it."

She was silent for a moment. All during the evening hours she'd thought about what she would say to him, how she would say it. "Jonas, what will you do?"

The flame of his lighter hissed, flared, then was quiet. "What I have to do."

The fear tasted like copper in her mouth, but it had nothing to do with herself and everything to do with Jonas. "If we make the exchange tonight, turn the second case over to Moralas. They'll have to come out in the open. Manchez, and the man who gives the orders."

"What are you getting at, Liz?"

"Manchez killed your brother."

Jonas looked beyond her. The sea was black. The sky

was black. Only the hum of the motor broke the silence. "He was the trigger."

"Are you going to kill him?"

Slowly, he turned back to her. The question had been quiet, but her eyes weren't. They sent messages, posed argument, issued pleas. "It doesn't involve you."

That hurt deeply, sharply. With a nod, she followed the shimmer of light on the water. "Maybe not. But if you let hate rule what you do, how you think, you'll never be free of it. Manchez will be dead, Jerry will still be dead and you..." She turned to look at him again. "You'll never really be alive again."

"I didn't come all this way, spend all this time, to let Manchez walk away. He kills for money and because he enjoys it. He enjoys it," Jonas repeated viciously. "You can see it in his eyes."

And she had. But she didn't give a damn about Manchez. "Do you remember telling me once that everyone was entitled to representation?"

He remembered. He remembered everything he'd once believed in. He remembered how Jerry had looked in the cold white light of the morgue. "It didn't have anything to do with this."

"I suppose you change the rules when it's personal."

"He was my brother."

"And he's dead." With a sigh she lifted her face so that the wind could cool her skin. "I'm sorry, Jonas. Jerry's dead and if you go through with what you've planned, you're going to kill something in yourself." And, though she couldn't tell him, something in her. "Don't you trust the law?"

He tossed his cigarette into the water, then leaned on the rail. "I've been playing with it for years. It's the last thing I'd trust."

She wanted to go to him but didn't know how. Still, no matter what he did, she was beside him. "Then you'll have to trust yourself. And so will I."

Slowly, he crossed to her. Taking her face in his hands, he tried to understand what she was telling him, what she was still holding back. "Will you?"

"Yes."

He leaned to press a kiss to her forehead. Inside there was a need, a fierce desire to tell her to head the boat out to sea and keep going. But that would never work, not for either of them. They stood on the boat together, and stood at the crossroads. "Then start now." He kissed her again before he turned and lifted one of the compartment seats. Liz frowned as she saw the wet suit.

"What are you doing?"

"I arranged to have Luis leave this here for me."

"Why? We can't both go down."

Jonas stripped down to his trunks. "That's right. I'm diving, you're staying with the boat."

Liz stood very straight. It wouldn't do any good to lose her temper. "The arrangements were made on all sides, Jonas. I'm diving."

"I'm changing the arrangements." He tugged the wet suit up to his waist before he looked at her. "I'm not taking any more chances with you."

"You're not taking chances with me. I am. Jonas, you don't know these waters. I do. You've never gone down here at night. I have."

"I'm about to."

"The last thing we need right now is for you to start behaving like an overprotective man."

He nearly laughed as he snapped the suit over his shoulders. "That's too bad, then, because that's just what we've got."

"I told Manchez and Trydent I was going down."

"I guess your reputation's shot when you lie to murderers and drug smugglers."

"Jonas, I'm not in the mood for jokes."

He strapped on his diver's knife, adjusted his weight belt, then reached for his mask. "Maybe not. And maybe you're not in the mood to hear this. I care about you. Too damn much." He reached out, gripping her chin. "My brother dragged you into this because he never wasted two thoughts about anyone else in his life. I pulled you in deeper because all I was thinking about was payback. Now I'm thinking about you, about us. You're not going down. If I have to tie you to the wheel, you're not going down."

"I don't want you to go." She balled her fists against his chest. "If I was down, all I'd think about was what I was doing. If I stay up here, I won't be able to stop thinking about what could happen to you."

"Time me." He lifted the tanks and held them out to her. "Help me get them on."

Hadn't she told herself weeks before that he wasn't a man who'd lose an argument? Her hands trembled a bit as she slipped the straps over his shoulders. "I don't know how to handle being protected."

He hooked the tanks as he turned back to her. "Practice."

She closed her eyes. It was too late for talk, too late

for arguments. "Bear northeast as you dive. The cave's at eighty feet." She hesitated only a moment, then picked up a spear gun. "Watch out for sharks."

When he was over the side, she lowered the case to him. In seconds, he was gone and the sea was black and still. In her mind, Liz followed him fathom by fathom. The water would be dark so that he would be dependent on his gauges and the thin beam of light. Night creatures would be feeding. Squid, the moray, barracuda. Sharks. Liz closed her mind to it.

She should have forced him to let her go. How? Pacing the deck, she pushed the hair back from her face. He'd gone to protect her. He'd gone because he cared about her. Shivering, she sat down to rub her arms warm again. Was this what it was like to be cared for by a man? Did it mean you had to sit and wait? She was up again and pacing. She'd lived too much of her life doing to suddenly become passive. And yet... To hear him say he cared. Liz sat again and waited.

She'd checked her watch four times before she heard him at the ladder. On a shudder of relief, she dashed over to the side to help him. "I'm going down the next time," she began.

Jonas pulled off his light, then his tanks. "Forget it." Before she could protest, he dragged her against him. "We've got an hour," he murmured against her ear. "You want to spend it arguing?"

He was wet and cold. Liz wrapped herself around him. "I don't like being bossed around."

"Next time you can boss me around." He dropped onto a bench and pulled her with him. "I'd forgotten what it was like down there at night. Fabulous." And it was nearly over, he told himself. The first step had been taken, the second one had to follow. "I saw a giant squid. Scared the hell out of him with the light. I swear he was thirty feet long."

"They get bigger." She rested her head on his shoulder and tried to relax. They had an hour. "I was diving with my father once. We saw one that was nearly sixty."

"Made you nervous?"

"No. I was fascinated. I remember I swam close enough to touch the tentacles. My father gave me a twenty-minute lecture when we surfaced."

"I imagine you'd do the same thing with Faith."

"I'd be proud of her," Liz began, then laughed. "Then I'd give her a twenty-minute lecture."

For the first time that night he noticed the stars. The sky was alive with them. It made him think of his mother's porch swing and long summer nights. "Tell me about her."

"You don't want to get me started."

"Yes, I do." He slipped an arm around her shoulder. "Tell me about her."

With a half smile, Liz closed her eyes. It was good to think of Faith, to talk of Faith. A picture began to emerge for Jonas of a young girl who liked school because there was plenty to do and lots of people. He heard the love and the pride, and the wistfulness. He saw the dark, sunny-faced girl in the photo and learned she spoke two languages, liked basketball and hated vegetables.

"She's always been sweet," Liz reflected. "But she's no angel. She's very stubborn, and when she's crossed, her temper isn't pretty. Faith wants to do things herself.

When she was two she'd get very annoyed if I wanted to help her down the stairs."

"Independence seems to run in the family."

Liz moved her shoulders. "We've needed it."

"Ever thought about sharing?"

Her nerves began to hum. Though she shifted only a bit, it was away from him. "When you share, you have to give something up. I've never been able to afford to give up anything."

It was an answer he'd expected. It was an answer he intended to change. "It's time to go back down."

Liz helped him back on with his tanks. "Take the spear gun. Jonas…" He was already at the rail before she ran to him. "Hurry back," she murmured. "I want to go home. I want to make love with you."

"Hell of a time to bring that up." He sent her a grin, curled and fell back into the water.

Within five minutes Liz was pacing again. Why hadn't she thought to bring any coffee? She'd concentrate on that. In little more than an hour they could be huddled in her kitchen with a pot brewing. It wouldn't matter that there would be police surrounding the house. She and Jonas would be inside. Together. Perhaps she was wrong about sharing. Perhaps… When she heard the splash at the side of the boat, she was at the rail like a shot.

"Jonas, did something happen? Why—" She found herself looking down the barrel of a .22.

"Señorita." Manchez tossed his mask and snorkel onto a bench as he climbed over the side. *"Buenas noches."*

"What are you doing here?" She struggled to sound indignant as the blood rushed from her face. No, she wasn't brave, she realized. She wasn't brave at all. "We had a deal."

"You're an amateur," he told her. "Like Sharpe was an amateur. You think we'd just forget about the money?"

"I don't know anything about the money Jerry took." She gripped the rail. "I've told you that all along."

"The boss decided you were a loose end, pretty lady. You do us a favor and make this delivery. We do you a favor. We kill you quickly."

She didn't look at the gun again. She didn't dare. "If you keep killing your divers, you're going to be out of business."

"We're finished in Cozumel. When your friend brings up the case, I take it and go to Merida. I live in style. You don't live at all."

She wanted to sit because her knees were shaking. She stood because she thought she might never be able to again. "If you're finished in Cozumel, why did you set up this drop?"

"Clancy likes things tidy."

"Clancy?" The name David Merriworth had mentioned, Liz remembered, and strained to hear any sound from the water.

"There's a few thousand in cocaine down there, that's all. A few thousand dollars in the case coming up. The boss figures it's worth the investment to make it look like you were doing the dealing with Sharpe. Then you two have an argument and shoot each other. Case closed."

"You killed Erika too, didn't you?"

"She asked too many questions." He lowered the gun. "You ask too many questions."

Light flooded the boat and the water so quickly that Liz's first instinct was to freeze. Before the next reaction had fully registered, she was tumbling into the water and diving blind.

How could she warn Jonas? Liz groped frantically in the water as lights played on the surface above her. She had no tanks, no mask, no protection. Any moment he'd be surfacing, unaware of any danger. He had no protection but her.

Without equipment, she'd be helpless in a matter of moments. She fought to stay down, keeping as close to the ladder as she dared. Her lungs were ready to burst when she felt the movement in the water. Liz turned toward the beam of light.

When he saw her, his heart nearly stopped. She looked like a ghost clinging to the hull of the boat. Her hair was pale and floating out in the current, her face was nearly as white as his light. Before his mind could begin to question, he was pushing his mouthpiece between her lips and giving her air. There could be no communication but emotion. He felt the fear. Jonas steadied the spear gun in his arm and surfaced.

"Mr. Sharpe." Moralas caught him in the beam of a spotlight. Liz rose up beside him. "We have everything under control." On the deck of her boat, Liz saw Manchez handcuffed and flanked by two divers. "Perhaps you will give my men and their prisoner a ride back to Cozumel."

She felt Jonas tense. The spear gun was set and aimed. Even through the mask, she could see his eyes burning, burning as only ice can. "Jonas, please." But he was already starting up the ladder. She hauled herself over the rail and tumbled onto the deck, cold and dripping. "Jonas, you can't. Jonas, it's over."

He barely heard her. All his emotion, all his concentration was on the man who stood only feet away. Their eyes were locked. It gave him no satisfaction to watch the blood drain from Manchez's face, or the knowledge leap frantically into his eyes. It was what he'd come for, what he'd promised himself. The medallion on the edge of his chain dangled and reminded him of his brother. His brother was dead. No satisfaction. Jonas lowered the gun.

Manchez tossed back his head. "I'll get out," he said quietly. The smile started to spread. "I'll get out."

The spear shot out and plowed into the deck between Manchez's feet. Liz saw the smile freeze on his face an instant before one formed on Jonas's. "I'll be waiting."

Could it really be over? It was all Liz could think when she awoke, warm and dry, in her own bed. She was safe, Jonas was safe, and the smuggling ring on Cozumel was broken. Of course, Jonas had been furious. Manchez had been watched, they had been watched, but the police had made their presence known only after Liz had been held at gunpoint.

But he'd gotten what he'd come for, she thought. His brother's killer was behind bars. He'd face a trial and justice. She hoped it was enough for Jonas.

The morning was enough for her. The normality of it. Happy, she rolled over and pressed her body against Jonas's. He only drew her closer.

"Let's stay right here until noon."

She laughed and nuzzled against his throat. "I have—"

"A business to run," he finished.

"Exactly. And for the first time in weeks I can run it without having this urge to look over my shoulder. I'm happy." She looked at him, then tossed her arms around his neck and squeezed. "I'm so happy."

"Happy enough to marry me?"

She went still as a stone, then slowly, very slowly drew away. "What?"

"Marry me. Come home with me. Start a life with me."

She wanted to say yes. It shocked her that her heart burned to say yes. Pulling away from him was the hardest thing she'd ever done. "I can't."

He stopped her before she could scramble out of bed. It hurt, he realized, more than he could possibly have anticipated. "Why?"

"Jonas, we're two different people with two totally separate lives."

"We stopped having separate lives weeks ago." He took her hands. "They're not ever going to be separate again."

"But they will." She drew her hands away. "After you're back in Philadelphia for a few weeks, you'll barely remember what I look like."

He had her wrists handcuffed in his hands. The fury that surfaced so seldom in him seemed always on simmer when he was around her. "Why do you do that?" he demanded. "Why can't you ever take what you're given?" He swung her around until she was beneath him on the bed. "I love you."

"Don't." She closed her eyes as the wish nearly eclipsed the reason. "Don't say that to me."

Shut out. She was shutting him out. Jonas felt the panic

come first, then the anger. Then the determination. "I will say it. If I say it enough, sooner or later you'll start to believe it. Do you think all these nights have been a game? Haven't you felt it? Don't you feel anything?"

"I thought I felt something once before."

"You were a child." When she started to shake her head, he gripped her tighter. "Yes, you were. In some ways you still are, but I know what goes through you when you're with me. I know. I'm not a ghost, I'm not a memory. I'm real and I want you."

"I'm afraid of you," she whispered. "I'm afraid because you make me want what I can't have. I won't marry you, Jonas, because I'm through taking chances with my life and I won't take chances with my child's life. Please let me go."

He released her, but when she stood, his arms went around her. "It isn't over for us."

She dropped her head against his chest, pressed her cheek close. "Let me have the few days we have left. Please let me have them."

He lifted her chin. Everything he needed to know was in her eyes. A man who knew and who planned to win could afford to wait. "You haven't dealt with anyone as stubborn as you are before this. And you haven't nearly finished dealing with me." Then his hand gentled as he stroked her hair. "Get dressed. I'll take you to work."

Because he acted as though nothing had been said, Liz relaxed. It was impossible, and she knew it. They'd known each other only weeks, and under circumstances that were bound to intensify any feelings. He cared. She believed that he cared, but love—the kind of love needed to build a marriage—was too much to risk.

She loved. She loved so much that she pushed him away when she wanted to pull him closer. He needed to go back to his life, back to his world. After time had passed, if he thought of her he'd think with gratitude that she had closed a door he'd opened on impulse. She would think of him. Always.

By the time Liz was walking toward the shop, she'd settled her mind. "What are you going to do today?"

"Me?" Jonas, too, had settled his mind. "I'm going to sit in the sun and do nothing."

"Nothing?" Incredulous, Liz stared at him. "All day?"

"It's known as relaxing, or taking a day off. If you do it several days running, it's called a vacation. I was supposed to have one in Paris."

Paris, she thought. It would suit him. She wondered briefly how the air smelled in Paris. "If you get bored, I'm sure one of the boats could use the extra crew."

"I've had enough diving for a few days, thanks." Jonas plopped down on a chaise in front of the shop. It was the best place to keep an eye on her.

"Miguel." Liz automatically looked around for Luis. "You're here early."

"I came with Luis. He's checking out the dive boat—got an early tour."

"Yes, I know." But she wouldn't trust Miguel to run the shop alone for long. "Why don't you help him? I'll take care of the counter."

"*Bueno*. Oh, there were a couple of guys looking at the fishing boat. Maybe they want to rent."

"I'll take a look. You go ahead." Walking back, she

crouched beside Jonas. "Keep an eye on the shop for me, will you? I've got a couple of customers over by the *Expatriate*."

Jonas adjusted his sunglasses. "What do you pay per hour?"

Liz narrowed her eyes. "I might cook dinner tonight."

With a smile, he got up to go behind the counter. "Take all the time you need."

He made her laugh. Liz strolled down the walkway and to the pier, drinking up the morning. She could use a good fishing cruise. The aqua bikes had been ordered, but they still had to be paid for. Besides, she'd like the ride herself. It made her think of Jonas and his unwanted catch a few weeks before. Liz laughed again as she approached the men beside her boat.

"Buenos días," she began. "Mr. Ambuckle." Beaming a smile, Liz held out a hand. "I didn't know you were back. Is this one of your quick weekend trips?"

"That's right." His almost bald head gleamed in the sun as he patted her hand. "When the mood strikes me I just gotta move."

"Thinking about some big-game fishing this time around?"

"Funny you should mention it. I was just saying to my associate here that I only go for the big game."

"Only the big game." Scott Trydent turned around and pushed back his straw hat. "That's right, Clancy."

"Now don't turn around, honey." Ambuckle's fingers clamped over hers before she could move. "You're going to get on the boat, nice and quiet. We have some talking to do, then we might just take a little ride."

"How long have you been using my dive shop to smuggle?" Liz saw the gun under Scott's jacket. She couldn't signal to Jonas, didn't dare.

"For the past couple of years I've found your shop's location unbeatable. You know, they ship that stuff up from Colombia and dump in Miami. The way the heat's been on the past few years, you take a big chance using the regular routes. It takes longer this way, but I lose less merchandise."

"And you're the organizer," she murmured. "You're the man the police want."

"I'm a businessman," he said with a smile. "Let's get on board, little lady."

"The police are watching," Liz told him as she climbed on deck.

"The police have Manchez. If he hadn't tried to pull a double cross, the last shipment would have gone down smooth."

"A double cross?"

"That's right," Scott put in as he flanked her. "Pablo decided he could make more free-lancing than by being a company man."

"And by reporting on his fellow employee, Mr. Trydent moves up in rank. I work my organization on the incentive program."

Scott grinned at Ambuckle. "Can't beat the system."

"You had Jerry Sharpe killed." Struggling to believe what was happening, Liz stared at the round little man who'd chatted with her and rented her tanks. "You had him shot."

"He stole a great deal of money from me." Ambuckle's face puckered as he thought of it. "A great deal. I had Manchez dispose of him. The truth is, I'd considered you as a liaison for some time. It seemed simpler, however, just to use your shop. My wife's very fond of you."

"Your wife." Liz thought of the neat, matronly woman in skirted bathing suits. "She knows you smuggle drugs, and she knows you kill people?"

"She thinks we have a great stockbroker." Ambuckle grinned. "I've been moving snow for ten years, and my wife wouldn't know coke from powdered sugar. I like to keep business and family separate. The little woman's going to be sick when she finds out you had an accident. Now we're going to take a little ride. And we're going to talk about the three hundred thousand our friend Jerry slipped out from under my nose. Cast off, Scott."

"No!" Thinking only of survival, Liz made a lunge toward the dock. Ambuckle had her on the deck with one shove. He shook his head, dusted his hands and turned to her. "I'd wanted to keep this from getting messy. You know, I switched gauges on your tanks, figuring you'd back off. Always had a soft spot for you, little lady. But business is business." With a wheezy sigh, he turned to Scott. "Since you've taken over Pablo's position, I assume you know how to deal with this."

"I certainly do." He took out a revolver. His eyes locked on Liz's. When she caught her breath, he turned the barrel toward Ambuckle. "You're under arrest." With his other hand, he pulled out a badge. "You have the right to remain silent…" It was the last thing Liz heard before she buried her face in her hands and wept.

Chapter 12

"I want to know what the hell's been going on." They were in Moralas's office, but Jonas wouldn't sit. He stood behind Liz's chair, his fingers curled tight over the back rung. If anyone had approached her, he would have struck first and asked questions later. He'd already flattened the unfortunate detective who'd tried to hold him back when he'd seen Liz on the deck of the *Expatriate* with Scott.

With his hands folded on his desk, Moralas gave Jonas a long, quiet look. "Perhaps the explanation should come from your countryman."

"Special Agent Donald Scott." The man Liz had known as Scott Trydent sat on the corner of Moralas's desk. "Sorry for the deception, Liz." Though his voice was calm and matter-of-fact, it couldn't mask the excitement that bubbled from him. As he sipped his coffee, he glanced up at Jonas. Explanations wouldn't go over easily with this one, he thought. But he'd always believed the ends justified the means. "I've been after that son of a bitch for three years." He drank again, savoring triumph. "It took us two before we could infiltrate the ring, and even then I couldn't make contact with the head man. To get to him I had to go through more channels than you do with the Company. He's been careful. For the past eight months I've been working with Manchez as Scott Trydent. He was the closest I could get to Ambuckle until two days ago."

"You used her." Jonas's hand went to Liz's shoulder. "You put her right in the middle."

"Yeah. The problem was, for a long time we weren't sure just how involved she was. We knew about your shop, Liz. We knew you were an experienced diver. In fact, there isn't anything about you my organization didn't know. For some time, you were our number-one suspect."

"Suspect?" She had her hands folded neatly in her lap, but the anger was boiling. "You suspected me."

"You left the U.S. over ten years ago. You've never been back. You have both the contacts and the means to have run the ring. You keep your daughter off the island for most of the year and in one of the best schools in Houston."

"That's my business."

"Details like that become our business. When you took Jerry Sharpe in and gave him a job, we leaned even further toward you. He thought differently, but then we weren't using him for his opinions."

She felt Jonas's fingers tighten and reached up to them as she spoke. "Using him?"

"I contacted Jerry Sharpe in New Orleans. He was someone else we knew everything about. He was a con, an operator, but he had style." He took another swig of coffee as he studied Jonas. "We made him a deal. If he could get on the inside, feed us information, we'd forget about a few…indiscretions. I liked your brother," Scott said to Jonas. "Really liked him. If he'd been able to settle a bit, he'd have made a hell of a cop. 'Conning the bad guys,' he called it."

"Are you saying Jerry was working for you?" Jonas felt his emotions race toward the surface. The portrait he'd barely been able to force himself to accept was changing.

"That's right." Scott took out a cigarette and watched the match flare as he struck it. "I liked him—I mean that. He had a way of looking at things that made you forget they were so lousy."

That was Jerry, Jonas thought. To give himself a moment, he walked to the window. He could see the water lapping calmly against the hulls of boats. He could see the sun dancing down on it and children walking along the sea wall. The scene had been almost the same the day he'd arrived on Cozumel. Some things remained the same; others altered constantly. "What happened?"

"He had a hard time following orders. He wanted to push them too fast too far. He told me once he had something to prove, to himself and to the other part of him. The better part of him."

Jonas turned slowly. The pain came again, an ache. Liz saw it in his eyes and went to stand with him. "Go on."

"He got the idea into his head to rip off the money from a shipment. I didn't know about it until he called me from Acapulco. He figured he'd put the head man in a position where he'd have to deal personally. I told him to stay put, that we were scrubbing him. He'd have been taken back to the States and put somewhere safe until the job was over." He tossed the match he'd been holding into an ashtray on Moralas's desk. "He didn't listen. He came back to Cozumel and tried to deal with Manchez himself. It was over before I knew. Even if I'd have known, I can't be sure I could've stopped it. We don't like to lose civilians, Mr. Sharpe. I don't like to lose friends."

The anger drained from him degree by degree. It would have been so like Jerry, Jonas thought. An adventure, the excitement, the impulsiveness. "Go on."

"Orders came down to put the pressure on Liz." Scott gave a half laugh that had nothing to do with humor. "Orders from both sides. It wasn't until after your trip to Acapulco that we were sure you weren't involved in the smuggling. You stopped being a suspect and became the decoy."

"I came to the police." She looked at Moralas. "I came to you. You didn't tell me."

"I wasn't aware of Agent Scott's identity until yesterday. I knew only that we had a man on the inside and that it was necessary to use you."

"You were protected," Scott put in. "There wasn't a day you weren't guarded by Moralas's men and by mine. Your being here complicated things," he said to Jonas. "You were pushing too close to the bone. I guess you and Jerry had more in common than looks."

Jonas felt the weight on the chain around his neck. "Maybe we did."

"Well, we'd come to the point where we had to settle for Manchez and a few others or go for broke. We went for broke."

"The drop we made. It was a setup."

"Manchez had orders to do whatever he had to to get back the money Jerry had taken. They didn't know about the safe-deposit box." He blew out a stream of smoke. "I had to play it pretty fast and loose to keep that under wraps. But then we didn't know about it either, until you led us to it. As far as Ambuckle was concerned, you had the money, and he was going to get it back. He wanted it to look as though you'd been running the smuggling operation together. When you were found dead, the heat would be off of him. He planned to lie low a while, then pick up business elsewhere. I had that from Manchez. You were set up," he agreed. "So was he. I got to Merriworth, made enough noise about how Manchez was about to double-cross to set him off. When Manchez was snorkeling to your boat, I was on the phone with the man I knew as Clancy. I got a promotion, and Clancy came back to deal with you himself."

Liz tried to see it as he did, as a chess game, as any game with pawns. She couldn't. "You knew who he was yesterday morning and you still had me get on that boat."

"There were a dozen sharpshooters in position. I had a gun, Ambuckle didn't. We wanted him to order Liz's murder, and we wanted him to tell her as much as possible. When this goes to court, we want it tidy. We want him put away for a long time. You're a lawyer, Sharpe. You know how these things can go. We can make a clean collar, have a stack of evidence and lose. I've watched too many of these bastards walk." He blew out smoke between set teeth. "This one's not walking anywhere but into federal prison."

"There is still the question of whether these men will be tried in your country or mine." Moralas spoke softly, and didn't move when Scott whirled on him.

"Look, Moralas—"

"This will be discussed later. You have my thanks and my apologies," he said to Jonas and Liz. "I regret we saw no other way."

"So do I," Liz murmured, then turned to Scott. "Was it worth it?"

"Ambuckle brought thousands of pounds of cocaine into the States. He's responsible for more than fifteen murders in the U.S. and Mexico. Yeah, it was worth it."

She nodded. "I hope you understand that I never want to see you again." After closing her hand around Jonas's she managed a smile. "You were a lousy student."

"Sorry we never had that drink." He looked back at Jonas. "Sorry about a lot of things."

"I appreciate what you told me about my brother. It makes a difference."

"I'm recommending him for a citation. They'll send it to your parents."

"It'll mean a great deal to them." He offered his hand and meant it. "You were doing your job—I understand that. We all do what we have to do."

"That doesn't mean I don't regret it."

Jonas nodded. Something inside him was free, completely free. "As to putting Liz through hell for the past few weeks…" Very calmly, Jonas curled his hand into a fist and planted it solidly on Scott's jaw. The thin man snapped a chair in half as he crashed into it on his way to the floor.

"Jonas!" Stunned, Liz could do no more than stare. Then, incredibly, she felt the urge to giggle. With one hand over her mouth, she leaned into Jonas and let the laughter come. Moralas remained contentedly at his desk, sipping coffee.

Scott rubbed his jaw gingerly. "We all do what we have to do," he murmured.

Jonas only turned his back. "Goodbye, Captain."

Moralas stayed where he was. "Goodbye, Mr. Sharpe." He rose and, in a rare show of feeling, took Liz's hand and kissed it. *"Vaya con dios."*

He waited until the door had shut behind them before he looked down at Scott again. "Your government will, of course, pay for the chair."

He was gone. She'd sent him away. After nearly two weeks, Liz awoke every morning with the same thoughts. Jonas was gone. It was for the best. After nearly two weeks she awoke every morning struggling to convince herself. If she'd followed her heart, she would have said yes the moment he'd asked her to marry him. She would have left everything she'd built behind and gone with him. And ruined his life, perhaps her own.

He was already back in his own world, poring through law books, facing juries, going to elegant dinner parties. By now, she was sure his time in Cozumel was becoming vague. After all, he hadn't written. He hadn't called. He'd left the day after Ambuckle had been taken into custody without another word about love. He'd conquered his ghosts when he'd faced Manchez and had walked away whole.

He was gone, and she was once more standing on her own. As she was meant to, Liz thought. She'd have no regrets. That she'd promised herself. What she'd given to Jonas had been given without conditions or expectations. What he'd given to her she'd never lose.

The sun was high and bright, she thought. The air was as mellow as quiet music. Her lover was gone, but she, too, was whole. A month of memories could be stretched to last a lifetime. And Faith was coming home.

Liz pulled her bike into a parking space and listened to the thunder of a plane taking off. Even now Faith and her parents were crossing the Gulf. Liz left her bike and walked toward the terminal. It was ridiculous to feel nervous, she told herself, but she couldn't prevent it. It was ridiculous to arrive at the airport nearly an hour early, but she'd have gone mad at home. She skirted around a bed of marigolds and geraniums. She'd buy flowers, she decided. Her mother loved flowers.

Inside the terminal, the air was cool and full of noise. Tourists came and went but rarely passed the shops without a last-minute purchase. Liz started in the first store and worked her way down, buying consistently and strictly on impulse. By the time she arrived at the gate, she carried two shopping bags and an armful of dyed carnations.

Any minute, she thought. She'd be here any minute. Liz shifted both bags to one hand and nervously brushed at her hair. Passengers waited for their flights by napping in the black plastic chairs or reading guidebooks. She watched a woman check her lipstick in a compact mirror and wondered if she had time to run into the ladies room to examine her own face. Gnawing on her lip, she decided she couldn't leave, even for a moment. Neither could she sit, so she paced back and forth in front of the wide windows and watched the planes come and go. It was late. Planes were always late when you were waiting for them. The sky was clear and blue. She knew it was equally clear in Houston because she'd been checking the weather for days. But the plane was late. Impatient, she walked back to security to ask about the status. She should have known better.

Liz got a shrug and the Mexican equivalent of It'll be here when it comes. In another ten minutes, she was ready to scream. Then she saw it. She didn't have to hear the flight announcement to know. With her heart thudding dully, she waited by the door.

Faith wore blue striped pants and a white blouse. Her hair's grown, Liz thought as she watched her daughter come down the steps. She's grown—though she knew it would never do to tell Faith so. She'd just wrinkle her nose and roll her eyes. Her palms were wet. Don't cry, don't cry, Liz ordered herself. But the tears were already welling. Then Faith looked up and saw her. With a grin and a wave she was racing forward. Liz dropped her bags and reached out for her daughter.

"Mom, I got to sit by the window, but I couldn't see our house." As she babbled, Faith held her mother's neck in a stranglehold. "I brought you a present."

With her face buried against Faith's throat, Liz drew in the scents—powder, soap and chocolate from the streak on the front of the white blouse. "Let me look at you." Drawing her back, Liz soaked up the sight of her. She's beautiful, Liz realized with a jolt. Not just cute or sweet or pretty any longer. Her daughter was beautiful.

I can't let her go again. It hit her like a wall. I'll never be able to let her go again. "You've lost a tooth," Liz managed as she brushed back her daughter's hair.

"Two." Faith grinned to show the twin spaces. "Grandma said I could put them under my pillow, but I brought them with me so I can put them under my real pillow. Will I get pesos?"

"Yes." Liz kissed one cheek, then the other. "Welcome home."

With her hand firmly in Faith's, Liz rose to greet her parents. For a moment she just looked at them, trying to see them as a stranger would. Her father was tall and still slim, though his hairline was creeping back. He was grinning at her the way he had whenever she'd done something particularly pleasing to him. Her mother stood beside him, lovely in her tidy way. She looked now, as she'd always looked to Liz, like a woman who'd never had to handle a crisis more stressful than a burned roast. Yet she'd been as solid and as sturdy as a rock. There were tears in her eyes. Liz wondered abruptly if the beginning of the summer left her mother as empty as the end of the summer left her.

"Momma." Liz reached out and was surrounded. "Oh, I've missed you. I've missed you all so much." *I want to go home.* The thought surged up inside her and nearly poured out. She needed to go home.

"Mom." Faith tugged on the pocket of her jeans. "Mom."

Giddy, Liz turned and scooped her up. "Yes." She covered her face with kisses until Faith giggled. "Yes, yes, yes!"

Faith snuggled in. "You have to say hello to Jonas."

"What?"

"He came with us. You have to say hi."

"I don't—" Then she saw him, leaning against the window, watching—waiting patiently. The blood rushed out of her head to her heart until she was certain something would burst. Holding onto Faith, Liz stood where she was. Jonas walked to her, took her face in both hands and kissed her hard.

"Nice to see you," he murmured, then bent down to pick up the bags Liz had dropped. "I imagine these are for you," he said as he handed Liz's mother the flowers.

"Yes." Liz tried to gather the thoughts stumbling through her mind. "I forgot."

"They're lovely." She sent her daughter a smile. "Jonas is going to drive us to the hotel. I invited him to dinner tonight. I hope you don't mind. You always make enough."

"No, I… Of course."

"We'll see you then." She gave Liz another brief kiss. "I know you want to get Faith home and have some time together. We'll see you tonight."

"But I—"

"Our bags are here. We're going to deal with customs."

Before Liz could say another word, she was alone with her daughter.

"Can we stop by and see Señor Pessado?"

"Yes," Liz said absently.

"Can I have some candy?"

Liz glanced down to the chocolate stain on Faith's blouse. "You've already had some."

Faith just smiled. She knew she could depend on Señor Pessado. "Let's go home now."

Liz waited until Faith was unpacked, until the crystal bird Faith had bought her was hanging in the window and her daughter had consumed two tacos and a pint of milk.

"Faith..." She wanted her voice to be casual. "When did you meet Mr. Sharpe?"

"Jonas? He came to Grandma's house." Faith turned the doll Liz had brought her this way and that for inspection.

"To Grandma's? When?"

"I don't know." She decided to call the doll Cassandra because it was pretty and had long hair. "Can I have my ice cream now?"

"Oh—yes." Liz walked over to get it out of the freezer. "Faith, do you know why he went to Grandma's?"

"He wanted to talk to her, I guess. To Grandpa, too. He stayed for dinner. I knew Grandma liked him because she made cherry pies. I liked him, too. He can play the piano really good." Faith eyed the ice cream and was satisfied when her mother added another scoop. "He took me to the zoo."

"What?" The bowl nearly slipped out of Liz's hand as she set it down. "Jonas took you to the zoo?"

"Last Saturday. We fed popcorn to the monkeys, but mostly we ate it." She giggled as she shoveled in ice cream. "He tells funny stories. I scraped my knee." Remembering suddenly, Faith pulled up her slacks to show off her wound.

"Oh, baby." It was small and already scabbed over, but Liz brushed a kiss over it anyway. "How'd you do this?"

"At the zoo. I was running. I can run really fast in my new sneakers, but I fell down. I didn't cry."

Liz rolled the slacks down. "I'm sure you didn't."

"Jonas didn't get mad or anything. He cleaned it all up with his handkerchief. It was pretty messy. I bled a lot." She smiled at that, pleased with herself. "He said I have pretty eyes just like you."

A little thrill of panic raced through her, but she couldn't stop herself. "Did he? What else did he say?"

"Oh, we talked about Mexico and about Houston. He wondered which I liked best."

Liz rested her hands on her daughter's knees. This is what matters, she realized. This was all that really mattered. "What did you tell him?"

"I like it best where you are." She scraped the bottom of the bowl. "He said he liked it best there, too. Is he going to be your boyfriend?"

"My—" Liz managed, just barely, to suppress the laugh. "No."

"Charlene's mother has a boyfriend, but he isn't as tall as Jonas and I don't think he ever took Charlene to the zoo. Jonas said sometime maybe we could go see the Liberty Bell. Do you think we can?"

Liz picked up the ice cream dish and began to wash it. "We'll see," she muttered.

"Listen, someone's coming." Faith was up like a shot and dashing for the front door. "It's Jonas!" With a whoop, she was out of the door and running full steam.

"Faith!" Liz hurried from the kitchen and reached the

porch in time to see Faith hurl herself at Jonas. With a laugh, he caught her, tossed her in the air then set her down again in a move so natural that it seemed he'd been doing so all his life. Liz knotted the dishcloth in her hands.

"You came early." Pleased, Faith hung on to his hand. "We were talking about you."

"Were you?" He tousled Faith's hair but looked up at Liz. "That's funny, because I was thinking about you."

"We're going to make paella because that's what Grandpa likes best. You can help."

"Faith—"

"Love to," Jonas interrupted. "After I talk to your mother." At the foot of the stairs he crouched down to Faith's level. "I'd really like to talk to your mom alone."

Faith's mouth screwed up. "Why?"

"I have to convince her to marry me."

He ignored Liz's gasp and watched for Faith's reaction. Her eyes narrowed and her mouth pursed. "She said you weren't her boyfriend. I asked."

He grinned and leaned closer. "I just have to talk her into it."

"Grandma says nobody can ever talk my mom into anything. She has a hard head."

"So do I, and I make a living talking people into things. But maybe you could put in a few good words for me later."

As Faith considered, her eyes brightened. "Okay. Mom, can I see if Roberto's home? You said he had new puppies."

Liz stretched out the cloth then balled it again. "Go ahead, but just for a little while."

Jonas straightened as he watched Faith race toward the house across the street. "You've done an excellent job with your daughter, Elizabeth."

"She's done a great deal of it herself."

He turned and saw the nerves on her face. It didn't displease him. But he remembered the way she'd looked when she had opened her arms to Faith at the airport. He wanted, he would, see her look that way again. "Do you want to talk inside?" he began as he walked up the steps. "Or right here?"

"Jonas, I don't know why you've come back, but—"

"Of course you know why I've come back. You're not stupid."

"We don't have anything to talk about."

"Fine." He closed the distance quickly. She didn't resist, though she told herself she would. When he dragged her against him, she went without hesitation. Her mouth locked hungrily to his, and for a moment, just for a moment, the world was right again. "If you don't want to talk, we'll go inside and make love until you see things a little more clearly."

"I see things clearly." Liz put her hands on his arms and started to draw away.

"I love you."

He felt the shudder, saw the flash of joy in her eyes before she looked away. "Jonas, this isn't possible."

"Wrong. It's entirely possible—in fact, it's already done. The point is, Liz, you need me."

Her eyes narrowed to slits. "What I need I take care of."

"That's why I love you," he said simply and took the wind out of her sails.

"Jonas—"

"Are you going to tell me you haven't missed me?" She opened her mouth, then shut it again. "Okay, so you take the Fifth on that one." He stepped back from her. "Are you going to deny that you've spent some sleepless nights in the past couple of weeks, that you've thought about what happened between us? Are you going to stand here and look at me now and tell me you're not in love with me?"

She'd never been able to lie well. Liz turned and meticulously spread the dishcloth over the porch rail. "Jonas, I can't run my life on my feelings."

"From now on you can. Did you like the present Faith brought you?"

"What?" Confused, she turned back. "Yes, of course I did."

"Good. I brought you one too." He took a box out of his pocket. Liz saw the flash of diamond and nearly had her hand behind her back before he caught it in his. Firmly, he slipped the ring on. "It's official."

She wouldn't even look at it. She couldn't stop herself. The diamond was shaped in a teardrop and as white and glossy as a wish. "You're being ridiculous," she told him, but couldn't make herself take it off.

"You're going to marry me." He took her shoulders and leaned her back against a post. "That's not negotiable. After that, we have several options. I can give up my practice and live in Cozumel. You can support me."

She let out a quick breath that might have been a laugh. "Now you're really being ridiculous."

"You don't like that one. Good, I didn't care for it either. You can come back to Philadelphia with me. I'll support you."

Her chin went up. "I don't need to be supported."

"Excellent. We agree on the first two options." He ran his hands through her hair and discovered he wasn't feeling as patient as he'd thought he would. "Now, you can come back to the States. We'll take a map and you can close your eyes and pick a spot. That's where we'll live."

"We can't run our lives this way." She pushed him aside to walk down the length of the porch and back. But part of her was beginning to believe they could. "Don't you see how impossible it is?" she demanded as much of herself as of him. "You have your career. I have my business. I'd never be a proper wife for someone like you."

"You're the only wife for someone like me." He grabbed her shoulders again. No, he wasn't feeling patient at all. "Damn it, Liz, you're the only one. If the business is important to you, keep it. Have Luis run it. We can come back a half a dozen times a year if you want. Start another business. We'll go to Florida, to California, anywhere you want where they need a good dive shop. Or…" He waited until he was sure he had her full attention. "You could go back to school."

He saw it in her eyes—the surprise, the dream, then the denial. "That's over."

"The hell it is. Look at you—it's what you want. Keep the shop, build another, build ten others, but give yourself something for yourself."

"It's been more than ten years."

He lifted a brow. "You said once you wouldn't change anything."

"And I meant it, but to go back now, after all this time."

"Afraid?"

Her eyes narrowed; her spine stiffened. "Yes."

He laughed, delighted with her. "Woman, in the past few weeks, you've been through hell and out again. And you're afraid of a few college courses?"

With a sigh, she turned away. "I might not be able to make it."

"So what?" He whirled her back again. "So you fall flat on your face. I'll be right there falling down with you. It's time for risking, Liz. For both of us."

"Oh, I want to believe you." She lifted a hand to rest it on his face. "I want to. I do love you, Jonas. So much."

She was locked against him again, lost in him. "I need you, Liz. I'm not going back without you."

She clung to him a moment, almost ready to believe. "But it's not just me. You have to understand I can't do whatever I'd like."

"Faith?" He drew her back again. "I've spent the past weeks getting to know her. My main objective when I started was to ingratiate myself. I figured the only way to get to you was through her."

So she'd already surmised. "Afternoons at the zoo?"

"That's right. Thing was, I didn't know she was as easy to fall for as her mother. I want her."

The hand Liz had lifted to her hair froze. "I don't understand."

"I want her to be mine—legally, emotionally. I want you to agree to let me adopt her."

"Adopt…" Whatever she might have expected from him, it hadn't been this. "But she's—"

"Yours?" he interrupted. "No, she's going to be ours. You're going to have to share her. And if you're set on her going to school in Houston, we'll live in Houston. Within the year I expect she should have a brother or sister because she needs family as much as we do."

He was offering her everything, everything she'd ever wanted and had refused to believe in. She had only to hold out her hand. The idea terrified her. "She's another man's child. How will you be able to forget that?"

"She's your child," he reminded her. "You told me yourself she was your child only. Now she's going to be mine." Taking her hands, he kissed them. "So are you."

"Jonas, do you know what you're doing? You're asking for a wife who'll have to start from scratch and a half-grown daughter. You're complicating your life."

"Yeah, and maybe I'm saving it."

And hers. Her blood was pumping again, her skin was tingling. For the first time in years she could look at her life and see no shadows. She closed her eyes and breathed deeply before she turned. "Be sure," she whispered. "Be absolutely sure. If I let myself go, if I say yes and you change your mind, I'll hate you for the rest of my life."

He took her by the shirtfront. "In one week, we're going to my parents' farm in Lancaster, calling the local minister, justice of the peace or witch doctor and we're getting married. Adoption papers are being drawn up. When we settle in as a family, we're all having the same name. You and Faith and I."

With a sigh, Liz leaned back again against the post and studied his face. It was beautiful, she decided. Strong, passionate, patient. Her life was going to be bound up with that face. It was as real as flesh and blood and as precious as dreams. Her lover was back, her child was with her and nothing was impossible.

"When I first met you, I thought you were the kind of man who always got what he wanted."

"And you were right." He took her hands again and held them. "Now what are we going to tell Faith?" he demanded.

Her lips curved slowly. "I guess we'd better tell her you talked me into it."

* * * * *

The Right Path

Chapter 1

The sky was cloudless—the hard, perfect blue of a summer painting. A breeze whispered through the roses in the garden. Mountains were misted by distance. A scent—flowers, sea, new grass—drifted on the air. With a sigh of pure pleasure, Morgan leaned farther over the balcony rail and just looked.

Had it really only been yesterday morning that she had looked out on New York's steel and concrete? Had she run through a chill April drizzle to catch a taxi to the airport? One day. It seemed impossible to go from one world to another in only a day.

But she was here, standing on the balcony of a villa on the Isle of Lesbos. There was no gray drizzle at all, but strong Greek sunlight. There was quiet, a deep blanketing stillness that contrasted completely with the fits and starts of New York traffic. If I could paint, Morgan mused, I'd paint this view and call it *Silence*.

"Come in," she called when there was a knock on the door. After one last deep breath, she turned, reluctantly.

"So, you're up and dressed." Liz swept in, a small, golden fairy with a tray-bearing maid in her wake.

"Room service." Morgan grinned as the maid placed the tray on a glass-topped table. "I'll begin to wallow in luxury from this moment." She took an appreciative sniff of the platters the maid uncovered. "Are you joining me?"

"Just for coffee." Liz settled in a chair, smoothing the skirts of her silk and lace robe, then took a long survey of the woman who sat opposite her.

Long loose curls in shades from ash blond to honey brown fell to tease pale shoulders. Almond-shaped eyes, almost too large for the slender face, were a nearly transparent blue. There was a straight, sharp nose and prominent cheekbones, a long, narrow mouth and a subtly pointed chin. It was a face of angles and contours that many a model starved herself for. It would photograph like a dream had Morgan ever been inclined to sit long enough to be captured on film.

What you'd get, Liz mused, would be a blur of color as Morgan dashed away to see what was around the next corner.

"Oh, Morgan, you look fabulous! I'm so glad you're here at last."

"Now that I'm here," Morgan returned, shifting her eyes back to the view, "I can't understand why I put off coming for so long. *Efxaristo,*" she added as the maid poured her coffee.

"Show-off," Liz said with mock scorn. "Do you know how long it took me to master a simple Greek hello, how are you? No, never mind." She waved her hand before Morgan could speak. The symphony of diamonds and sapphires in her wedding ring caught the flash of sunlight. "Three years married to Alex and living in Athens and Lesbos, and I still stumble over the language. Thank you, Zena," she added in English, dismissing the maid with a smile.

"You're simply determined not to learn." Morgan bit enthusiastically into a piece of toast. She wasn't hungry, she discovered. She was ravenous. "If you'd open your mind, the words would seep in."

"Listen to you." Liz wrinkled her nose. "Just because you speak a dozen languages."

"Five."

"Five is four more than a rational person requires."

"Not a rational interpreter," Morgan reminded her and dug wholeheartedly into her eggs. "And if I hadn't spoken Greek, I wouldn't have met Alex and you wouldn't be *Kryios* Elizabeth Theoharis. Fate," she announced with a full mouth, "is a strange and wonderful phenomenon."

"Philosophy at breakfast," Liz murmured into her coffee. "That's one of the things I've missed about you. Actually, I'd hate to think what might have happened if I hadn't been home on layover when Alex popped up. You wouldn't have introduced us." She commandeered a piece of toast, adding a miserly dab of plum jelly. "I'd still be serving miniature bottles of bourbon at thirty thousand feet."

"Liz, my love, when something's meant, it's meant." Morgan cut into a fat sausage. "I'd love to take credit for your marital bliss, but one brief introduction wasn't responsible for the fireworks that followed." She glanced up at the cool blond beauty and smiled. "Little did I know I'd lose my roommate in less than three weeks. I've never seen two people move so fast."

"We decided we'd get acquainted after we were married." A grin warmed Liz's face. "And we have."

"Where is Alex this morning?"

"Downstairs in his office." Liz moved her shoulders absently and left half her toast untouched. "He's building another ship or something."

Morgan laughed outright. "You say that in the same tone you'd use if he were building a model train. Don't you know you're supposed to become spoiled and disdainful when you marry a millionaire—especially a foreign millionaire?"

"Is that so? Well, I'll see what I can do." She topped off her coffee. "He'll probably be horribly busy for the next few weeks, which is one more reason I'm glad you're here."

"You need a cribbage partner."

"Hardly," Liz corrected as she struggled with a smile. "You're the worst cribbage player I know."

"Oh, I don't know," Morgan began as her brows drew together.

"Perhaps you've improved. Anyway," Liz went on, concealing with her coffee cup what was now a grin, "not to be disloyal to my adopted country, but it's just so good to have my best friend, and an honest-to-God American, around."

"*Spasibo.*"

"English at all times," Liz insisted. "And I know that wasn't even Greek. You aren't translating government hyperbole at the U.N. for the next four weeks." She leaned forward to rest her elbows on the table. "Tell me the truth, Morgan, aren't you ever terrified you'll interpret some nuance incorrectly and cause World War III?"

"Who me?" Morgan opened her eyes wide. "Not a chance. Anyway, the trick is to think in the language you're interpreting. It's that easy."

"Sure it is." Liz leaned back. "Well, you're on vacation, so you only have to think in English. Unless you want to argue with the cook."

"Absolutely not," Morgan assured her as she polished off her eggs.

"How's your father?"

"Marvelous, as always." Relaxed, content, Morgan poured more coffee. When was the last time she had taken the time for a second cup in the morning? Vacation, Liz had said. Well, she was damn well going to learn how to enjoy one. "He sends you his love and wants me to smuggle some ouzo back to New York."

"I'm not going to think about you going back." Liz rose and swirled around the balcony. The lace border at the hem of her robe swept over the tile. "I'm going to find a suitable mate for you and establish you in Greece."

"I can't tell you how much I appreciate your handling things for me," Morgan returned dryly.

"It's all right. What are friends for?" Ignoring the sarcasm, Liz leaned back on the balcony. "Dorian's a likely candidate. He's one of Alex's top men and really attractive. Blond and bronzed with a profile that belongs on a coin. You'll meet him tomorrow."

"Should I tell Dad to arrange my dowry?"

"I'm serious." Folding her arms, Liz glared at Morgan's grin. "I'm not letting you go back without a fight. I'm going to fill your days with sun and sea, and dangle hordes of gorgeous men in front of your nose. You'll forget that New York and the U.N. exist."

"They're already wiped out of my mind…for the next four weeks." Morgan tossed her hair back over her shoulders. "So, satiate and dangle. I'm at your mercy. Are you going to drag me to the beach this morning? Force me to lie on the sand and soak up rays until I have a fabulous golden tan?"

"Exactly." With a brisk nod, Liz headed for the door. "Change. I'll meet you downstairs."

Thirty minutes later, Morgan decided she was going to like Liz's brand of brainwashing. White sand, blue water. She let herself drift on the gentle waves. *Too wrapped up in your work.* Isn't that what Dad said? *You're letting the job run you instead of the other way around.* Closing her eyes, Morgan rolled to float on her back. Between job pressure and the nasty breakup with Jack, she mused, I need a peace transfusion.

Jack was part of the past. Morgan was forced to admit that he had been more a habit than a passion. They'd suited each other's requirements. She had wanted an intelligent male companion; he an attractive woman whose manners would be advantageous to his political career.

If she'd loved him, Morgan reflected, she could hardly think of him so objectively, so…well, coldly. There was no ache, no loneliness. What there was, she admitted, was relief. But with the relief had come the odd feeling of being at loose ends. A feeling Morgan was neither used to nor enjoyed.

Liz's invitation had been perfectly timed. And this, she thought, opening her eyes to study that perfect sweep of sky, was paradise. Sun, sand, rock, flowers—the whispering memory of ancient gods and goddesses. Mysterious Turkey was close, separated only by the narrow Gulf of Edremit. She closed her eyes again and would have dozed if Liz's voice hadn't disturbed her.

"Morgan! Some of us have to eat at regular intervals."

"Always thinking of your stomach."

"And *your* skin," Liz countered from the edge of the water. "You're going to fry. You can overlook lunch, but not sunburn."

"All right, Mommy." Morgan swam in, then stood on shore and shook like a wet dog. "How come you can swim and lie in the sun and still look ready to walk into a ballroom?"

"Breeding," Liz told her and handed over the short robe. "Come on, Alex usually tears himself away from his ships for lunch."

I could get used to eating on terraces, Morgan thought after lunch was finished. They relaxed over iced coffee and fruit. She noted that Alexander Theoharis was still as fascinated with his small, golden wife as he had been three years before in New York.

Though she'd brushed off Liz's words that morning, Morgan felt a certain pride at having brought them together. A perfect match, she mused, Alex had an Old World charm—dark aquiline looks made dashing by a thin white scar above his eyebrow. He was only slightly above average height but with a leanness that was more aristocratic than rangy. It was the ideal complement for Liz's dainty blond beauty.

"I don't see how you ever drag yourself away from here," Morgan told him. "If this were all mine, nothing would induce me to leave."

Alex followed her gaze across the glimpse of sea to the mountains. "But when one returns, it's all the more magnificent. Like a woman," he continued, lifting Liz's hand to kiss, "paradise demands constant appreciation."

"It's got mine," Morgan stated.

"I'm working on her, Alex." Liz laced her fingers with his. "I'm going to make a list of all the eligible men within a hundred miles."

"You don't have a brother, do you, Alex?" Morgan asked, sending him a smile.

"Sisters only. My apologies."

"Forget it, Liz."

"If we can't entice you into matrimony, Alex will have to offer you a job in the Athens office."

"I'd steal Morgan from the U.N. in a moment," Alex reminded her with a move of his shoulders. "I couldn't lure her away three years ago. I tried."

"We have a month to wear her down this time." She shot Alex a quick glance. "Let's take her out on the yacht tomorrow."

"Of course." He agreed immediately. "We'll make a day of it. Would you like that, Morgan?"

"Oh, well, I'm constantly spending the day on a yacht on the Aegean, but"—her lake-blue eyes lit with laughter—"since Liz wants to, I'll try not to be too bored."

"She's such a good sport," Liz confided to Alex.

* * *

It was just past midnight when Morgan made her way down to the beach again. Sleep had refused to come. Morgan welcomed the insomnia, seeing it as an excuse to walk out into the warm spring night.

The light was liquid. The moon was sliced in half but held a white, gleaming brightness. Cypresses which flanked the steps down to the beach were silvered with it. The scent of blossoms, hot and pungent during the day, seemed more mysterious, more exotic, by moonlight.

From somewhere in the distance, she heard the low rumble of a motor. A late-night fisherman, she thought, and smiled. It would be quite an adventure to fish under the moon.

The beach spread in a wide half circle. Morgan dropped both her towel and wrap on a rock, then ran into the water. Against her skin it was so cool and silky that she toyed with the idea of discarding even the brief bikini. Better not, she thought with a low laugh. No use tempting the ghosts of the gods.

Though the thought of adventure appealed to her, she kept to the open bay and suppressed the urge to explore the inlets. They'd still be there in the daylight, she reminded herself. She swam lazily, giving her strokes just enough power to keep her afloat. She hadn't come for the exercise.

Even when her body began to feel the chill, she lingered. There were stars glistening on the water, and silence. Such silence. Strange, that until she had found it, she hadn't known she was looking for it.

New York seemed more than a continent away; it

seemed centuries away. For the moment, she was content that it be so. Here she could indulge in the fantasies that never seemed appropriate in the rush of day-to-day living. Here she could let herself believe in ancient gods, in shining knights and bold pirates. A laugh bubbled from her as she submerged and rose again. Gods, knights, and pirates…well, she supposed she'd take the pirate if she had her pick. Gods were too bloodthirsty, knights too chivalrous, but a pirate…

Shaking her head, Morgan wondered how her thoughts had taken that peculiar turn. It must be Liz's influence, she decided. Morgan reminded herself she didn't want a pirate or any other man. What she wanted was peace.

With a sigh, she stood knee-deep in the water, letting the drops stream down her hair and skin. She was cold now, but the cold was exhilarating. Ignoring her wrap, she sat on the rock and pulled a comb from its pocket and idly ran it through her hair. Moon, sand, water. What more could there be? She was, for one brief moment, in total harmony with her own spirit and with nature's.

Shock gripped her as a hand clamped hard over her mouth. She struggled, instinctively, but an arm was banded around her waist—rough cloth scraping her naked skin. Dragged from the rock, Morgan found herself molded against a solid, muscular chest.

Rape? It was the first clear thought before the panic. She kicked out blindly as she was pulled into the cover of trees. The shadows were deep there. Fighting wildly, she raked with her nails wherever she could reach, feeling only a brief satisfaction at the hiss of an undrawn breath near her ear.

"Don't make a sound." The order was in quick, harsh Greek. About to strike out again, Morgan felt her blood freeze. A glimmer of knife caught the moonlight just before she was thrust to the ground under the length of the man's body. "Wildcat," he muttered. "Keep still and I won't have to hurt you. Do you understand?"

Numb with terror, Morgan nodded. With her eyes glued to his knife, she lay perfectly still. I can't fight him now, she thought grimly. Not now, but somehow, somehow I'll find out who he is. He'll pay.

The first panic was gone, but her body still trembled as she waited. It seemed an eternity, but he made no move, no sound. It was so quiet, she could hear the waves lapping gently against the sand only a few feet away. Over her head, through the spaces in the leaves, stars still shone. It must be a nightmare, she told herself. It can't be real. But when she tried to shift under him, the pressure of his body on hers proved that it was very, very real.

The hand over her mouth choked her breath until vague colors began to dance before her eyes. Morgan squeezed them tight for a moment to fight the faintness. Then she heard him speak again to a companion she couldn't see.

"What do you hear?"

"Nothing yet—in a moment." The voice that answered was rough and brisk. "Who the devil is she?"

"It doesn't matter. She'll be dealt with."

The roaring in her ears made it difficult to translate the Greek. Dealt with? she thought, dizzy again from fear and the lack of air.

The second man said something low and furious about women, then spat into the dirt.

"Just keep your ears open," Morgan's captor ordered. "And leave the woman to me."

"Now."

She felt him stiffen, but her eyes never left the knife. He was gripping it tighter now, she saw the tensing of his fingers on the handle.

Footsteps. They echoed on the rock steps of the beach. Hearing them, Morgan began to struggle again with the fierce strength of panic and of hope. With a whispered oath, he put more of his weight on her. He smelt faintly of the sea. As he shifted she caught a brief glimpse of his face in a patchy stream of moonlight. She saw dark, angular features, a grim mouth, and narrowed jet eyes. They were hard and cold and ruthless. It was the face of a man prepared to kill. *Why?* She thought as her mind began to float. I don't even know him.

"Follow him," he ordered his companion. Morgan heard a slight stirring in the leaves. "I'll take care of the woman."

Morgan's eyes widened at the sharp glimmer of the blade. She tasted something—bitter, copper—in her throat, but didn't recognize it as terror. The world spun to the point of a pin, then vanished.

The sky was full of stars, silver against black. The sea whispered. Against her back, the sand was rough. Morgan rose on her elbow and tried to clear her head. Fainted? Good God, had she actually fainted? Had she simply fallen asleep and dreamed it all? Rubbing her fingers against her temple, she wondered if her fantasies about pirates had caused her to hallucinate.

A small sound brought her swiftly to her feet. No, it

had been real, and he was back. Morgan hurled herself at the shadow as it approached. She'd accepted the inevitability of death once without a struggle. This time, he was going to have a hell of a fight on his hands.

The shadow grunted softly as she struck, then Morgan found herself captured again, under him with the sand scraping her back.

"*Diabolos!* Be still!" he ordered in furious Greek as she tried to rip at his face.

"The hell I will!" Morgan tossed back in equally furious English. She fought with every ounce of strength until he pinned her, spread-eagle beneath him. Breathless, fearless in her rage, she stared up at him.

Looking down, he studied her with a frown. "You're not Greek." The statement, uttered in surprised and impatient English, stopped her struggles. "Who are you?"

"None of your business." She tried, and failed, to jerk her wrists free of his hold.

"Stop squirming," he ordered roughly, as his fingers clamped down harder. He wasn't thinking of his strength or her fragility, but that she wasn't simply a native who had been in the wrong place at the wrong time. His profession had taught him to get answers and adjust for complications. "What were you doing on the beach in the middle of the night?"

"Swimming," she tossed back. "Any idiot should be able to figure that out."

He swore, then shifted as she continued to struggle beneath him. "Damn it, be still!" His brows were lowered, not in anger now but concentration. "Swimming," he repeated as his eyes narrowed again. He'd watched her walk out of the sea—perhaps it was as innocent as that. "American," he mused, ignoring Morgan's thrashing. Weren't the Theoharises expecting an American woman? Of all the ill-timed... "You're not Greek," he murmured again.

"Neither are you," Morgan said between clenched teeth.

"Half." His thoughts underwent some rapid readjustments. The Theoharises' American houseguest, out for a moonlight swim—he'd have to play this one carefully or there'd be hell to pay. Quite suddenly, he flashed her a smile. "You had me fooled. I thought you could understand me."

"I understand perfectly," she retorted. "And you won't find it an easy rape now that you don't have your knife out."

"Rape?" Apparently astonished, he stared at her. His laughter was as sudden as the smile. "I hadn't given that much thought. In any case, Aphrodite, the knife was never intended for you."

"Then what do you mean by dragging me around like that? Flashing a knife in my face and nearly suffocating me?" Fury was much more satisfying than fear, and Morgan went with it. "Let me go!" She pushed at him with her body, but couldn't nudge him.

"In a moment," he said pleasantly. The moonlight played on her skin, and he enjoyed it. A fabulous face, he mused, now that he had time to study it. She'd be a woman accustomed to male admiration. Perhaps charm would distract her from the rather unique aspect of their meeting. "I can only say that what I did was for your own protection."

"Protection!" she flung back at him and tried to wrench her arms free.

"There wasn't time for amenities, fair lady. My apologies if my...technique was unrefined." His tone seemed to take it for granted that she would understand. "Tell me, why were you out alone, sitting like Lorelei on the rock and combing your hair?"

"That's none of your business." His voice had dropped, becoming low and seductive. The dark eyes had softened and appeared depthless. She could almost believe she had imagined the ruthlessness she'd glimpsed in the shadows. But she felt the light throbbing where his fingers had gripped her flesh. "I'm going to scream if you don't let me go."

Her body was tempting now that he had time to appreciate it, but he rose with a shrug. There was still work to be done that night. "My apologies for your inconvenience."

"Oh, is that right?" Struggling to her feet, Morgan began to brush at the sand that clung to her skin. "You have your nerve, dragging me off into the bushes, smothering me, brandishing a knife in my face, then apologizing like you've just stepped on my toe." Suddenly cold, she wrapped her arms around herself. "Just who are you and what was this all about?"

"Here." Stooping, he picked up the wrap he had dropped in order to hold her off. "I was bringing this to you when you launched your attack." He grinned as she shrugged into the wrap. It was a pity to cover the lengthy, intriguing body. "Who I am at the moment isn't relevant.

As for the rest"—again the smooth, easy shrug—"I can't tell you."

"Just like that?" With a quick nod, Morgan turned and stalked to the beach steps. "We'll see what the police have to say about it."

"I wouldn't if I were you."

The advice was quiet, but vibrated with command. Hesitating, Morgan turned at the base of the steps to study him. He wasn't threatening now. What she felt wasn't fear, but his authority. He was quite tall, she noticed suddenly. And the moonlight played tricks with his face, making it almost cruel one moment, charming the next. Now it held all the confidence of Lucifer regrouping after the Fall.

Looking at him, she remembered the feel of hard, wiry muscles. He was standing easily, hands thrust into the pockets of jeans. The aura of command fit him perfectly. His smile didn't disguise it, nor did his casual stance. Damn pirates, she thought, feeling a quick twinge. Only lunatics find them attractive. Because she felt vulnerable, Morgan countered with bravado.

"Wouldn't you?" She lifted her chin and walked back to him.

"No," he answered mildly. "But perhaps, unlike me, you look for complications. I'm a simple man." He took a long, searching look of her face. *This is not,* he decided instantly, *a simple woman.* Though in his mind he cursed her, he went on conversationally. "Questions, reports to fill out, hours wasted on red tape. And then, even if you had my name"—he shrugged and flashed the grin again—"no one would believe you, Aphrodite. No one."

She didn't trust that grin—or the sultry way he called

her by the goddess's name. She didn't trust the sudden warmth in her blood. "I wouldn't be so sure," Morgan began, but he cut her off, closing the slight distance between them.

"And I didn't rape you." Slowly, he ran his hands down her hair until they rested on her shoulders. His fingers didn't bite into her flesh now, but skimmed lazily. She had the eyes of a witch, he thought, and the face of a goddess. His time was short, but the moment was not to be missed. "Until now, I haven't even given in to the urge to do this."

His mouth closed over hers, hot and stunningly sweet. She hadn't been prepared for it. She pushed against him, but it was strictly out of reflex and lacked strength. He was a man who knew a woman's weakness. Deliberately, he brought her close, using style rather than force.

The scent of the sea rose to surround her, and heat— such a furnace heat that seemed to come from within and without at the same time. Almost leisurely, he explored her mouth until her heart thudded wildly against the quick, steady beat of his. His hands were clever, sliding beneath the wide sleeves of her robe to tease and caress the length of her arms, the slope of her shoulders.

When her struggles ceased, he nibbled at her lips as if he would draw out more taste. Slow, easy. His tongue tempted hers then retreated, then slipped through her parted lips again to torment and savor. For a moment, Morgan feared she would faint for a second time in his arms.

"One kiss," he murmured against her lips, "is hardly a criminal offense." She was sweeter than he had imagined and, he realized as desire stirred hotly, deadlier. "I could take another with little more risk."

"No." Coming abruptly to her senses, Morgan pushed away from him. "You're mad. And you're madder still if you think I'm going to let this go. I'm going—" She broke off as her hand lifted to her throat in a nervous gesture. The chain which always hung there was missing. Morgan glanced down, then brought her eyes back to his, furious, glowing.

"What have you done with my medal?" she demanded. "Give it back to me."

"I'm afraid I don't have it, Aphrodite."

"I want it back." Bravado wasn't a pose this time; she was livid. She stepped closer until they were toe to toe. "It's not worth anything to you. You won't be able to get more than a few drachmas for it."

His eyes narrowed. "I didn't take your medal. I'm not a thief." The temper in his voice was cold, coated with control. "If I were going to steal something from you, I would have found something more interesting than a medal."

Her eyes filled in a rush, and she swung out her hand to slap him. He caught her wrist, adding frustration to fury.

"It appears the medal is important," he said softly, but his hand was no longer gentle. "A token from a lover?"

"A gift from someone I love," Morgan countered. "I wouldn't expect a man like you to understand its value." With a jerk, she pulled her wrist from his hold. "I won't forget you," she promised, then turned and flew up the stairs.

He watched her until she was swallowed by the darkness. After a moment he turned back to the beach.

Chapter 2

The sun was a white flash of light. Its diamonds skimmed the water's surface. With the gentle movement of the yacht, Morgan found herself half-dozing.

Could the moonlit beach and the man have been a dream? she wondered hazily. Knives and rough hands and sudden draining kisses from strangers had no place in the real world. They belonged in one of those strange, half-remembered dreams she had when the rush and demands of work and the city threatened to become too much for her. She'd always considered them her personal release valve. Harmless, but absolutely secret—something she'd never considered telling Jack or any of her co-workers.

If it hadn't been for the absence of her medal, and the light trail of bruises on her arms, Morgan could have believed the entire incident had been the product of an overworked imagination.

Sighing, she shifted her back to the sun, pillowing her head on her hands. Her skin, slick with oil, glistened. Why was she keeping the whole crazy business from Liz and Alex? Grimacing, she flexed her shoulders. They'd be horrified if she told them she'd been assaulted. Morgan could all but see Alex placing her under armed guard for the rest of her stay on Lesbos. He'd make certain there was an investigation—complicated, time-consuming, and in all probability fruitless. Morgan could work up a strong hate for the dark man for being right.

And what, if she decided to pursue it, could she tell the police? She hadn't been hurt or sexually assaulted. There'd been no verbal threat she could pin down, not even the slimmest motivation for what had happened. And what had happened? she demanded of herself. A man had dragged her into the bushes, held her there for no clear reason, then had let her go without harming her.

The Greek police wouldn't see the kiss as a criminal offense. She hadn't been robbed. There was no way on earth to prove the man had taken her medal. And damn it, she added with a sigh, as much as she'd like to assign all sorts of evil attributes to him, he just didn't fit the role of a petty thief. Petty anything, she thought grudgingly. Whatever he did, she was certain he did big…and did well.

So what was she going to do about it? True, he'd frightened and infuriated her—the second was probably a direct result of the first—but what else was there?

If and when they caught him, it would be his word against hers. Somehow, Morgan thought his word would carry more weight.

So I was frightened—my pride took a lump. She shrugged and shifted her head on her hands. It's not worth upsetting Liz and Alex. Midnight madness, she mused. Another strange adventure in the life and times of Morgan James. File it and forget it.

Hearing Alex mount the steps to the sun deck, Morgan rested her chin on her hands and smiled at him. On the lounger beside her, Liz stirred and slept on.

"So, the sun has put her to sleep." Alex mounted the last of the steps, then settled into the chair beside his wife.

"I nearly dozed off myself." With a yawn, Morgan stretched luxuriously before she rolled over to adjust the lounger to a sitting position. "But I didn't want to miss anything." Gazing over the water, she studied the clump of land in the distance. The island seemed to float, as insubstantial as a mist.

"Chios," Alex told her, following her gaze. "And"—he gestured, waiting for her eyes to shift in the direction of his—"the coast of Turkey."

"So close," Morgan mused. "It seems as though I could swim to it."

"At sea, the distance can be deceiving." He flicked a lighter at the end of a black cigarette. The fragrance that rose from it was faintly sweet and exotic. "You'd have to be a hardy swimmer. Easy enough with a boat, though. There are some who find the proximity profitable." At Morgan's blank expression, Alex laughed. "Smuggling, innocence. It's still popular even though the punishment is severe."

"Smuggling," she murmured, intrigued. Then the word put her in mind of pirates again and her curious expression turned into a frown. A nasty business, she reminded herself, and not romantic at all.

"The coast," Alex made another gesture, sweeping, with the elegant cigarette held between two long fingers. "The many bays and peninsulas, offshore islands, inlets. There's simple access from the sea to the interior."

She nodded. Yes, a nasty business—they weren't talking about French brandy or Spanish lace. "Opium?"

"Among other things."

"But, Alex." His careless acceptance caused her frown to deepen. Once she'd sorted it through, Morgan's own sense of right and wrong had little middle ground. "Doesn't it bother you?"

"Bother me?" he repeated, taking a long, slow drag on the cigarette. "Why?"

Flustered with the question, she sat up straighter. "Aren't you concerned about that sort of thing going on so close to your own home?"

"Morgan." Alex spread his hands in an acceptance of fate. The thick chunk of gold on his left pinky gleamed dully in the sunlight. "My concern would hardly stop what's been going on for centuries."

"But still, with crime practically in your own backyard…" She broke off, thinking about the streets of Manhattan. Perhaps she was the pot calling the kettle black. "I supposed I'd thought you'd be annoyed," she finished.

His eyes lit with a touch of amusement before he shrugged. "I leave the matter—and the annoyance—to the patrols and authorities. Tell me, are you enjoying your stay so far?"

Morgan started to speak again, then consciously smoothed away the frown. Alex was Old World enough not to want to discuss unpleasantries with a guest. "It's wonderful here, Alex. I can see why Liz loves it."

He flashed her a grin before he drew in strong tobacco. "You know Liz wants you to stay. She's missed you. At times, I feel very guilty because we don't get to America to see you often enough."

"You don't have to feel guilty, Alex." Morgan pushed on sunglasses and relaxed again. After all, she reflected, smuggling had nothing to do with her. "Liz is happy."

"She'd be happier with you here."

"Alex," Morgan began with a smile for his indulgence of his wife. "I can't simply move in as a companion, no matter how much both of us love Liz."

"You're still dedicated to your job at the U.N.?" His tone had altered slightly, but Morgan sensed the change. It was business now.

"I like my work. I'm good at it, and I need the challenge."

"I'm a generous employer, Morgan, particularly to one with your capabilities." He took another long, slow drag, studying her through the mist of smoke. "I asked you to come work for me three years ago. If I hadn't been"—he glanced down at Liz's sleeping figure—"distracted"—he decided with a mild smile—"I would have taken more time to convince you to accept."

"Distracted?" Liz pushed her sunglasses up to her forehead and peered at him from under them.

"Eavesdropping," Morgan said with a sniff. A uniformed steward set three iced drinks on the table. She lifted one and drank. "Your manners always were appalling."

"You have a few weeks yet to think it over, Morgan."

Tenacity beneath a smooth delivery was one of Alex's most successful business tactics. "But I warn you, Liz will be more persistent with her other solution." He shrugged, reaching for his own drink. "And I must agree—a woman needs a husband and security."

"How very Greek of you," Morgan commented dryly.

His grin flashed without apology. "I'm afraid one of Liz's candidates will be delayed. Dorian won't join us until tomorrow. He's bringing my cousin Iona with him."

"Marvelous." Liz's response was drenched in sarcasm. Alex sent her a frown.

"Liz isn't fond of Iona, but she's family." The quiet look he sent his wife told Morgan the subject had been discussed before. "I have a responsibility."

Liz took the last glass with a sigh of acceptance. Briefly she touched her hand to his. "We have a responsibility," she corrected. "Iona's welcome."

Alex's frown turned into a look of love so quickly, Morgan gave a mock groan. "Don't you two ever fight? I mean, don't you realize it isn't healthy to be so well balanced?"

Liz's eyes danced over the rim of her glass. "We have our moments, I suppose. A week ago I was furious with him for at least—ah, fifteen minutes."

"That," Morgan said positively, "is disgusting."

"So," Alex mused, "you think a man and woman must fight to be…healthy?"

Shaking back her hair, Morgan laughed. "*I* have to fight to be healthy."

"Morgan, you haven't mentioned Jack at all. Is there a problem?"

"Liz." Alex's disapproval was clear in the single syllable.

"No, it's all right, Alex." Taking her glass, Morgan rose and moved to the rail. "It's not a problem," she said slowly. "At least I hope it's not." She stared into her drink, frowning, as if she wasn't quite sure what the glass contained. "I've been running on this path—this very straight, very defined path. I could run it blindfolded." With a quick laugh, Morgan leaned out on the rail to let the wind grab at her hair. "Suddenly, I discovered it wasn't a path, but a rut and it kept getting deeper. I decided to change course before it became a pit."

"You always did prefer an obstacle course," Liz murmured. But she was pleased with Jack's disposal, and took little trouble to hide it.

The sea churned in a white froth behind the boat. Morgan turned from her study of it. "I don't intend to fall at Dorian's feet, Liz—or anyone else you might have in mind—just because Jack and I are no longer involved."

"I should hope not," Liz returned with some spirit. "That would take all the fun out of it."

With a sigh of exasperated affection, Morgan turned back to the rail.

The stark mountains of Lesbos rose from the sea. Jagged, harsh, timeless. Morgan could make out the pure white lines of Alex's villa. She thought it looked like a virgin offering to the gods—cool, classic, certainly feminine. Higher still was a rambling gray structure which seemed hewn from the rock itself. It faced the sea; indeed, it loomed over it. As if challenging Poseidon to claim it, it clung to the cliff. Morgan saw it as arrogant, rough, masculine. The flowering vines which grew all around it didn't soften the appearance, but added a haunted kind of beauty.

There were other buildings—a white-washed village, snuggled cottages, one or two other houses on more sophisticated lines, but the two larger structures hovered over the rest. One was elegant; one was savage.

"Who does that belong to?" Morgan called over her shoulder. "It's incredible."

Following her gaze, Liz grinned and rose to join her. "I should have known that would appeal to you. Sometimes I'd swear it's alive. Nicholas Gregoras, olive oil, and more recently, import-export." She glanced at her friend's profile. "Maybe I'll include him for dinner tomorrow if he's free, though I don't think he's your type."

Morgan gave her a dry look. "Oh? And what is my type?"

"Someone who'll give you plenty to fight about. Who'll give you that obstacle course."

"*Hmm.* You know me too well."

"As for Nick, he's rather smooth and certainly a charmer." Liz tapped a fingernail against the rail as she considered. "Not as blatantly handsome as Dorian, but he has a rather basic sort of sex appeal. Earthier, and yet…" She trailed off, narrowing her eyes she tried to pigeonhole him. "Well, he's an odd one. I suppose he'd have to be to live in a house like that. He's in his early thirties, inherited the olive oil empire almost ten years ago. Then he branched into import-export. He seems to have a flair for it. Alex is very fond of him because they go back to short pants together."

"Liz, I only wanted to know who owned the house. I didn't ask for a biography."

"These facts are part of the service." She cupped her hands around her lighter and lit a cigarette. "I want to give you a clear picture of your options."

"Haven't you got a goatherd up your sleeve?" Morgan demanded. "I rather like the idea of a small, white-washed cottage and baking black bread."

"I'll see what I can do."

"I don't suppose it occurs to you or Alex that I'm content to be single—the modern, capable woman on her own? I know how to use a screwdriver, how to change a flat tire…"

"'Methinks she doth protest too much,'" Liz quoted mildly.

"Liz—"

"I love you, Morgan."

On a frustrated sigh, Morgan lifted her drink again. "Damn it, Liz," she murmured.

"Come on, let me have my fun," she coaxed, giving Morgan a friendly pat on the cheek. "As you said yourself, it's all up to fate anyway."

"Hoist by my own petard. All right, bring on your Dorians and your Nicks and your Lysanders."

"Lysander?"

"It's a good name for a goatherd."

With a chuckle, Liz flicked her cigarette into the churning water. "Just wait and see if I don't find one."

"Liz…" Morgan hesitated for a moment, then asked casually, "do many people use the beach where we swam yesterday?"

"*Hmm?* Oh." She tucked a pale blond strand behind her ear. "Not really. It's used by us and the Gregoras villa for the most part. I'd have to ask Alex who owns it, I've never given it any thought. The bay's secluded and only easily accessible by the beach steps which run between the properties. Oh, yes, there's a cottage Nick owns which he rents out occasionally," she remembered. "It's occupied now by an American. Stevens...no," she corrected herself. "Stevenson. Andrew Stevenson, a poet or a painter or something. I haven't met him yet." She gave Morgan a frank stare. "Why? Did you plan for an all over tan?"

"Just curious." Morgan rearranged her thoughts. If she was going to file it and forget it, she had to stop letting the incident play back in her mind. "I'd love to get a close look at that place." She gestured toward the gray villa. "I think the architect must have been just a little mad. It's fabulous."

"Use some charm on Nick and get yourself an invitation," Liz suggested.

"I might just do that." Morgan studied the villa consideringly. She wondered if Nick Gregoras was the man whose footsteps she had heard when she had been held in the bushes. "Yes, I might just."

That evening, Morgan left the balcony doors wide. She wanted the warmth and scents of the night. The house was quiet but for the single stroke of a clock that signaled the hour. For the second night in a row she was wide awake. Did people really sleep on vacations? she wondered. What a waste of time.

She sat at the small rosewood desk in her room, writing a letter. From somewhere between the house and the sea, an owl cried out twice. She paused to listen, hoping it would call again, but there was only silence. How could she describe how it felt to see Mount Olympus rising from the sea? Was it possible to describe the timelessness, the strength, the almost frightening beauty?

She shrugged, and did what she could to explain the sensation to her father on paper. He'd understand, she mused as she folded the stationery. Who understood better her sometimes whimsical streaks of fancy than the man she'd inherited them from? And, she thought with a lurking smile, he'd get a good chuckle at Liz's determination to marry her off and keep her in Greece.

She rose, stretched once, then turned and collided with a hard chest. The hand that covered her mouth used more gentleness this time, and the jet eyes laughed into hers. Her heart rose, then fell like an elevator with its cable clipped.

"*Kalespera,* Aphrodite. Your word that you won't scream, and you have your freedom."

Instinctively she tried to jerk away, but he held her still without effort, only lifting an ironic brow. He was a man who knew whose word to accept and whose word to doubt.

Morgan struggled for another moment, then finding herself outmatched, reluctantly nodded. He released her immediately.

She drew in the breath to shout, then let it out in a frustrated huff. A promise was a promise, even if it was to a devil. "How did you get in here?" she demanded.

"The vines to your balcony are sturdy."

"You climbed?" Her incredulity was laced with helpless admiration. The walls were sheer, the height was dizzying. "You must be mad."

"That's a possibility," he said with a careless smile.

He seemed none the worse for wear after the climb. His hair was disheveled, but then she'd never seen it otherwise. There was a shadow of beard on his chin. His eyes held no strain or fatigue, but rather a light of adventure that drew her no matter how hard she tried to resist. In the lamplight she could see him more clearly than she had the night before. His features weren't as harsh as she had thought and his mouth wasn't grim. It was really quite beautiful, she realized with a flood of annoyance.

"What do you want?"

He smiled again, letting his gaze roam down her leisurely with an insolence she knew wasn't contrived but inherent. She wore only a brief cinnamon-colored teddy that dipped low at the breast and rose high at the thighs. Morgan noted the look, and that he stood squarely between her and the closet where she had left her robe. Rather than acknowledge the disadvantage, she tilted her chin.

"How did you know where to find me?"

"It's my business to find things out," he answered. Silently, he approved more than her form, but her courage as well. "Morgan James," he began. "Visiting friend of Elizabeth Theoharis. American, living in New York. Unmarried. Employed at the U.N. as interpreter. You speak Greek, English, French, Italian and Russian."

She tried not to let her mouth fall open at his careless rundown on her life. "That's a very tidy summary," she said tightly.

"Thank you. I try to be succinct."

"What does any of that have to do with you?"

"That's yet to be decided." He studied her, thinking again. It might be that he could employ her talents and position for his own uses. The package was good, very good. And so, more important at the moment, was the mind.

"You're enjoying your stay on Lesbos?"

Morgan stared at him, then slowly shook her head. No, he wasn't a ruffian or a rapist. That much she was sure of. If he were a thief, which she still reserved judgment on, he was no ordinary one. He spoke too well, moved too well. What he had was a certain amount of odd charm, a flair that was hard to resist, and an amazing amount of arrogance. Under different circumstances, she might even have liked him.

"You have incredible gall," she decided.

"You continue to flatter me."

"All right." Tight-lipped, Morgan strode over to the open balcony doors and gestured meaningfully. "I gave you my word I wouldn't scream, and I didn't. But I have no intention of standing here making idle conversation with a lunatic. Out!"

With his lips still curved in a smile, he sat on the edge of the bed and studied her. "I admire a woman of her word." He stretched out jean-clad legs and crossed his feet. "I find a great deal to admire about you, Morgan. Last night you showed good sense and courage—rare traits to find together."

"Forgive me if I'm not overwhelmed."

He caught the sarcasm, but more important, noted the change in her eyes. She wasn't as angry as she tried to be. "I did apologize," he reminded her and smiled.

Her breath came out in a long-suffering sigh. She could detest him for making her want to laugh when she should be furious. Just who the devil was he? He wasn't the mad rapist she had first thought—he wasn't a common thief. So just what was he? Morgan stopped herself before she asked—she was better off in ignorance.

"It didn't seem like much of an apology to me."

"If I make a more…honest attempt," he began with a bland sincerity that made her lips twitch, "would you accept?"

Firmly, she banked down on the urge to return his smile. "If I accept it, will you go away?"

"But I find your company so pleasant."

An irrepressible light of humor flickered in her eyes. "The hell you do."

"Aphrodite, you wound me."

"I'd like to draw and quarter you. Are you going to go away?"

"Soon." Smiling, he rose again. What was that scent that drifted from her? he wondered. It was not quite sweet, not quite tame. Jasmine—wild jasmine. It suited her. He moved to the dresser to toy with her hand mirror. "You'll meet Dorian Zoulas and Iona Theoharis tomorrow," he said casually. This time Morgan's mouth did drop. "There's little on the island I'm not aware of," he said mildly.

"Apparently," she agreed.

Now he noted a hint of curiosity in her tone. It was what he had hoped for. "Perhaps, another time, you'll give me your impression of them."

Morgan shook her head more from bafflement than offense. "I have no intention of there being another time, or of gossiping with you. I hardly see why—"

"Why not?" he countered.

"I don't *know* you," she said in frustration. "I don't know this Dorian or Iona either. And I don't understand how you could possibly—"

"True," he agreed with a slight nod. "How well do you know Alex?"

Morgan ran a hand through her hair. Here I am, wearing little more than my dignity, exchanging small talk with a maniac who climbed in the third-story window. "Look, I'm not discussing Alex with you. I'm not discussing anyone or anything with you. Go away."

"We'll leave that for later too, then," he said mildly as he crossed back to her. "I have something for you." He reached into his pocket, then opened his hand and dangled a small silver medal by its chain.

"Oh, you did have it!" Morgan grabbed, only to have him whip it out of her reach. His eyes hardened with fury.

"I told you once, I'm no thief." The change in his voice and face had been swift and potent. Involuntarily, she took a step away. His mouth tightened at the movement before he went on in a more controlled tone. "I went back and found it in the grove. The chain had to be repaired, I'm afraid."

With his eyes on hers, he held it out again. Taking it, Morgan began to fasten it around her neck. "You're a very considerate assailant."

"Do you think I enjoyed hurting you?"

Her hands froze at the nape of her neck. There was no teasing banter in his tone now, no insolent light of amusement in his eyes. This was the man she recognized from the shadows. Waves of temper came from him, hardening his voice, burning in his jet eyes. With her hands still lifted, Morgan stared at him.

"Do you think I enjoyed frightening you into fainting, having you think I would murder you? Do you think it gives me pleasure to see there are bruises on you and know that I put them there?" He whirled away, stalking the room. "I'm not a man who makes a habit of misusing women."

"I wouldn't know about that," she said steadily.

He stopped, and his eyes came back to hers. Damn, she was cool, he thought. And beautiful. Beautiful enough to be a distraction when he couldn't afford one.

"I don't know who you are or what you're mixed up in," she continued. Her fingers trembled a bit as she finished fastening the chain, but her voice was calm and unhurried. "Frankly, I don't care as long as you leave me alone. Under different circumstances, I'd thank you for the return of my property, but I don't feel it applies in this case. You can leave the same way you came in."

He had to bank down on an urge to throttle her. It wasn't often he was in the position of having a half-naked woman order him from her bedroom three times in one evening. He might have found it amusing if he hadn't been fighting an overwhelming flood of pure and simple desire.

The hell with fighting it, he thought. A woman who kept her chin lifted in challenge deserved to be taken up on it.

"Courage becomes you, Morgan," he said coolly. "We might do very well together." Reaching out, he fingered the medal at her throat and frowned at it. With a silent oath, he tightened his grip on the chain and brought his eyes back to hers.

There was no fear in those clear blue pools now, but a light, maddening disdain. A woman like this, he thought, could make a man mad, make him suffer and ache. And by God, a woman like this would be worth it.

"I told you to go," she said icily, ignoring the sudden quick thud of her pulse. It wasn't fear—Morgan told herself she was through with fear. But neither was it the anger she falsely named it.

"And so I will," he murmured and let the chain drop. "In the meantime, since you don't offer, I take."

Once again she found herself in his arms. It wasn't the teasing, seductive kiss of the night before. Now he devoured her. No one had kissed her like this before— as if he knew every secret she hoarded. He would know, somehow, where she needed to be touched.

The hot, insistent flow of desire that ran through her left her too stunned to struggle, too hungry to reason. How could she want him? her mind demanded. How could she want a man like this to touch her? But her mouth was moving under his, she couldn't deny it. Her tongue met his. Her hands gripped his shoulders, but didn't push him away.

"There's honey on your lips, Morgan," he murmured. "Enough to drive a man mad for another taste."

He took his hand on a slow journey down her back, pressing silk against her skin before he came to the hem. His fingers were strong, callused, and as clever as a musician's. Without knowing, without caring what she did,

Morgan framed his face with her hands for a moment before they dove into his hair. The muttered Greek she heard from him wasn't a love word but an oath as he dragged her closer.

How well she knew that body now. Long and lean and wiry with muscle. She could smell the sea on it, almost taste it beneath that hot demand as his mouth continued to savage hers.

The kiss grew deeper, until she moaned, half in fear of the unexplored, half in delight of the exploration. She'd forgotten who she was, who he was. There was only pleasure, a dark, heavy pleasure. Through her dazed senses she felt a struggle—a storm, a fury. Then he drew her away to study her face.

He wasn't pleased that his heartbeat was unsteady. Or that the thoughts whirling in his head were clouded with passion. This was no time for complications. And this was no woman to take risks with. With an effort, he slid his hands gently down her arms. "More satisfying than a thank you," he said lightly, then glanced with a grin toward the bed. "Are you going to ask me to stay?"

Morgan pulled herself back with a jolt. He must have hypnotized her, she decided. There was no other rational explanation. "Some other time, perhaps," she managed, as carelessly as he.

Amusement lightened his features. Capturing her hand, he kissed it formally. "I'll look forward to it, Aphrodite."

He moved to the balcony, throwing her a quick grin before he started his descent. Unable to prevent herself, Morgan ran over to watch him climb down.

He moved like a cat, confident, fearless, a shadow

clinging to the stark white walls. Her heart stayed lodged in her throat as she watched him. He sprang to the ground and melted into the cover of trees without looking back. Whirling, Morgan shut the doors to the balcony. And locked them.

Chapter 3

Morgan swirled her glass of local wine but drank little. Though its light, fruity flavor was appealing, she was too preoccupied to appreciate it. The terrace overlooked the gulf with its hard blue water and scattering of tiny islands. Small dots that were boats skimmed the surface, but she took little notice of them. Most of her mind was occupied in trying to sort out the cryptic comments of her late-night visitor. The rest was involved with following the conversation around her.

Dorian Zoulas was all that Liz had said—classically handsome, bronzed, and sophisticated. In the pale cream suit, he was a twentieth-century Adonis. He had intelligence and breeding, tempered with a golden beauty that was essentially masculine. Liz's maneuvers might have caused Morgan to treat him with a polite aloofness if she hadn't seen the flashes of humor in his eyes. Morgan had realized immediately that he not only knew the way his hostess's mind worked, but had decided to play the game.

The teasing challenge in his eyes relaxed her. Now she could enjoy a harmless flirtation without embarrassment.

Iona, Alex's cousin, was to Morgan's mind less appealing. Her dark, sultry looks were both stunning and disturbing. The gloss of beauty and wealth didn't quite polish over an edge that might have come from poor temperament or nerves. There was no humor in the exotic sloe eyes or pouting mouth. Iona was, Morgan mused, like a volcano waiting to erupt. Hot, smoky, and alarming.

The adjectives brought her night visitor back to her mind. They fit him just as neatly as they fit Iona Theoharis, and yet...oddly, Morgan found she admired them in the man and found them disturbing in the woman. Double standard? she wondered, then shook her head. No, the energy in Iona seemed destructive. The energy in the man was compelling. Annoyed with herself, Morgan turned from her study of the gulf and pushed aside her disturbing thoughts.

She gave Dorian her full attention. "You must find it very peaceful here after Athens."

He turned in his chair to face her. With only a smile, he intimated that there was no woman but she on the terrace—a trick Morgan found pleasant. "The island's a marvelous place...tranquil. But I thrive on chaos. As you live in New York, I'm sure you understand."

"Yes, but at the moment, tranquility is very appealing." Leaning against the rail, she let the sun play warm on her back. "I've been nothing but lazy so far. I haven't even whipped up the energy to explore."

"There's quite a bit of local color, if that's what you have in mind." Dorian slipped a thin gold case from his pocket, and opening it, offered Morgan a cigarette. At the shake of her head, he lit one for himself, then leaned back in a manner that was both relaxed and alert. "Caves and inlets, olive groves, a few small farms and flocks," he continued. "The village is very quaint and unspoiled."

"Exactly what I want." Morgan nodded and sipped her drink. "But I'm going to take it very slow. I'll collect shells and find a farmer who'll let me milk his goat."

"Terrifying aspirations," Dorian commented with a quick smile.

"Liz will tell you, I've always been intrepid."

"I'd be happy to help you with your shells." He continued to smile as his eyes skimmed her face with an approval she couldn't have missed. "But as to the goat…"

"I'm surprised you're content with so little entertainment." Iona's husky voice broke into the exchange.

Morgan shifted her gaze to her and found it took more of an effort to smile. "The island itself is entertainment enough for me. Remember, I'm a tourist. I've always thought vacations where you rush from one activity to the next aren't vacations at all."

"Morgan's been lazy for two full days," Liz put in with a grin. "A new record."

Morgan cast her a look, thinking of her nighttime activities. "I'm shooting for two weeks of peaceful sloth," Morgan murmured. *Starting today,* she added silently.

"Lesbos is the perfect spot for idleness." Dorian blew out a slow, fragrant stream of smoke. "Rustic, quiet."

"But perhaps this bit of island isn't as quiet as it appears." Iona ran a manicured nail around the rim of her glass.

Morgan saw Dorian's brows lift as if in puzzlement while Alex's drew together in disapproval.

"We'll do our best to keep it quiet during Morgan's visit," Liz said smoothly. "She rarely stays still for long, and since she's determined to this time, we'll see that she has a nice, uneventful vacation."

Morgan made some sound of agreement and managed not to choke over her drink. Uneventful! If Liz only knew.

"More wine, Morgan?" Dorian rose, bringing the bottle to her.

Iona began to tap her fingers on the arm of her wrought iron chair. "I suppose there are people who find boredom appealing."

"Relaxation," Alex said with a slight edge in his voice, "comes in many forms."

"And of course," Liz went on, skimming her hand lightly over the back of her husband's, "Morgan's job is very demanding. All those foreign dignitaries and protocol and politics."

Dorian sent Morgan an appreciative smile as he poured more wine into her glass. "I'm sure someone with Morgan's talents would have many fascinating stories to tell."

Morgan cocked a brow. It had been a long time since she had been given a purely admiring male smile—undemanding, warm without being appraising. She could learn to enjoy it. "I might have a few," she returned.

The sun was sinking into the sea. The rosy light streamed through the open balcony doors and washed the room. Red sky at night, Morgan mused. Wasn't that supposed to mean clear sailing? She decided to take it as an omen.

Her first two days on Lesbos had been a far cry from the uneventful vacation Liz had boasted of, but that was behind her now. With luck, and a little care, she wouldn't run into that attractive lunatic again.

Morgan caught a glimpse of her own smile in the mirror and hastily rearranged her expression. Perhaps when she got back to New York, she'd see a psychiatrist. When you started to find lunatics appealing, you were fast becoming one yourself. Forget it, she ordered herself firmly as she went to the closet. There were more important things to think about—like what she was going to wear to dinner.

After a quick debate, Morgan chose a drifting white dress—thin layers of crêpe de chine, full-sleeved, full-skirted. Dorian had inspired her to flaunt her femininity a bit. Jack, she recalled, had preferred the tailored look. He had often offered a stern and unsolicited opinion on her wardrobe, finding her taste both inconsistent and flighty. There might be a multicolored gypsy-style skirt hanging next to a prim business suit. He'd never understood that both had suited who she was. Just another basic difference, Morgan mused as she hooked the line of tiny pearl buttons.

Tonight she was going to have fun. It had been a long while since she'd flirted with a man. Her thoughts swung back to a dark man with tousled hair and a shadowed chin. Hold on, Morgan, she warned herself. *That* was hardly in the same league as a flirtation. Moving over, she closed the balcony doors and gave a satisfied nod as she heard the click of the lock. And that, she decided, takes care of that.

Liz glided around the salon. It pleased her that Morgan hadn't come down yet. Now she could make an entrance. For all her blond fragility, Liz was a determined woman. Loyalty was her strongest trait; where she loved, it was unbendable. She wanted Morgan to be happy. Her own marriage had given her nothing but happiness. Morgan would have the same if Liz had any say in it.

With a satisfied smile, she glanced around the salon. The light was low and flattering. The scent of night blossoms drifting in through the open windows was the perfect touch. The wines she'd ordered for dinner would add the final prop for romance. Now, if Morgan would cooperate...

"Nick, I'm so glad you could join us." Liz went to him, holding out both hands. "It's so nice that we're all on the island at the same time for a change."

"It's always a pleasure to see you, Liz," he returned with a warm, charming smile. "And a relief to be out of the crowds in Athens for a few weeks." He gave her hands a light squeeze, then lifted one to his lips. His dark eyes skimmed her face. "I swear, you're lovelier every time I see you."

With a laugh, Liz tucked her arm through his. "We'll have to invite you to dinner more often. Did I ever thank you properly for that marvelous Indian chest you found me?" Smiling, she guided him toward the bar. "I adore it."

"Yes, you did." He gave her hand a quick pat. "I'm glad I was able to find what you had in mind."

"You never fail to find the perfect piece. I'm afraid Alex wouldn't know an Indian chest from a Hepplewhite."

Nick laughed. "We all have our talents, I suppose."

"But your work must be fascinating." Liz glanced up at him with her wide-eyed smile as she began to fix him a drink. "All those treasures and all the exotic places you travel to."

"There are times it's more exciting just to be home."

She shot him a look. "You make that hard to believe, since you're so seldom here. Where was it last month? Venice?"

"A beautiful city," he said smoothly.

"I'd love to see it. If I could drag Alex away from his ships…" Liz's eyes focused across the room. "Oh dear, it looks like Iona is annoying Alex again." On a long breath, she lifted her eyes to Nick's. Seeing the quick understanding, she gave a rueful smile. "I'm going to have to play diplomat."

"You do it charmingly, Liz. Alex is a lucky man."

"Remind him of that from time to time," she suggested. "I'd hate for him to take me for granted. Oh, here comes Morgan. She'll keep you entertained while I do my duty."

Following Liz's gaze, Nick watched as Morgan entered the room. "I'm sure she will," was his murmured reply. He liked the dress she wore, the floating white that was at once alluring and innocent. She'd left her hair loose so that it fell over her shoulders almost as if it had come off a pillow. Quite beautiful, he thought as he felt the stir. He'd always had a weakness for beauty.

"Morgan." Before Morgan could do any more than smile her hello at Liz, Liz took her arm. "You'll keep

Nick happy for a moment, I have a job to do. Morgan James, Nicholas Gregoras." With the quick introduction, Liz was halfway across the room.

Morgan stared in stunned silence. Nick lifted her limp hand to his lips. "You," she managed in a choked whisper.

"Aphrodite, you're exquisite. Even fully dressed."

With his lips lingering over her knuckles, he met her eyes. His were dark and pleased. Regaining her senses, Morgan tried to wrench her hand free. Without changing expression, Nick tightened his grip and held her still.

"Careful, Morgan," he said mildly. "Liz and her guest will wonder at your behavior. And explanations would"— he grinned, exactly as she remembered—"cause them to wonder about your mental health."

"Let go of my hand," she said quietly and smiled with her lips only. "Or I swear, I'll deck you."

"You're magnificent." Making a small bow, he released her. "Did you know your eyes literally throw darts when you're annoyed?"

"Then I've the pleasure of knowing you're riddled with tiny holes," she returned. "Let me know when one hits the heart, *Mr.* Gregoras."

"Nick, please," he said in a polished tone. "We could hardly start formalities now after all we've…been through together."

Morgan gave him a brilliant smile. "Very well, Nick, you odious swine. What a pity this isn't the proper time to go into how detestable you are."

He inclined his head. "We'll arrange for a more appropriate opportunity. Soon," he added with the faintest hint of steel. "Now, let me get you a drink."

Liz breezed up, pleased with the smiles she had seen exchanged. "You two seem to be getting along like old friends."

"I was just telling Mr. Gregoras how enchanting his home looks from the sea." Morgan sent him a quick but lethal glance.

"Yes, Morgan was fascinated by it," Liz told him. "She's always preferred things that didn't quite fit a mold, if you know what I mean."

"Exactly." Nick let his eyes sweep over Morgan's face. A man could get lost in those eyes, he thought, if he wasn't careful. Very careful. "Miss James has agreed to a personal tour tomorrow afternoon." He smiled, watching her expression go from astonishment to fury before she controlled it.

"Marvelous!" Pleased, Liz beamed at both of them. "Nick has so many treasures from all over the world. His house is just like Aladdin's cave."

Smiling, Morgan thought of three particularly gruesome wishes, all involving her intended host. "I can't wait to see it."

Through dinner, Morgan watched, confused, then intrigued by Nick's manner. This was not the man she knew. This man was smooth, polished. Gone was the intensity, the ruthlessness, replaced by an easy warmth and charm.

Nicholas Gregoras, olive oil, import-export. Yes, she could see the touches of wealth and success—and the authority she'd understood from the first. But command sat differently on him now, with none of the undertones of violence.

He could sit at the elegant table, laughing with Liz and Alex over some island story with the gleam of cut crystal in his hand. The smoky-gray suit was perfectly tailored and fit him with the same ease as the dark sweatshirt and jeans she'd first seen him in. His arrogance had a more sophisticated tone now. All the rough edges were smoothed.

He seemed relaxed, at home—with none of that vital, dangerous energy. How could this be the same man who had flourished a knife, or climbed the sheer wall to her balcony?

Nick handed her a glass of wine and she frowned. But he was the same man, she reminded herself. And just what game was he playing? Lifting her eyes, Morgan met his. Her fingers tightened on the stem of the glass. The look was brief and quickly veiled, but she saw the inner man. The force was vital. If he was playing games, she thought, sipping her wine to calm suddenly tight nerves, it wasn't a pleasant one. And she wanted no part of it—or of him.

Turning to Dorian, Morgan left Nick to Iona. Intelligent, witty, and with no frustrating mysteries, Dorian was a more comfortable dinner companion. Morgan fell into the easy exchange and tried to relax.

"Tell me, Morgan, don't you find the words of so many languages a bit crowded in the mind?"

She toyed with her moussaka, finding her stomach too jittery to accept the rich sauce. Damn the man for interfering even with her appetite. "I do my thinking in one at a time," she countered.

"You take it too lightly," Dorian insisted. "It's an accomplishment to be proud of. Even a power."

"A power?" Her brows drew together for a moment,

then cleared as she smiled. "I suppose it is, though I'd never really thought about it. It just seemed too limiting to only be able to communicate and think in one language, then once I got started, I couldn't seem to stop."

"Having the language, you'd be at home in many countries."

"Yes, I guess that's why I feel so—well, easy here."

"Alex tells me he's trying to entice you into his company." With a smile, Dorian toasted her. "I've drafted myself as promoter. Working with you would add to the company benefits."

Iona's rich laughter floated across the table. "Oh, Nicky, you say the most ridiculous things."

Nicky, Morgan thought with a sniff. I'll be ill any minute. "I think I might enjoy your campaign," Morgan told Dorian with her best smile.

"Take me out on your boat tomorrow, Nicky. I simply must have some fun."

"I'm sorry, Iona, not tomorrow. Perhaps later in the week." Nick softened the refusal with the trace of a finger down her hand.

Iona's mouth formed a pout. "I might die of boredom by later in the week."

Morgan heard Dorian give a quiet sigh. Glancing over, she noted the quick look of exasperation he sent Iona. "Iona tells me she ran into Maria Popagos in Athens last week." The look of exasperation was gone, and his voice was gentle. "She has what—four children now, Iona?"

They treat her like a child, Morgan thought with distaste. And she behaves like one—a spoiled, willful, not quite healthy child.

Through the rest of the meal, and during coffee in the salon, Morgan watched Iona's moods go from sullen to frantic. Apparently used to it, or too good mannered to notice, Dorian ignored the fluctuations. And though she hated to give him the credit for it, so did Nick. But Morgan noted, with a flutter of sympathy, that Alex grew more distracted as the evening wore on. He spoke to his cousin in undertones as she added more brandy to her glass. Her response was a dramatic toss of her head before she swallowed the liquor and turned her back on him.

When Nick rose to leave, Iona insisted on walking with him to his car. She cast a look of triumph over her shoulder as they left the salon arm-in-arm. Now who, Morgan mused, was that aimed at? Shrugging, she turned back to Dorian and let the evening wind down naturally. There would be time enough to think things through when she was alone in her room again.

Morgan floated with the dream. The wine had brought sleep quickly. Though she had left the balcony doors securely locked, the night breeze drifted through the windows. She sighed, and shifted with its gentle caress on her skin. It was a soft stroking, like a butterfly's wing. It teased across her lips then came back to warm them. She stirred with pleasure. Her body was pliant, receptive. As the phantom kiss increased in pressure, she parted her lips. She drew the dream lover closer.

Excitement was sleepy. The tastes that seeped into her were as sweet and as potent as the wine that still misted her brain. With a sigh of lazy, languid pleasure, she floated with it. In the dream, her arms wrapped around the faceless lover—the pirate, the phantom. He whispered her name and deepened the kiss as his hands drew down the sheet that separated them. Rough fingers, familiar fingers, traced over her skin. A body, too hard, too muscular for a dream, pressed against hers. The lazy images became more tangible, and the phantom took on form. Dark hair, dark eyes, and a mouth that was grimly beautiful and oh, so clever.

Warmth became heat. With a moan, she let passion take her. The stroking along her body became more insistent at her response. Her mouth grew hungry, demanding. Then she heard the breathy whisper of a Greek endearment against her ear.

Suddenly, the filmy curtain of sleep lifted. The weight on her body was real, achingly real—and achingly familiar. Morgan began a confused struggle.

"The goddess awakes. More's the pity."

She saw him in the shaft of moonlight. Her body was alive with needs, her mind baffled with the knowledge that he had induced them. "What are you doing!" she demanded, and found her breathing was quick and ragged. His mouth had been on hers, she knew. She could still taste him. And his hands… "This is the limit! If you think for one minute I'm going to sit still for you crawling into my bed while I'm sleeping—"

"You were very agreeable a moment ago."

"Oh! What a despicable thing to do."

"You're very responsive," Nick murmured, and traced her ear with his fingertip. Beneath his hand he could feel the thunder of her heartbeat. He knew, though he fought to slow it, that his own beat as quickly. "It seemed to please you to be touched. It pleased me to touch you."

His voice had lowered again, as she knew it could—dark, seductive. The muscles in her thighs loosened. "Get off of me," she ordered in quick defense.

"Sweet Morgan." He nipped her bottom lip—felt her tremble, felt a swift rush of power. It would be so easy to persuade her...and so risky. With an effort, he gave her a friendly smile. "You only postpone the inevitable."

She kept her eyes level as she tried to steady her breathing. Something told her that if all else he had said had been lies, his last statement was all too true. "I didn't promise not to scream this time."

He lifted a brow as though the possibility intrigued him. "It might be interesting to explain this...situation to Alex and Liz. I could claim I was overcome with your beauty. It has a ring of truth. But you won't scream in any case."

"Just what makes you so sure?"

"You'd have given me away—or tried to by now—if you were going to." Nick rolled aside.

Sitting up, Morgan pushed at her hair. Did he always have to be right? she wondered grimly. "What do you want now? And how the hell did you get in this time? I locked..." Her voice trailed off as she saw the balcony doors were wide open.

"Did you think a lock would keep me out?" With a laugh, Nick ran a finger down her nose. "You have a lot to learn."

"Now, you listen to me—"

"No, save the recriminations for later. They're understood in any case." Absently, he rubbed a lock of her hair between his thumb and forefinger. "I came back to make certain you didn't develop a convenient headache that would keep you from coming to the house tomorrow. There are one or two things I want to discuss with you."

"I've got a crate full of things to discuss with you," Morgan hissed furiously. "Just what were you doing that night on the beach? And who—"

"Later, Aphrodite. I'm distracted at the moment. That scent you wear, for instance. It's very…" He lifted his eyes to hers, "alluring."

"Stop it." She didn't trust him when his voice dropped to that tone. She didn't trust him at all, she reminded herself and gave him a level look. "What's the purpose behind that ridiculous game you were playing tonight?"

"Game?" His eyes widened effectively. "Morgan, my love, I don't know what you're talking about. I was quite natural."

"Natural be damned."

"No need to swear at me," he said mildly.

"There's every need," she countered. How could he manage to be charming under such ridiculous circumstances? "You were the perfect guest this evening," Morgan went on, knocking his hand aside as he began to toy with the thin strap of her chemise. "Charming—"

"Thank you."

"And false," she added, narrowing her eyes.

"Not false," Nick disagreed. "Simply suitable, considering the occasion."

"I suppose it would have looked a bit odd if you'd pulled a knife out of your pocket."

His fingers tightened briefly, then relaxed. She wasn't going to let him forget that—and he wasn't having an easy time blanking out that moment she had gone limp with terror beneath him. "Few people have seen me other than as I was tonight," he murmured, and began to give the texture of her hair his attention. "Perhaps it's your misfortune to count yourself among them."

"I don't want to see you *any* way, from now on."

Humor touched his eyes again as they shifted to hers. "Liar. I'll pick you up tomorrow at one."

Morgan tossed out a phrase commonly heard in the less elite portions of Italy. Nick responded with a pleased laugh.

"*Agapetike,* I should warn you, in my business I've had occasion to visit some Italian gutters."

"Good, then you won't need a translation."

"Just be ready." He let his gaze sweep down her, then up again. "You might find it easier to deal with me in the daylight—and when you're more adequately attired."

"I have no intention of dealing with you at all," Morgan began in a furious undertone. "Or of continuing this ridiculous charade by going with you tomorrow."

"Oh, I think you will." Nick's smile was confident and infuriating. "You'd find yourself having a difficult time explaining to Liz why you won't come when you've already expressed an interest in my home. Tell me, what was it that appealed to you about it?"

"The insanity of the architecture."

He laughed again and took her hand. "More compliments. I adore you, Aphrodite. Come, kiss me good-night."

Morgan drew back and scowled. "I certainly will not."

"You certainly will." In a swift movement he had her pinned under him again. When she cursed him, he laughed and the insolence was back. "Witch," he murmured. "What mortal can resist one?"

His mouth came down quickly, lingering until she had stopped squirming beneath him. Gradually, the force went out of the kiss, but not the power. It seeped into her, so that she couldn't be sure if it was hers or his. Then it was only passion—clean and hot and senseless. On a moan, Morgan accepted it, and him.

Feeling the change in her, Nick relaxed a moment and simply let himself enjoy.

She had a taste that stayed with him long after he left her. Each time he touched her he knew, eventually, he would have to have it all. But not now. Now there was too much at stake. She was a risk, and he had already taken too many chances with her. But that taste...

He gave himself over to the kiss knowing the danger of letting himself become vulnerable, even for a moment, by losing himself in her. If she hadn't been on the beach that night. If he hadn't had to reveal himself to her. Would things have been different than they were now? he wondered as desire began to claw at him. Would he have been able to coax her into his arms, into his bed, with a bit of flair and a few clever words? If they had met for the first time tonight, would he have wanted her this badly, this quickly?

Her hands were in his hair. He found his mouth had roamed to her throat. Her scent seemed to concentrate there, and the taste was wild and dangerous. He lived with danger and enjoyed it—lived by his wits and won. But this woman, this feeling she stirred in him, was a risk he could calculate. Yet it was done. There was no changing the course he had to take. And no changing the fact that she was involved.

He wanted to touch her, to tear off that swatch of silk she wore and feel her skin warm under his hand. He dared not. He was a man who knew his own limitations, his own weaknesses. Nick didn't appreciate the fact that Morgan James had become a weakness at a time when he could least afford one.

Murmuring his name, Morgan slid her hands beneath the loose sweatshirt, to run them over the range of muscle. Nick felt need shoot like a spear, white-tipped, to the pit of his stomach. Using every ounce of will, he banked down on it until it was a dull ache he could control. He lifted his head and waited for those pale, clouded blue eyes to open. Something dug into his palm, and he saw that he had gripped her medal in his hand without realizing it. Nick had to quell the urge to swear, then give himself a moment until he knew he could speak lightly. "Sleep well, Aphrodite," he told her with a grin. "Until tomorrow."

"You—" She broke off, struggling for the breath and the wit to hurl abuse at him.

"Tomorrow," Nick repeated as he brought her hand to his lips.

Morgan watched him stride to the balcony, then lower himself out of sight. Lying perfectly still, she stared at the empty space and wondered what she had gotten herself into.

Chapter 4

The house was cool and quiet in the mid-morning hush. Gratefully, Morgan accepted Liz's order to enjoy the beach. She wanted to avoid Iona's company, and though she hated to admit it, she didn't think she could handle Liz's carefree chatter about the dinner party. Liz would have expected her to make some witty observations about Nick that Morgan just didn't feel up to. Relieved that Dorian had business with Alex, and wouldn't feel obliged to keep her company, she set out alone.

Morgan wanted the solitude—she did her best thinking when she was alone. In the past few days she had accumulated quite a bit to think about. Now she decided to work it through one step at a time.

What had Nicholas Gregoras been doing that night on the beach? He'd had the scent of the sea on him, so it followed that he had been out on the water. She remembered the sound of a motor. She'd assumed it belonged to a fisherman but Nick was no fisherman. He'd been desperate not to be seen by someone…desperate enough to have been carrying a knife. She could still see the look on his face as she had lain beneath him in the shadows of the cypress. He'd been prepared to use the knife.

Somehow the knowledge that this was true disturbed her more now than it had when he'd been a stranger. Kicking bad-temperedly at a stone, she started down the beach steps.

And who had been with him? Morgan fretted. Someone had followed his orders without any question. Who had used the beach steps while Nick had held her prisoner in the shadows? Alex? The man who rented Nick's cottage? Frustrated, Morgan slipped out of her shoes and began to cross the warm sand. Why would Nick be ready to kill either one of them rather than be discovered by them? By anyone, she corrected. It could have been a servant of one of the villas, a villager trespassing.

One question at a time, Morgan cautioned herself as she kicked idly at the sand. First, was it logical to assume that the footsteps she had heard were from someone who had also come from the sea? Morgan thought it was. And second, she decided that the person must have been headed to one of the villas or a nearby cottage. Why else would they have used that particular strip of beach? Logical, she concluded, walking aimlessly. So why was Nick so violently determined to go unseen?

Smuggling. It was so obvious. So logical. But she had continued to push the words aside. She didn't want to think of him involved in such a dirty business. Somewhere, beneath the anger and resentment she felt for him, Morgan had experienced a totally different sensation. There was something about him—something she couldn't really pinpoint in words. Strength, perhaps. He was the kind of man you could depend on when no one else could—or would—help. She wanted to trust him. There was no logic to it, it simply was.

But was he a smuggler? Had he thought she'd seen something incriminating? Did the footsteps she'd heard belong to a patrol? Another smuggler? A rival? If he'd believed her to be a threat, why hadn't he simply used the knife on her? If he were a cold-blooded killer...no. Morgan shook her head at the description. While she could almost accept that Nick would kill, she couldn't agree with the adjective. And that led to hundreds of other problems.

Questions and answers sped through her mind. Stubborn questions, disturbing answers. Morgan shut her eyes on them. I'm going to get some straight answers from him this afternoon, she promised herself. It was his fault she was involved. Morgan dropped to the sand and brought her knees to her chest. She had been minding her own business when he had literally dragged her into it. All she had wanted was a nice, quiet vacation.

"Men!"

"I refuse to take that personally."

Morgan spun her head around and found herself staring into a wide, friendly smile.

"Hello. You seem to be angry with my entire gender." He rose from a rock and walked to her. He was tall and very slender, with dark gold curls appealingly disarrayed around a tanned face that held both youth and strength. "But I think it's worth the risk. I'm Andrew Stevenson." Still smiling, he dropped to the sand beside her.

"Oh." Recovering, Morgan returned the smile. "The poet or the painter? Liz wasn't sure."

"Poet," he said with a grimace. "Or so I tell myself."

Glancing down, she saw the pad he held. It was dog-eared and covered with a fine, looping scribble. "I've interrupted your work, I'm sorry."

"On the contrary, you've given me a shot of inspiration. You have a remarkable face."

"I think," Morgan considered, "that's a compliment."

"Dear lady, yours is a face a poet dreams of." He let his eyes roam it for a moment. "Do you have a name, or are you going to vanish in a mist and leave me bewitched?"

"Morgan." The fussy compliment, delivered with bland sincerity made her laugh. "Morgan James, and are you a good poet, Andrew Stevenson?"

"I can't say no." Andrew continued to study her candidly. "Modesty isn't one of my virtues. You said Liz. I assume that's Mrs. Theoharis. You're staying with them?"

"Yes, for a few weeks." A new thought crossed her mind. "You're renting Nicholas Gregoras's cottage?"

"That's right. Actually, it's a free ride." Though he set down the pad, he began to trace patterns in the sand as if he couldn't keep his hands quite still. "We're cousins." Andrew noted the surprise on her face. His smile deepened. "Not the Greek side. Our mothers are related."

"Oh, so his mother's American." This at least explained his ease with the language.

"A Norling of San Francisco," he stated with a grin for the title. "She remarried after Nick's father died. She's living in France."

"So, you're visiting Lesbos and your cousin at the same time."

"Actually, Nick offered me the retreat when he learned I was working on an epic poem—a bit Homeric, you see." His eyes were blue, darker than hers, and very direct on her face. Morgan could see nothing in the open, ingenuous look to link him with Nick. "I wanted to stay on Lesbos awhile, so it worked out nicely. The home of Sappho. The poetry and legend have always fascinated me."

"Sappho," Morgan repeated, turning her thoughts from Nick. "Oh, yes, the poetess."

"The Tenth Muse. She lived here, in Mitilini." His gaze, suddenly dreamy, swept down the stretch of beach. "I like to think Nick's house is on the cliff where she hurled herself into the sea, desperate for Phaon's love."

"An interesting thought." Morgan looked up to where a portion of a gray stone wall was visible. "And I suppose her spirit floats over the house searching for her love." Somehow, she liked the idea and smiled. "Lord knows, it's the perfect house for a poetic haunting."

"Have you been inside?" Andrew asked her, his tone as dreamy as his eyes now. "It's fantastic."

"No, I'm getting a personal tour this afternoon." Morgan kept her voice light as she swore silently in several languages.

"A personal tour?" Abruptly direct again, Andrew tilted his head, with brows lifted in speculation. "You must have made quite an impression on Nick. But then," he added with a nod, "you would. He sets great store by beauty."

Morgan gave him a noncommital smile. He could hardly know that it wasn't her looks or charm that had secured the invitation. "Do you often write on the beach? I can't keep away from it myself." Morgan hesitated briefly, then plunged. "I came down here a couple of nights ago and swam by moonlight."

There was no shock or anxiety in his eyes at this information. Andrew grinned. "I'm sorry I missed that. You'll find me all over this part of the island. Here, up on the cliffs, in the olive groves. I go where the mood strikes me."

"I'm going to do some exploring myself." She thought wistfully of a carefree hour in the inlets.

"I'm available if you'd like a guide." His gaze skimmed over her face again, warm and friendly. "By now, I know this part of the island as well as a native. If you find you want company, you can usually find me wandering around or in the cottage. It isn't far."

"I'd like that." A gleam of amusement lit her eyes. "You don't happen to keep a goat, do you?"

"Ah—no."

Laughing at his expression, Morgan patted his hand. "Don't try to understand," she advised. "And now I'd better go change for my tour."

Andrew rose with her and captured her hand. "I'll see you again." It was a statement, not a question. Morgan responded to the gentle pressure.

"I'm sure you will; the island's very small."

Andrew smiled as he released her hand. "I'd rather call it kismet." He watched Morgan walk away before he settled back on his rock, facing the sea.

Nicholas Gregoras was very prompt. By five minutes past one, Morgan found herself being shoved out the door by an enthusiastic Liz. "Have fun, darling, and don't hurry back. Nick, Morgan will adore your house; all those winding passages and the terrifying view of the sea. She's very courageous, aren't you, Morgan?"

"I'm practically stalwart," she muttered while Nick grinned.

"Well, run along and have fun." Liz shooed them out the door as if they were two reluctant children being sent to school.

"You should be warned," Morgan stated as she slid into Nick's car, "Liz considers you a suitable candidate for my hand. I think she's getting desperate picturing me as her unborn child's maiden aunt."

"Aphrodite." Nick settled beside her and took her hand. "There isn't a male alive who could picture you as anyone's maiden aunt."

Refusing to be charmed, Morgan removed her hand from his, then studied the view out the side window. "I met your poet in residence this morning on the beach."

"Andrew? He's a nice boy. How did you find him?"

"Not like a boy." Turning back to Nick, Morgan frowned. "He's a very charming man."

Nick lifted a brow fractionally. "Yes, I suppose he is. Somehow, I always think of him as a boy, though there's barely five years between us." He moved his shoulders. "He does have talent. Did you charm him?"

"'Inspire' was his word," she returned, annoyed.

Nick flashed her a quick grin. "Naturally. One romantic should inspire another."

"I'm not a romantic." The conversation forced her to

give him a great deal more of her attention than she had planned. "I'm very practical."

"Morgan, you're an insatiable romantic." Her annoyance apparently amused him, because a smile continued to hover on his mouth. "A woman who combs her hair on a moonlit beach, wears filmy white, and treasures a valueless memento thrives on romance."

Uncomfortable with the description, Morgan spoke coolly. "I also clip coupons and watch my cholesterol."

"Admirable."

She swallowed what might have been a chuckle. "You, Nicholas Gregoras, are a first-rate bastard."

"Yes. I hate to be second-rate at anything."

Morgan flounced back in her seat, but lost all resentment as the house came into full view. "Oh, Lord," she murmured. "It's wonderful!"

It looked stark and primitive and invulnerable. The second story lashed out over the sea like an out-stretched arm—not offering payment, but demanding it. None of the power she had felt out at sea was diminished at close range. The flowering shrubs and vines which trailed and tangled were placed to disguise the care of their planting. The result was an illusion of wild abandon. Sleeping Beauty's castle, she thought, a century after she pricked her finger.

"What a marvelous place." Morgan turned to him as he stopped the car at the entrance. "I've never seen anything like it."

"That's the first time you've smiled at me and meant it." He wasn't smiling now, but looking at her with a trace of annoyance. He hadn't realized just how much he'd wanted to see that spontaneous warmth in her eyes—directed at him. And now that he had, he wasn't certain what to do about it. With a quick mental oath, Nick slid from the car.

Ignoring him, Morgan climbed out and tried to take in the entire structure at once. "You know what it looks like," she said, half to herself. "It looks like Zeus hurled a lightning bolt into the mountain and the house exploded into existence."

"An interesting theory." Nick took her hand and started up the stone steps. "If you'd known my grandfather, you'd realize how close that is to the truth."

Morgan had primed herself to begin hurling questions and demanding explanations as soon as they had arrived. When she stepped into the entrance hall, she forgot everything.

Wide and speckled in aged white, the hall was sporadically slashed with stark colors from wall hangings and primitive paintings. On one wall, long spears were crossed—weapons for killing, certainly, but with an ancient dignity she had to admire. The staircase leading to the upper floors arched in a half circle with a banister of dark, unvarnished wood. The result was one of earthy magnificence. It was far from elegant, but there was a sense of balance and savage charm.

"Nicholas." Turning a full circle, Morgan sighed. "It's really wonderful. I expect a cyclops to come stalking down the stairs. Are there centaurs in the courtyard?"

"I'll take you through, and we'll see what we can do." She was making it difficult for him to stick to his plan. She wasn't supposed to charm him. That wasn't in the script. Still, he kept her hand in his as he led her through the house.

Liz's comparison to Aladdin's cave was completely apt. Room after room abounded with treasures—Venetian glass, Fabergé boxes, African masks, Native American pottery, Ming vases. All were set together in a hodge-podge of cultures. What might have seemed like a museum was instead a glorious clutter of wonders. As the house twisted and turned, revealing surprise after surprise, Morgan became more fascinated. Elegant Waterford crystal was juxtaposed with a deadly looking seventeenth-century crossbow. She saw exquisite porcelain and a shrunken head from Ecuador.

Yes, the architect was mad, she decided, noting lintels with wolves' heads or grinning elves carved into them. Wonderfully mad. The house was a fairy tale—not the tame children's version, but with all the whispering shadows and hints of gremlins.

A huge curved window on the top floor gave her the sensation of standing suspended on the edge of the cliff. It jutted out, arrogantly, then fell in a sheer drop into the sea. Morgan stared down, equally exhilarated and terrified.

Nick watched her. There was a need to spin her around and seize, to possess while that look of dazzled courage was still on her face. He was a man accustomed to taking what he wanted without a second thought. She was something he wanted.

Morgan turned to him. Her eyes were still alive with the fascination of the sea and hints of excited fear. "Andrew said he hoped this was the cliff where Sappho hurled herself into the sea. I'm ready to believe it."

"Andrew's imaginative."

"So are you," she countered. "You live here."

"Your eyes are like some mythological lake," he murmured. "Translucent and ethereal. I should call you Circe rather than Aphrodite." Abruptly, he gripped her hair in his hand, tugging it until her face was lifted to his. "I swear you're more witch than goddess."

Morgan stared at him. There was no teasing in his eyes this time, no arrogance. What she saw was longing. And the longing, more than passion, seduced her. "I'm only a woman, Nicholas," she heard herself say.

His fingers tightened. His expression darkened. Then even as she watched, his mood seemed to shift. This time, he took her arm rather than her hand. "Come, we'll go down and have a drink."

As they entered the salon, Morgan reasserted her priorities. She had to get answers—she *would* get answers. She couldn't let a few soft words and a pair of dark eyes make her forget why she'd come. Before she could speak, however, a man slipped into the doorway.

He was small, with creased, leather skin. His hair was gray with age, but thick. So were his arms—thick and muscled. He made her think of a small-scaled, very efficient tank. His moustache was a masterpiece. It spread under his nose to drop free along the sides of his mouth, reaching his chin in two flowing arches. He smiled, showing several gaps in lieu of teeth.

"Good afternoon." He spoke in respectful Greek, but his eyes were dancing.

Intrigued, Morgan gave him an unsmiling stare. *"Yiasou."*

"Stephanos, Miss James. Stephanos is my, ah, caretaker."

The checkerboard grin widened at the term. "Your servant, my lady." He bowed, but there was nothing deferential in the gesture. "The matter we discussed has been seen to, Mr. Gregoras." Turning to Nick, the old man spoke with exaggerated respect. "You have messages from Athens."

"I'll tend to them later."

"As you wish." The small man melted away. Morgan frowned. There had been something in the exchange that wasn't quite what it should be. Shaking her head, she watched Nick mix drinks. It wasn't Nick's relationship with his servants that she was interested in.

Deciding that plunging head first was the most direct route, Morgan leaped. "What were you doing on the beach the other night?"

"I rather thought we'd concluded I was assaulting you." His voice was very mild.

"That was only part of the evening's entertainment." She swallowed and took another dive. "Had you been smuggling?"

To his credit, Nick hesitated only briefly. As his back was to her, Morgan didn't see his expression range from surprise to consideration. A very sharp lady, he mused. Too damn sharp.

"And how did you come by such an astonishing conclusion?" He turned to hand her a delicate glass.

"Don't start that charade with me," Morgan fumed, snatching the glass. "I've seen you stripped." She sat down and aimed a level stare.

Nick's mouth twitched. "What a fascinating way you have of putting things."

"I asked if you were a smuggler."

Nick sat across from her, taking a long study of her face as he ticked off possibilities. "First, tell me why you think I might be."

"You'd been out on the water that night. I could smell the sea on you."

Nick gazed down into the liquid in his glass, then sipped. "It's fanciful, to say the least, that my being out on the water equals smuggling."

Morgan ground her teeth at the cool sarcasm and continued. "If you'd been out on a little fishing trip, you'd hardly have dragged me into the trees waving a knife."

"One might argue," he murmured, "that fishing was precisely my occupation."

"The coast of Turkey is very convenient from this part of the island. Alex told me smuggling was a problem."

"Alex?" Nick repeated. There was a quick, almost imperceptible change in his expression. "What was Alex's attitude toward smuggling?"

Morgan hesitated. The question had broken into her well-thought-out interrogation. "He was…resigned, like one accepts the weather."

"I see." Nick swirled his drink as he leaned back. "And did you and Alex discuss the intricacies of the procedure?"

"Of course not!" she snapped, infuriated that he had cleverly turned the interrogation around on her. "Alex would hardly be intimate with such matters. But," she continued, "I think you are."

"Yes, I can see that."

"Well?"

He sent her a mildly amused smile that didn't quite reach his eyes. "Well what?"

"Are you going to deny it?" She wanted him to, Morgan realized with something like a jolt. She very, very badly wanted him to deny it.

Nick considered her for a moment. "If I deny it, you won't believe me. It's easy to see you've already made up your mind." He tilted his head, and now the amusement crept into his eyes. "What will you do if I admit it?"

"I'll turn you over to the police." Morgan took a bold sip of her drink. Nick exploded with laughter.

"Morgan what a sweet, brave child you are." He leaned over to take her hand before she could retort. "You don't know my reputation, but I assure you, the police would think you mad."

"I could prove—"

"What?" he demanded. His eyes were steady on hers, probing. The polished veneer was slowly fading. "You can't prove what you don't know."

"I know that you're not what you pretend to be." Morgan tried to pull her hand from his, but he held it firm. "Or maybe it's more accurate to say you're something you pretend not to be."

Nick watched her in silence, torn between annoyance and admiration. "Whatever I am, whatever I'm not, has nothing to do with you."

"No one wishes more than I that that was the truth."

Battling a new emotion, he sat back and studied her over the rim of his glass. "So your conclusions that I might be involved in smuggling would prompt you to go to the police. That wouldn't be wise."

"It's a matter of what's right." Morgan swallowed, then blurted out what was torturing her mind. "The knife—would you have used it?"

"On you?" he asked, his eyes as expressionless as his voice.

"On anyone."

"A general question can't be given a specific answer."

"Nicholas, for God's sake—"

Nick set down his drink, then steepled his fingers. His expression changed, and his eyes were suddenly dangerous. "If I were everything you seem to think, you're incredibly brave or incredibly foolish to be sitting here discussing it with me."

"I think I'm safe enough," she countered and straightened her shoulders. "Everyone knows where I am."

"I could always dispose of you another time if I considered you an obstacle." Morgan's eyes flickered with momentary fear, quickly controlled. It was one more thing he could admire her for.

"I can take care of myself."

"Can you?" he murmured, then shrugged as his mood shifted again. "Well, in any case, I have no intention of wasting beauty especially when I intend to enjoy its benefits. Your talents could be useful to me."

Her chin shot up. "I have no intention of being your tool. Smuggling opium is a filthy way to make money. It's a far cry from crossing the English Channel with French silks and brandy."

"With mists curling and eye-patched buccaneers?" Nick countered with a smile. "Is that how your practical mind sees it, Morgan?"

She opened her mouth to retort, but found herself smiling. "I refuse to like you, Nicholas."

"You don't have to like me, Morgan. Like is too tame for my tastes in any case." Outwardly relaxed, he picked up his glass again. "Don't you like your drink?"

Without taking her eyes from his, Morgan set it down. "Nicholas, I only want a straight answer—I deserve one. You're perfectly right that I can't go to the police, no matter what you tell me. You really have nothing to fear from me."

Something flashed in his eyes at her final statement, then was quickly banked. He considered his options before he spoke. "I'll tell you this much, I am—concerned with smuggling. I'd be interested to know of any conversations you might hear on the subject."

Frowning, Morgan rose to wander the room. He was making it difficult for her to remember the straight and narrow path of right and wrong. The path took some confusing twists and turns when emotions were involved. Emotions! She brought herself up short. No, no emotions here. She had no feelings toward him.

"Who was with you that night?" Keep to the plan, she told herself. Questions and answers. Save the introspection for later. "You were giving someone orders."

"I thought you were too frightened to notice." Nick sipped at his drink.

"You were speaking to someone," Morgan went on doggedly. "Someone who did precisely what you told him without question. Who?"

Nick weighed the pros and cons before he answered.

With her mind she'd figure it out for herself soon enough. "Stephanos."

"That little old man?" Morgan stopped in front of Nick and stared down. Stephanos was not Morgan's image of a ruthless smuggler.

"That little old man knows the sea like a gardener knows a rose bush." He smiled at her incredulous expression. "He also has the advantage of being loyal. He's been with me since I was a boy."

"How convenient all this is for you." Depressed, Morgan wandered to a window. She was getting her answers, but she discovered they weren't the ones she wanted. "A home on a convenient island, a convenient servant, a convenient business to ease distribution. Who passed by the grove that night whom you wanted to avoid?"

Frightened or not, he thought angrily, she'd been far too observant. "That needn't concern you."

Morgan whirled. "You got me into this, Nicholas. I have a right to know."

"Your rights end where I say they do." He rose as his temper threatened. "Don't push me too far, Morgan. You wouldn't like the results. I've told you all I intend to for now. Be content with it."

She backed away a step, furious with herself for being frightened. He swore at the movement, then gripped her shoulders.

"I have no intention of harming you, damn it. If I had, there's already been ample opportunity. What do you picture?" he demanded, shaking her. "Me cutting your throat or tossing you off a cliff?"

Her eyes were dry and direct, more angry now than frightened. "I don't know what I picture."

Abruptly he realized he was hurting her. Cursing himself, he eased the grip to a caress. He couldn't keep letting her get under his skin this way. He couldn't let it matter what she thought of him. "I don't expect you to trust me," he said calmly. "But use common sense. Your involvement was a matter of circumstance, not design. I don't want to see you hurt, Morgan. That much you can take as the truth."

And that much she believed. Intrigued, she studied his face. "You're a strange man, Nicholas. Somehow, I can't quite see you doing something as base as smuggling opium."

"Intuition, Morgan?" Smiling, Nick tangled his fingers in her hair. It was soft, as he remembered, and tempting. "Are you a woman who believes in her intuition, or in her reason?"

"Nicholas—"

"No. No more questions or I'll have to divert you. I'm very"—a frown hovered, then flashed into a grin—"very susceptible to beauty. You have a remarkable supply. Coupled with a very good mind, the combination is hard to resist." Nick lifted the medal at her throat, examined it, then let it fall before he moved back from her. "Tell me, what do you think of Dorian and Iona?"

"I resent this. I resent all of this." Morgan spun away from him. He shouldn't be allowed to affect her so deeply, so easily, then switch off like a light. "I came to Lesbos to get away from pressures and complications."

"What sort of pressures and complications?"

She turned back to him, eyes hot. "They're my business. I had a life before I went down to that damned beach and ran into you."

"Yes," he murmured and picked up his drink. "I'm sure you did."

"Now, I find myself tossed into the middle of some grade-B thriller. I don't like it."

"It's a pity you didn't stay in bed that night, Morgan." Nick drank deeply, then twirled his glass by the stem. "Maybe I'm Greek enough to say the gods didn't will it so. For the moment your fate's linked with mine and there's nothing either of us can do about it."

She surprised him by laying a hand on his chest. He didn't like the way his heart reacted to the touch. Needs... he couldn't need. Wants were easily satisfied or ignored, but needs ate at a man.

"If you feel that way, why won't you give me a straight answer?"

"I don't choose to." His eyes locked on hers, cementing her to the spot. In them she saw desire—his and a mirror of her own. "Take me for what I am, Morgan."

She dropped her hand. Frightened not of him now, but of herself. "I don't want to take you at all."

"No?" He pulled her close, perversely enjoying her resistance. "Let's see just how quickly I can make a liar of you."

She could taste anger on his mouth, and just as clearly she could taste need. Morgan stopped resisting. The path of right and wrong took a few more confusing twists when she was in his arms. Whoever, whatever he was, she wanted to be held by him.

Her arms wound around his neck to draw him closer. She heard him murmur something against her mouth; the kiss held a savageness, a demand she was answering with equal abandon.

Had this passion always been there, sleeping inside her? It wasn't asleep any longer. The force of it had her clinging to him, had her mouth urgent and hungry against his. Something had opened inside her, letting him pour through. His hands were in her hair, then running down her back in a swift stroke of possession. She arched against him as if daring him to claim her—taunting him to try.

Somehow she knew, as her body fit truly to his, that they would come back to each other, again and again, against their will, against all reason. She might fight it from moment to moment, but there would be a time. The knowledge filled her with hunger and fear.

"Morgan." Her name wrenched from him on a sigh of need. "I want you—by the gods, I want you. Come, stay here with me tonight. Here, where we can be alone."

His mouth was roaming her face. She wanted to agree. Her body was aching to agree to anything—to everything. Yet, she found herself drawing back. "No."

Nick lifted his face. His expression was amused and confident. "Afraid?"

"Yes."

His brows rose at the unexpected honesty, then drew together in frustration. The look in her eyes made it impossible for him to press his advantage. "*Diabolos,* you're an exasperating woman." He strode away and poured more liquor into his glass. "I could toss you over my shoulder, haul you up to the bedroom, and be done with it."

Though her legs were watery, Morgan forced herself to remain standing. "Why don't you?"

He whirled back, furious. She watched as he slowly pulled out the control. "You're more accustomed to a wine and candlelight seduction, I imagine. Soft promises. Soft lies." Nick drank deep, then set down his glass with a bang. "Is that what you want from me?"

"No." Morgan met his fury steadily while her hand reached instinctively for the medal at her throat. "I don't want you to make love to me."

"Don't take me for a fool!" He took a step toward her, then stopped himself. Another step and neither of them would have a choice. "Your body betrays you every time I touch you."

"That has nothing to do with it," she said calmly. "I don't want you to make love to me."

He waited a beat until the desire and frustration could be tamed a bit. "Because you believe I'm an opium smuggler?"

"No," she said, surprising both of them. She felt her strength waver a moment, then told him the truth. "Because I don't want to be one of your amusements."

"I see." Carefully, Nick dipped his hands into his pockets. "I'd better take you back before you discover I find nothing amusing in lovemaking."

A half-hour later, Nick slammed back into the house. His temper was foul. He stalked into the salon, poured himself another drink, and slumped into a chair. Damn the woman, he didn't have the time or patience to deal with her. The need for her was still churning inside him like a pain, sharp and insistent. He took a long swallow of liquor to dull it. Just physical, he told himself. He'd have to find another woman—any other woman—and release some of the tension.

"Ah, you're back." Stephanos entered. He noted the black temper and accepted it without comment. He'd seen it often enough in the past. "The lady is more beautiful than I remembered." Nick's lack of response left him unperturbed. He moved to the bar and poured himself a drink. "How much did you tell her?"

"Only what was necessary. She's sharp and remarkably bold." Nick eyed the liquid in his glass with a scowl. "She accused me flat out of smuggling." At Stephanos's cackle of laughter, Nick drained more liquor. "Your sense of humor eludes me at the moment, old man."

Stephanos only grinned. "Her eyes are sharp—they linger on you." Though Nick made no response, Stephanos's grin remained. "Did you speak to her of Alex?"

"Not at length."

"Is she loyal?"

"To Alex?" Nick frowned into his drink. "Yes, she would be. Where she cares, she'd be loyal." He set down the glass, refusing to give in to the urge to hurl it across the room. "Getting information out of her won't be easy."

"You'll get it nonetheless."

"I wish to hell she'd stayed in bed that night," Nick said savagely.

The gap-toothed grin appeared before Stephanos tossed back the drink in one long swallow. He let out a wheezy sigh of appreciation. "She lingers in your mind. That makes you uncomfortable." He laughed loud and long at Nick's scowl, then sighed again with the effort of it. "Athens is waiting for your call."

"Athens can fry in hell."

Chapter 5

Morgan's frame of mind was as poor as Nick's when she entered the Theoharis villa. Somewhere on the drive back from Nick's she had discovered that what she was feeling wasn't anger. It wasn't fear or even resentment. In a few days Nick had managed to do something Jack hadn't done in all the months she had known him. He'd hurt her.

It had nothing to do with the bruises that were already fading on her arms. This hurt went deeper, and had begun before she had even met him. It had begun when he had chosen the life he was leading.

Nothing to do with me. Nothing to do with me, Morgan told herself again and again. But she slammed the front door as she swept into the cool white hall. Her plans to go immediately to her room before she could snarl at anyone were tossed to the winds by a call and a wave from Dorian.

"Morgan, come join us."

Fixing on a smile, Morgan strolled out to the terrace.

Iona was with him sprawled on a lounge in a hot-pink playsuit that revealed long, shapely legs but covered her arms with white lace cuffs at the wrists. She sent Morgan a languid greeting, then went back to her sulky study of the gulf. Morgan felt the tension hovering in the air and wondered if it had been there before or if she had brought it with her.

"Alex is on a transatlantic call," Dorian told her as he held out a chair. "And Liz is dealing with some domestic crisis in the kitchen."

"Without an interpreter?" Morgan asked. She smiled, telling herself Nick wasn't going to ruin her mood and make her as sulky as Alex's cousin.

"It's ridiculous." Iona gestured for Dorian to light her cigarette. "Liz should simply fire the man. Americans are habitually casual with servants."

"Are they?" Morgan felt her back go up at the slur on her friend and her nationality. "I wouldn't know."

Iona's dark eyes flicked over her briefly. "I don't imagine you've had many dealings with servants."

Before Morgan could retort, Dorian stepped in calmly. "Tell me, Morgan, what did you think of Nick's treasure trove?"

The expression in his eyes asked her to overlook Iona's bad manners, and told her something she'd begun to suspect the night before. He's in love with her, she mused, and felt a stab of pity. With an effort, Morgan relaxed her spine. "It's a wonderful place, like a museum without being regimented or stiff. It must have taken him years to collect all those things."

"Nick's quite a businessman," Dorian commented. Another look passed between him and Morgan. This time she saw it was gratitude. "And, of course, he uses his knowledge and position to secure the best pieces for himself."

"There was a Swiss music box," she remembered. "He said it was over a hundred years old. It played *Für Elise*." Morgan sighed, at ease again. "I'd kill for it."

"Nick's a generous man—when approached in the proper manner." Iona's smile was sharp as a knife. Morgan turned her head and met it.

"I wouldn't know anything about that either," she said coolly. Deliberately, she turned back to Dorian. "I met Nick's cousin earlier this morning."

"Ah, yes, the young poet from America."

"He said he wanders all over this part of the island. I'm thinking of doing the same myself. It's such a simple, peaceful place. I suppose that's why I was so stunned when Alex said there was a problem with smuggling."

Dorian merely smiled as if amused. Iona stiffened. As Morgan watched, the color drained from her face, leaving it strained and cold and anything but beautiful. Surprised by the reaction, Morgan studied her carefully. Why, she's afraid, she realized. Now why would that be?

"A dangerous business," Dorian commented conversationally. Since his eyes were on Morgan, Iona's reaction went unnoticed by him. "But common enough—traditional in fact."

"An odd tradition," Morgan murmured.

"The network of patrols is very large, I'm told, and closely knotted. As I recall, five men were killed last year, gunned down off the Turkish coast." He lit a cigarette of his own. "The authorities confiscated quite a cache of opium."

"How terrible." Morgan noticed that Iona's pallor increased.

"Just peasants and fishermen," he explained with a shrug. "Not enough intelligence between them to have organized a large smuggling ring. It's rumored the leader is brilliant and ruthless. From the stories passed around in the village, he goes along on runs now and then, but wears a mask. Apparently, not even his cohorts know who he is. It might even be a woman." He flashed a grin at the idea. "I suppose that adds an element of romance to the whole business."

Iona rose and dashed from the terrace.

"You must forgive her." Dorian sighed as his eyes followed her. "She's a moody creature."

"She seemed upset."

"Iona's easily upset," he murmured. "Her nerves…"

"You care for her quite a lot."

His gaze came back to lock on Morgan's before he rose and strode to the railing.

"I'm sorry, Dorian," Morgan began immediately. "I didn't mean to pry."

"No, forgive me." He turned back and the sun streamed over his face, gleaming off the bronzed skin, combing through his burnished gold hair. Adonis, Morgan thought again, and for the second time since she had come to Lesbos wished she could paint. "My feelings for Iona are… difficult and, I had thought, more cleverly concealed."

"I'm sorry," Morgan said again, helplessly.

"She's spoiled, willful." With a laugh, Dorian shook

his head. "What is it that makes one person lose his heart to another?"

Morgan looked away at the question. "I don't know. I wish I did."

"Now I've made you sad." Dorian sat back down beside Morgan and took her hands. "Don't pity me. Sooner or later, what's between Iona and me will be resolved. I'm a patient man." He smiled then, his eyes gleaming with confidence. "For now, we'll talk of something else. I have to confess, I'm fascinated by the smuggling legends."

"Yes. It is interesting. You said the rumor is that no one, not even the men who work for him, know who the leader is."

"That's the story. Whenever I'm on Lesbos, I keep hoping to stumble across some clue that would unmask him."

Morgan murmured something as her thoughts turned uncomfortably to Nick. "Yet you don't seem terribly concerned about the smuggling itself."

"Ah, the smuggling." Dorian moved his shoulders. "That's something for the authorities to worry about. But the thrill of the hunt, Morgan." His eyes gleamed as they moved past her. "The thrill of the hunt."

"You wouldn't believe it!" Liz bustled out and plopped into a chair. "A half-hour with a temperamental Greek cook. I'd rather face a firing squad. Give me a cigarette, Dorian." Her smile and everyday complaint made the subject of smuggling absurd. "So tell me, Morgan, how did you like Nick's house?"

Pink streaks joined sky and sea as dawn bloomed. The air was warm and moist. After a restless night, it was the best of beginnings.

Morgan strolled along the water's edge and listened to the first serenading of birds. This was the way she had planned to spend her vacation—strolling along the beach, watching sunrises, relaxing. Isn't that what her father and Liz had drummed into her head?

Relax, Morgan. Get off the treadmill for a while. You never give yourself any slack.

She could almost laugh at the absurdity. But then, neither Liz nor her father had counted on Nicholas Gregoras.

He was an enigma, and she couldn't find the key. His involvement in smuggling was like a piece of a jigsaw puzzle that wouldn't quite fit. Morgan had never been able to tolerate half-finished puzzles. She scuffed her sandals in the sand. He was simply not a man she could categorize, and she wanted badly to shake the need to try.

On the other hand, there was Iona. Morgan saw the puzzle there as well. Alex's sulky cousin was more than a woman with an annoying personality. There was some inner agitation—something deep and firmly rooted. And *Alex knows something of it,* she mused. *Dorian, too, unless she missed her guess.* But what? And how much? Iona's reaction to talk of smuggling had been a sharp contrast to both Alex's and Dorian's. They'd been resigned—even amused. Iona had been terrified. Terrified of discovery? Morgan wondered. But that was absurd.

Shaking her head, Morgan pushed the thought aside. This morning she was going to do what she had come to Greece to do. Nothing. At least, nothing strenuous. She was going to look for shells, she decided, and after rolling up the hem of her jeans, splashed into a shallow inlet.

They were everywhere. The bank of sand and the shallow water were glistening with them. Some had been crushed underfoot or beaten smooth by the slow current. Crouching, she stuffed the pockets of her jacket with the best of them.

She noticed the stub of a black cigarette half-buried in the sand. So, Alex comes this way, she thought with a smile. Morgan could see Liz and her husband strolling hand in hand through the shallows.

As the sun grew higher, Morgan became more engrossed. If only I'd brought a tote, she thought, then shrugged and began to pile shells in a heap to retrieve later. She'd have them in a bowl on her windowsill at home. Then, whenever she was trapped indoors on a cold, rainy afternoon, she could look at them and remember Greek sunshine.

There were dozens of gulls. They flapped around her, circled, and called out. Morgan found the high, piercing sound the perfect company for a solitary morning. As the time passed, she began to find that inner peace she had experienced so briefly on the moonlit beach.

The hunt had taken her a good distance from the beach. Glancing up, she saw, with pleasure, the mouth of a cave. It wasn't large and was nearly hidden from view, but she thought it was entitled to an exploration. With a frown for her white jeans, Morgan decided to take a peek inside the entrance and come back when she was more suitably dressed. She moved to it with the water sloshing up to her calves. Bending down, she tugged another shell from its bed of sand. As her gaze swept over toward the cave, her hand froze.

The face glistened white in the clear water. Dark eyes

stared back at her. Her scream froze in her throat, locked there by terror. She had never seen death before—not unpampered, staring death. Morgan stepped back jerkily, nearly slipping on a rock. As she struggled to regain her balance, her stomach heaved up behind the scream so that she could only gag. Even through the horror, she could feel the pressure of dizziness. She couldn't faint, not here, not with that only a foot away. She turned and fled.

She scrambled and spilled over rocks and sand. The only clear thought in her head was to get away. On a dead run, breath ragged, she broke from the concealment of the inlet out to the sickle of beach.

Hands gripped her. Blindly, Morgan fought against them with the primitive fear that the thing in the inlet had risen up and come after her.

"Stop it! Damn it, I'll end up hurting you again. Morgan, stop this. What's wrong with you?"

She was being shaken roughly. The voice pierced the first layer of shock. She stared and saw Nick's face. "Nicholas?" The dizziness was back and she went limp against him as waves of fear and nausea wracked her. Trembling, she couldn't stop the trembling, but knew she'd be safe now. He was there. "Nicholas," she managed again as though his name alone was enough to shield her.

Nick caught her tighter and shook her again. Her face was deathly pale, her skin clammy. He'd seen enough of horror to recognize it in her eyes. In a moment, he knew, she'd faint or be hysterical. He couldn't allow either.

"What happened?" he demanded in a voice that commanded an answer.

Morgan opened her mouth, but found she could only

shake her head. She buried her face against his chest in an attempt to block out what she had seen. Her breath was still ragged, coming in dry sobs that wouldn't allow for words. She'd be safe now, she told herself as she fought the panic. He'd keep her safe.

"Pull yourself together, Morgan," Nick ordered curtly, "and tell me what happened."

"Can't…" She tried to burrow herself into him.

In one quick move he jerked her away, shaking her. "I said tell me." His voice was cold, emotionless. He knew only one way to deal with hysteria, and her breath was still rising in gasps.

Dazed by the tone of his voice, she tried again, then jolted, clinging to him when she heard the sound of footsteps.

"Hello. Am I intruding?" Andrew's cheerful voice came from behind her, but she didn't look back. The trembling wouldn't stop.

Why was he angry with her? Why wasn't he helping her? The questions whirled in her head as she tried to catch her breath. Oh, God, she needed him to help her.

"Is something wrong?" Andrew's tone mirrored both concern and curiosity as he noted Nick's black expression and Morgan's shaking form.

"I'm not sure." Nick forced himself not to curse his cousin and spoke briefly. "Morgan was running across the beach. I haven't been able to get anything out of her yet." He drew her away, his fingers digging roughly in her skin as she tried to hold firm. She saw nothing in his face but cool curiosity. "Now, Morgan"—there was an edge of steel now—"tell me."

"Over there." Her teeth began to chatter as the next stage of reaction set in. Swallowing, she clamped them together while her eyes pleaded with him. His remained hard and relentless on hers. "Near the cove." The effort of the two short sentences swam in her head. She leaned toward him again. "Nicholas, please."

"I'll have a look." He grabbed her arms, dragging them away from him, wishing he didn't see what she was asking of him—knowing he couldn't give it to her.

"Don't leave, please!" Desperate, she grabbed for him again only to be shoved roughly into Andrew's arms.

"Damn it, get her calmed down," Nick bit off, tasting his own fury. She had no right—no right to ask for things he couldn't give. He had no right—no right to want to give them to her. He swore again, low and pungent under his breath as he turned away.

"Nicholas!" Morgan struggled out of Andrew's arms, but Nick was already walking away. She pressed a hand to her mouth to stop herself from calling him again. He never looked back.

Arms encircled her. Not Nick's. She could feel the gentle comfort of Andrew as he drew her against his chest. Her fingers gripped his sweater. Not Nick. "Here now." Andrew brought a hand to her hair. "I had hoped to entice you into this position under different circumstances."

"Oh, Andrew." The soft words and tender stroking had the ice of shock breaking into tears. "Andrew, it was so horrible."

"Tell me what happened, Morgan. Say it fast. It'll be easier then." His tone was quiet and coaxing as he stroked her hair. Morgan gave a shuddering sigh.

"There's a body at the mouth of the cave."

"A body!" He drew her back to stare into her face. "Good God! Are you sure?"

"Yes, yes, I saw—I was…" She covered her face with her hands a moment until she thought she could speak.

"Easy, take it easy," he murmured. "And let it come out."

"I was collecting shells in the inlet. I saw the cave. I was going to peek inside, then I…" She shuddered once, then continued. "Then I saw the face—under the water."

"Oh, Morgan." He drew her into his arms again and held her tight. He didn't say any more, but in silence gave her everything she had needed. When the tears stopped, he kept her close.

Nick moved rapidly across the sand. His frown deepened as he saw Morgan molded in his cousin's arms. As he watched, Andrew bent down to kiss her hair. A small fire leaped inside him that he smothered quickly.

"Andrew, take Morgan up to the Theoharis villa and phone the authorities. One of the villagers has had a fatal accident."

Nodding, Andrew continued to stroke Morgan's hair. "Yes, she told me. Terrible that she had to find it." He swallowed what seemed to be his own revulsion. "Are you coming?"

Nick looked down as Morgan turned her face to his. He hated the look in her eyes as she stared at him—the blankness, the hurt. She wouldn't forgive him easily for this. "No, I'll stay and make sure no one else happens across it. Morgan…" He touched her shoulders, detesting himself. There was no response, her eyes were dry now, and empty. "You'll be all right. Andrew will take you home."

Without a word, Morgan turned her face away again.

His control slipped a bit as Nick shot Andrew a hard glance. "Take care of her."

"Of course," Andrew murmured, puzzled by the tone. "Come on, Morgan, lean on me."

Nick watched them mount the beach steps. When they were out of sight, he went back to search the body.

Seated in the salon, her horror dulled with Alex's best brandy, Morgan studied Captain Tripolos of Mitilini's police department. He was short, with his build spreading into comfortable lines that stopped just short of fat. His gray hair was carefully slicked to conceal its sparseness. His eyes were dark and sharp. Through the haze of brandy and shock, Morgan recognized a man with the tenacity of a bulldog.

"Miss James." The captain spoke in quick, staccato English. "I hope you understand, I must ask you some questions. It is routine."

"Couldn't it wait?" Andrew was stationed next to Morgan on the sofa. As he spoke he slipped an arm around her shoulders. "Miss James has had a nasty shock."

"No, Andrew, it's all right." Morgan laid her hand over his. "I'd rather be done with it. I understand, Captain." She gave him a straight look which he admired. "I'll tell you whatever I can."

"Efxaristo." He licked the end of his pencil, settled himself in his chair, and smiled with his mouth only.

"Perhaps you could start by telling me exactly what happened this morning, from the time you arose."

Morgan began to recount the morning as concisely as she could. She spoke mechanically, with her hands limp and still in her lap. Though her voice trembled once or twice, Tripolos noted that her eyes stayed on his. She was a strong one, he decided, relieved that she wasn't putting him to the inconvenience of tears or jumbled hysterics.

"Then I saw him under the water." Morgan accepted Andrew's hand with gratitude. "I ran."

Tripolos nodded. "You were up very early. Is this your habit?"

"No. But I woke up and had an impulse to walk on the beach."

"Did you see anyone?"

"No." A shudder escaped, but her gaze didn't falter. She went up another notch in Tripolos's admiration. "Not until Nicholas and Andrew."

"Nicholas? Ah, Mr. Gregoras." He shifted his eyes to where Nick sprawled on a sofa across the room with Alex and Liz. "Had you ever seen the…deceased before?"

"No." Her hand tightened convulsively on Andrew's as the white face floated in front of her eyes. With a desperate effort of will, she forced the image away. "I've only been here a few days and I haven't been far from the villa yet."

"You're visiting from America?"

"Yes."

He made a quiet cluck of sympathy. "What a pity a murder had to blight your vacation."

"Murder?" Morgan repeated. The word echoed in

her head as she stared into Tripolos's calm eyes. "But I thought...wasn't it an accident?"

"No." Tripolos glanced idly down at his notepad. "No, the victim was stabbed—in the back," he added with distaste. It was as if he considered murder one matter and back-stabbing another. "I hope I won't have to disturb you again." He rose and bowed over her hand. "Did you find many shells this morning, Miss James?"

"Yes I—I gathered quite a few." She felt compelled to reach in her jacket pocket and produce some. "I thought they were...lovely."

"Yes." He smiled, then turned to the others. "I regret we will have to question everyone on their whereabouts from last evening to this morning. Of course," he continued with a shrug, "we will no doubt find the murder was a result of a village quarrel, but with the body found so close to both villas..." He trailed off as he pocketed his pad and pencil. "One of you might recall some small incident that will help settle the matter."

Settle the matter? Morgan thought on a wave of hysteria. Settle the matter. But a man's dead. I'm dreaming. I must be dreaming.

"Easy, Morgan," Andrew whispered in her ear. "Have another sip." Gently, he urged the brandy back to her lips.

"You have our complete cooperation, Captain," Alex stated, and rose. "It isn't pleasant for any of us to have such a thing happen so near our homes. It's particularly upsetting that a guest of mine should have found the man."

"I understand, of course." Tripolos nodded wearily, rubbing a hand over his square chin. "It would be less confusing if I spoke with you one at a time. Perhaps we could use your office?"

"I'll show you where it is." Alex gestured to the door. "You can speak to me first if you like."

"Thank you." Tripolos gave the room a general bow before retreating behind Alex. Morgan watched his slow, measured steps. He'd haunt a man to the grave, she thought, and shakily swallowed the rest of the brandy.

"I need a drink," Liz announced, moving toward the liquor cabinet. "A double. Anyone else?"

Nick's eyes skimmed briefly over Morgan. "Whatever you're having." He gestured with his hand, signaling Liz to refill Morgan's glass.

"I don't see why he has to question us." Iona moved to the bar, too impatient to wait for Liz to pour. "It's absurd. Alex should have refused. He has enough influence to avoid all of this." She poured something potent into a tall glass and drank half of it down.

"There's no reason for Alex to avoid anything." Liz handed Nick his drink before splashing another generous portion of brandy into Morgan's glass. "We have nothing to hide. What can I fix you, Dorian?"

"Hide? I said nothing about hiding," Iona retorted as she swirled around the room. "I don't want to answer that policeman's silly questions just because *she* was foolish enough to stumble over some villager's body," she said, gesturing toward Morgan.

"A glass of ouzo will be fine, Liz," Dorian stated before Liz could fire a retort. His gaze lit on Iona. "I hardly think we can blame Morgan, Iona. We'd have been questioned in any case. As it is, she's had to deal with finding the man as well as the questions. Thank you, Liz," he added as she placed a glass in his hand and shot him a grim smile.

"I cannot stay in this house today." Iona prowled the room, her movements as jerky as a nervous finger on a trigger. "Nicky, let's go out in your boat." She stopped and dropped to the arm of his chair.

"The timing's bad, Iona. When I'm finished here, I have paperwork to clear up at home." He sipped his drink and patted her hand. His eyes met Morgan's briefly, but long enough to recognize condemnation. Damn you, he thought furiously, you have no right to make me feel guilty for doing what I have to do.

"Oh, Nicky." Iona's hand ran up his arm. "I'll go mad if I stay here today. Please, a few hours on the sea?"

Nick sighed in capitulation while inside he fretted against a leash that was too long, and too strong, for him to break. He had reason to agree, and couldn't let Morgan's blank stare change the course he'd already taken. "All right, later this afternoon."

Iona smiled into her drink.

The endless questioning continued. Liz slipped out as Alex came back in. And the waiting went on. Conversation came in fits and starts, conducted in undertones. As Andrew left the room for his conference, Nick wandered to Morgan's new station by the window.

"I want to talk to you." His tone was quiet, with the steel under it. When he put his hand over hers, she jerked it away.

"I don't want to talk to you."

Deliberately, he slipped his hands into his pockets. She

was still pale. The brandy had steadied her but hadn't brought the color back to her cheeks. "It's necessary, Morgan. At the moment, I haven't the opportunity to argue about it."

"That's your problem."

"We'll go for a drive when the captain's finished. You need to get away from here for a while."

"I'm not going anywhere with you. Don't tell me what I need now." She kept her teeth clamped and spoke without emotion. "I needed you then."

"Damn it, Morgan." His muttered oath had all the power of a shout. She kept her eyes firmly on Liz's garden. Some of the roses, she thought dispassionately, were overblown now. The hands in his pockets were fists, straining impotently. "Don't you think I know that? Don't you think I—" He cut himself off before he lost control. "I couldn't give you what you needed—not then. Don't make this any more impossible for me than it is."

She turned to him now, meeting his fury with frost. "I have no intention of doing that." Her voice was as low as his but with none of his vibrating emotion. "The simple fact is I don't want anything from you now. I don't want anything to do with you."

"Morgan…" There was something in his eyes now that threatened to crack her resolve. Apology, regret, a plea for understanding where she'd never expected to see one. "Please, I need—"

"I don't care what you need," she said quickly, before he could weaken her again. "Just stay away from me. Stay completely away from me."

"Tonight," he began, but the cold fury in her eyes stopped him.

"Stay away," Morgan repeated.

She turned her back on him and walked across the room to join Dorian. Nick was left with black thoughts and the inability to carry them out.

Chapter 6

Morgan was surprised she'd slept. She hadn't been tired when Liz and Alex had insisted she lie down, but had obeyed simply because her last words with Nick had sapped all of her resistance. Now as she woke she saw it was past noon. She'd slept for two hours.

Groggy, heavy-eyed, Morgan walked into the bath to splash cool water on her face. The shock had passed, but the nap had brought her a lingering weariness instead of refreshment. Beneath it all was a deep shame—shame that she had run, terrified, from a dead man. Shame that she had clung helplessly to Nick and been turned away. She could feel even now that sensation of utter dependence—and utter rejection.

Never again, Morgan promised herself. She should have trusted her head instead of her heart. She should have known better than to ask or expect anything from a man like him. A man like him had nothing to give. You'd always find hell if you looked to a devil. And yet...

And yet it had been Nick she had needed, and trusted—him she had felt safe with the moment his arms had come around her. My mistake, Morgan thought grimly, and studied herself in the mirror over the basin. There were still some lingering signs of shock—the pale cheeks and too wide eyes, but she felt the strength returning.

"I don't need him," she said aloud, wanting to hear the words. "He doesn't mean anything to me."

But he's hurt you. Someone who doesn't matter can't hurt you.

I won't let him hurt me again, Morgan promised herself. Because I won't ever go to him again, I won't ever ask him again, no matter what.

She turned away from her reflection and went downstairs.

Even as she entered the main hall, Morgan heard the sound of a door closing and footsteps. Glancing behind her, she saw Dorian.

"So, you've rested." He came to her and took her hand. In the gesture was all the comfort and concern she could have asked for.

"Yes. I feel like a fool." At his lifted brow, Morgan moved her shoulders restlessly. "Andrew all but carried me back up here."

With a low laugh, he slipped an arm around her shoulders and led her into the salon. "You American women—do you always have to be strong and self-reliant?"

"I always have been." She remembered weeping in Nick's arms—clinging, pleading—and straightened her spine. "I have to depend on myself."

"I admire you for it. But then, you don't make a habit

of stumbling over dead bodies." He cast a look at her pale cheeks and gentled his tone. "There, it was foolish of me to remind you. Shall I fix you another drink?"

"No— No, I've enough brandy in me as it is." Morgan managed a thin smile and moved away from him.

Why was it she was offered a supporting arm by everyone but the one who mattered? No, Nick couldn't matter, she reminded herself. She couldn't let him matter, and she didn't need a supporting arm from anyone.

"You seem restless, Morgan. Would you rather be alone?"

"No." She shook her head as she looked up. His eyes were calm. She'd never seen them otherwise. There'd be strength in him, she thought, and wished bleakly it had been Dorian she had run to that morning. Going to the piano, she ran a finger over the keys. "I'm glad the captain's gone. He made me nervous."

"Tripolos?" Dorian drew out his cigarette case. "I doubt he's anything to worry about. I doubt even the killer need worry," he added with a short laugh. "The Mitilini police force isn't known for its energy or brilliance."

"You sound as if you don't care if the person who killed that man is caught."

"Village quarrels mean nothing to me," he countered. "I'm concerned more with the people I know. I don't like to think you're worried about Tripolos."

"He doesn't worry me," she corrected, frowning as he lit a cigarette. Something was nagging at the back of her mind, struggling to get through. "He just has a way of looking at you while he sits there, comfortable and not quite tidy." She watched the column of smoke curl up from the tip of the long, black cigarette. With an effort,

Morgan shook off the feeling of something important, half remembered. "Where is everyone?"

"Liz is with Alex in his office. Iona's gone on her boat ride."

"Oh, yes, with Nicholas." Morgan looked down at her hands, surprised that they had balled into fists. Deliberately, she opened them. "It must be difficult for you."

"She needed to escape. The atmosphere of death is hard on her nerves."

"You're very understanding." Disturbed and suddenly headachy, Morgan wandered to the window. "I don't think I would be—if I were in love."

"I'm patient, and I know that Nick means less than nothing to her. A means to an end." He paused for a moment, before he spoke again, thoughtfully. "Some people have no capacity for emotion—love or hate."

"How empty that would be," Morgan murmured.

"Do you think so?" He gave her an odd smile. "Somehow, I think it would be comfortable."

"Yes, comfortable perhaps but…" Morgan trailed off as she turned back. Dorian was just lifting the cigarette to his lips. As Morgan's eyes focused on it, she remembered, with perfect clarity, seeing the stub of one of those expensive brands in the sand, only a few yards from the body. A chill shot through her as she continued to stare.

"Morgan, is something wrong?" Dorian's voice broke through so that she blinked and focused on him again.

"No, I—I suppose I'm not myself yet. Maybe I'll have that drink after all."

She didn't want it, but needed a moment to pull her thoughts together. The stub of a cigarette didn't have to mean anything, she told herself as Dorian went to the bar. Anyone from the villa could have wandered through that inlet a dozen times.

But the stub had been fresh, Morgan remembered—half in, half out of the sand, unweathered. The birds hadn't picked at it. Surely if someone had been that close to the body, they would have seen. They would have seen, and they would have gone to the police. Unless…

No, that was a ridiculous thought, she told herself as she felt a quick tremor. It was absurd to think that Dorian might have had anything to do with a villager's murder. Dorian or Alex, she thought as that sweet, foreign smoke drifted over her.

They were both civilized men—civilized men didn't stab other men in the back. Both of them had such beautiful, manicured hands and careful manners. Didn't it take something evil, something cold and hard to kill? She thought of Nick and shook her head. No, she wouldn't think of him now. She'd concentrate on this one small point and work it through to the end.

It didn't make any sense to consider Dorian or Alex as killers. They were businessmen, cultured. What possible dealings could they have had with some local fisherman? It was an absurd thought, Morgan told herself, but couldn't quite shake the unease that was creeping into her. There'd be a logical explanation, she insisted. There was always a logical explanation. She was still upset, that was all. Blowing some minor detail out of proportion.

Whose footsteps were on the beach steps that first night? a small voice insisted. Who was Nick hiding from? Or waiting for? That man hadn't been killed in a village quarrel, her thoughts ran on. She hadn't believed it for a moment, any more than she'd really believed the man had died accidentally. Murder...smuggling. Morgan closed her eyes and shuddered.

Who was coming in from the sea when Nick had held her in the shadow of the cypress? Nick had ordered Stephanos to follow him. Alex? Dorian? The dead man perhaps? She jolted when Dorian offered her the snifter.

"Morgan, you're still so pale. You should sit."

"No... I guess I'm still a little jumpy, that's all." Morgan cupped the snifter in both hands but didn't drink. She would ask him, that was all. She would simply ask him if he'd been to the inlet. But when her eyes met his, so calm, so concerned, she felt an icy tremor of fear. "The inlet—" Morgan hesitated, then continued before her courage failed her. "The inlet was so beautiful. It seemed so undisturbed." But so many shells had been crushed underfoot, she remembered abruptly. Why hadn't she thought of that before? "Do you—do a lot of people go there?"

"I can't speak for the villagers," Dorian began, watching as she perched on the arm of a divan. "But I'd think most of them would be too busy with their fishing or in the olive groves to spend much time gathering shells."

"Yes." She moistened dry lips. "But still, it's a lovely spot, isn't it?"

Morgan kept her eyes on his. Was it her imagination, or had his eyes narrowed? A trick of the smoke that wafted between them? Her own nerves?

"I've never been there," Dorian said lightly. "I suppose it's a bit like a native New Yorker never going to the top of the Empire State Building." Morgan's gaze followed his fingers as he crushed out the cigarette in a cut-glass ashtray. "Is there something else, Morgan?"

"Something—no." Hastily, she looked back up to meet his eyes. "No, nothing. I suppose like Iona, the atmosphere's getting to me, that's all."

"Small wonder." Sympathetic, he crossed to her. "You've been through too much today, Morgan. Too much talk of death. Come out in the garden," he suggested. "We'll talk of something else."

Refusal was on the tip of her tongue. She didn't know why, only that she didn't want to be with him. Not then. Not alone. Even as she cast around for a reasonable excuse, Liz joined them.

"Morgan, I'd hoped you were resting."

Grateful for the interruption, Morgan set down her untouched brandy and rose. "I rested long enough." A quick scan of Liz's face showed subtle signs of strain. "You look like you should lie down awhile."

"No, but I could use some air."

"I was just taking Morgan out to the garden." Dorian touched a hand to Liz's shoulder. "You two go out and relax. Alex and I have some business we should clear up."

"Yes." Liz lifted her hand to his. "Thank you, Dorian. I don't know what Alex or I would have done without you today."

"Nonsense." He brushed her cheek with his lips. "Go, take your mind off this business."

"I will. See if you can get Alex to do the same." The plea was light, but unmistakable before Liz hooked her arm through Morgan's.

"Dorian." Morgan felt a flush of shame. He'd been nothing but kind to her, and she'd let her imagination run wild. "Thank you."

He lifted a brow at the gratitude, then smiled and kissed her cheek in turn. He smelt of citrus groves and sunshine. "Sit with the flowers for a while, and enjoy."

As he walked into the hall, Liz turned and headed toward the garden doors. "Should I order us some tea?"

"Not for me. And stop treating me like a guest."

"Good Lord, was I doing that?"

"Yes, ever since—"

Liz shot Morgan a quick look as she broke off, then grimaced. "This whole business really stinks," Liz stated inelegantly, and plopped down on a marble bench.

Surrounded by the colors and scents of the garden, isolated from the house and the outside world by vines, Morgan and Liz frowned at each other.

"Damn, Morgan, I'm so sorry that you had to be the one. No, don't shrug and try to look casual," she ordered as Morgan did just that. "We've known each other too long and too well. I know what it must have been like for you this morning. And I know how you must be feeling right now."

"I'm all right, Liz." She chose a small padded glider and curled her legs under her. "Though I'll admit I won't be admiring seashells for a while. Please," she continued as Liz's frown deepened. "Don't do this. I can see that you and Alex are blaming yourselves. It was just—just a horrible coincidence that I happened to take a tour of that inlet this morning. A man was killed; someone had to find him."

"It didn't have to be you."

"You and Alex aren't responsible."

Liz sighed. "My practical American side knows that, but…" She shrugged, then managed to smile. "But I think I'm becoming a bit Greek. You're staying in my house." Liz lit a cigarette resignedly as she rose to pace the tiny courtyard.

A black cigarette, Morgan noticed with a tremor of anxiety—slim and black. She'd forgotten Liz had picked up the habit of occasionally smoking one of Alex's brand.

She stared up into Liz's oval, classic face, then shut her eyes. She must be going mad if she could conceive, even for an instant, that Liz was mixed up in smuggling and back-stabbing. This was a woman she'd known for years—lived with. Certainly if there was one person she knew as well as she knew herself, it was Liz.

But how far—how far would Liz go to protect the man she loved?

"And I have to admit," Liz went on as she continued to pace, "though it sticks me in the same category as Iona, that policeman made me nervous. He was just too"—she searched for an adjective—"respectful," she decided. "Give me a good old American grilling."

"I know what you mean," Morgan murmured. She had to stop thinking, she told herself. If she could just stop thinking, everything would be all right again.

"I don't know what he expected to find out, questioning us that way." Liz took a quick, jerky puff, making her wedding ring flash with cold, dazzling light.

"It was just routine, I suppose." Morgan couldn't take

her eyes from the ring—the light, the stones. Love, honor, and obey—forsaking all others.

"And creepy," Liz added. "Besides, none of us even knew this Anthony Stevos."

"The captain said he was a fisherman."

"So is every second man in the village."

Morgan allowed the silence to hang. Carefully, she reconstructed the earlier scene in the salon. What were the reactions? If she hadn't been so dimmed with brandy and shock, would she have noticed something? There was one more person she'd seen lighting one of the expensive cigarettes. "Liz," she began slowly, "don't you think Iona went a little overboard? Didn't she get a bit melodramatic about a few routine questions?"

"Iona thrives on melodrama," Liz returned with grim relish. "Did you see the way she fawned all over Nick? I don't see how he could bear it."

"He didn't seem to mind," Morgan muttered. No, not yet, she warned herself. You're not ready to deal with that yet. "She's a strange woman," Morgan continued. "But this morning…" And yesterday, she remembered. "Yesterday when I spoke of smuggling… I think she was really afraid."

"I don't think Iona has any genuine feelings," Liz said stubbornly. "I wish Alex would just cross her off as a bad bet and be done with it. He's so infuriatingly conscientious."

"Strange, Dorian said almost the same thing." Morgan plucked absently at an overblown rose. It was Iona she should concentrate on. If anyone could do something deadly and vile, it was Iona. "I don't see her that way."

"What do you mean?"

"Iona." Morgan stopped plucking at the rose and gave Liz her attention. "I see her as a woman of too many feelings rather than none at all. Not all healthy certainly, perhaps even destructive—but strong, very strong emotions."

"I can't abide her," Liz said with such unexpected venom, Morgan stared. "She upsets Alex constantly. I can't tell you how much time and trouble and money he's put into that woman. And he gets nothing back but ingratitude, rudeness."

"Alex has very strong family feelings," Morgan began. "You can't protect him from—"

"I'd protect him from anything," Liz interrupted passionately. "Anything and anyone." Whirling, she hurled her cigarette into the bushes where it lay smoldering. Morgan found herself staring at it with dread. "Damn," Liz said in a calmer tone. "I'm letting all this get to me."

"We all are." Morgan shook off the sensation of unease and rose. "It hasn't been an easy morning."

"I'm sorry, Morgan, it's just that Alex is so upset by all this. And as much as he loves me, he just isn't the kind of man to share certain areas with me. His trouble—his business. He's too damn Greek." With a quick laugh, she shook her head. "Come on, sit down. I've vented my spleen."

"Liz, if there were something wrong—I mean, something really troubling you, you'd tell me, wouldn't you?"

"Oh, don't start worrying about me now." Liz nudged Morgan back down on the glider. "It's just frustrating when you love someone to distraction and they won't let you help. Sometimes it drives me crazy that Alex insists on trying to keep the less-pleasant aspects of his life away from me."

"He loves you," Morgan murmured and found she was gripping her hands together.

"And I love him."

"Liz…" Morgan took a deep breath and plunged. "Do you and Alex walk through the inlet often?"

"Hmmm?" Obviously distracted, Liz looked back over her shoulder as she walked toward her bench. "Oh, no, actually, we usually walk on the cliffs—if I can drag him away from his office. I can't think when's the last time I've been near there. I only wish," she added in a gentler tone, "I'd been with you this morning."

Abruptly and acutely ashamed at the direction her thoughts had taken, Morgan looked away. "I'm glad you weren't. Alex had his hands full enough with one hysterical female."

"You weren't hysterical," Liz corrected in a quiet voice. "You were almost too calm by the time Andrew brought you in."

"I never even thanked him." Morgan forced herself to push doubts and suspicions aside. They were as ugly as they were ridiculous. "What did you think of Andrew?"

"He's a very sweet man." Sensing Morgan's changing mood, Liz adjusted her own thoughts. "He appeared to put himself in the role of your champion today." She smiled, deliberately looking wise and matronly. "I'd say he was in the first stages of infatuation."

"How smug one becomes after three years of marriage."

"He'd be a nice diversion for you," Liz mused, unscathed. "But he's from the genteel-poor side of Nick's family. I rather fancy seeing you set up in style. Then again," she continued as Morgan sighed, "he'd be nice company for you...for a while."

Dead on cue, Andrew strolled into the courtyard. "Hello. I hope I'm not intruding."

"Why, no!" Liz gave him a delighted smile. "Neighboring poets are always welcome."

He grinned, a flash of boyishness. With that, he went up several notches on Liz's list. "Actually, I was worried about Morgan." Bending over, he cupped her chin and studied her. "It was such an awful morning, I wanted to see how you were doing. I hope you don't mind." His eyes were dark blue, like the water in the bay—and with the same serenity.

"I don't." She touched the back of his hand. "At all. I'm really fine. I was just telling Liz I hadn't even thanked you for everything you did."

"You're still pale."

His concern made her smile. "A New York winter has something to do with that."

"Determined to be courageous?" he asked with a tilted smile.

"Determined to do a better job of it than I did this morning."

"I kind of liked the way you held on to me." He gave her hand a light squeeze. "I want to steal her for an evening," he told Liz, shifting his gaze from Morgan's face. "Can you help me convince her a diversion is what she needs?"

"You have my full support."

"Come have dinner with me in the village." He bent down to Morgan again. "Some local color, a bottle of ouzo, and a witty companion. What more could you ask for?"

"What a marvelous idea!" Liz warmed to Andrew and the scheme. "It's just what you need, Morgan."

Amused, Morgan wondered if she should just let them pat each other on the back for a while. But it was what she needed—to get away from the house and the doubts. She smiled at Andrew. "What time should I be ready?"

His grin flashed again. "How about six? I'll give you a tour of the village. Nick gave me carte blanche with his Fiat while I'm here, so you won't have to ride on an ass."

Because her teeth were tight again, Morgan relaxed her jaw. "I'll be ready."

The sun was high over the water when Nick set his boat toward the open sea. He gave it plenty of throttle, wanting the speed and the slap of the wind.

Damn the woman! he thought on a new surge of frustration. Seething, he tossed the butt of a slender black cigarette into the churning waves. If she'd stay in bed instead of wandering on beaches at ridiculous hours, all of this could have been avoided. The memory of the plea in her voice, the horror in her eyes flashed over him. He could still feel the way she had clung to him, needing him.

He cursed her savagely and urged more speed from the motor.

Shifting his thoughts, Nick concentrated on the dead man. Anthony Stevos, he mused, scowling into the sun. He knew the fisherman well enough—what he had occasionally fished for—and the Athens phone number he had found deep inside Stevos's pants pocket.

Stevos had been a stupid, greedy man, Nick thought dispassionately. Now he was a dead one. How long would it take Tripolos to rule out the village brawl and hit on the truth? Not long enough, Nick decided. He was going to have to bring matters to a head a bit sooner than he had planned.

"Nicky, why are you looking so mean?" Iona called to him over the motor's roar. Automatically, he smoothed his features.

"I was thinking about that pile of paperwork on my desk." Nick cut the motor off and let the boat drift in its own wake. "I shouldn't have let you talk me into taking the afternoon off."

Iona moved to where he sat. Her skin glistened, oiled slick, against a very brief bikini. Her bosom spilled over in invitation. She had a ripe body, rounded and full and arousing. Nick felt no stir as she swung her hips moving toward him.

"*Agapetikos,* we'll have to take your mind off business matters." She wound herself into his lap and pressed against him.

He kissed her mechanically, knowing that, after the bottle of champagne she'd drunk, she'd never know the difference. But her taste lingered unpleasantly on his lips. He thought of Morgan, and with a silent, furious oath, crushed his mouth against Iona's.

"*Mmm.*" She preened like a stroked cat. "Your mind isn't on your paperwork now, Nicky. Tell me you want me. I need a man who wants me."

"Is there a man alive who wouldn't want a woman such as you?" He ran a hand down her back as her mouth searched greedily for his.

"A devil," she muttered with a slurred laugh. "Only a devil. Take me, Nicky." Her head fell back, revealing eyes half closed and dulled by wine. "Make love to me here, in the open, in the sun."

And he might have to, he thought with a grinding disgust in his stomach. To get what he needed. But first, he would coax what he could from her while she was vulnerable.

"Tell me, *matia mou*," he murmured, tasting the curve of her neck while she busily undid the buttons of his shirt. "What do you know of this smuggling between Lesbos and Turkey?"

Nick felt her stiffen, but her response—and, he knew, her wits—were dulled by the champagne. In her state of mind, he thought, it wouldn't take much more to loosen her tongue. She'd been ready to snap for days. Deliberately, he traced his tongue across her skin and felt her sigh.

"Nothing," she said quickly and fumbled more desperately at his buttons. "I know nothing of such things."

"Come, Iona," he murmured seductively. She was a completely physical woman, one who ran on sensations alone. Between wine and sex and her own nerves, she'd talk to him. "You know a great deal. As a businessman"— he nipped at her earlobe—"I'm interested in greater profit. You won't deny me a few extra·drachmas, will you?"

"A few million," she murmured, and put her hand on his to show him what she wanted. "Yes, there's much I know."

"And much you'll tell me?" he asked. "Come, Iona. You and the thought of millions excite me."

"I know the man that stupid woman found this morning was murdered because he was greedy."

Nick forced himself not to tense. "But greed is so difficult to resist." He went with her as she stretched full length on the bench. "Do you know who murdered him, Iona?" She was slipping away from him, losing herself to the excess of champagne. On a silent oath, Nick nipped at her skin to bring her back.

"I don't like murder, Nicky," she mumbled, "and I don't like talking to the police even more." She reached for him, but her hands fumbled. "I'm tired of being used," she said pettishly, then added, "Perhaps it's time to change allegiance. You're rich, Nicky. I like money. I need money."

"Doesn't everyone?" Nick asked dryly.

"Later, we'll talk later. I'll tell you." Her mouth was greedy on his. Forcing everything from his mind, Nick struggled to find some passion, even the pretense of passion, in return. God, he needed a woman; his body ached for one. And he needed Iona. But as he felt her sliding toward unconsciousness, he did nothing to revive her.

Later, as Iona slept in the sun, Nick leaned over the opposite rail and lit a cigarette from the butt of another. The clinging distaste both infuriated and depressed him. He knew that he would have to use Iona, be used by her—if not this time, then eventually. He had to tap her knowledge to learn what he wanted to know. It was a matter of his own safety—and his success. The second had always been more important to him than the first.

If he had to be Iona's lover to gain his own end, then

he'd be her lover. It meant nothing. Swearing, he drew deeply on the cigarette. It meant nothing, he repeated. It was business.

He found he wanted a shower, a long one, something to cleanse himself of the dirt which wouldn't wash away. Years of dirt, years of lies. Why had he never felt imprisoned by them until now?

Morgan's face slipped into his mind. Her eyes were cold. Flinging the cigarette out to sea, he went back to the wheel and started the engine.

Chapter 7

During a leisurely drink after a leisurely tour, Morgan decided the village was perfect. White-washed houses huddled close together, some with pillars, some with arches, still others with tiny wooden balconies. The tidiness, the freshness of white should have lent an air of newness. Instead, the village seemed old and timeless and permanent.

She sat with Andrew at a waterfront *kafenion,* watching the fishing boats sway at the docks, and the men who spread their nets to dry.

The fishermen ranged from young boys to old veterans. All were bronzed, all worked together. There were twelve to each net—twenty-four hands, some wrinkled and gnarled, some smooth with youth. All strong. As they worked they shouted and laughed in routine companionship.

"Must have been a good catch," Andrew commented.

He watched Morgan's absorption with the small army of men near the water's edge.

"You know, I've been thinking." She ran a finger down the side of her glass. "They all seem so fit and sturdy. Some of those men are well past what we consider retirement age in the States. I suppose they'll sail until they die. A life on the water must be a very satisfying existence." Pirates...would she ever stop thinking of pirates?

"I don't know if any of these people think much about satisfaction. It's simply what they do. They fish or work in Nick's olive groves. They've been doing one or the other for generations." Toying with his own drink, Andrew studied them too. "I do think there's a contentment here. The people know what's expected of them. If their lives are simple, perhaps it's an enviable simplicity."

"Still, there's the smuggling," Morgan murmured.

Andrew shrugged. "It's all part of the same mold, isn't it? They do what's expected of them and earn a bit of adventure and a few extra drachmas."

She shot him a look of annoyed surprise. "I didn't expect that attitude from you."

Andrew looked back at her, both brows raised. "What attitude?"

"This—this nonchalance over crime."

"Oh, come on, Morgan, it's—"

"Wrong," she interrupted. "It should be stopped." Morgan swallowed the innocently clear but potent ouzo.

"How do you stop something that's been going on for centuries in one form or another?"

"It's current form is ugly. I should think the men of influence like Alex and… Nicholas, with homes on the island, would put pressure on whoever should be pressured."

"I don't know Alex well enough to comment," Andrew mused, filling her glass again. "But I can't imagine Nick getting involved in anything that didn't concern himself or his business."

"Can't you?" Morgan murmured.

"If that sounds like criticism, it's not." He noted he had Morgan's full attention, but that her eyes were strangely veiled. "Nick's been very good to me, lending me the cottage and the money for my passage. Lord knows when I'll be able to pay him back. And it irks quite a bit to have to borrow, but poetry isn't the most financially secure career."

"I think I read somewhere that T.S. Eliot was a bank teller."

Andrew returned her understanding smile with a wry grimace. "I could work out of Nick's California office." He shrugged and drank. "His offer wasn't condescending, just absentminded. It's rough on the ego." He looked past her, toward the docks. "Maybe my ship will come in."

"I'm sure it will, Andrew. Some of us are meant to follow dreams."

His gaze came back to her. "And artists are meant to suffer a bit, rise beyond the more base needs of money and power?" His smile was brittle, his eyes cool. "Let's order." Morgan watched him shake off the mood and smile with his usual warmth. "I'm starved."

The evening sky was muted as they finished their meal. There were soft, dying colors flowing into the western sea. In the east, it was a calm, deep violet waiting for the first stars. Morgan was content with the vague glow brought on by spiced food and Greek ouzo. There was intermittent music from a mandolin. Packets of people shuffled in and out of the café, some of them breaking into song.

Their waiter cum proprietor was a wide man with a thin moustache and watery eyes. Morgan figured the eyes could be attributed to the spices and cook smoke hanging in the air. American tourists lifted his status. Because he was impressed with Morgan's easily flowing Greek, he found opportunities to question and gossip as he hovered around their table.

Morgan toyed with a bit of *psomaki* and relaxed with the atmosphere and easy company. She'd found nothing but comfort and good will in the Theoharis villa, but this was something different. There was an earthier ambience she had missed in Liz's elegant home. Here there would be lusty laughter and spilled wine. As strong as Morgan's feelings were for both Liz and Alex, she would never have been content with the lives they led. She'd have rusted inside the perpetual manners.

For the first time since that morning, Morgan felt the nagging ache at the base of her skull begin to ease.

"Oh, Andrew, look! They're dancing." Cupping her chin on her hands, Morgan watched the line of men hook arms.

As he finished up the last of a spicy sausage, Andrew glanced over. "Want to join in?"

Laughing, she shook her head. "No, I'd spoil it—but you could," she added with a grin.

"You have," Andrew began as he filled her glass again,

"a wonderful laugh. It's rich and unaffected and trails off into something sensuous."

"What extraordinary things you say, Andrew." Morgan smiled at him, amused. "You're an easy man to be with. We could be friends."

Andrew lifted his brows. Morgan was surprised to find her mouth briefly captured. There was a faint taste of the island on him—spicy and foreign. "For starters." At her stunned expression, he leaned back and grinned. "That face you're wearing doesn't do great things for my ego, either." He pulled a pack of cigarettes out of his jacket pocket, then dug for a match. Morgan stopped staring at him to stare at the thin black box.

"I didn't know you smoked," she managed after a moment.

"Oh, not often." He found a match. The tiny flame flared, flickering over his face a moment, casting shadows, mysteries, suspicions. "Especially since my taste runs to these. Nick takes pity on me and leaves some at my cottage whenever he happens by. Otherwise, I suppose I'd do without altogether." When he noticed Morgan's steady stare, he gave her a puzzled smile. "Something wrong?"

"No." She lifted her glass and hoped she sounded casual. "I was just thinking—you'd said you roam all over this part of the island. You must have been in that inlet before."

"It's a beautiful little spot." He reached over for her hand. "Or it was. I guess I haven't been there in over a week. It might be quite a while before I go back now."

"A week," Morgan murmured.

"Don't dwell on it, Morgan."

She lifted her eyes to his. They were so clear, so concerned. She was being a fool. None of them—Alex, Dorian, Andrew—none of them were capable of what was burning into her thoughts. How was she to know that some maniac from the village hadn't had a taste for expensive tobacco and back-stabbing? It made more sense, a great deal more sense than her ugly suspicions.

"You're right." She smiled again and leaned toward him. "Tell me about your epic poem."

"Good evening, Miss James, Mr. Stevenson."

Morgan twisted her head and felt the sky cloud over. She looked up into Tripolos's pudgy face. "Hello, Captain."

If her greeting lacked enthusiasm, Tripolos seemed unperturbed. "I see you're enjoying a bit of village life. Do you come often?"

"This is Morgan's first trip," Andrew told him. "I convinced her to come out to dinner. She needed something after this morning's shock."

Tripolos clucked sympathetically. Morgan noted the music and laughter had stilled. The atmosphere in the café was hushed and wary.

"Very sensible," the captain decided. "A young lady must not dwell on such matters. I, unfortunately, must think of little else at the moment." He sighed and looked wistfully at the ouzo. "Enjoy your evening."

"Damn, damn, *damn!*" she muttered when he walked away. "Why does he affect me this way? Every time I see him, I feel like I've got the Hope diamond in my pocket."

"I know what you mean." Andrew watched people fall

back to create a path for Tripolos. "He almost makes you wish you had something to confess."

"Thank God, it's not just me." Morgan lifted her glass again, noticed her hands were trembling, and drained it. "Andrew," she began in calm tones, "unless you have some moral objection, I'm going to get very drunk."

Sometime later, after learning Andrew's views on drinking were flexible, Morgan floated on a numbing cloud of ouzo. The thin light of the moon had replaced the colors of sunset. As the hour grew later, the café crowd grew larger, both in size and volume. Music was all strings and bells. If the interlude held a sheen of unreality, she no longer cared. She'd had enough of reality.

The waiter materialized with yet another bottle. He set it on the table with the air of distributing a rare wine.

"Busy night," Morgan commented, giving him a wide if misty, smile.

"It is Saturday," he returned, explaining everything.

"So, I've chosen my night well." She glanced about, seeing a fuzzy crush of people. "Your customers seem happy."

He followed her survey with a smug smile, wiping a hand on his apron. "I feared when the Mitilini captain came, my business would suffer, but all is well."

"The police don't add to an atmosphere of enjoyment. I suppose," she added slowly, "he's investigating the death of that fisherman."

He gave Morgan a quick nod. "Stevos came here often, but he was a man with few companions. He was not one for dancing or games. He found other uses for his time." The waiter narrowed his eyes. "My customers do not like to answer questions." He muttered something uncomplimentary, but Morgan wasn't sure if it was directed at Stevos or Tripolos.

"He was a fisherman," she commented, struggling to concentrate on the Greek's eyes. "But it appears his comrades don't mourn him."

The waiter moved his shoulders eloquently, but she saw her answer. There were fishermen, and fishermen. "Enjoy your evening, *kyrios*. It is an honor to serve you."

"You know," Andrew stated when the waiter drifted to another table, "it's very intimidating listening to all that Greek. I couldn't pick up on it. What was he saying?"

Not wanting to dwell on the murder again, Morgan merely smiled. "Greek males are red-blooded, Andrew, but I explained that I was otherwise engaged for this evening." She locked her hands behind her head and looked up at the stars. "Oh, I'm glad I came. It's so lovely. No murders—no smuggling tonight. I feel marvelous, Andrew. When can I read some of your poetry?"

"When your brain's functioning at a normal level." Smiling, he tilted more ouzo into her glass. "I think your opinion might be important."

"You're a nice man." Morgan lifted her glass and studied him as intensely as possible. "You're not at all like Nicholas."

"What brought that on?" Andrew frowned, setting the bottle back down again.

"You're just not." She held out her glass. "To Americans," she told him. "One hundred percent pure."

After tapping her glass with his, Andrew drank and

shook his head. "I have a feeling we weren't toasting the same thing."

She felt Nick begin to push into her thoughts and she thrust him away. "What does it matter? It's a beautiful night."

"So it is." His finger traced lightly over the back of her hand. "Have I told you how lovely you are?"

"Oh, Andrew, are you going to flatter me?" With a warm laugh, she leaned closer. "Go ahead, I love it."

With a wry grin, he tugged her hair. "You're spoiling my delivery."

"Oh, dear…how's this?" Morgan cupped her chin on her hands again and gave him a very serious stare.

On a laugh, Andrew shook his head. "Let's walk for a while. I might find a dark corner where I can kiss you properly."

Rising, he helped Morgan to her feet. She exchanged a formal and involved good-night with the proprietor before Andrew could navigate her away from the crowd.

Those not gathered in the *kafenion* were long since in bed. The white houses were closed and settled for the night. Now and then a dog barked, and another answered. Morgan could hear her own footsteps echo down the street.

"It's so quiet," she murmured. "All you can really hear is the water and the night itself. Ever since that first morning when I woke up on Lesbos, I've felt as if I belonged. Nothing that's happened since has spoiled that for me, Andrew." She whirled herself around in his arms and laughed. "I don't believe I'm *ever* going home again. How can I face New York and the traffic and the snow again?

Rushing to work, rushing home. Maybe I'll become a fisherman, or give in to Liz and marry a goatherd."

"I don't think you should marry a goatherd," Andrew said practically, and drew her closer. Her scent was tangling his senses. Her face, in the moonlight, was an ageless mystery. "Why don't you give the fishing a try? We could set up housekeeping in Nick's cottage."

It would serve him right, her mind muttered. Lifting her mouth, Morgan waited for the kiss.

It was warm and complete. Morgan neither knew nor cared if the glow was a result of the kiss or the liquor. Andrew's lips weren't demanding, weren't urgent and possessive. They were comforting, requesting. She gave him what she could.

There was no rocketing passion—but she told herself she didn't want it. Passion clouded the mind more successfully than an ocean of ouzo. She'd had enough of hunger and passions. They brought pain with disillusionment. Andrew was kind, uncomplicated. He wouldn't turn away when she needed him. He wouldn't give her sleepless nights. He wouldn't make her doubt her own strict code of right and wrong. He was the knight—a woman was safe with a knight.

"Morgan," he murmured, then rested his cheek on her hair. "You're exquisite. Isn't there some man I should consider dueling with?"

Morgan tried to think of Jack, but could form no clear picture. There was, however, a sudden, atrociously sharp image of Nick as he dragged her close for one of his draining kisses.

"No," she said too emphatically. "There's no one. Absolutely no one."

Andrew drew her away and tilted her chin with his finger. He could see her eyes in the dim glow of moonlight. "From the strength of your denial, I'd say my competition's pretty formidable. No"—he laid a finger over her lips as she started to protest—"I don't want to have my suspicions confirmed tonight. I'm selfish." He kissed her again, lingering over it. "Damn it, Morgan, you could be habit forming. I'd better take you home while I remember I'm a gentleman and you're a very drunk lady."

The villa shimmered white under the night sky. A pale light glowed in a first-floor window for her return.

"Everyone's asleep," Morgan stated unnecessarily as she let herself out of the car. Andrew rounded the hood. "I'll have to be very quiet." She muffled irrepressible giggles with a hand over her mouth. "Oh, I'm going to feel like an idiot tomorrow if I remember any of this."

"I don't think you'll remember too much," Andrew told her as he took her arm.

Morgan managed the stairs with the careful dignity of someone who no longer feels the ground under her feet. "It would never do to disgrace Alex by landing on my face in the foyer. He and Dorian are *so* dignified."

"And I," Andrew returned, "will have to resume my drive with the utmost caution. Nick wouldn't approve if I ran his Fiat off a cliff."

"Why, Andrew." Morgan stood back and studied him owlishly. "You're almost as sloshed as I am."

"Not quite, but close enough. However"—he let out a

long breath and wished he could lie down—"I conducted myself with the utmost restraint."

"Very nicely done." She went off into a muffled peal of giggles again. "Oh, Andrew." She leaned against him so heavily that he had to shift his balance to support her. "I did have a good time—a wonderful time. I needed it more than I realized. Thank you."

"In you go." He opened the door and gave her a nudge inside. "Be careful on the stairs," he whispered. "Should I wait and listen for the sounds of an undignified tumble?"

"Just be on your way and don't take the Fiat for a swim." She stood on her toes and managed to brush his chin with her lips. "Maybe I should make you some coffee."

"You'd never find the kitchen. Don't worry, I can always park the car and walk if worse comes to worst. Go to bed, Morgan, you're weaving."

"That's you," she retorted before she closed the door.

Morgan took the stairs with painful caution. The last thing she wanted to do was wake someone up and have to carry on any sort of reasonable conversation. She stopped once and pressed her hands to her mouth to stop a fresh bout of giggles. Oh, it felt so good, so good not to be able to think. But this has to stop, she told herself firmly. No more of this, Morgan, straighten up and get upstairs before all is discovered.

She managed to pull herself to the top landing, then had to think carefully to remember in which direction her room lay. To the left, of course, she told herself with a shake of the head. But which way is left, for God's sake? She spent another moment working it out before she crept down the hall. She gripped the doorknob, then waited for the door to stop swaying before she pushed it open.

"Ah, success," she murmured, then nearly spoiled it by stumbling over the rug. Quietly, she shut the door and leaned back against it. Now, if she could just find the bed. A light switched on, as if by magic. She smiled absently at Nick.

"*Yiasou*, you seem to be a permanent fixture."

The fury in his eyes rolled off the fog as she stepped unsteadily out of her shoes.

"What the hell have you been up to?" he demanded. "It's nearly three o'clock in the morning!"

"Oh, how rude of me not to have phoned to tell you I'd be late."

"Don't get cute, damn it, I'm not in the mood." He stalked over to her and grabbed her arms. "I've been waiting for you half the night, Morgan, I…" His voice trailed off as he studied her. His expression altered from fury to consideration then reluctant amusement. "You're totally bombed."

"Completely," she agreed, and had to take a deep breath to keep from giggling again. "You're so observant, Nicholas."

Amusement faded as her hand crept up his shirt front. "How the hell am I supposed to have a rational conversation with a woman who's seeing two of everything?"

"Three," she told him with some pride. "Andrew's only up to two. I quite surpassed him." Her other hand slid up to toy with one of his buttons. "Did you know you have wonderful eyes. I've never seen eyes so dark. Andrew's are blue. He doesn't kiss anything like you do. Why don't you kiss me now?"

He tightened his grip for a moment, then carefully released her. "So, you've been out with young Andrew." He wandered the room while Morgan swayed and watched him.

"*Young* Andrew and I would have asked you to join us, but it just slipped our minds. Besides, you can be really boring when you're proper and charming." She had a great deal of trouble with the last word and yawned over it. "Do we have to talk much longer? My tongue's getting thick."

"I've had about enough of being proper and charming myself," he muttered, picking up a bottle of her scent and setting it down again. "It serves its purpose."

"You do it very well," she told him and struggled with her zipper. "In fact, you're nearly perfect at it."

"Nearly?" His attention caught, he turned in time to see her win the battle with the zipper. "Morgan, for God's sake, don't do that now. I—"

"Yes, except you do slip up from time to time. A look in your eyes—the way you move. I suppose it's convincing all around if I'm the only one who's noticed. Then again, it might be because everyone else knows you and expects the inconsistency. Are you going to kiss me or not?" She dropped the dress to the floor and stepped out of it.

He felt his mouth go dry as she stood, clad only in a flimsy chemise, watching him mistily. Desire thudded inside him, hot, strong, and he forced himself back to what she was saying.

"Noticed what?"

Morgan made two attempts to pick up the dress. Each time she bent, the top of the chemise drifted out to show the swell of her breasts. Nick felt the thud lower to his stomach. "Noticed what?" she repeated as she left the dress where it was. "Oh, we're back to that. It's definitely the way you move."

"Move?" He struggled to keep his eyes on her face and away from her body. But her scent was already clouding his brain, and her smile—her smile challenged him to do something about it.

"It's like a panther," Morgan told him, "who knows he's being hunted and plans to turn the attack to his advantage when he's ready."

"I see." He frowned, not certain he liked her analogy. "I'll have to be more careful."

"Your problem," Morgan said cheerfully. "Well, since you don't want to kiss me, I'll say good-night, Nicholas. I'm going to bed. I'd see you down your vine, but I'm afraid I'd fall off the balcony."

"Morgan, I need to talk to you." He moved quickly and took her arm before she could sink onto the bed. That, he knew, would be too much pressure for any man. But she lost her already uncertain balance and tumbled into his arms. Warm and pliant, she leaned against him, making no objection as he molded her closer.

"Have you changed your mind?" she murmured, giving him a slow, sleepy-eyed smile. "I thought of you when Andrew kissed me tonight. It was very rude of me—or of you, I'm not sure which. Perhaps I'll think of Andrew if you kiss me now."

"The hell you will." He dragged her against him, teetering on the edge. Morgan let her head fall back.

"Try me," she invited.

"Morgan—the hell with all of it!"

Helplessly, he devoured her mouth. She was quickly

and totally boneless, arousing him to desperation by simple surrender. Desire was a fire inside him, spreading dangerously.

For the first time, he let himself go. He could think of nothing, nothing but her and the way her body flowed in his hands. She was softer than anything he'd ever hoped to know. So soft, she threatened to seep into him, become a part of him before he could do anything to prevent it. The need was raging, overpowering, taking over the control he'd been master of for as long as he could remember. But now, he burned to forfeit it.

With her, everything could be different. With her, he'd be clean again. Could she turn back the clock?

He could feel the brush of the bedspread against his thigh and knew, in one movement, he could be on it with her. Then nothing would matter but that he had her—a woman. But it wasn't any woman he wanted. It had been her since the first night she had challenged him on that deserted beach. It had been her since the first time those light, clear eyes had dared him. He was afraid—and he feared little—that it would always be her.

Mixed with the desire came a quick twist of pain. With a soft oath, he pulled her away, keeping his grip firm on her arms.

"Pay attention, will you?" His voice was rough and unsteady, but she didn't seem to notice. She smiled up at him and touched his cheek with her palm.

"Wasn't I?"

He checked the urge to shake her and spoke calmly. "I need to talk to you."

"Talk?" She smiled again. "Do we have to talk?"

"There are things I need to tell you—this morning…" He fumbled with the words, no longer certain what he wanted to say, what he wanted to do. How could her scent be stronger than it had been a moment ago? He was drowning in it.

"Nicholas." Morgan sighed sleepily. "I drank an incredible amount of ouzo. If I don't sleep it off, I may very well die. I'm sure the body only tolerates a certain amount of abuse. I've stretched my luck tonight."

"Morgan." His breath was coming too quickly. His own pulse like thunder in his ears. He should let her go, he knew. He should simply let her go—for both their sakes. But his arms stayed around her. "Straighten up and listen to me," he demanded.

"I'm through listening." She gave a sleepy, sultry laugh. "Through listening. Make love with me or go."

Her eyes were only slits, but the clear, mystical blue pulled him in. No struggle, no force would drag him out again. "Damn you," he breathed as they fell onto the bed. "Damn you for a witch."

It was all hell smoke and thunder. He couldn't resist it. Her body was as fluid as wine—as sweet and as potent. Now he could touch her wherever he chose and she only sighed. As his mouth crushed possessively on hers, she yielded, but in yielding held him prisoner. Even knowing it, he was helpless. There'd be a payment—a price in pain—for succumbing to the temptation. He no longer cared for tomorrows. Now, this moment, he had her. It was enough.

He tore the filmy chemise from her, too anxious, too

desperate, but she made no protest as the material ripped away. On a groan of need, he devoured her.

Tastes—she had such tastes. They lingered on his tongue, spun in his head. The crushed wild honey of her mouth, the rose-petal sweetness of her skin, drove him to search for more, and to find everything. He wasn't gentle—he was long past gentleness, but the quiet moans that came from her spoke of pleasure.

Words, low and harsh with desire, tumbled from him. He wasn't certain if he cursed her again or made her hundreds of mad promises. For the moment, it was all the same. Needs ripped through him—needs he understood, needs he'd felt before. But there was something else, something stronger, greedier. Then his flesh was against her flesh, and everything was lost. Fires and flames, a furnace of passion engulfed him, driving him beyond control, beyond reason. She was melting into him. He felt it as a tangible ache but had no will to resist.

Her hands were hot on his skin, her body molten. He could no longer be certain who led and who followed. Beneath his, her mouth was soft and willing, but he tasted her strength. Under him, her body was pliant, unresisting, but he felt her demand. Her skin would be white, barely touched by the sun. He burned to see it, but saw only the glimmer of her eyes in the darkness.

Then she pulled his mouth back to hers and he saw nothing, nothing but the blur of raging colors that were passion. The wild, sweet scent of jasmine seeped into him, arousing, never soothing, until he thought he'd never smell anything else.

With a last force of will, he struggled for sanity. He

wouldn't lose himself in her—to her. He couldn't. Without self-preservation he was nothing, vulnerable. Dead.

Even as he took her in a near violent rage, he surrendered.

Chapter 8

The sunlight that poured through the windows, through the open balcony doors, throbbed and pulsed in Morgan's head. With a groan she rolled over, hoping oblivion would be quick and painless. The thudding only increased. Morgan shifted cautiously and tried for a sitting position. Warily she opened her eyes then groaned at the flash of white morning sun. She closed them again in self-preservation. Slowly, gritting her teeth for courage, she allowed her lids to open again.

The spinning and whirling which had been enjoyable the night before, now brought on moans and mutters. With queasy stomach and aching eyes, she sat in the center of the bed until she thought she had the strength to move. Trying to keep her head perfectly still, she eased herself onto the floor.

Carelessly, she stepped over her discarded dress and found a robe in the closet. All she could think of were ice packs and coffee. Lots of coffee.

Then she remembered. Abruptly, blindingly. Morgan whirled from the closet to stare at the bed. It was empty— maybe she'd dreamed it. Imagined it. In useless defense she pressed her hands to her face. No dream. He had been there, and everything she remembered was real. And she remembered...the anger in his eyes, her own misty, taunting invitation. The way his mouth had pressed bruisingly to hers, her own unthinking, abandoned response.

The passion—it had been all she had thought it would be. Unbearable, wonderful, consuming. He'd cursed her. She could remember his words. Then he had taken her places she'd never even glimpsed before. She'd given him everything, then mindlessly challenged him to take more. She could still feel those taut, tensing muscles in his back, hear that ragged, desperate breathing at her ear.

He had taken her in fury, and it hadn't mattered to her. Then he had been silent. She had fallen asleep with her arms still around him. And now he was gone.

On a moan, Morgan dropped her hands to her sides. Of course he was gone. What else did she expect? The night had meant nothing to him—less than nothing. If she hadn't had so much to drink...

Oh, convenient excuse, Morgan thought on a wave of disgust. She still had too much pride to fall back on it. No, she wouldn't blame the ouzo. Walking to the bed, she picked up the torn remains of her chemise. She'd wanted him. God help her, she cared for him—too much. No, she wouldn't blame the ouzo. Balling the chemise in her fist, Morgan hurled it into the bottom of the closet. She had only herself to blame.

With a snap, Morgan closed the closet door. It was over,

she told herself firmly. It was done. It didn't have to mean any more to her than it had to Nick. For a moment, she leaned her forehead against the smooth wooden panel and fought the urge to weep. No, she wouldn't cry over him. She'd never cry over him. Straightening, Morgan told herself it was the headache that was making her feel so weak and weepy. She was a grown woman, free to give herself, to take a man, when and where she chose. Once she'd gone down and had some coffee, she'd be able to put everything in perspective.

She swallowed the threatening tears and walked to the door.

"Good morning, *kyrios*." The tiny maid greeted Morgan with a smile she could have done without. "Would you like your breakfast in your room now?"

"No, just coffee." The scent of food didn't agree with her stomach or her disposition. "I'll go down for it."

"It's a beautiful day."

"Yes, beautiful." With her teeth clenched, Morgan moved down the hall.

The sound of crashing dishes and a high-pitched scream had Morgan gripping the wall for support. She pressed her hand to her head and moaned. Did the girl have to choose this morning to be clumsy!

But when the screaming continued, Morgan turned back. The girl knelt just inside the doorway. Scattered plates and cups lay shattered over the rug where the food had splattered.

"Stop it!" Leaning down, Morgan grabbed her shoulders and shook Zena out of self-defense. "No one's going to fire you for breaking a few dishes."

The girl shook her head as her eyes rolled. She pointed a trembling finger toward the bed before she wrenched herself from Morgan's hold and fled.

Turning, Morgan felt the room dip and sway. A new nightmare crept in to join the old. With her hand gripping the doorknob; she stared.

A shaft of sunlight spread over Iona as she lay on her back, flung sideways across the bed. Her head hung over the edge, her hair streaming nearly to the floor. Morgan shook off the first shock and dizziness and raced forward. Though her fingers trembled, she pressed them to Iona's throat. She felt a flutter, faint, but she felt it. The breath she hadn't been aware she'd held came out in a rush of relief. Moving on instinct, she pulled Iona's unconscious form until she lay back on the bed.

It was then she saw the syringe lying on the tumbled sheets.

"Oh, my God."

It explained so much. Iona's moodiness, those tight, jerky nerves. She'd been a fool not to suspect drugs before. She's overdosed, Morgan thought in quick panic. What do I do? There must be something I'm supposed to do.

"Morgan—dear God!"

Turning her head only, Morgan looked at Dorian standing pale and stiff in the doorway. "She's not dead," Morgan said quickly. "I think she's overdosed—get a doctor—an ambulance."

"Not dead?"

She heard the flat tone of his voice, heard him start to come toward her. There was no time to pamper his feelings. "Do it quickly!" she ordered. "There's a pulse, but it's faint."

"What's Iona done now?" Alex demanded in a tone of strained patience. "The maid's hysterical, and—oh, sweet Lord!"

"An ambulance!" Morgan demanded as she kept her fingers on Iona's pulse. Perhaps if she kept them there, it would continue to beat. "In the name of God, *hurry!*" She turned then in time to see Alex rush from the room as Dorian remained frozen. "There's a syringe," she began with studied calm. She didn't want to hurt him, but continued as his gaze shifted to her. His eyes were blank. "She must have o.d.'d. Did you know she used drugs, Dorian?"

"Heroin." And a shudder seemed to pass through him. "I thought it had stopped. Are you sure she's—"

"She's alive." Morgan gripped his hand as he came to the bed. A wave of pity washed over her—for Iona, for the man whose hand she held in her own. "She's alive, Dorian. We'll get help for her."

His hand tightened on hers for a moment so that Morgan had to choke back a protest. "Iona," he murmured. "So beautiful—so lost."

"She's not lost, not yet!" Morgan said fiercely. "If you know how to pray, pray that we found her in time."

His eyes came back to Morgan's, clear, expressionless. She thought as she looked at him she'd never seen anything so empty. "Pray," he said quietly. "Yes, there's nothing else to be done."

It seemed to take hours, but when Morgan watched the helicopter veer off to the west, the morning was still young. Iona, still unconscious, was being rushed to Athens. Dorian rode with her and the doctor while Alex and Liz began hurried preparations for their own flight.

Still barefoot and in her robe, Morgan watched the helicopter until it was out of sight. As long as she lived, she thought, she'd never forget that pale, stony look on Dorian's face—or the lifeless beauty on Iona's. With a shudder, she turned away and saw Alex just inside the doorway.

"Tripolos," he said quietly. "He's in the salon."

"Oh, not now, Alex." Overcome with pity, she held out both hands as she went to him. "How much more can you stand?"

"It's necessary." His voice was tight with control and he held her hands limply. "I apologize for putting you through all this, Morgan—"

"No." She interrupted him and squeezed his hands. "Don't treat me that way, Alex. I thought we were friends."

"*Diabolos*," he murmured. "Such friends you have. Forgive me."

"Only if you stop treating me as though I were a stranger."

On a sigh, he slipped his arm around her shoulders. "Come, we'll face the captain."

Morgan wondered if she would ever enter the salon without seeing Captain Tripolos seated in the wide, high-back chair. She sat on the sofa as before, faced him, and waited for the questions.

"This is difficult for you," Tripolos said at length. "For all of you." His gaze roamed over the occupants of the room, from Morgan to Alex to Liz. "We will be as discreet as is possible, Mr. Theoharis. I will do what I can to avoid the press, but an attempted suicide in a family as well known as yours…" He let the rest trail off.

"Suicide," Alex repeated softly. His eyes were blank, as if the words hadn't penetrated.

"It would seem, from the preliminary report, that your cousin took a self-induced overdose. Heroin. But I hesitate to be more specific until the investigation is closed. Procedure, you understand."

"Procedure."

"You found Miss Theoharis, Miss James?"

Morgan gave a quick, nervous jolt at the sound of her name, then settled. "No, actually, the maid found her. I went in to see what was wrong. Zena had dropped the tray and was carrying on…when I went in I saw Iona."

"And you called for an ambulance?"

"No." She shook her head, annoyed. He knew Alex had called, but wanted to drag the story from her piece by piece. Resigned, Morgan decided to accommodate him. "I thought at first she was dead—then I felt a pulse. I got her back into bed."

"Back into bed?"

Tripolos's tone had sharpened, ever so faintly, but Morgan caught it. "Yes, she was half out of it, almost on the floor. I wanted to lay her down." She lifted her hands helplessly. "I honestly don't know what I wanted to do, it just seemed like the right thing."

"I see. Then you found this?" He held up the syringe, now in a clear plastic bag.

"Yes."

"Did you know your cousin was a user of heroin, Mr. Theoharis?"

Alex stiffened at the question. Morgan saw Liz reach out to take his hand. "I knew Iona had a problem—with drugs. Two years ago she went to a clinic for help. I thought she had found it. If I had believed she was still… ill," he managed. "I wouldn't have brought her into my home with my wife and my friend."

"Mrs. Theoharis, were you unaware of Miss Theoharis's problem?"

Morgan heard the breath hiss out between Alex's teeth, but Liz spoke quickly. "I was perfectly aware of it." Alex's head whipped around but she continued calmly. "That is, I was aware that my husband arranged for her to have treatment two years ago, though he tried to shield me." Without looking at him, Liz covered their joined hands with her free one.

"Would you, Mr. Theoharis, have any notion where your cousin received her supply?"

"None."

"I see. Well, since your cousin lives in Athens, perhaps it would be best if I worked with the police there, in order to contact her close friends."

"Do what you must," Alex said flatly. "I only ask that you spare my family as much as possible."

"Of course. I will leave you now. My apologies for the intrusion, yet again."

"I must phone my family," Alex said dully when the door closed behind Tripolos. As if seeking comfort, his hand went to his wife's hair. Then he rose and left without another word.

"Liz," Morgan began. "I know it's a useless phrase, but if there's anything I can do…"

Liz shook her head. She shifted her eyes from the doorway back to her friend's. "It's all so unbelievable. That she's lying there, so near death. What's worse, I never liked her. I made no secret of it, but now…" She rose and walked to the window. "She's Alex's family, and he feels that deeply. Now, in his heart, he's responsible for whatever happens to her. And all I can think of is how cold I was to her."

"Alex is going to need you." Morgan rose and walked over to put a hand on her shoulder. "You can't help not liking her, Liz. Iona isn't an easy person to like."

"You're right, of course." With a deep breath Liz turned and managed a weak smile. "It's been a hell of a vacation so far, hasn't it? No, don't say anything." She squeezed Morgan's hand. "I'm going to see if Alex needs me. There'll be arrangements to be made."

The villa was silent as Morgan went up to change. As she buttoned her shirt, she stood by the terrace doors, staring out at the view of garden, sea, and mountain. How could it be that so much ugliness had intruded in such a short time? she wondered. Death and near death. This wasn't the place for it. But even Paradise named its price, she thought, and turned away.

The knock on her door was quiet. "Yes, come in."

"Morgan, am I disturbing you?"

"Oh, Alex." As she looked up, Morgan's heart welled with sympathy. The lines of strain and grief seemed etched into his face. "I know how horrible all this is for you, and I don't want to add to your problems. Perhaps I should go back to New York."

"Morgan." He hesitated for a moment. "I know it's a lot to ask, but I don't do it for myself. For Liz. Will you stay for Liz? Your company is all I can give her for a time." He released Morgan's hands and moved restlessly around the room. "We'll have to fly to Athens. I can't say how long—until Iona is well or—" He broke off as if he wasn't yet prepared for the word. "I'll have to stay with my family for a few days. My aunt will need me. If I could send Liz back knowing you'd be here with her, it would make it so much easier."

"Of course, Alex. You know I will."

He turned and gave her a phantom of a smile. "You're a good friend, Morgan. We'll have to leave you for at least a day and a night. After that, I'll send Liz back. I can be sure she'll leave Athens if you're here." With a sigh, he took her hand absently. "Dorian might choose to stay in Athens as well. I believe he…has feelings for Iona I didn't realize before. I'll ask Nick to look after you while we're gone."

"No." She bit her tongue on the hurried protest. "No, really, Alex, I'll be fine. I'm hardly alone, with the servants in the house. When will you leave?"

"Within the hour."

"Alex, I'm sure it was an accident."

"I'll have to convince my aunt of that." He held out his hands, searching his own palms for a moment. "Though as to what I believe…" His look had hardened when he lifted his eyes again. "Iona courts disaster. She feeds on misery. I'll tell you now, because I won't ever be able to speak freely to anyone else. Not even Liz." His face was a grim mask now. Cold. "I detest her." He spit the words out as if they were poison. "Her death would be nothing but a blessing to everyone who loves her."

When Alex, Liz, and Dorian were gone, Morgan left the villa. She needed to walk—needed the air. This time she avoided her habit of heading for the beach. She was far from ready for that. Instead, she struck out for the cliffs, drawn to their jagged, daring beauty.

How clean the air was! Morgan wanted no floral scents now, just the crisp tang of the sea. She walked without destination. Up, only up, as if she could escape from everything if she could only get higher. If the gods had walked here, she thought, they would have come to the cliffs, to hear the water beat against rock, to breathe the thin, pure air.

She saw, to her pleasure, a scruffy, straggly goat with sharp black eyes. He stared at her a moment as he gnawed on a bit of wild grass he'd managed to find growing in between the rocks. But when she tried to get closer, he scrambled up, lightly, and disappeared over the other side of the cliff.

With a sigh, Morgan sat down on a rock perched high above the water. With some surprise, she saw tiny blue-headed flowers struggling toward the sun out of a crevice hardly wider than a thumbnail. She touched them, but couldn't bring herself to pluck any. Life's everywhere, she realized, if you only know where to look.

"Morgan."

Her hand closed over the blooms convulsively at the

sound of his voice. She opened it slowly and turned her head. Nick was standing only a short distance away, his hair caught by the breeze that just stirred the air. In jeans and a T-shirt, his face unshaven, he looked more like the man she had first encountered. Undisciplined. Unprincipled. Her heart gave a quick, bounding leap before she controlled it.

Without a word, Morgan rose and started down the slope.

"Morgan." He caught her quickly, then turned her around with a gentleness she hadn't expected from him. Her eyes were cool, but beneath the frost, he saw they were troubled. "I heard about Iona."

"Yes, you once told me there was little that happened on the island you didn't know."

Her toneless voice slashed at him, but he kept his hands easy on her arms. "You found her."

She wouldn't let that uncharacteristic caring tone cut through her defenses. She could be—would be—as hard and cold as he had been. "You're well informed, Nicholas."

Her face was unyielding, and he didn't know how to begin. If she would come into his arms, he could show her. But the woman who faced him would lean on no one. "It must have been very difficult for you."

She lifted a brow, as though she were almost amused. "It was easier to find someone alive than to find someone dead."

He winced at that—a quick jerk of facial muscles, then dropped his hands. She'd asked him for comfort once, and now that he wanted to give it, needed to give it, it was too late. "Will you sit down?"

"No, it's not as peaceful here as it was."

"Stop slashing at me!" he exploded, grabbing her arms again.

"Let me go."

But the faint quaver in her voice told him something her words hadn't. She was closer to her own threshold than perhaps even she knew. "Very well, if you'll come back to the house with me."

"No."

"Yes." Keeping a hand on her arm, Nick started up the rough path. "We'll talk."

Morgan jerked her arm but his grip was firm. He propelled her up the rough path without looking at her. "What do you want, Nicholas? More details?"

His mouth thinned as he pulled her along beside him. "All right. You can tell me about Iona if you like."

"I don't like," she tossed back. They were already approaching the steps to his house. Morgan hadn't realized they were so close. What devil had prompted her to walk that way? "I don't want to go with you."

"Since when have I cared what you want?" he asked bitterly and propelled her through the front door. "Coffee," he demanded as Stephanos appeared in the hall.

"All right, I'll give you the details," Morgan raged as she whirled inside the door of the salon. "And then, by God, you'll leave me be! I found Iona unconscious, hardly alive. There was a syringe in bed with her. It seems she was an addict." She paused, unaware that her breath was starting to heave. "But you knew that, didn't you, Nicholas? You know all manner of things."

She'd lost all color, just as she had when she'd run

across the beach and into his arms. He felt a twinge, an ache, and reached out for her.

"Don't touch me!" Nick's head jerked back as if she'd slapped him. Morgan pressed her hands against her mouth and turned away. "Don't touch me."

"I won't put my hands on you," Nick managed as they balled into fists. "Sit down, Morgan, before you keel over."

"Don't tell me what to do." Her voice quavered, and she detested it. Making herself turn back, she faced him again. "You have no right to tell me what to do."

Stephanos entered, silent, watchful. As he set the coffee tray down, he glanced over at Morgan. He saw, as Nick couldn't, her heart in her eyes. "You'll have coffee, miss," he said in a soft voice.

"No, I—"

"You should sit." Before Morgan could protest, Stephanos nudged her into a chair. "The coffee's strong."

Nick stood, raging at his impotence as Stephanos clucked around her like a mother hen.

"You'll have it black," he told her. "It puts color in your cheeks."

Morgan accepted the cup, then stared at it. "Thank you."

Stephanos gave Nick one long, enigmatic look, then left them.

"Well, drink it," Nick ordered, furious that the old man had been able to hack through her defenses when he felt useless. "It won't do you any good in the cup."

Because she needed to find strength somewhere, Morgan drank it down quickly. "What else do you want?"

"Damn it, Morgan, I didn't bring you here to grill you about Iona."

"No? You surprise me." Steadier, she set the cup aside and rose again. "Though why anything you do should surprise me, I don't know."

"There's nothing too vile you wouldn't attribute to me, is there?" Ignoring the coffee, Nick strode to the bar. "Perhaps you think I killed Stevos and left the body for you to find."

"No," she said calmly, because she could speak with perfect truth. "He was stabbed in the back."

"So?"

"You'd face a man when you killed him."

Nick turned away from the bar, the glass still empty in his hand. His eyes were black now, as black as she'd ever seen them. There was passion in them barely, just barely, suppressed. "Morgan, last night—"

"I won't discuss last night with you." Her voice was cold and final, cutting through him more accurately than any blade.

"All right, we'll forget it." This time he filled the glass. He'd known there would be a price to pay; somehow he hadn't thought it would be quite so high. "Would you like an apology?"

"For what?"

He gave a short laugh as his hand tightened on the glass. He tossed back the liquor. "God, woman, you've a streak of ice through you I hadn't seen."

"Don't talk to me of ice, Nicholas." Her voice rose with a passion she'd promised herself she wouldn't feel. "You sit here in your ancestral home, playing your dirty chess games with lives. I won't be one of your pawns. There's a woman barely alive in an Athens hospital. You make your money feeding her illness. Do you think you're remote from the blame because you cross the strait in the dead of night like some swashbuckling pirate?"

Very carefully, he set down the glass and turned. "I know what I am."

She stared at him until her eyes began to fill again. "So do I," she whispered. "God help me."

Turning, she fled. He didn't go after her.

Moments later, Stephanos came back into the room. "The lady's upset," he said mildly.

Nick turned his back to fill his glass again. "I know what the lady is."

"The past two days have been difficult for her." He clucked his tongue. "She came to you for comfort?"

Nick whirled but managed to bite back the words. Stephanos watched calmly. "No, she didn't come to me. She'd go to the devil himself before she came to me again." With an effort, he controlled the rage and his tone. "And it's for the best, I can't let her interfere now. As things stand, she'll be in the way."

Stephanos caressed his outrageous moustache and whistled through his teeth. "Perhaps she'll go back to America."

"The sooner the better," Nick muttered and drained his glass. At the knock on the door, he swore. "See who the hell it is and get rid of them if you can."

"Captain Tripolos," Stephanos announced a few moments later. There was a gleam in his eye as he melted out of sight.

"Captain." Nick fought off the need to swear again. "You'll join me for coffee?"

"Thank you." Tripolos settled into a chair with a few wheezes and sighs. "Was that Miss James I just saw going down the cliff path?"

"Yes." With some effort, Nick prevented his knuckles from whitening against the handle of the pot. "She was just here."

Both men watched each other with what seemed casual interest. One was Morgan's panther—the other a crafty bear.

"Then she told you about Miss Theoharis."

"Yes." Nick offered the cream. "A nasty business, Captain. I intend to call Athens later this morning to see what news there is. Is Iona's condition why you're here?"

"Yes. It's kind of you to see me, Mr. Gregoras. I know you are a very busy man."

"It's my duty to cooperate with the police, Captain," Nick countered as he sat back with his coffee. "But I don't know how I can help you in this case."

"As you were with Miss Theoharis all of yesterday afternoon, I hoped you could shed some light on her frame of mind."

"Oh, I see." Nick sipped his coffee while his mind raced with possibilities. "Captain, I don't know if I can help you. Naturally, Iona was distressed that the man's murder was practically on her doorstep. She was edgy—but then, she often is. I can't say I saw anything different in her."

"Perhaps you could tell me what you did on your boat trip?" Tripolos suggested. "If Miss Theoharis said anything which seemed to indicate she was thinking of suicide?"

Nick lifted a brow. "We weren't overly engaged in conversation."

"Of course."

Nick wondered how long they could continue to fence. He decided to execute a few flourishes of his own. "I will say that Iona seemed a trifle nervous. That is, as I said, however, a habitual trait. You'll find that the people who know her will describe Iona as a…restive woman. I can say with complete honesty that it never entered my mind that she was contemplating suicide. Even now, to be candid, I find the idea impossible."

Tripolos settled back comfortably. "Why?"

Generalities, Nick concluded, would suffice. "Iona's too fond of herself to seek death. A beautiful woman, Captain, and one greedy for life's pleasures. It's merely an opinion, you understand. You know much more about this sort of thing." He shrugged. "My opinion is that it was an accident."

"An accident, Mr. Gregoras, is unlikely." He was fishing for a reaction, and Nick gave him another curious lift of brow. "There was too much heroin in her system for any but an amateur to take by mistake. And Miss Theoharis is no stranger to heroin. The marks of the needle tell a sad story."

"Yes, I see."

"Were you aware that Miss Theoharis was an addict?"

"I didn't know Iona very well, Captain. Socially, of course, but basically, she's a cousin of a friend—a beautiful woman who isn't always comfortable to be around."

"Yet you spent the day with her yesterday."

"A beautiful woman," Nick said again, and smiled. "I'm sorry I can't help you."

"Perhaps you'd be interested in a theory of mine."

Nick didn't trust those bland eyes but continued to smile. "Of course."

"You see, Mr. Gregoras," Tripolos went on. "If it was an accident, and if your instincts are correct, there is only one answer."

"One answer?" Nick repeated then allowed his expression to change slowly. "Do you mean you think someone attempted to…murder Iona?"

"I'm a simple policeman, Mr. Gregoras." Tripolos looked plumply humble. "It is my nature to look at such matters from a suspicious point of view. May I be frank?"

"By all means," Nick told him, admiring the captain's plodding shrewdness. Frank be damned, Nick mused, he's going to try to give me enough rope to hang myself.

"I am puzzled, and as a man who knows the Theoharis family well, I would like your opinion."

"Whatever I can do."

Tripolos nodded. "I will tell you first—and of course, you understand this cannot leave this room?"

Nick merely inclined his head and sipped his coffee.

"I will tell you Anthony Stevos was part of a smuggling ring operating on Lesbos."

"I must admit, the thought had crossed my mind." Amused, Nick took out a box of cigarettes, offering one to Tripolos.

"It's no secret that a group has been using this island's nearness to Turkey to smuggle opium across the strait."

Tripolos admired the thin wisp of elegant tobacco before he bent closer to Nick for a light.

"You think this Stevos was murdered by one of his cohorts?"

"That is my theory." Tripolos drew in the expensive smoke appreciatively. "It is the leader of this group that is my main concern. A brilliant man, I am forced to admit." Reluctant respect crossed his face. "He is very clever and has so far eluded any nets spread for his capture. It is rumored he rarely joins in the boat trips. When he does, he is masked."

"I've heard the rumors, naturally," Nick mused behind a mist of smoke. "I put a great deal of it down to village gossip and romance. A masked man, smuggling—the stuff of fiction."

"He is real, Mr. Gregoras, and there is nothing romantic about back-stabbing."

"No, you're quite right."

"Stevos was not a smart man. He was being watched in hopes he would lead us to the one we want. But…" As was his habit, Tripolos let the sentence trail off.

"I might ask, Captain, why you're telling me what must be police business."

"As an important man in our community," Tripolos said smoothly, "I feel I can take you into my confidence."

The old fox, Nick thought, and smiled. "I appreciate that. Do you think this masked smuggler is a local man?"

"I believe he is a man who knows the island." Tripolos gave a grim smile in return. "But I do not believe he is a fisherman."

"One of my olive pickers?" Nick suggested blandly, blowing out a stream of smoke. "No, I suppose not."

"I believe," Tripolos continued, "from the reports I have received on Miss Theoharis's activities in Athens, that she is aware of the identity of the man we seek."

Nick came to attention. "Iona?"

"I am of the opinion that Miss Theoharis is very involved in the smuggling operation. Too involved for her own safety. If…when," he amended, "she comes out of her coma, she'll be questioned."

"It's hard for me to believe that Alex's cousin would be a part of something like that." *He's getting entirely too close,* Nick realized, and swore silently at the lack of time. "Iona's a bit untamed," he went on, "but smuggling and murder. I can't believe it."

"I am very much afraid someone tried to murder Miss Theoharis because she knew too much. I will ask you, Mr. Gregoras, as one who is acquainted with her, how far would Miss Theoharis have gone for love—or for money?"

Nick paused as if considering carefully while his mind raced at readjustments to plans already formed. "For love, Captain, I think Iona would do little. But for money"— he looked up—"for money, Iona could justify anything."

"You are frank," Tripolos nodded. "I am grateful. Perhaps you would permit me to speak with you again on this matter. I must confess"—Tripolos's smile was sheepish, but his eyes remained direct—"it is a great help to discuss my problems with a man like yourself. It allows me to put things in order."

"Captain, I'm glad to give you any help I can, of course." Nick gave him an easy smile.

For some time after Tripolos left, Nick remained in his chair. He scowled at the Rodin sculpture across the room as he calculated his choices.

"We move tonight," he announced as Stephanos entered.

"It's too soon. Things are not yet safe."

"Tonight," Nick repeated and shifted his gaze. "Call Athens and let them know about the change in plan. See if they can't rig something up to keep this Tripolos off my back for a few hours." He laced his fingers together and frowned. "He's dangled his bait, and he's damn well expecting me to bite."

"It's too dangerous tonight," Stephanos insisted. "There's another shipment in a few days."

"In a few days, Tripolos will be that much closer. We can't afford to have things complicated with the local police now. And I have to be sure." Jet eyes narrowed, and his mouth became a grim line. "I haven't gone through all this to make a mistake at this point. I have to speed things up before Tripolos starts breathing down the wrong necks."

Chapter 9

The cove was blanketed in gloom. Rocks glistened, protecting it from winds—and from view. There was a scent—lush wet leaves, wild blossoms that flourished in the sun and hung heavy at night. But somehow it wasn't a pleasant fragrance. It smelt of secrets and half-named fears.

Lovers didn't hold trysts there. Legend said it was haunted. At times, when a man walked near enough on a dark, still night, the voices of spirits murmured behind the rocks. Most men took another route home and said nothing at all.

The moon shed a thin, hollow light over the face of the water, adding to rather than detracting from the sense of whispering stillness, of mystic darkness. The water itself sighed gently over the rocks and sand. It was a passive sound, barely stirring the air.

The men who gathered near the boat were like so many shadows—dark, faceless in the gloom. But they were men, flesh and blood and muscle. They didn't fear the spirits in the cove.

They spoke little, and only in undertones. A laugh might be heard from time to time, quick and harsh in a place of secrets, but for the most part they moved silently, competently. They knew what had to be done. The time was nearly right.

One saw the approach of a new shadow and grunted to his companion. Stealthily, he drew a knife from his belt, gripping its crude handle in a strong, work-worn hand. The blade glittered dangerously through the darkness. Work stopped; men waited.

As the shadow drew closer, he sheathed the knife and swallowed the salty taste of fear. He wouldn't have been afraid to murder, but he was afraid of this man.

The thick, sturdy fingers trembled as they released the knife. "We weren't expecting you."

"I do not like to always do the expected." The answer was in brisk Greek as a pale finger of moonlight fell over him. He wore black—all black, from lean black slacks to a sweater and leather jacket. Lean and tall, he might have been god or devil.

A hood concealed both his head and face. Only the gleam of dark eyes remained visible—and deadly.

"You join us tonight?"

"I am here," he returned. He wasn't a man who answered questions, and no more were asked. He stepped aboard as one used to the life and sway of boats.

It was a typical fishing vessel. Its lines were simple. The decks were clean but rough, the paint fresh and black.

Only the expense and power of its motor separated it from its companions.

Without a word, he crossed the deck, ignoring the men who fell back to let him pass. They were hefty, muscled men with thick wrists and strong hands. They moved away from the lean man as if he could crush them to bone with one sweep of his narrow hand. Each prayed the slitted eyes would not seek him out.

He placed himself at the helm, then gazed casually over his shoulder. At the look, the lines were cast off. They would row until they were out to sea and the roar of the motor would go unnoticed.

The boat moved at an easy pace, a lone speck in a dark sea. The motor purred. There was little talk among the men. They were a silent group in any case, but when the man was with them, no one wanted to speak. To speak was to bring attention to yourself—not many dared to do so.

He stared out into the water and ignored the wary glances thrown his way. He was remote, a figure of the night. His hood rippled in the salt-sprayed wind—a carefree, almost adventurous movement. But he was still as a stone.

Time passed; the boat listed with the movement of the sea. He might have been a figurehead. Or a demon.

"We are short-handed." The man who had greeted him merged with his shadow. His voice was low and coarse. His stomach trembled. "Do you wish me to find a replacement for Stevos?"

The hooded head turned—a slow, deliberate motion.

The man took an instinctive step in retreat and swallowed the copper taste that had risen to his throat.

"I will find my own replacement. You would all do well to remember Stevos." He lifted his voice on the warning as his eyes swept the men on deck. "There is no one who cannot be...replaced." He used a faint emphasis on the final word, watching the dropping of eyes with satisfaction. He needed their fear, and he had it. He could smell it on them. Smiling beneath the hood, he turned back to the sea.

The journey continued, and no one else spoke to him—or about him. Now and then a sailor might cast his eyes toward the man at the helm. The more superstitious crossed themselves or made the ancient sign against evil. When the devil was with them, they knew the full power of fear. He ignored them, treated them as though he were alone on the boat. They thanked God for it.

Midway between Lesbos and Turkey, the motor was shut off. The sudden silence resounded like a thunderclap. No one spoke as they would have done if the figure hadn't been at the helm. There were no crude jokes or games of dice.

The boat shifted easily in its own wake. They waited, all but one swatting in the cool sea breeze. The moon winked behind a cloud, then was clear again.

The motor of an approaching boat was heard as a distant cough, but the sound grew steadier, closer. A light signaled twice, then once again before the glow was shut off. The second motor, too, gave way to silence as another fishing vessel drifted alongside the first. The two boats merged into one shadow.

The night was glorious—almost still and silvered by the moon. Men waited, watching that dark, silent figure at the helm.

"The catch is good tonight," a voice called out from the second boat. The sound drifted, disembodied over the water.

"The fish are easily caught while sleeping."

There was a short laugh as two men leaned over the side and hauled a dripping net, pregnant with fish, onto the deck. The vessel swayed with the movement, then steadied.

The hooded man watched the exchange without word or gesture. His eyes shifted from the second vessel to the pile of fish lying scattered and lifeless on the deck. Both motors roared into life again and separated; one to the east, one to the west. The moon glimmered white. The breeze picked up. The boat was again a lone speck on a dark sea.

"Cut them open."

The men looked up sharply into the slitted eyes. "Now?" one of them dared to ask. "Don't you want them taken to the usual place?"

"Cut them open," he repeated. His voice sent a chill through the quiet night. "I take the cache with me."

Three men knelt beside the fish. Their knives worked swiftly and with skill while the scent of blood and sweat and fear prickled the air. A small pile of white packets grew as they were torn from the bellies of fish. The mutilated corpses were tossed back into the sea. No one would bring that catch to their table.

He moved quickly but without any sense of hurry, slipping packets into the pockets of his jacket. To a man they scrambled back from him, as if his touch might bring death—or worse. Satisfied, he gave them a brief survey before he resumed his position at the helm.

Their fear brought him a grim pleasure. And the cache was his for the taking. For the first time, he laughed—a long, cold sound that had nothing to do with humor. No one spoke, in even a whisper, on the journey back.

Later, a shadow among shadows, he moved away from the cove. He was wary that the trip had gone so easily, exhilarated that it was done. There had been no one to question him, no one with the courage to follow, though he was one man and they were many. Still, as he crossed the strip of beach, he moved with caution, for he wasn't a fool. He had more than just a few frightened fishermen to consider. And he would have more to deal with before he was done.

The walk was long, and steep, but he took it at an easy pace. The hollow call of an owl caused him to pause only briefly to scan the trees and rocks through the slits in the mask. From his position, he could see the cool white lines of the Theoharis villa. He stood where he was a moment—watching, thinking. Then he spun away to continue his climb.

He moved over rocks as easily as a goat—walking with a sure, confident stride in the darkness. He'd covered that route a hundred times without a light. And he kept clear of the path—a path meant men. He stepped around the rock where Morgan had sat that morning, but he didn't see the flowers. Without pausing, he continued.

There was a light in the window. He'd left it burning

himself before he had set out. Now for the first time he thought of comfort—and a drink to wash the taste of other men's fear from his throat.

Entering the house, he strode down the corridor and entered a room. Carelessly, he dumped the contents of his pockets on an elegant Louis XVI table, then removed his hood with a flourish.

"Well, Stephanos." Nick's teeth flashed in a grin. "The fishing was rich tonight."

Stephanos acknowledged the packets with a nod. "No trouble?"

"One has little trouble with men who fear the air you breathe. The trip was as smooth as a whore's kiss." Moving away, he poured two drinks and handed one to his companion. The sense of exhilaration was still on him—the power that comes from risking death and winning. He drained his drink in one swallow. "A seedy crew, Stephanos, but they do their job. They're greedy, and"—he lifted the hood, then let it fall on the cache of opium, black on white—"terrified."

"A terrified crew is a cooperative one," Stephanos commented. He poked a stubby finger at the cache of opium. "Rich fishing indeed. Enough to make a man comfortable for a long time."

"Enough to make him want more," Nick stated with a grin. "And more. *Diabolos,* the smell of fish clings to me." He wrinkled his nose in disgust. "Send our cache to Athens, and see they send a report to me of its purity. I'm going to wash off this stink and go to bed."

"There's a matter you might be interested in."

"Not tonight." Nick didn't bother to turn around. "Save your gossip for tomorrow."

"The woman, Nicholas." Stephanos saw him stiffen and pause. There was no need to tell him which woman. "I learned she doesn't go back to America. She stays here while Alex is in Athens."

"Diabolos!" Nick swore and turned back into the room. "I can't be worried about a woman."

"She stays alone until Alex sends his lady back."

"The woman is not my concern," he said between his teeth.

As was his habit, Stephanos sniffed the liquor to add to his appreciation. "Athens was interested," he said mildly. "Perhaps she could still be of use."

"No." Nick took an agitated turn around the room. Nerves that had been cold as ice began to thaw. Damn her, he thought, she'll make me careless even thinking of her. "That woman is more trouble than use. No," he repeated as Stephanos lifted his brows. "We'll keep her out of it."

"Difficult, considering—"

"We'll keep her out of it," Nick repeated in a tone that made Stephanos stroke his moustache.

"As you wish, *kyrios.*"

"Go to the devil." Annoyed with the mock respectful tone, Nick picked up his glass, then set it down again. "She's no use to us," he said with more calm. "More of a stumbling block. We'll hope she keeps her elegant nose inside the villa for a few days."

"And if she pokes her elegant nose out?" Stephanos inquired, enjoying his liquor.

Nick's mouth was a grim line. "Then I'll deal with her."

"I think perhaps," he murmured as Nick strode from the room, "she has already dealt with you, old friend." He laughed and poured himself another drink. "Indeed, the lady's dealt you a killing blow."

After he had bathed, Nick couldn't settle. He told himself it was the excess energy from the night, and his success. But he found himself standing at his window, staring down at the Theoharis villa.

So she was alone, he thought, asleep in that big soft bed. It meant nothing to him. He'd climbed that damn wall to her room for the last time. He'd gone there the night before on impulse, something he'd known better than to do. He'd gone to see her, with some mad idea of justifying his actions to her.

Fool, he called himself as his hands curled tight around the stone railing. Only a fool justifies what he does. He'd gone to her and she'd taunted him, driven him to give up something he had no business giving up. His heart. Damn her, she'd wrenched it out of him.

His grip tightened as he remembered what it had been like to have her—to taste her and fill himself with her. It had been a mistake, perhaps the most crucial one he'd ever made. It was one matter to risk your life, another to risk your soul.

He shouldn't have touched her, Nick thought on yet another wave of anger. He'd known it even as his hands had reached for her. She hadn't known what she was doing, drunk on the ouzo Andrew had bought her. Andrew—he felt a moment's rage and banked it. There'd been moments when he hated Andrew, knowing he'd kissed her.

Hated Dorian because Morgan had smiled at him. And Alex because he could touch her in friendship.

And, he knew, Morgan would hate him for what had passed between them that night. Hadn't he heard it in the icy words she'd flung at him? He'd rather have handed her his own knife than to have the words of a woman slash at him that way. She would hate him for taking her when she was vulnerable—while that damn medal hung around her neck. And she would hate him for what he was.

On a rising wave of temper, Nick whirled away from the window. Why should it concern him? Morgan James would slip out of his life like a dream in only a few weeks in any case. He'd chosen his path before, long before he'd seen her. It was his way. If she hated him for what he was, then so be it. He wouldn't allow her to make him feel dirty and soiled.

If she'd touched his heart, he could deal with it. Sprawling into a chair, Nick scowled into the darkness. He would deal with it, he promised himself. After all he'd done, and all he'd faced, no blue-eyed witch would take him under.

Morgan felt completely alone. The solitude and silence she had so prized only a few days before now weighed down on her. The house was full of servants, but that brought her no comfort, no company. Alex and Liz and Dorian were gone. She wandered listlessly through the morning as she had wandered restlessly through the night. The house felt like a prison—clean and white and empty. Trapped inside it, she was too vulnerable to her own thoughts.

And because her thoughts centered too often on Nick,

she found the idea of lying in the bed they had shared too painful. How could she sleep in peace in a place where she could still feel his hands on her, his lips ruthlessly pressing on hers? How could she sleep in a room that seemed to carry that faint sea-smell that so often drifted from him?

So she couldn't sleep, and her thoughts—and needs—haunted her. What could have happened to her to cause her to love such a man? And how long could she fight it? If she surrendered to it, she'd suffer for the rest of her life.

Knowing she was only adding to her own depression, Morgan changed into a bathing suit and headed for the beach.

It was ridiculous to be afraid of the beach, afraid of the house, she told herself. She was here to enjoy both for the next three weeks. Locking herself in her room wouldn't change anything that had happened.

The sand glistened, white and brilliant. Morgan found that on facing it again, the horror didn't materialize. Tossing aside her wrap, she ran into the sea. The water would ease the weariness, the tension. And maybe, just maybe, she would sleep tonight.

Why should she be keeping herself in a constant state of nerves over the death of a man she didn't even know? Why should she allow the harmless stub of a cigarette to haunt her? It was time to accept the simple explanations and keep her distance. The man had been killed as a result of a village brawl, and that was that. It had nothing to do with her, or anyone she knew. It was tragic, but it wasn't personal.

She wouldn't think about Iona, she told herself. She wouldn't think about smuggling or murders or—here she hesitated a moment and dived under a wave—Nicholas. For now, she wouldn't think at all.

Morgan escaped. In a world of water and sun, she thought only of pleasures. She drifted, letting the tension sink beneath the waves. She'd forgotten, in her own misery, just how clean and alive the water made her feel. For a few moments she would go back to that first day, to that feeling of peace she'd found without even trying.

Liz was going to need her in the next day or two. And Morgan wouldn't be any help at all if she were haggard and tense. Yes, tonight she'd sleep—she'd had enough of nightmares.

More relaxed than she had been in days, Morgan swam back toward shore. The sand shifted under her feet with the gentle current. Shells dotted the shoreline, clean and glistening. She stood and stretched as the water lapped around her knees. The sun felt glorious.

"So Helen rises from the sea."

Lifting her hand, Morgan shielded her eyes and saw Andrew. He sat on the beach by her towel, watching her.

"It's easy to understand how she set kingdoms at odds." He stood and moved to the water's verge to join her. "How are you, Morgan?"

"I'm fine." She accepted the towel he handed her and rubbed it briskly over her hair.

"Your eyes are shadowed. A blue sea surrounded by clouds." He traced her cheek with a fingertip. "Nick told me about Iona Theoharis." He took her hand and led her back to the white sand. Dropping the towel, Morgan sat beside him. "It's a bit soon for you to have to handle something like that, Morgan. I'm sorry you had to be the one to find her."

"It seems to be a talent of mine." She shook her head. "I'm much better today, really." Smiling, she touched his cheek. "Yesterday I felt…actually I don't think I felt much of anything yesterday. It was like I was watching everything through a fisheye lens. Everything was distorted and unreal. Today it's real, but I can cope with it."

"I suppose that's nature's way of cushioning the senses."

"I feel this incredible sorrow for Alex and Liz—and for Dorian." She leaned back on her elbows, wanting to feel the sun as it dried the water on her skin. "It's so hard on them, Andrew. It leaves me feeling helpless." She turned her face to his, pushing at her streaming hair. "I hope this doesn't sound hard, but I feel, after these past two days, I think I've just realized how glad I am to be alive."

"I'd say that's a very healthy, very normal reaction." He, too, leaned back on his elbows, narrowing his eyes against the sun as he studied her.

"Oh, I hope so. I've been feeling guilty about it."

"You can't be guilty about wanting to live, Morgan."

"No. Suddenly I realized how much I want to do. How much I want to see. Do you know, I'm twenty-six, and this is the first time I've been anywhere? My mother died when I was a baby and my father and I moved to New York from Philadelphia. I've never seen anything else." As drops of water trickled down her skin, she shook her damp hair back. "I can speak five languages, and this is the first time I've been in a country where English isn't needed. I want to go to Italy and France." She turned to face him more directly. Her eyes, though still shadowed, were huge with adventure. "I want to see Venice and ride in a gondola. I want to walk on the Cornish moors and on the Champs d'élysées." She laughed and it felt marvelous. "I want to climb mountains."

"And be a fisherman?" He smiled and laid a hand over hers.

"Oh, I did say that, didn't I?" She laughed again. "I'll do that, too. Jack always said my taste was rather eclectic."

"Jack?"

"He's a man I knew back home." Morgan found the ease with which she put him in the past satisfying. "He was in politics. I think he wanted to be king."

"Were you in love with him?"

"No, I was used to him." She rolled her eyes and grinned. "Isn't that a terrible thing to say?"

"I don't know—you tell me."

"No," she decided. "Because it's the truth. He was very cautious, very conventional, and, I'm sorry to say, very boring. Not at all like…" Her voice trailed off.

Andrew followed her gaze and spotted Nick at the top of the cliff. He stood, legs apart, hands thrust in his pockets, staring down at them. His expression was unreadable in the distance. He turned, without a wave or a sign of greeting, and disappeared behind the rocks.

Andrew shifted his gaze back to Morgan. Her expression was totally readable.

"You're in love with Nick."

Morgan brought herself back sharply. "Oh, no. No, of course not. I hardly know him. He's a very disagreeable man. He has a brutal temper, and he's arrogant and bossy and without any decent feelings. He shouts."

Andrew took in this impassioned description with a lifted brow. "We seem to be talking about two different people."

Morgan turned away, running sand through her fingers. "Maybe. I don't like either one of them."

Andrew let the silence hang a moment as he watched her busy fingers. "But you're in love with him."

"Andrew—"

"And you don't want to be," he finished, looking thoughtfully out to sea. "Morgan, I've been wondering, if I asked you to marry me, would it spoil our friendship?"

"What?" Astonished, she spun her head back around. "Are you joking?"

Calmly, he searched her face. "No, I'm not joking. I decided that asking you to bed would put a strain on our friendship. I wondered if marriage would. Though I didn't realize you were in love with Nick."

"Andrew," she began, uncertain how to react. "Is this a question or a proposal?"

"Let's take the question first."

Morgan took a deep breath. "An offer of marriage, especially from someone you care for, is always flattering to the ego. But egos are unstable and friendships don't require flattery." Leaning over, she brushed his mouth with hers. "I'm very glad you're my friend, Andrew."

"Somehow I thought that would be your reaction. I'm a romantic at heart." Shrugging, he gave her a rueful smile. "An island, a beautiful woman with a laugh like a night wind. I could see us setting up house in the cottage. Fires in the winter, flowers in the spring."

"You're not in love with me, Andrew."

"I could be." Taking her hand, he turned it palm up and studied it. "It isn't your destiny to fall in love with a struggling poet."

"Andrew—"

"And it isn't mine to have you." Smiling again, he kissed her hand. "Still, it's a warm thought."

"And a lovely one. Thank you for it."

He nodded before he rose. "I might decide Venice offers inspiration." Andrew studied the protruding section of the gray stone wall before turning back to her. "Maybe we'll see each other there." He smiled, the flashing boyish smile, and Morgan felt a twinge of regret. "Timing, Morgan, is such an essential factor in romance."

She watched him cross the sand and mount the steps before she turned back to the sea.

Chapter 10

The villa whispered and trembled like an old woman. Even after all her promises to herself that morning, Morgan couldn't sleep. She rolled and tossed in her bed, frantically bringing herself back from dreams each time she started to drift off. It was too easy for Nick to slip into her mind in a dream. Through sheer force of will, Morgan had blocked him out for most of the day. She wouldn't surrender to him now, for only a few hours sleep.

Yet awake and alone, she found herself remembering the inlet—the face under the water, the slim black stub of a cigarette. And Iona, pale and barely alive, with her thick mane of hair streaming nearly to the floor.

Why was it she couldn't rid herself of the thought that one had something to do with the other?

There was too much space, too much quiet in the villa to be tolerated in solitude. Even the air seemed hot and oppressive. As fatigue began to take over, Morgan found herself caught between sleep and wakefulness, that vulnerable land where thoughts can drift and tease.

She could hear Alex's voice, cold and hard, telling her that Iona would be better off dead. There were Dorian's eyes, so calm, so cool, as he lifted a thin black cigarette to his lips. Andrew smiling grimly as he waited for his ship to come in. Liz vowing passionately that she would protect her husband from anyone and anything. And the knife blade, so sharp and deadly. She knew without seeing that Nick's hand gripped the handle.

On a half scream, Morgan sat up and willed herself awake. No, she wouldn't sleep, not alone. She didn't dare.

Before giving herself time to think, she rose and slipped on jeans and a shirt. The beach had given her peace that afternoon. Maybe it would do the same for her tonight.

Outside, she found the openness comforting. There were no walls here or empty rooms. There were stars and the scent of blossoms. She could hear the cypress leaves whisper. The feeling of dread slid from her with every step. She headed for the beach.

The moon was nearly full now, and white as bone. The breeze off the water was degrees cooler than the air had been in her room. She followed the path without hesitation, without fear. Some instinct told her nothing would harm her that night.

After rolling up her pants legs, she stood, letting the water lap over her ankles, warm and silky. Gratefully, she breathed in the moist sea air and felt it soothe her. She stretched her arms toward the stars.

"Will you never learn to stay in bed?"

Morgan spun around to find herself face-to-face with

Nick. Had he already been there? she wondered. She hadn't heard him walk behind her. Straightening, she eyed him coolly. Like her, he wore jeans and no shoes. His shirt hung unbuttoned over his bare chest. What madness was it, she wondered, that made her long to go to him. Whatever madness drew her to him, she suppressed.

"That's not your concern." Morgan turned her back on him.

Nick barely prevented himself from yanking her back around. He'd been standing sleepless at his window when he'd seen her leave the house. Almost before he had known what he was doing, he was coming down the beach steps to find her. And it was ice, that same ice, she greeted him with.

"Have you forgotten what happens to women who wander night beaches alone?" The words rang with mockery as he tangled his fingers in her hair. He'd touch her if he chose, he thought furiously. No one would stop him.

"If you plan to drag me around this time, Nicholas, I warn you, I'll bite and scratch."

"That should make it interesting." His fingers tightened as she tossed her head to dislodge his grip. "I'd think you'd have had your fill of beaches today, Aphrodite. Or are you expecting Andrew again?"

She ignored the taunt and the peculiar thrill that came whenever he called her by that name. "I'm not expecting anyone. I came here to be alone. If you'd go away, I could enjoy myself."

Hurting, wanting, Nick spun her around. His fingers bruised her skin so that she made a surprised sound of pain before she could clamp it down. "Damn you, Morgan, don't push me any more. You'll find me a different breed from young Andrew."

"Take your hands off me." She managed to control her voice to a hard, cold steadiness. Her eyes glimmered with frost as they stared into his. She wouldn't cower before him again, and she wouldn't yield. "You'd do well to take lessons from Andrew"—deliberately, she tossed her head and smiled—"or Dorian on how to treat a woman."

Nick swore with quick Greek expertise. Unable to do otherwise, he gripped her tighter, but this time she made no sound. Morgan watched as the dark fury took total command of his face. He was half devil now, violent, with barely a trace of the man others knew. It gave her a perverse enjoyment to know she had driven him to it.

"So you offer yourself to Dorian as well?" He bit off the words as he fought to find some hold on his control. "How many men do you need?"

A flood of fury rose, but she stamped it down. "Isn't it strange, Nicholas," she said calmly, "how your Greek half seems to take over when you're angry? I simply can't see how you and Andrew can be related, however remotely."

"You enjoy leading him on, don't you?" The comparison stroked his fury higher. Morgan found she was gritting her teeth to prevent a whimper at the pain. She wouldn't give him the satisfaction. "Heartless bitch," he hissed at her. "How long do you intend to dangle and tease?"

"How dare you!" Morgan pushed against him. Anger, unreasonable and full, welled up in her for all the sleepless hours he'd given her, and all the pain. "How dare you criticize me for anything! You, with the filthy games you play, and the lies. You care about *no one*—no one but yourself. I detest you and everything you are!" Wrenching free, Morgan fled into the sea, blind and senseless with rage.

"Stupid woman!" Nick tore through two sentences of furious Greek before he caught her and pulled her around. The water lapped around her hips as he shook her. When her feet slipped on the bottom, he dragged her back up. He couldn't think now, couldn't reason. His voice whipped out with the violence of his thoughts. "I'll be damned if you'll make me crawl. Damned if I'll beg for your good feelings. I do what I have to do; it's a matter of necessity. Do you think I enjoy it?"

"I don't care about your necessities or your smuggling or your murders! I don't care about anything that has to do with you. I hate you!" She took a swing at his chest and nearly submerged again. "I hate everything about you. I hate myself for ever letting you touch me!"

The words cut at him, deeper than he wanted them to. He fought not to remember what it had felt like to hold her, to press his mouth against her and feel her melt against him. "That's fine. Just keep your distance and we'll get along perfectly."

"There's nothing I want more than to keep away from you." Her eyes glittered as the words brought her a slash of pain. "Nothing I want more than to never see your face again or hear your name."

He controlled himself with an effort—for there was nothing he wanted more at that moment than to crush her against him and beg, as he'd never begged anyone, for whatever she'd give him. "Then that's what you'll have,

Aphrodite. Play your games with Dorian if you like, but tread carefully with Andrew. Tread carefully, or I'll break your beautiful neck."

"Don't you threaten me. I'll see Andrew just as often as I like." Morgan pushed at her dripping hair and glared at him. "I don't think he'd appreciate your protection. He asked me to marry him."

In one swift move, Nick lifted her off her feet and dragged her against his chest. Morgan kicked out, succeeding only in drenching both of them. "What did you tell him?"

"It's none of your business." She struggled, and though she was slick as an eel in the water, his hold remained firm. "Put me *down!* You can't treat me this way."

Fury was raging in him, uncontrollable, savage. No, he wouldn't stand by and watch her with another man. "Damn you, I said what did you tell him!"

"No!" she shouted, more in anger than in fear. "I told him *no.*"

Nick relaxed his grip. Morgan's feet met the sea bottom again as he formed a brittle smile. Her face was white as chalk and he cursed himself. God, would he do nothing but hurt her? Would she do nothing but hurt him? If there weren't so many walls in his way…if he could break down even one of them, he'd have her.

"That's fine." His voice was far from steady, but she had no way of knowing it was from panic rather than temper. "I won't stand by and watch you lead Andrew along. He's an innocent yet." He released her, knowing it might be the last time he'd ever touch her. "I don't suppose you chose to tell him about the lover you left behind."

"Lover?" Morgan pushed at her hair as she took a step back. "What lover?"

Nick lifted the medallion at her neck, then let it fall before he gave into the need to rip it from her. "The one who gave you the trinket you treasure so much. When a woman carries another man's brand, it's difficult to overlook it."

Morgan closed her hand over the small piece of silver. She had thought nothing could make her more angry than she already was. She was blind and trembling with it. "Another man's brand," she repeated in a whisper. "How typical of you. No one brands me, Nicholas. No one, no matter how I love."

"Your pardon, Aphrodite," he returned coolly. "An expression only."

"My father gave me this," she tossed at him. "He gave it to me when I was eight years old and broke my arm falling out of a tree. He's the kindest and most loving person I've ever known. You, Nicholas Gregoras, are a stupid man."

She turned and darted toward the beach, but he caught her again while the water was still around her ankles. Ignoring her curses and struggles, Nick turned her to face him. His eyes bored into hers. His breath was coming in gasps, but not from rage. He needed an answer, and quickly, before he exploded.

"You don't have a lover in America?"

"I said let me *go!*" She was glorious in fury—eyes glittering, skin white as the moonlight. With her head thrown back, she dared him to defy her. In that moment he thought he would have died for her.

"Do you have a lover in America?" Nick demanded again, but his voice was quiet now.

Morgan threw up her chin. "I haven't a lover *anywhere*."

On an oath that sounded more like a prayer, Nick drew her close. The heat from his body fused through the soaked shirts as if they had been naked. Morgan's breath caught at the pressure and the sudden gleam of triumph in his eyes.

"You do now."

Capturing her mouth, he pulled her to the sand.

His lips were urgent, burning. His talk of branding raced through her head, but Morgan accepted the fire eagerly. And already he was stripping off her shirt as if he couldn't bear even the thin separation between them.

Morgan knew he would always love like this. Intensely, without thought, without reason. She gloried in it. Desire this strong took no denial. Her own fingers were busy with his shirt, ripping at the seam in her hurry to be flesh to flesh. She heard him laugh with his mouth pressed against her throat.

There was no longer any right or wrong. Needs were too great. And love. Even as passion drove her higher, Morgan knew and recognized her love. She had waited for it all of her life. With the heat building, there was no time to question how it could be Nick. She only knew it was, whatever, whoever, he was. Nothing else mattered.

When his hands found her naked breasts, he groaned and crushed his lips to hers again. She was so soft, so slender. He struggled not to bruise her, not again, but desire was wild and free in him. He'd never wanted a woman like this. Not like this. Even when he had taken her the first time, he hadn't felt this clean silver streak of power.

She was consuming him, pouring inside his mind. And the taste. Dear God, would he never get enough of the taste of her? He found her breast with his mouth and filled himself.

Morgan arched and dove her fingers into his hair. He was murmuring something, but his breathing was as ragged as hers and she couldn't understand. When his mouth was back on hers, there was no need to. She felt him tugging her jeans over her hips, but was too delirious to realize she had pulled at his first. She felt the skin stretched tight over his bones, the surprising narrowness of his body.

Then his lips and hands were racing over her—not in the angry desperation she remembered from the night before, but in unquestionable possession. There was no gentleness, but neither was there a fierceness. He took and took as though no one had a better right. Those strong lean fingers stroked down her, making her gasp out loud in pleasure, then moan in torment when they lay still.

His mouth was always busy, tongue lightly torturing, teeth taking her to the edge of control. There seemed to be no part of her, no inch he couldn't exploit for pleasure. And the speed never slacked.

Cool sand, cool water, and his hot, clever mouth—she was trapped between them. There was moonlight, rippling white, but she was a willing prisoner of the darkness. In the grove of cypresses a night bird called out—one long, haunting note. It might have been her own sigh. She tasted the sea on his skin, knew he would taste it on hers as well. Somehow, that small intimacy made her hold him tighter.

They might have been the only ones, washed ashore, destined to be lovers throughout their lives without the need for anyone else. The scent of the night wafted over her—his scent. They would always be the same to her.

Then she heard nothing, knew nothing, as he drove her beyond reason with his mouth alone.

She was grasping at him, demanding and pleading in the same breathless whispers for him to give her that final, delirious relief. But he held her off, pleasing himself, and pleasing her until she thought her body would simply implode at the pressure that was building.

With a wild, hungry kiss he silenced her while leading her closer to the edge. Though she could feel his heart racing against hers, he seemed determined to hold them there—an instant, an hour—hovering between heaven and hell.

When he drove them over, Morgan wasn't certain on which side they had fallen—only that they had fallen together.

Morgan lay quiet, cushioned against Nick's bare shoulder. The waves gently caressed her legs. In the aftermath of the demands of passion she was light and cool and stunned. She could feel the blood still pounding in his chest and knew no one, no one had ever wanted her like this. The sense of power it might have given her came as an ache. She closed her eyes on it.

She hadn't even struggled, she thought. Not even a token protest. She had given herself without thought—

not in submission to his strength, but in submission to her own desires. Now, as the heat of passion ebbed, she felt the hard edge of shame.

He was a criminal—a hard, self-seeking man who trafficked in misery for profit. And she had given him her body and her heart. Perhaps she had no control over her heart, but Morgan was honest enough to know she ruled her own body. Shivering, she drew away from him.

"No, stay." Nick nuzzled in her hair as he held her against his side.

"I have to go in," she murmured. Morgan drew her body away as far as his arm would permit. "Please, let me go."

Nick shifted until his face hovered over hers. His lips were curved in amusement; his face was relaxed and satisfied. "No," he said simply. "You won't walk away from me again."

"Nicholas, please." Morgan turned her head aside. "It's late. I have to go."

He became still for a moment, then took her face firmly in his hand and turned it back to his. He saw the gleam of tears, tightly controlled, and swore. "It occurs to you suddenly that you've just given yourself to a criminal and enjoyed it."

"Don't!" Morgan shut her eyes. "Just let me go in. Whatever I've done, I've done because I wanted to."

Nick stared down at her. She was dry-eyed now, but her eyes were bleak. Swearing again, he reached for his partially dry shirt and pulled Morgan into a sitting position. Athens, he thought again, could fry in hell.

"Put this on," he ordered, swinging it over her shoulders. "We'll talk."

"I don't want to talk. There's no need to talk."

"I said we'll talk, Morgan." Nick pushed her arm into a sleeve. "I won't have you feeling guilty over what just happened." She could feel the simmering anger pulsing from him as he pulled his shirt over her breasts. "I won't have that," he muttered. "It's too much. I can't explain everything now…there are some things I won't ever explain."

"I'm not asking for explanations."

His eyes locked on hers. "You ask every time you look at me." Nick pulled a cigarette from the pocket of the shirt, then lit it. "My business in import-export has made me quite a number of contacts over the years. Some of whom, I imagine, you wouldn't approve of." He mused over this for a moment as he blew out a hazy stream of smoke.

"Nicholas, I don't—"

"Shut up, Morgan. When a man's decided to bare his soul, a woman shouldn't interrupt. God knows how dark you'll find it," he added, as he drew in smoke again. "When I was in my early, impressionable twenties, I met a man who considered me suitable for a certain type of work. I found the work itself fascinating. Danger can become addicting, like any other drug."

Yes, she thought as she stared out over the water. If nothing else, she could understand that.

"I began to—freelance." He smiled at the term, but it had little to do with humor. "For his organization. For the most part I enjoyed it. In any case, I was content with it.

It's amazing that a way of life, ten years of my life should become a prison in a week's time."

Morgan had drawn her knees close to her chest while she stared out over the water. Nick laid a hand on her hair, but she still didn't look at him. He was finding it more difficult to tell her than he had imagined. Even after he'd finished, she might turn away from him. He'd be left with nothing—less than nothing. He drew hard on his cigarette, then stared at the red glow at the tip.

"Morgan, there are things I've done…" He swore briefly under his breath. "There are things I've done I wouldn't tell you about even if I were free to. You wouldn't find them pleasant."

Now she lifted her face. "You've killed people."

He found it difficult to answer when she was looking at him with tired despair in her eyes. But his voice was cool with control. "When it was necessary."

Morgan lowered her head again. She hadn't wanted to think him a murderer. If he had denied it, she would have tried to have taken him at his word. She hadn't wanted to believe he was capable of what she considered the ultimate sin. The taking of a life.

Nick scowled at the cigarette and hurled it into the sea. I could have lied to her, he thought furiously. Why the hell didn't I just lie—I'm an expert at it. Because I can't lie to her, he realized with a tired sigh. Not anymore. "I did what I had to do, Morgan," he said flatly. "I can't erase the way I've lived for ten years. Right or wrong, it was my choice. I can't apologize for it."

"No, I'm not asking you to. I'm sorry if it seems that way." She drew herself up again and faced him. "Please,

Nicholas, let's leave it at this. Your life's your own. You don't have to justify it to me."

"Morgan—" If she had hurled abuse at him, stabbed him with ice, he might have been able to keep silent. But he couldn't be silent while she struggled to understand. He would tell her, and the decision he'd been struggling with for days would be made. "For the last six months, I've been working on breaking the smuggling ring that runs between Turkey and Lesbos."

Morgan stared at him as though she'd never seen him before. "Breaking it? But I thought...you told me—"

"I've never told you much of anything," he said curtly. "I let you assume. It was better that way. It was necessary."

For a moment she sat quietly, trying to sort out her thoughts. "Nicholas, I don't understand. Are you telling me you're a policeman?"

He laughed at the thought, and part of his anger drained. "No, Aphrodite, spare me that."

Morgan frowned. "A spy then?"

The rest of his anger vanished. He cupped her face in his hands. She was so unbearably sweet. "You will romanticize it, Morgan, I'm a man who travels and follows orders. Be content with that, it's all I can give you."

"That first night on the beach..." At last the puzzle pieces were taking a shape she could understand. "You were watching for the man who runs the smuggling ring. That was who Stephanos followed."

Nick frowned and dropped his hands. She believed him without question or hesitation. Already she'd forgotten that he'd killed—and worse. Why, when she was making it so easy for him did he find it so hard to go on?

"I had to get you out of the way. I knew he'd cross that section of beach on his way to Stevos's cottage. Stevos was eliminated because he knew, as I don't yet, the man's exact position in the organization. I think he asked for a raise and got a knife in the back."

"Who is he, Nicholas?"

"No." His eyes came back to hers. His face was hard again, unreachable. "Even if I were sure, I wouldn't tell you. Don't ask me questions I can't answer, Morgan. The more I tell you, the more dangerous your position becomes." His eyes grew darker. "I was ready to use you once, and my organization is very interested in your talent with languages, but I'm a selfish man. You're not going to be involved." His tone was final and just a little furious. "I told my associate you weren't interested."

"That's a bit presumptuous," Morgan began. She frowned until he twisted his head and looked at her again. "I'm capable of making my own decisions."

"You haven't one to make," Nick countered coolly. "And once I know for certain the identity of the head of the ring, my job's finished. Athens will have to learn how to function without me."

"You're not going to do this…" She gestured vaguely, not knowing what title to give his work. "This sort of thing anymore?"

"No." Nick stared back out to sea. "I've been in it long enough."

"When did you decide to stop?"

When I first made love with you, he thought, and nearly said it. But it wasn't quite true. There was one more thing he would have to tell her. "The day I took Iona on the boat." Nick let out an angry breath and turned to her. He had his doubts that she would forgive him for what he was going to say. "Iona's in this, Morgan, deeply."

"In the smuggling? But——"

"I can only tell you that she is, and that part of my job was to get information out of her. I took her out on the boat, fully intending to make love to her to help loosen her tongue." Morgan kept her eyes steady and he continued, growing angrier. "She was cracking under pressure. I was there to help her along. That's why someone tried to kill her."

"Kill her?" Morgan tried to keep her voice level as she dealt with what he was telling her. "But Captain Tripolos said it was attempted suicide."

"Iona would no more have committed suicide than she would have tended goats."

"No," she said slowly. "No, of course you're right."

"If I could have worked on her a little longer, I would have had all that I needed."

"Poor Alex," she murmured. "He'll be crushed if it comes out that she was mixed up in this. And Dorian..." She remembered his empty eyes and his words. *Poor Iona—so beautiful—so lost*. Perhaps he already suspected. "Isn't there something you can do?" She looked up at Nick, this time with trust. "Do the police know? Captain Tripolos?"

"Tripolos knows a great deal and suspects more." Nick took her hand now. He wanted the link badly. "I don't work directly with the police, it slows things down. At the moment," he added cheerfully, "Tripolos has me pegged as the prime suspect in a murder, an attempted murder, and sees me in the role of the masked smuggler. Lord, I'd have given him a thrill last night."

"You enjoy your work, don't you?" Morgan studied him, recognizing the light of adventure in his eyes. "Why are you stopping?"

His smile faded. "I told you I was with Iona. It wasn't the first time I used that method. Sex can be a weapon or a tool, it's a fact of life." Morgan dropped her gaze to the sand. "She'd had too much champagne to be cooperative, but there would have been another time. Since that day, I haven't felt clean." He slid his hand under her chin and lifted it. "Not until tonight."

She was studying him closely, searching. In his eyes she saw something she had only seen once before—regret, and a plea for understanding. Lifting her arms, she brought his mouth down to hers. She felt more than his lips—the heady wave of his relief.

"Morgan." He pressed her back to the sand again. "If I could turn back the clock and have this past week to live over..." He hesitated, then buried his face in her hair. "I probably wouldn't do anything differently."

"You apologize beautifully, Nicholas."

He couldn't keep his hands off her. They were roaming again, arousing them both. "This thing should come to a head tomorrow night, then I'll be at loose ends. Come away somewhere with me for a few days. Anywhere."

"Tomorrow?" She struggled to keep her mind on his words while her body heated. "Why tomorrow?"

"A little complication I caused last night. Come, we're covered with sand. Let's take a swim."

"Complication?" Morgan repeated as he hauled her to her feet. "What kind of complication?"

"I don't think our man will tolerate the loss of a shipment," he murmured as he slipped his shirt from her shoulders.

"You stole it!"

He was pulling her into the water. His blood was already pounding for her as he saw the moonlight glow white over her body. "With incredible ease." When she was past her waist, he drew her against him. The water lapped around them as he began to explore her again. "Stephanos and I watched the connection from a safe distance on several runs." His mouth brushed over hers, then traced down to her throat. "We'd just come back from one the night I found you on the beach. Now, about those few days."

"What will you do tomorrow night?" Morgan drew back enough to stop his roaming hands and mouth. A hint of fear had worked its way in. "Nicholas, what's going to happen?"

"I'm waiting for some conclusive information from Athens. When it comes, I'll know better how to move. At any rate, I'll be there when the boat docks with its cache tomorrow night."

"Not alone?" She gripped his shoulders. "He's already killed a man."

Nick rubbed his nose against hers. "Do you worry for me, Aphrodite?"

"Don't joke!"

He heard the very real panic in her voice and spoke soothingly. "By late tomorrow afternoon, Tripolos will be brought up to date. If everything goes as planned, I can brief him personally." He smiled down at the frown on her face. "He'll gain all official credit for whatever arrests are made."

"But that's unfair!" Morgan exclaimed. "After all your work, and the time, why shouldn't you—"

"Shut up, Morgan, I can't make love to a woman who's constantly complaining."

"Nicholas, I'm trying to understand."

"Understand this." Impatience shimmered in his voice as he pulled her close again. "I've wanted you from the minute I saw you sitting on that damn rock, and I haven't begun to have enough. You've driven me mad for days. Not anymore, Aphrodite. Not anymore."

He lowered his mouth, and all else was lost.

Chapter 11

Her jeans were still damp as Morgan struggled into them laughing. "You would make me so furious I'd run into the water fully dressed."

Nick fastened the snap on his own. "The feeling was mutual."

Turning her head, she looked at him as he stood, naked to the waist, shaking what sand he could from his shirt. A gleam of mischief lit her eyes. "Oh?" Taking a step closer, Morgan ran her palms up his chest—taking her time—enjoying the hard, firm feel of it before she linked them around his neck. "Did it make you furious thinking I was wearing a token from a lover waiting for me back home?"

"No," he lied with a careless smile. Gripping his shirt in both hands, Nick hooked it around her waist to draw her closer. "Why should that concern me?"

"Oh." Morgan nipped lightly at his bottom lip. "Then perhaps you'd like to hear about Jack."

"I damn well wouldn't," he muttered before his mouth

crushed down on hers. Even as her lips answered his, Nick heard the low sound of her muffled laughter. "Witch." Then he took her deeper, deeper, until her laughter was only a sigh. "Maybe you prefer me when I'm angry."

"I prefer you," she said simply, and rested her head on his shoulder.

His arms tightened, strong, possessive. Yet somehow he knew strength alone would never keep her. "Dangerous woman," Nick murmured. "I knew it the first time I held you."

With a laugh, Morgan tossed back her head. "The first time you held me, you cursed me."

"And I continue to do so." But his lips sought hers again without an oath.

"I wish there was only tonight." Suddenly, she was clinging to him with her heart racing. "No tomorrows, only now. I don't want the sun to come up."

Nick buried his face in her hair as the guilt swamped him. He'd brought her fear from the first instant. Even loving her, he could bring her nothing else. He had no right to tell her now that his heart was hers for the asking. Once he told her, she might beg him to abandon his responsibility, leave his job half finished. And he would do just as she asked, he realized…and never feel like a man again.

"Don't wish your days away, Morgan," he told her lightly. "The sun comes up tomorrow, then goes down. And when it comes up again, we'll have nothing but time."

She had to trust him, had to believe that he would be safe—that the danger he lived with would be over in little more than twenty-four hours.

"Come back with me now." Lifting her head again, Morgan gave him a smile. Her worry and fears wouldn't help him. "Come back to the villa and make love with me again."

"You tempt me, Aphrodite." Bending, he kissed both her cheeks in a gesture she found unbearably gentle and sweet. "But you're asleep on your feet. There'll be other nights. I'll take you back."

She allowed him to turn her toward the beach steps. "You might not find it as easy to leave me there alone as you think," she commented with another smile.

With a quiet laugh, he drew her closer to his side. "Not easy perhaps, but—" His head whipped up abruptly, as if he were scenting the air. Narrowed and cold, his eyes swept the darkness of the cliffs above them.

"Nicholas, what—"

But his hand clamped over her mouth as he pulled her, once again, into the shadows of the cypress. Her heart leaped to her throat as it had before, but this time Morgan didn't struggle.

"Be still and don't speak," Nick whispered. Removing his hand, he pushed her back against the trunk of a tree. "Not a sound, Morgan."

She nodded, but he wasn't looking at her. His eyes were trained on the cliffs. Standing at the edge of the covering, Nick watched and waited. Then he heard it again—the quiet scrape of boot on rock. Tensing, he strained his eyes and at last saw the shadow. So, he thought with a grim smile as he watched the black form move swiftly over the rocks, he's come for his cache. But you won't find it, Nick told the shadow silently. And I'll be like a hound on your tail.

Soundlessly, he moved back to Morgan. "Go back to the villa and stay there." All warmth had dropped away from him. His voice was as cold as his eyes.

"What did you see?" she demanded. "What are you going to do?"

"Do as I say." Taking her arm, he pulled her toward the beach steps. "Go quickly, I haven't got time to waste. I'll lose him."

Him. Morgan felt a flutter of fear. She swallowed it. "I'm going with you."

"Don't be a fool." Impatient, Nick dragged her along. "Go back to the villa, I'll speak to you in the morning."

"No." Morgan pulled out of his hold. "I said I'm going with you. You can't stop me."

She was standing straight as an arrow, eyes blazing with a combination of fear and determination. Nick swore at her, knowing every second he stayed meant his man was farther away. "I don't have time—"

"Then you'd better stop wasting it," Morgan said calmly. "I'm coming."

"Then come," he said under his breath as he turned away from her. She won't last five minutes on the cliffs without shoes, he thought. She'd limp her way back to the villa in ten. He moved quickly up the beach steps without waiting for her. Gritting her teeth, Morgan raced after him.

As he left the steps to start his scramble up the cliff, Nick paid little attention to her. He cast his eyes to the sky and wished the night were not so clear. A cloud over the moon would allow him to risk getting closer to the man he followed. He gripped a rock and hauled himself up farther—a few pebbles loosened and skidded down. When he glanced back, he was surprised to see Morgan keeping pace with him.

Damn the woman, he thought with a twinge of reluctant admiration. Without a word, he held out his hand and pulled her up beside him. "Idiot," he hissed, wanting to shake her and kiss her all at once. "Will you go back? You don't have any shoes."

"Neither do you," Morgan gritted.

"Stubborn fool."

"Yes."

Cursing silently, Nick continued the climb. He couldn't risk the open path in the moonlight, so kept to the rocks. Though it wouldn't be possible to keep his quarry in sight, Nick knew where he was going.

Morgan clamped her teeth shut as the ball of her foot scraped against a rock. With a quick hiss of breath, she kept going. She wasn't going to whimper and be snapped at. She wasn't going to let him go without her.

On a rough ledge, Nick paused briefly to consider his options. Circling around would take time. If he'd been alone—and armed, he would have taken his chances with the narrow path now. Odds were that the man he followed was far enough ahead and confident enough to continue his journey without looking over his shoulder. But he wasn't alone, he thought on a flare of annoyance. And he had no more than his hands to protect Morgan if they were spotted.

"Listen to me," he whispered, hoping to frighten her

as he grabbed her by the shoulders. "The man's killed—and killed more than once, I promise you. When he finds his cache isn't where it should be, he'll know he's being hunted. Go back to the villa."

"Do you want me to call the police?" Morgan asked calmly, though he'd succeeded very well in frightening her.

"No!" The word whipped out, no louder than a breath. "I can't afford to give up the chance to see who he is." Frustrated, he glared at her. "Morgan, I don't have a weapon, if he—"

"I'm not leaving you, Nicholas. You're wasting time arguing about it."

He swore again, then slowly controlled his temper. "All right, damn you. But you'll do exactly as I say or I promise you, I'll knock you unconscious and shove you behind a rock."

She didn't doubt it. Morgan lifted her chin. "Let's go."

Agilely, Nick pulled himself over the ridge and onto the path. Before he could reach back to assist her, Morgan was kneeling on the hard ground beside him. He thought, as he looked into her eyes, that she was a woman men dreamed of. Strong, beautiful, loyal. Taking her hand, he dashed up the path, anxious to make up the time he'd wasted arguing with her. When he felt they'd been in the open long enough, he left the path for the rocks again.

"You know where he's going," Morgan whispered, breathing quickly. "Where?"

"A small cave near Stevos's cottage. He thinks to pick up last night's cache." He grinned suddenly. Morgan heard it in his voice. "He won't find it, and then, by God, he'll sweat. Keep low now—no more talk."

She could see the beauty of the night clearly in the moonlight. The sky was velvet, pierced with stars, flooded by the moon. Even the thin, scruffy bushes working their way through rock held an ethereal allure. The sound of the sea rose from below them, soft with distance. An owl sent up a quiet hooting music of lazy contentment. Morgan thought, if she could look, she might find more blue-headed flowers. Then Nick was pulling her over the next ridge and pressing her to the ground.

"It's just up ahead. Stay here."

"No, I—"

"Don't argue," he said roughly. "I can move faster without you. Don't move and don't make a sound."

Before she could speak, he was scrambling away, silently, half on his belly, half on his knees. Morgan watched him until he was concealed by another huddle of rocks. Then, for the first time since they had begun, she started to pray.

Nick couldn't move quickly now. If he had misjudged the timing, he'd find himself face-to-face with his quarry. He needed to save that pleasure for the following night. But to know—to know who he had been hounding for six months was a bonus Nick couldn't resist.

There were more rocks and a few trees for cover, and he used them as he skirted the dead man's rough cottage. An attempt had been made to clear the ground for a vegetable garden, but the soil had never been worked. Nick wondered idly what had become of the woman who had sometimes shared Stevos's bed and washed his shirts. Then he heard the quiet scrape of boot on rock again. Less than a hundred yards away, Nick estimated. Eyes gleaming in the darkness, he crept toward the mouth of the cave.

He could hear the movements inside, quiet, confident. Slipping behind a rock, he waited, patient, listening. The furious oath that echoed inside the cave brought Nick a rich thrill of pleasure.

Taste the betrayal, he told the man inside. And choke on it.

The movements inside the cave became louder. Nick's smile spread. He'd be searching now, Nick concluded. Looking for signs to tell him if his hiding place had been looted. But no, you haven't been robbed, Nick thought. Your little white bags were lifted from right under your nose.

He saw him then, striding out of the cave—all in black, still masked. Take it off, Nick ordered him silently. Take it off and let me see your face.

The figure stood in the shadows of the mouth of the cave. Fury flowed from him in waves. His head turned from side to side as if he were searching for something... or someone.

They heard the sound at the same instant. The shifting of pebbles underfoot, the rustling of bushes. Dear God, Morgan! Nick thought and half rose from his concealment. As he tensed, he saw the black-clad figure draw a gun and melt back into the shadows.

With his heart beating in his throat, Nick gripped the rock and prepared to lunge. He could catch the man off-guard, he thought rapidly, gain enough time to shout a warning to Morgan so that she could get away. Fear licked at him—not for himself, but at the thought that she might not run fast enough.

The bush directly across the path trembled with movement. Nick sucked in his breath to lunge.

Bony, and with more greed than wit, a dusty goat stepped forward to find a more succulent branch.

Nick sunk down behind the rock, furious that he was trembling. Though she had done nothing more than what he had told her, he cursed Morgan fiercely.

With a furious oath, the man in black stuck the gun back in his belt as he strode down the path. As he passed Nick, he whipped off his mask.

Nick saw the face, the eyes, and knew.

Morgan huddled behind the rock where Nick had shoved her, her arms wrapped around her knees. It seemed she'd already waited an eternity. She strained to hear every sound—the whisper of the wind, the sigh of leaves. Her heart hadn't stopped its painful thudding since he'd left her.

Never again, Morgan promised herself. Never again would she sit and wait. Never again would she sit helpless and trembling, on the verge of hot, useless tears. If anything happened—she clamped down on the incomplete thought. Nothing was going to happen to Nick. He'd be back any moment. But the moments dragged on.

When he dropped down beside her, she had to stifle a scream. Morgan had thought her ears were tuned to hear even the dust blow on the wind, but she hadn't heard his approach. She didn't even say his name, just went into his arms.

"He's gone," Nick told her.

The memory of that one shuddering moment of terror washed over him. He crushed his mouth to hers as though he were starving. All of her fears whipped out, one by one, until there was nothing in her but a well of love.

"Oh, Nicholas, I was so frightened for you. What happened?"

"He wasn't pleased." With a grin that was both ruthless and daring, he pulled her to her feet. "No, he wasn't pleased. He'll be on the boat tomorrow."

"But did you see who—"

"No questions." He silenced her again with his mouth, roughly, as though the adventure were only beginning. "I don't want to have to lie to you again." With a laugh, Nick drew her toward the path and the moonlight. "Now, my stubborn, courageous witch, I'll take you back. Tomorrow when your feet are too sore to stand, you'll curse me."

He wouldn't tell her any more, Morgan thought. And for now, perhaps it was best. "Share my bed tonight." She smiled as she hooked her arm around his waist. "Stay another hour with me, and I won't curse you."

Laughing, he ran a hand down her hair. "What man could resist such an ultimatum?"

Morgan awoke as a soft knock sounded at her door. The small maid peeked inside.

"Your pardon, *kyrios,* a phone call from Athens."

"Oh…thank you, Zena, I'll be right there." Rising quickly, Morgan hurried to the phone in Liz's sitting room, belting her robe as she went. "Hello?"

"Morgan, did I wake you? It's past ten."

"Liz?" Morgan tried to shake away the cobwebs. It had been dawn before she had slept.

"Do you know anyone else in Athens?"

"I'm a bit groggy." Morgan yawned, then smiled with memories. "I went for a late-night swim. It was wonderful."

"You sound very smug," Liz mused. "We'll have to discuss it later. Morgan, I feel terrible about it, but I'm going to have to stay here until tomorrow. The doctors are hopeful, but Iona's still in a coma. I can't leave Alex to cope with his family and everything else alone."

"Please, don't worry about me. I'm sorry, Liz. I know it's difficult for both of you." She thought of Iona's involvement in the smuggling and felt a fresh wave of pity. "How is Alex holding up? He seemed so devastated when he left here."

"It would be easier if the whole family didn't look to him for answers. Oh, Morgan, it's so ugly." Strain tightened her voice and Morgan heard her take a deep breath to control it. "I don't know how Iona's mother will handle it if she dies. And suicide—it just makes it harder."

Morgan swallowed the words she wanted to say. Nick had spoken to her in confidence; she couldn't betray it even for Liz. "You said the doctors are hopeful."

"Yes, her vital signs are leveling, but—"

"What about Dorian, Liz? Is he all right?"

"Barely." Morgan heard Liz sigh again. "I don't know how I could have been so blind not to see how he felt about her. He's hardly left her bedside. If Alex hadn't bullied him, I think he might have slept in the chair beside her last night instead of going home. From the way he looks this morning, I don't think he got any sleep anyway."

"Please give him my best—and Alex, too." On a long frustrated breath she sat down. "Liz, I feel so helpless." She thought of smuggling, attempted murder and shut her eyes. "I wish there were something I could do for you."

"Just be there when I get back." Though her tone lightened, Morgan recognized the effort. "Enjoy the beach for me, look for your goatherd. If you're going to take moonlight swims, you should have some company for them." When Morgan was silent Liz continued slowly. "Or did you?"

"Well, actually..." Smiling, Morgan trailed off.

"Tell me, have you settled on a goatherd or a poet?"

"Neither."

"It must be Nick then," Liz concluded. "Imagine that—all I had to do was invite him to dinner."

Morgan lifted a brow and found herself grinning. "I don't know what you're talking about." Life was everywhere, she remembered, if you only knew where to look.

"*Mmm-hmmm.* We'll talk about it tomorrow. Have fun. The number's there if you need me for anything. Oh, there's some marvelous wine in the cellar," she added, and for the first time, the smile in her voice seemed genuine. "If you feel like a cozy evening—help yourself."

"I appreciate it, Liz, but—"

"And don't worry about me or any of us. Everything's going to be fine. I just know it. Give Nick my love."

"I will," Morgan heard herself saying.

"I thought so. See you tomorrow."

Smiling, Morgan replaced the receiver.

* * *

"And so," Stephanos finished, lovingly stroking his moustache, "after several glasses of ouzo, Mikal became more expansive. The last two dates he gave me when our man joined the fishing expedition were the last week in February and the second week in March. That doesn't include the evening we encountered Morgan James, or when you took the trip in his stead."

Smiling, Nick flipped through the reports on his desk. "And from the end of February to the first week of April, he was in Rome. Even without my stroke of luck last night, that would have ruled him out. With the phone call I just got from Athens, I'd say we've eliminated him altogether from having any part in this. Now we know our man works alone. We move."

"And you move with an easy heart?" Stephanos noted. "What did Athens say?"

"The investigation on that end is complete. He's clean. His books, his records, his phone calls and correspondence. From this end, we know he hasn't been on the island to take part in any of the runs." Nick leaned back in his chair. "I have no doubt that since our man learned of the loss of his last shipment, he'll make the trip tonight. He won't want another to slip through his fingers." He tapped idly on the papers which littered his desk. "Now that I have the information I've been waiting for, we won't keep Athens waiting any longer. We'll have him tonight."

"You were out very late last night," Stephanos commented, taking out an ugly pipe and filling it.

"Keeping tabs on me, Stephanos?" Nick inquired with a lift of brow. "I haven't been twelve for a very long time."

"You are in very good humor this morning." He continued to fill his pipe, tapping the tobacco with patient care. "You haven't been so for many days."

"You should be glad my mood's broken. But then, you're used to my moods, aren't you, old man?"

Stephanos shrugged in agreement or acceptance. "The American lady is fond of walking on the beach. Perhaps you encountered her last night?"

"You're becoming entirely too wise in your old age, Stephanos." Nick struck a match and held it over the bowl of the pipe.

"Not too old to recognize the look of a man satisfied with a night of pleasure," Stephanos commented mildly and sucked to get flame. "A very beautiful lady. Very strong."

Lighting a cigarette, Nick smiled at him. "So you've mentioned before. I'd noticed myself. Tell me, Stephanos, are you also not too old to have ideas about strong, beautiful ladies?"

Stephanos cackled. "Only the dead have no ideas about strong, beautiful ladies, Nicholas. I'm a long way from dead."

Nick flashed him a grin. "Keep your distance, old man. She's mine."

"She is in love with you."

The cigarette halted on its journey to Nick's lips. His smiled faded. Stephanos stood grinning broadly as he was pierced with one of his friend's, lancing looks. "Why do you say that?"

"Because it is true, I've seen it." He puffed enjoyably

on his pipe. "It is often difficult to see what is standing before your eyes. How much longer is she alone?"

Nick brought his thoughts back and scowled at the papers on his desk. "I'm not certain. Another day or so at least, depending on Iona's condition. In love with me," he murmured and looked back at Stephanos.

He knew she was attracted, that she cared—perhaps too much for her own good. But in love with him…. He'd never allowed himself to consider the possibility.

"She will be alone tonight," Stephanos continued blandly, appreciating Nick's stunned look. "It wouldn't do for her to wander from the villa." He puffed a few moments in silence. "If all does not go smoothly, you would want her safely behind locked doors."

"I've already spoken to her. She understands enough to listen and take care." Nick shook his head. Today of all days he had to think clearly. "It's time we invited Captain Tripolos in. Call Mitilini."

Morgan enjoyed a late breakfast on the terrace and toyed with the idea of walking to the beach. He might come, she thought. I could phone and ask him to come. No, she decided, nibbling on her lip as she remembered all he had told her. If tonight is as important as he thinks, he needs to be left alone. I wish I knew more. I wish I knew what he was going to do. What if he gets hurt or… Morgan clamped down on the thought and wished it were tomorrow.

"Kyrios." At the maid's quiet summons, Morgan gasped and spun. "The captain from Mitilini is here to speak with you."

"What?" Panic rose and Morgan swallowed it. If Nick had spoken to him, Tripolos would hardly be waiting to see her, she thought frantically. Perhaps Nick wasn't ready yet. What could Tripolos possibly want with her?

"Tell him I'm out," she decided quickly. "Tell him I've gone to the beach or the village."

"Very good, *kyrios*." The maid accepted her order without question, then watched as Morgan streaked from the terrace.

For the second time, Morgan climbed the steep cliff path. This time, she knew where she was going. She could see Tripolos's official car parked at the villa's entrance as she rounded the first bend. She increased her pace, running until she was certain she herself was out of view.

Her approach had been noticed, however. The wide doors of Nick's villa opened before she reached the top step. Nick came out to meet her.

"*Yiasou*. You must be in amazing shape to take the hill at that speed."

"Very funny," she panted as she ran into his arms.

"Is it that you couldn't keep away from me or is something wrong?" He held her close a moment, then drew her back just far enough to see her face. It was flushed with the run, but there was no fear in her eyes.

"Tripolos is at the villa." Morgan pressed her hand to her heart and tried to catch her breath. "I slipped out the back because I didn't know what I should say to him. Nicholas, I have to sit down. That's a very steep hill."

He was searching her face silently. Still struggling for her breath, Morgan tilted her head and returned the survey. She laughed and pushed the hair from her eyes. "Nicholas, why are you staring at me like that?"

"I'm trying to see what's standing in front of my eyes."

She laughed again. "Well, I am, you fool, but I'm going to collapse from exhaustion any minute."

With a sudden grin, Nick swept her off her feet and into his arms. She circled his neck as his mouth came down on hers.

"What are you doing?" she asked, when he let her breathe again.

"Taking what's mine."

His lips came back to hers and lingered. Slowly, almost lazily, he began to tease her tongue with his until he felt her breath start to shudder into his mouth. He promised himself that when everything was over, he would kiss her again, just like this—luxuriously with the heat of the sun warming her skin. When the night's work was finally over, he thought, and for a moment his lips were rough and urgent. Needs rushed through him almost painfully before he banked them.

"So…" He strolled into the house, still carrying her. "The captain came to see you. He's very tenacious."

Morgan took a deep breath to bring herself back from the power of the kiss. "You said you were going to speak with him today, but I didn't know if you were ready. If you'd gotten the information you needed. And to confess and humiliate myself, I'm a coward. I didn't want to face him again."

"Coward, Aphrodite? No, that's something you're not." He laid his cheek against hers a moment, making her wonder what was going on in his head. "I called Mitilini," he continued, "I left a message for Tripolos. After our talk, he should lose all interest in you."

"I'll be devastated." He grinned and took her lips again. "Would you put me down? I can't talk to you this way."

"I'm enjoying it." Ignoring her request, he continued into the salon. "Stephanos, I believe Morgan might like something cool. She had quite a run."

"No, nothing really. *Efxaristo.*" Faintly embarrassed, she met Stephanos's checkerboard grin. When he backed out of sight, she turned her head back to Nick. "If you know who the man is who's running the smuggling, can't you just tell Captain Tripolos and have him arrested?"

"It's not that simple. We want to catch him when the cache is in his possession. There's also the matter of cleaning up the place in the hills where he keeps his goods stored before he ships them on. That part," he added with an absent interest, "I'll leave to Tripolos."

"Nicholas, what will you do?"

"What has to be done."

"Nicholas—"

"Morgan," he interrupted. Standing her on feet, he placed his hands on her shoulders. "You don't want a step-by-step description. Let me finish this without bringing you in any more than I already have."

He lowered his mouth, taking hers with uncharacteristic gentleness. He brought her close, but softly, as if he held something precious. Morgan felt her bones turn to water.

"You have a knack for changing the subject," she murmured.

"After tonight, it's the only subject that's going to interest me. Morgan—"

"A thousand pardons." Stephanos hovered in the doorway. Nick looked up impatiently.

"Go away, old man."

"Nicholas!" Morgan drew out of his arms, sending him a look of reproof. "Has he always been rude, Stephanos?"

"Alas my lady, since he took his thumb out of his mouth."

"Stephanos," Nick began in warning, but Morgan gave a peal of laughter and kissed him.

"Captain Tripolos requests a few moments of your time, Mr. Gregoras," Stephanos said, respectfully and grinned.

"Give me a moment, then send him in, and bring the files from the office."

"Nicholas." Morgan clung to his arm. "Let me stay with you. I won't get in the way."

"No." His refusal was short and harsh. He saw the hurt flicker in her eyes and sighed. "Morgan, I can't allow it even if I wanted to. This isn't going to touch you. I can't let it touch you. That's important to me."

"You're not going to send me away," she began heatedly.

He arched a brow and looked very cool. "I'm not under the same pressure I was last night, Morgan. And I will send you away."

"I won't go."

His eyes narrowed. "You'll do precisely what I say."

"Like hell."

Fury flickered, smoldered, then vanished in a laugh. "You're an exasperating woman, Aphrodite. If I had the time, I'd beat you." To prove his point, he drew her close and touched his lips to her. "Since I don't I'll ask you to wait upstairs."

"Since you *ask*."

"Mr. Gregoras. Ah, Miss James." Tripolos lumbered into the room. "How convenient. I was inquiring for Miss James at the Theoharis villa when your message reached me."

"Miss James is leaving," Nick told him. "I'm sure you'll agree her presence isn't necessary. Mr. Adonti from Athens has asked me to speak with you on a certain matter."

"Adonti?" Tripolos repeated. Nick watched surprise and interest move across the pudgy face before his eyes became direct. "So, you are acquainted with Mr. Adonti's organization?"

"Well acquainted," Nick returned mildly. "We've had dealings over the years."

"I see." He studied Nick with a thoughtful purse of his lips. "And Miss James?"

"Miss James chose an inopportune time to visit friends," Nick said and took her arm. "That's all. If you'll excuse me, I'll just see her out. Perhaps you'd care for a drink while you're waiting." With a gesture toward the bar, Nick drew Morgan out into the hall.

"He looked impressed with the name you just dropped."

"Forget the name," Nick told her briefly. "You've never heard it."

"All right," she said without hesitation.

"What have I done to deserve this trust you give me?" he demanded suddenly. "I've hurt you again and again. I couldn't make up for it in a lifetime."

"Nicholas—"

"No." He cut her off with a shake of his head. In an uncharacteristic gesture of nerves or frustration, he dragged a hand through his hair. "There's no time. Stephanos will show you upstairs."

"As you wish," Stephanos agreed from behind them. Handing Nick a folder, he turned to the stairs. "This way, my lady."

Because Nick had already turned back to the salon, Morgan followed the old man without a word. She'd been given more time with him, she told herself. She couldn't ask for any more than that.

Stephanos took her into a small sitting room off the master bedroom. "You'll be comfortable here," he told her. "I'll bring you coffee."

"No. No, thank you, Stephanos." She stared at him, and for the second time he saw her heart in her eyes. "He'll be all right, won't he?"

He grinned at her so that his moustache quivered. "Can you doubt it?" he countered before he closed the door behind him.

Chapter 12

There was nothing more frustrating than waiting, Morgan decided after the first thirty minutes. Especially for someone who simply wasn't made for sitting still.

The little room was shaped like a cozy box and done in warm, earthy colors with lots of polished wood that gleamed in the early afternoon light. It was filled with small treasures. Morgan sat down and scowled at a Dresden shepherdess. At another time she might have admired the flowing grace of the lines, the fragility. Now she could only think that she was of no more practical use than that pale piece of porcelain. She had, in a matter of speaking, been put on the shelf.

It was ridiculous for Nick to constantly try to…shield her. Morgan's sigh was quick and impatient. Hadn't that been Liz's words when she had spoken of Alex's actions? After all, Morgan thought as she rose again, she was hardly some trembling, fainting scatterbrain who couldn't deal with whatever there was to face. She remembered trembling *and* fainting dead away in his arms. With a rueful smile, she paced to the window. Well, it wasn't as though she made a habit of it.

In any case, her thoughts ran on, he should know that she would, and could, face anything now that they were together. If he understood how she felt about him, then… but did he? she thought abruptly. She'd shown him, certainly she'd shown him in every possible way open to her, but she hadn't told him.

How can I? Morgan asked herself as she sunk into another chair. When a man had lived ten years of his life following his own rules, courting danger, looking for adventures, did he want to tie himself to a woman and accept the responsibilities of love?

He cared for her, Morgan reflected. Perhaps more than he was comfortable with. And he wanted her—more than any man had ever wanted her. But love…love wouldn't come easily to a man like Nicholas. No, she wouldn't pressure him with hers now. Even the unselfish offer of it would be pressure, she thought, when he had so much on his mind. She was only free to go on showing him, trusting him.

Even that seemed to throw him off-balance a bit, she mused, smiling a little. It was as if he couldn't quite accept that someone could see him as he was, know the way he had lived and still give him trust. Morgan wondered if he would have been more comfortable if she had pulled back from him a little after the things he had told her. He would have understood her condemnations more readily than her acceptance. Well, he'll just have to get used to it, she decided. He'll just have to get used to it because I'm not going to make it easy for him to back away.

Restless, she walked to the window. Here was a different view, Morgan thought, from one she so often looked out on from her bedroom window. Higher, more dangerous. More compelling, she thought with a quick thrill. The rocks seemed more jagged, the sea less tame. How it suited the man she'd given her heart to.

There was no terrace there, and suddenly wanting the air and sun, Morgan went through to his bedroom and opened his balcony doors. She could hear the sea hissing before she reached the rail. With a laugh, she leaned farther out.

Oh, she could live with the challenge of such a view every day, she thought, and never tire of it. She could watch the sea change colors with the sky, watch the gulls swoop over the water and back to the nests they'd built in the cliff walls. She could look down on the Theoharis villa and appreciate its refined elegance, but she would choose the rough gray stone and dizzying height.

Morgan tossed back her head and wished for a storm. Thunder, lightning, wild wind. Was there a better spot on earth to enjoy it? Laughing, she dared the sky to boil and spew out its worst.

"My God, how beautiful you are."

The light of challenge still in her eyes, Morgan turned. Leaning against the open balcony door, Nick stared at her. His face was very still, his gaze like a lance. The passion was on him, simmering, bubbling, just beneath the surface. It suited him, Morgan thought, suited those long, sharp bones in his face, those black eyes and the mouth that could be beautiful or cruel.

As she leaned back on the railing, the breeze caught at the ends of her hair. Her eyes took on the color of the sky. Power swept over her, and a touch of madness. "You want me, I can see it. Come and show me."

It hurt, Nick discovered. He'd never known, until Morgan, that desire could hurt. Perhaps it was only when you loved that your needs ached in you. How many times had he loved her last night? he wondered. And each time, it had been like a tempest in him. Now, he promised himself, this time, he would show her a different way.

Slowly, he went to her. Taking both of her hands, he lifted them, then pressed his lips to the palms. When he brought his gaze to hers, Nick saw that her eyes were wide and moved, her lips parted in surprise. Something stirred in him—love, guilt, a need to give.

"Have I shown you so little tenderness, Morgan?" he murmured.

"Nicholas…" She could only whisper his name as her pulses raged and her heart melted.

"Have I given you no soft words, no sweetness?" He kissed her hands again, one finger at a time. She didn't move, only stared at him. "And you still come to me. I'm in your debt," he said quietly in Greek. "What price would you ask me?"

"No, Nicholas, I…" Morgan shook her head, unable to speak, nearly swaying with the weakness this gentle, quiet man brought her.

"You asked me to show you how I wanted you." He put his hands to her face as if she were indeed made of

Dresden porcelain, then touched his lips almost reverently to hers. A sound came from her, shaky and small. "Come and I will."

He lifted her, not with a flourish as he had on the porch, but as a man lifts something he cherishes. "Now..." He laid her down with care. "In the daylight, in my bed."

Again, he took her hand, tracing kisses over the back and palm, then to the wrist where her pulse hammered. All the while he watched her as she lay back, staring at him with something like astonished wonder.

How young she looks, Nick thought as he gently drew her finger into his mouth. And how fragile. Not a witch now, or a goddess, but only a woman. His woman. And her eyes were already clouding, her breath already trembling. He'd shown her the fire and the storm, he thought, but not once—not once had he given her spring.

Bending, he nibbled lightly at her lips, allowing his hands to touch no more than her hair.

It might have been a dream, so weak and weightless did she feel. Nick kissed her eyes closed so that Morgan saw no more than a pale red glow. Then his lips continued, over her forehead, her temples, down the line of her cheekbones—always soft, always warm. The words he whispered against her skin flowed like scented oil over her. She would have moved to bring him closer if her arms had not been too heavy to lift. Instead, she lay in the flood of his tenderness.

His mouth was at her ear, gently torturing with a trace of tongue, a murmured promise. Even as she moaned in surrender, he moved lower to taste and tease the curve of her neck. With kisses like whispers, and whispers like wine, he took her deeper. Gentleness was a drug for both of them.

Hardly touching her, he loosened the buttons of her blouse and slipped it from her. Though he felt the firm pressure of her breasts against him, he took his mouth to the slope of her shoulder instead. He could feel the strength there, the grace, and he tarried.

Morgan's eyes were closed, weighed down with gold-tipped lashes. Her breath rushed out between her lips. He knew he could watch those flickers of pleasure move over her face forever. With his hands once more buried in her hair, Nick kissed her. He felt the yielding and the hunger before he moved on.

Slowly, savoring, he took his lips down to the soft swell—circling, nibbling until he came to the tender underside of her breast. On a moan, Morgan fretted under him as if she were struggling to wake from a dream. But he kept the pace slow and soothed her with words and soft, soft kisses.

With aching gentleness he stroked his tongue over the peak, fighting a surge of desperation when he found it hot and ready. Her movements beneath him took on a rhythmic sinuousness that had the blood pounding in his brain. Her scent was there, always there on the verge of his senses even when she wasn't with him. Now he wallowed in it. As he suckled, he allowed his hands to touch her for the first time.

Morgan felt the long stroke of his hands, the quick scrape of those strong rough fingers that now seemed sensitive enough to tune violins. They caressed lightly, like a breeze. They made her ache.

Soft, slow, gentle, his mouth traveled down the center of her body, lingering here, exploring there until he paused where her slacks hugged across her stomach. When she felt him unfasten them, she trembled. She arched to help him, but Nick drew them down inch by inch, covering the newly exposed flesh with moist kisses so that she could only lie steeped in a pool of pleasure.

And when she was naked, he continued to worship her with his lips, with his suddenly gentle hands. She thought she could hear her own skin hum. The muscles in her thighs quivered as he passed over them, and her desire leaped from passive to urgent.

"Nicholas," she breathed. "Now."

"You've scratched your feet on the rocks," he murmured, pressing his lips against the ball of her foot. "It's a sin to mar such skin, my love." Watching her face, he ran his tongue over the arch. Her eyes flew open, dazed with passion. "I've longed to see you like this." His voice grew thick as his control began to slip. "With sunlight streaming over you, your hair flowing over my pillow, your body trembling for me."

As he spoke, he began the slow, aching journey back, gradually back to her lips. Needs pressed at him and demanded he hurry, but he wouldn't be rushed. He told himself he could linger over the taste and the feel of her for days.

Her arms weren't heavy now, but strong as they curled around him. Every nerve, every pore of her body seemed tuned to him. The harmony seemed impossible, yet it sung through her. His flesh was as hot and damp as hers, his breath as unsteady.

"You ask how I want you," he murmured, thrilling to her moan as he slipped into her. "Look at me and see."

His control hung by a thread. Morgan pulled his mouth to hers and snapped it.

Nick held Morgan close, gently stroking her back while her trembles eased. She clung to him, almost as much in wonder as in love. How was she to have known he had such tenderness in him? How was she to have known she would be so moved by it? Blinking back tears, she pressed her lips to his throat.

"You've made me feel beautiful," she murmured.

"You are beautiful." Tilting her head back, Nick smiled at her. "And tired," he added, tracing a thumb over the mauve smudges under her eyes. "You should sleep, Morgan, I won't have you ill."

"I won't be ill." She snuggled against him, fitting herself neatly against the curve of his body. "And there'll be time for sleeping later. We'll go away for a few days, like you said."

Twining a lock of her hair around his finger, Nick gazed up at the ceiling. A few days with her would never be enough, but he still had the night to get through. "Where would you like to go?"

Morgan thought of her dreams of Venice and Cornish moors. With a sigh, she closed her eyes and drew in Nick's scent. "Anywhere. Right here." Laughing, she propped herself on his chest. "Wherever it is, I intend to keep you in bed a good deal of the time."

"Is that so?" His mouth twitched as he tugged on her

hair. "I might begin to think you have designs only on my body."

"It is a rather nice one." In a long stroke, she ran her hands down his shoulders, enjoying the feel of firm flesh and strong bone. "Lean and muscled…" She trailed off when she spotted a small scar high on his chest. A frown creased her brow as she stared at it. It seemed out of place on that smooth brown skin. "Where did you get this?"

Nick tilted his head, shifting his gaze down. "Ah, an old battle scar," he said lightly.

From a bullet, Morgan realized all at once. Horror ripped through her and mirrored in her eyes. Seeing it, Nick cursed his loose tongue.

"Morgan—"

"No, please." She buried her face against his chest and held tight. "Don't say anything. Just give me a minute."

She'd forgotten. Somehow the gentleness and beauty of their lovemaking had driven all the ugliness out of her mind. It had been easy to pretend for a little while that there was no threat. Pretending's for children, she reminded herself. He didn't need to cope with a child now. If she could give him nothing else, she would give him what was left of her strength. Swallowing fear, she pressed her lips to his chest then rolled beside him again.

"Did everything go as you wanted with Captain Tripolos?"

A strong woman, Nick thought, linking his hand with hers. An extraordinary woman. "He's satisfied with the information I've given him. A shrewd man for all his plodding technique."

"Yes, I thought he was like a bulldog the first time I encountered him."

Chuckling, Nick drew her closer. "An apt description, Aphrodite." He shifted then, reaching to the table beside him for a cigarette. "I think he's one of the few policemen I find it agreeable to work with."

"Why do you—" She broke off as she looked up and focused on the slim black cigarette. "I'd forgotten," Morgan murmured. "How could I have forgotten?"

Nick blew out a stream of smoke. "Forgotten what?"

"The cigarette." Morgan sat up, pushing at her tumbled hair. "The stub of the cigarette near the body."

He lifted a brow, but found himself distracted by the firm white breasts easily within reach. "So?"

"It was fresh, from one of those expensive brands like you're smoking." She let out an impatient breath. "I should have told you before, but it hardly makes any difference at this point. You already know who killed Stevos—who runs the smuggling."

"I never told you I did."

"You didn't have to." Annoyed with herself, Morgan frowned and missed Nick's considering look.

"Why didn't I?"

"You'd have told me if you hadn't seen his face. When you wouldn't answer me at all, I knew you had."

He shook his head as a reluctant smile touched his lips. "*Diabolos,* it's a good thing I didn't cross you earlier in my career. I'm afraid it would have been over quickly. As it happens," he added, "I saw the cigarette myself."

"I should have known you would," she muttered.

"I can assure you Tripolos didn't miss it either."

"That damn cigarette has driven me to distraction." Morgan gave an exasperated sigh. "There were moments I suspected everyone I knew—Dorian, Alex, Iona, even Liz and Andrew. I nearly made myself sick over it."

"You don't name me." Nick studied the cigarette in his hand.

"No, I already told you why."

"Yes," he murmured, "with an odd sort of compliment I haven't forgotten. I should have eased your mind sooner, Morgan, about what I do. You might have slept better."

Leaning over, she kissed him. "Stop worrying about my sleep. I'm going to start thinking I look like a tired hag."

He slid a hand behind her neck to keep her close. "Will you rest if I tell you that you do?"

"No, but I'll hit you."

"Ah, then I'll lie and tell you you're exquisite."

She hit him anyway, a quick jab in the ribs.

"So, now you want to play rough." Crushing out his cigarette, Nick rolled her beneath him. She struggled for a moment, then eyed him narrowly.

"Do you know how many times you've pinned me down like this?" Morgan demanded.

"No, how many?"

"I'm not sure." Her smile spread slowly. "I think I'm beginning to like it."

"Perhaps I can make you like it better." He muffled her laugh with his lips.

He didn't love her gently now, but fiercely. As desperate as he, Morgan let the passion rule her. Fear that it might be the last time caused her response and demands to be urgent. She lit a fire in him.

Now, where his hands had trailed slowly, they raced. Where his mouth had whispered, it savaged. Morgan threw herself into the flames without a second thought. Her mouth was greedy, searching for his taste everywhere while her hands rushed to touch and arouse.

Her body had never felt so agile. It could melt into his one moment, then slither away to drive him to madness. She could hear his desire in the short, harsh breath, feel it in the tensing and quivering of his muscles as she roamed over them, taste it in the dampness that sheened his skin. It matched her own, and again they were in harmony.

She arched against him as his mouth rushed low—but it was more a demand than an invitation. Delirious with her own strength and power, Morgan dug her fingers into his hair and urged him to take her to that first giddy peak. Even as she cried out with it, she hungered for more. And he gave more, while he took.

But she wasn't satisfied with her own pleasure. Ruthlessly she sought to undermine whatever claim he still held to sanity. Her hands had never been so clever, or so quick. Her teeth nipped at his skin before she soothed the tiny pains with a flick of her tongue. She heard him groan and a low, sultry laugh flowed from her. His breath caught when she reached him, then came out in an oath. Morgan felt the sunlight explode into fragments as he plunged into her.

Later, much later, when he knew his time with her was nearly up, Nick kissed her with lingering tenderness.

"You're going," Morgan said, struggling not to cling to him.

"Soon. I'll have to take you back to the villa in a little while." Sitting up, he drew her with him. "You'll stay inside. Lock the doors, tell the servants to let no one in. No one."

Morgan tried to promise, and found she couldn't form the words. "When you're finished, you'll come?"

Smiling, he tucked her hair behind her ear. "I suppose I can handle your window vines again."

"I'll wait up for you and let you in the front door."

"Aphrodite." Nick pressed a kiss to her wrist. "Where's your romance?"

"Oh, God!" Morgan threw her arms around his neck and clung. "I wasn't going to say it—I promised myself I wouldn't. Be careful." Biting back tears, she pressed her face against his throat. "Please, please be careful. I'm terrified for you."

"No, don't." Feeling the dampness against his skin, he held her tighter. "Don't cry for me."

"I'm sorry." With a desperate effort, she forced back the tears. "I'm not helping you."

Nick drew her away and looked at the damp cheeks and shimmering eyes. "Don't ask me not to go, Morgan."

"No." She swallowed again. "I won't. Don't ask me not to worry."

"It's the last time," he said fiercely.

The words made her shudder, but she kept her eyes on his. "Yes, I know."

"Just wait for me." He pulled her back against him. "Wait for me."

"With a bottle of Alex's best champagne," she promised in a stronger voice.

He pressed a kiss to her temple. "We'll have some of mine now, before I take you back. A toast," he told her as he drew her away again. "To tomorrow."

"Yes." She smiled. It almost reached her eyes. "I'll drink with you to tomorrow."

"Rest a moment." With another kiss, he laid her back against the pillow. "I'll go bring some up."

Morgan waited until the door had closed behind him before she buried her face in the pillow.

Chapter 13

It was dark when she woke. Confused, disoriented, Morgan struggled to see where she was. The room was all shifting shadows and silence. There was a cover over her—something soft and light with a fringe of silk. Beneath it, she was warm and naked.

Nicholas, she thought in quick panic. She'd fallen asleep and he'd gone. On a moan, she sat up, drawing her knees to her chest. How could she have wasted those last precious moments together? How long? She thought abruptly. How long had he been gone? With trembling fingers, she reached for the lamp beside the bed.

The light eased some of her fears, but before she could climb out of bed to find a clock, she saw the note propped against the lamp. Taking it, Morgan studied the bold, strong writing. *Go back to sleep* was all it said.

How like him, she thought, and nearly laughed. Morgan kept the note in her hand, as if to keep Nick close, as she rose to look for her clothes. It didn't take her long to discover they were gone.

"The louse!" Morgan said aloud, forgetting the tender thoughts she had only moments before. So, he wasn't taking any chances making certain she stayed put. Naked, hands on her hips, she scowled around the room. Where the devil does he think I'd go? she asked herself. I have no way of knowing where he is...or what he's doing, she thought on a fresh flood of worry.

Wait. Suddenly cold, Morgan pulled the cover from the bed and wrapped herself in it. All I can do is wait.

The time dripped by, minute by endless minute. She paced, then forced herself to sit, then paced again. It would be morning in only a few more hours, she told herself. In the morning, the wait would be over. For all of them.

She couldn't bear it, she thought in despair one moment. She had to bear it, she told herself the next. Would he never get back? Would morning never come? On a sound of fury, she tossed the cover aside. She might have to wait, Morgan thought grimly as she marched to Nick's closet. But she'd be damned if she'd wait naked.

Nick shifted the muscles in his shoulders and blocked out the need for a cigarette. Even the small light would be dangerous now. The cove was bathed in milky moonlight and silence. There would be a murmur now and then from behind a rock. Not from a spirit, but from a man in uniform. The cove still held secrets. Lifting his binoculars, Nick again scanned the sea.

"Any sign?" Tripolos seemed remarkably comfortable

in his squat position behind a rock. He popped a tiny mint into his mouth and crunched quietly. Nick merely shook his head and handed the glasses to Stephanos.

"Thirty minutes," Stephanos stated, chewing on the stem of his dead pipe. "The wind carries the sound of the motor."

"I hear nothing." Tripolos gave the old man a doubtful frown.

Nick chuckled as the familiar feeling of excitement rose. "Stephanos hears what others don't. Just tell your men to be ready."

"My men are ready." His gaze flicked over Nick's profile. "You enjoy your work, Mr. Gregoras."

"At times," Nick muttered, then grinned. "This time, by God."

"And soon it's over," Stephanos said from beside him.

Nick turned his head to meet the old man's eyes. He knew the statement covered more than this one job, but the whole of what had been Nick's career. He hadn't told him, but Stephanos knew. "Yes," he said simply, then turned his eyes to the sea again.

He thought of Morgan and hoped she was still asleep. She'd looked so beautiful—and so exhausted when he'd come back into the room. Her cheeks had been damp. Damn, he couldn't bear the thought of her tears. But he'd felt a wave of relief that she'd been asleep. He didn't have to see her eyes when he left her.

She's safer there than if I'd taken her back, Nick told himself. With luck, she'd still be asleep when he got back and then he'd have spared her hours of worry. Stashing her clothes had been an impulse that had eased his mind.

Even Morgan wouldn't go wandering around without a stitch on her back.

His grin flashed again. If she woke and looked for them, she'd curse him. The idea gave him a moment's pleasure. He could see her, standing in the center of his room with only the moonlight covering her as she raged.

He felt the low aching need in the pit of his stomach, and promised himself he'd keep her just that way—naked fire—until the sun went down again.

Lifting the binoculars, he scanned the dark sea. "They're coming."

The moon threw the boat into silhouette. A dozen men watched her approach from clumps of rock and shadows. She came in silence, under the power of oars.

She was secured with little conversation and a few deft movements of rope. There was a scent Nick recognized. The scent of fear. A fresh bubble of excitement rose, though his face was deadly calm. He's there, Nick thought. And we have him.

The crew left the boat to gather in the shadows of the beach. A hooded figure moved to join them. At Nick's signal, the cove was flooded with light. The rocks became men.

"In the King's name," Tripolos stated grandly, "this vessel will be searched for illegal contraband. Put up your weapons and surrender."

Shouts and the scrambling of men shattered the glass-like quiet of the cove. Men seeking to escape, and men seeking to capture tangled in the sudden chaos of sound and light. Gunfire shocked the balmy air. There were cries of pain and fury.

The smugglers would fight with fist and blade. The battle would be short, but grim. The sounds of violence bounced hollowly off the rocks and drifted out on the air.

Nick saw the hooded figure melt away from the confusion and streak from the cove. Swearing, he raced after it, thrusting his gun back in his belt. A burly form collided with him as another man sought escape. Each swore at the obstacle, knowing the only choice was to remove it.

Together, they rolled over the rocks, away from the noise and the light. Thrown into darkness, they tumbled helplessly until the ground leveled. A blade glistened, and Nick grasped the thick wrist with both hands to halt its plunge to his throat.

The crack of shots had Morgan springing up from her chair. Had she heard, or just imagined? she wondered as her heart began to thud. Could they be so close? As she stared into the darkness, she heard another shot, and the echo. Fear froze her.

He's all right, she told herself. He'll be here soon, and it'll be over. I know he's all right.

Before the sentence had finished racing through her mind, she was running down the steps and out of the villa.

Telling herself she was only being logical, Morgan headed for the beach. She was just going to meet him. He'd be coming along any minute, and she would see for herself that he wasn't hurt. Nick's jeans hung loosely at her hips as she streaked down the cliff path. Her breath was gasping now, the only sound as her feet padded on the hard dirt. Morgan thought it would almost be a relief to hear the guns again. If she heard them, she might be able to judge the direction. She could find him.

Then, from the top of the beach steps, she saw him walking across the sand. With a sob of shuddering relief, she flew down them to meet him.

He continued, too intent on his own thoughts to note her approach. Morgan started to shout his name, but the word strangled in her throat. She stopped running. Not Nicholas, she realized as she stared at the hooded figure. The moves were wrong, the walk. And he'd have no reason to wear the mask. Even as her thoughts began to race, he reached up and tore off the hood. Moonlight fell on golden hair.

Oh God, had she been a fool not to see it? Those calm, calm eyes—too calm, she thought frantically. Had she ever seen any real emotion in him? Morgan took a step in retreat, looking around desperately for some cover. But he turned. His face hardened as he saw her.

"Morgan, what are you doing out here?"

"I—I wanted to walk." She struggled to sound casual. There was no place for her to run. "It's a lovely night. Almost morning, really." As he advanced on her she moistened her lips and kept talking. "I didn't expect to see you. You surprised me. I thought—"

"You thought I was in Athens," Dorian finished with a smile. "But as you see, I'm not. And, I'm afraid, Morgan, you've seen too much." He held up the hood, dangling it a moment before he dropped it to the sand.

"Yes." There was no use dissembling. "I have."

"It's a pity." His smile vanished as though it had never been. "Still, you could be useful. An American hostage," he said thoughtfully as he scanned her face. "Yes, and a woman." Grabbing her arm, Dorian began to pull her across the sand.

She jerked and struggled against his hold. "I won't go with you."

"You have no choice"—he touched the handle of his knife—"unless you prefer to end up as Stevos did."

Morgan swallowed as she stumbled across the beach. He said it so casually. *Some people have no capacity for emotion—love, hate.* He hadn't been speaking of Iona, Morgan realized, but himself. He was as dangerous as any animal on the run.

"You tried to kill Iona too."

"She'd become a nuisance. Greedy not only for money, but to hold me. She thought to blackmail me into marriage." He gave a quick laugh. "I had only to tempt her with the heroin. I had thought the dose I gave her was enough."

Purposely, Morgan fell to her knees as though she'd tripped. "You would have finished her that morning if I hadn't found her first."

"You have a habit of being in the wrong place." Roughly, Dorian hauled her to her feet. "I had to play the worried lover for a time—dashing back and forth between Lesbos and Athens. A nuisance. Still, if I'd been allowed one moment alone with her in the hospital…" Then he shrugged, as if the life or the death of a woman meant nothing. "So, she'll live and she'll talk. It was time to move in any case."

"You lost your last shipment," Morgan blurted out, desperate to distract him from his hurried pace toward the beach steps. If he got her up there—up there in the rocks…and the dark….

Dorian froze and turned to her. "How do you know this?"

"I helped steal it," she said impulsively. "Your place in the hills, the cave—"

The words choked off as his hand gripped her throat. "So you've taken what's mine. Where is it?"

Morgan shook her head.

"Where?" Dorian demanded as his fingers tightened.

A god, she thought staring into his face as the moonlight streamed over it. He had the face of a god. Why hadn't she remembered her own thought that gods were bloodthirsty? Morgan put a hand to his wrist as if in surrender. His fingers eased slightly.

"Go to hell."

Swiftly, he swept the back of his hand across her face, knocking her to the sand. His eyes were a calm empty blue as he looked down at her. "You'll tell me before I'm through with you. You'll beg to tell me. There'll be time," he continued as he walked toward her, "when we're off the island."

"I'll tell you nothing." With the blood singing in her ears, Morgan inched away from him. "The police know who you are, there isn't a hole big enough for you to hide in."

Reaching down, he grabbed her by the hair and hauled her painfully to her feet. "If you prefer to die—"

Then she was free, going down to her knees again as Dorian stumbled back and fell onto the sand.

"Nick." Dorian rubbed the blood from his mouth as his

gaze traveled up. "This is a surprise." It dropped again to the revolver Nick held in his hand. "Quite a surprise."

"Nicholas!" Scrambling up, Morgan ran to him. He never looked at her. His arm was rigid as iron when she gripped it. "I thought—I was afraid you were dead."

"Get up," he told Dorian with a quick gesture of the gun. "Or I'll put a bullet in your head while you lie there."

"Were you hurt?" Morgan shook his arm, wanting some sign. She'd seen that cold hard look before. "When I heard the shots—"

"Only detained." Nick pushed her aside, his gaze fixed on Dorian. "Get rid of the gun. Toss it over there." He jerked his head and leveled his own revolver. "Two fingers. If you breathe wrong, you won't breathe again."

Dorian lifted out his gun in a slow, steady motion and tossed it aside. "I have to admit you amaze me, Nick. It's been you who's been hounding me for months."

"My pleasure."

"And I would have sworn you were a man concerned only with collecting his trinkets and making money. I've always admired your ruthlessness in business—but it seems I wasn't aware of *all* of your business." One graceful brow rose. "A policeman?"

Nick gave a thin smile. "I answer to one man only," he said quietly. "Adonti." The momentary flash of fear in Dorian's eyes gave him great pleasure. "You and I might have come to this sooner. We nearly did last night."

A shadow touched Dorian's face briefly, then was gone. "Last night?"

"Did you think it was only a goat who watched you?" Nick asked with a brittle laugh.

"No." Dorian gave a brief nod. "I smelled something more—foolish of me not to have pursued it."

"You've gotten careless, Dorian. I took your place on your last run and made your men tremble."

"You," Dorian breathed.

"A rich cache," Nick added, "according to my associates in Athens. It might have been over for you then, but I waited until I was certain Alex wasn't involved. It was worth the wait."

"Alex?" Dorian laughed with the first sign of true pleasure. "Alex wouldn't have the stomach for it. He thinks only of his wife and his ships and his honor." He gave Nick a thoughtful glance. "But it seems I misjudged you. I thought you a rich, rather singleminded fool, a bit of a nuisance with Iona this trip, but hardly worth a passing thought. My congratulations on your talent for deceit, and"—he let his gaze travel and rest on Morgan—"your taste."

"Efxaristo."

Morgan watched in confusion, then in terror, as Nick tossed his gun down to join Dorian's. They lay side by side, black and ugly, on the white sand.

"It's my duty to turn you over to Captain Tripolos and the Greek authorities." Calmly, slowly, Nick drew out a knife. "But it will be my pleasure to cut out your heart for putting your hands on my woman."

"No! Nicholas, don't!"

Nick stopped Morgan's panicked rush toward him with a terse command. "Go back to the villa and stay there."

"Please," Dorian interrupted with a smile as he got to his feet. "Morgan must stay. Such an interesting development." He pulled out his own knife with a flourish. "She'll be quite a prize for the one who lives."

"Go," Nick ordered again. His hand tensed on the knife. He was half Greek, and Greek enough to have tasted blood when he had seen Dorian strike her. Morgan saw the look in his eyes.

"Nicholas, you can't. He didn't hurt me."

"He left his mark on your face," he said softly, and turned the knife in his hand. "Stay out of the way."

Touching her hand to her cheek, she stumbled back.

They crouched and circled. As she watched, the knives caught the moonlight and held it. Glittering silver, dazzling and beautiful.

At Dorian's first thrust, Morgan covered her mouth to hold back a scream. There was none of the graceful choreography of a staged fight. This was real and deadly. There were no adventurous grins or bold laughs with the thrusts and parries. Both men had death in his eyes. Morgan could smell the sweat and the sweet scent of blood from both of them.

Starlight dappled over their faces, giving them both a ghostly pallor. All she could hear was the sound of their breathing, the sound of the sea, the sound of steel whistling through the air. Nick was leading him closer to the surf—away from Morgan. Emotion was frozen in him. Anger, such anger, but he knew too much to let it escape. Dorian fought coldly. An empty heart was its own skill.

"I'll pleasure myself with your woman before the night's over," Dorian told him as blade met blade. His lips curved as he saw the quick, naked fury in Nick's eyes.

Morgan watched with horror as a bright stain spread

down Nick's sleeve where Dorian had slipped through his guard. She would have screamed, but there was no breath in her. She would have prayed, but even her thoughts were frozen.

The speed with which they came together left her stunned. One moment they were separate, and the next they were locked together as one tangled form. They rolled to the sand, a confusion of limbs and knives. She could hear the labored breathing and grunted curses. Then Dorian was on top of him. Morgan watched, numb with terror, as he plunged his knife. It struck the sand, a whisper away from Nick's face. Without thought, Morgan fell on the guns.

Once, the revolver slipped through her wet hands, back onto the sand. Gritting her teeth, she gripped it again. As she knelt, she aimed toward the entwined bodies. Coldly, willing herself to do what she had always despised, she prepared to kill.

A cry split the air, animal and primitive. Not knowing which one of them it had been torn from, Morgan clutched the gun with both hands and kept it aimed on the now motionless heap in the sand. She could still hear breathing—but only from one. If Dorian stood up, she swore to herself, and to Nick, that she would pull the trigger.

A shadow moved. She heard the labored breathing and pressed her lips together. Against the trigger, her finger shook lightly.

"Put that damn thing down, Morgan, before you kill me."

"Nicholas." The gun slipped from her nerveless hand.

He moved to her, limping a little. Reaching down, he drew her to her feet. "What were you doing with the gun,

Aphrodite?" he said softly, when he felt her tremble under his hands. "You couldn't have pulled the trigger."

"Yes." Her eyes met his. "I could."

He stared at her for a moment and saw she was speaking nothing less than the truth. With an oath, he pulled her against him. "Damn it, Morgan, why didn't you stay in the villa? I didn't want this for you."

"I couldn't stay in the house, not after I heard the shooting."

"Yes, you hear shooting, so naturally you run outside."

"What else could I do?"

Nick opened his mouth to swear, then shut it again. "You've stolen my clothes," he said mildly. He wouldn't be angry with her now, he promised himself as he stroked her hair. Not while she was shaking like a leaf. But later, by God, later...

"You took mine first." He couldn't tell if the sound she made was a laugh or a sob. "I thought..." Suddenly, she felt the warm stickiness against her palm. Looking down, she saw his blood on her hand. "Oh, God, Nicholas, you're hurt!"

"No, it's nothing, I—"

"Oh, damn you for being macho and stupid. You're *bleeding!*"

He laughed and crushed her to him again. "I'm not being macho and stupid, Aphrodite, but if it makes you happy, you can nurse all of my scratches later. Now, I need a different sort of medicine." He kissed her before she could argue.

Her fingers gripped at his shirt as she poured everything she had into that one meeting of lips. Fear drained from her, and with it, whatever force had driven her. She went limp against him as his energy poured over her.

"I'm going to need a lot of care for a very long time," he murmured against her mouth. "I might be hurt a great deal more seriously than I thought. No, don't." Nick drew her away as he felt her tears on his cheeks. "Morgan, don't cry. It's the one thing I don't think I can face tonight."

"No, I won't cry," she insisted as the tears continued to fall. "I won't cry. Just don't stop kissing me. Don't stop." She pressed her mouth to his. As she felt him, warm and real against her, the tears and trembling stopped.

"Well, Mr. Gregoras, it seems you intercepted Mr. Zoulas after all."

Nick swore quickly, but without heat. Keeping Morgan close, he looked over her head at Tripolos. "Your men have the crew?"

"Yes." Lumbering over, he examined the body briefly. He noted, without comment, that there was a broken arm as well as the knife wound. With a gesture, he signaled one of his men to take over. "Your man is seeing to their transportation," he went on.

Nick kept Morgan's back to the body and met Tripolos's speculative look calmly. "It seems you had a bit of trouble here," the captain commented. His gaze drifted to the guns lying on the sand. He drew his own conclusions. "A pity he won't stand trial."

"A pity," Nick agreed.

"You dropped your gun in the struggle to apprehend him, I see."

"It would seem so."

Tripolos stooped with a wheeze and handed it back to him. "Your job is finished?"

"Yes, my job is finished."

Tripolos made a small bow. "My gratitude, Mr Gregoras." He smiled at the back of Morgan's head. "And my congratulations."

Nick lifted a brow in acknowledgment. "I'll take Miss James home now. You can reach me tomorrow if necessary. Good night, Captain."

"Good night," Tripolos murmured and watched them move away.

Morgan leaned her head against his shoulder as they walked toward the beach steps. Only a few moments before she had fought to keep from reaching them. Now they seemed like the path to the rest of her life.

"Oh, look, the stars are going out." She sighed. There was nothing left, no fear, no anxiety. No more doubts. "I feel as if I've waited for this sunrise all my life."

"I'm told you want to go to Venice and ride on a gondola."

Morgan glanced up in surprise, then laughed. "Andrew told you."

"He mentioned Cornwall and the Champs d'élysées as well."

"I have to learn how to bait a hook, too," she murmured. Content, she watched as day struggled with night.

"I'm not an easy man, Morgan."

"*Hmm?* No," she agreed fervently. "No, you're not."

He paused at the foot of the steps and turned her to face him. The words weren't easy for him now. He wondered why he had thought they would be. "You know the worst of me already. I'm not often gentle, and I'm demanding. I'm prone to black, unreasonable moods."

Morgan smothered a yawn and smiled at him. "I'd be the last one to disagree."

He felt foolish. And, he discovered, afraid. Would a woman accept words of love when she had seen a man kill? Did he have any right to offer them? Looking down, he saw her, slim and straight in his clothes—jeans that hung over her hips—a shirt that billowed and hid small, firm breasts and a waist he could nearly span with his hands. Right or wrong, he couldn't go on without her.

"Morgan…"

"Nicholas?" Her smile became puzzled as she fought off a wave of weariness. "What is it?"

His gaze swept back to hers, dark, intense, perhaps a little desperate.

"Your arm," she began and reached for him.

"No! *Diabolos.*" Gripping her by the shoulders, he shook her. "It's not my arm, listen to me."

"I am listening," she tossed back with a trace of heat. "What's wrong with you?"

"This." He covered her mouth with his. He needed the taste of her, the strength. When he drew her away, his hands had gentled, but his eyes gleamed.

With a sleepy laugh, she shook her head. "Nicholas, if you'll let me get you home and see to your arm—"

"My arm's a small matter, Aphrodite."

"Not to me."

"Morgan." Nick stopped her before she could turn toward the steps again. "I'll make a difficult and exasperating husband, but you won't be bored." Taking her hands, he kissed them as he had on his balcony. "I love you enough to let you climb your mountains, Morgan. Enough to climb them with you if that's what you want."

She wasn't tired now, but stunned into full alertness. Morgan opened her mouth, but found herself stupidly unable to form a word.

"Damn it, Morgan, don't just stare at me." Frustration and temper edged his voice. "Say yes, for God's sake!" Fury flared in his eyes. "I won't let you say no!"

His hands were no longer in hers, but gripping her arms again. She knew, any moment, he would start shaking her. But there was more in his eyes than anger. She saw the doubts, the fears, the fatigue. Love swept into her, overwhelmingly.

"Won't you?" she murmured.

"No." His fingers tightened. "No, I won't. You've taken my heart. You won't leave with it."

Lifting a hand, she touched his cheek, letting her finger trace over the tense jaw. "Do you think I could climb mountains without you, Nicholas?" She drew him against her and felt his shudder of relief. "Let's go home."

* * * * *

LET'S TALK
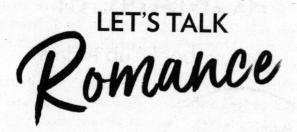
Romance

For exclusive extracts, competitions
and special offers, find us online:

 facebook.com/millsandboon

@millsandboonuk

@millsandboon

Or get in touch on 0844 844 1351*

For all the latest titles coming soon, visit
millsandboon.co.uk/nextmonth

*Calls cost 7p per minute plus your phone company's price per minute access charge